HEART OF THE GAME

The Heart's Victory

and

Rules of the Game

ALSO BY NORA ROBERTS

Hot Ice • Sacred Sins • Brazen Virtue • Sweet Revenge •
Public Secrets • Genuine Lies • Carnal Innocence •
Divine Evil • Honest Illusions • Private Scandals • Hidden
Riches • True Betrayals • Montana Sky • Sanctuary •
Homeport • The Reef • River's End • Carolina Moon •
The Villa • Midnight Bayou • Three Fates • Birthright •
Northern Lights • Blue Smoke • Angels Fall • High Noon •
Tribute • Black Hills • The Search • Chasing Fire •
The Witness • Whiskey Beach • The Collector •
Tonight and Always • The Liar • The Obsession •
Come Sundown • Shelter in Place • Under Currents •
Hideaway • Legacy

Irish Born Trilogy
Born in Fire • Born in Ice • Born in Shame

Dream Trilogy
Daring to Dream • Holding the Dream • Finding the Dream

Chesapeake Bay Saga
Sea Swept • Rising Tides • Inner Harbor • Chesapeake Blue

Gallaghers of Ardmore Trilogy
Jewels of the Sun • Tears of the Moon • Heart of the Sea

Three Sisters Island Trilogy
Dance Upon the Air • Heaven and Earth • Face the Fire

Key Trilogy
Key of Light • Key of Knowledge • Key of Valor

In the Garden Trilogy
Blue Dahlia • Black Rose • Red Lily

Circle Trilogy
Morrigan's Cross • Dance of the Gods • Valley of Silence

Sign of Seven Trilogy
Blood Brothers • *The Hollow* • *The Pagan Stone*

Bride Quartet
Vision in White • *Bed of Roses* • *Savor the Moment* • *Happy Ever After*

The Inn Boonsboro Trilogy
The Next Always • *The Last Boyfriend* • *The Perfect Hope*

The Cousins O'Dwyer Trilogy
Dark Witch • *Shadow Spell* • *Blood Magick*

The Guardians Trilogy
Stars of Fortune • *Bay of Sighs* • *Island of Glass*

Chronicles of The One
Year One • *Of Blood and Bone* • *The Rise of Magicks*

The Dragon Heart Legacy
The Awakening • *The Becoming*

EBOOKS BY NORA ROBERTS

Cordina's Royal Family
Affaire Royale • *Command Performance* • *The Playboy Prince* • *Cordina's Crown Jewel*

The Donovan Legacy
Captivated • *Entranced* • *Charmed* • *Enchanted*

The O'Hurleys
The Last Honest Woman • *Dance to the Piper* • *Skin Deep* • *Without a Trace*

Night Tales
Night Shift • *Night Shadow* • *Nightshade* • *Night Smoke* • *Night Shield*

• *Witness in Death* • *Judgment in Death* • *Betrayal in Death*
• *Seduction in Death* • *Reunion in Death* • *Purity in Death*
• *Portrait in Death* • *Imitation in Death* • *Divided in Death*
• *Visions in Death* • *Survivor in Death* • *Origin in Death*
• *Memory in Death* • *Born in Death* • *Innocent in Death* •
Creation in Death • *Strangers in Death* • *Salvation in Death*
• *Promises in Death* • *Kindred in Death* • *Fantasy in Death* •
Indulgence in Death • *Treachery in Death* • *New York to Dallas*
• *Celebrity in Death* • *Delusion in Death* • *Calculated in Death*
• *Thankless in Death* • *Concealed in Death* • *Festive in Death* •
Obsession in Death • *Devoted in Death* • *Brotherhood in Death*
• *Apprentice in Death* • *Echoes in Death* • *Secrets in Death* •
Dark in Death • *Leverage in Death* • *Connections in Death* •
Vendetta in Death • *Golden in Death* • *Shadows in Death* •
Faithless in Death • *Forgotten in Death* •
Abandoned in Death

ANTHOLOGIES

From the Heart • *A Little Magic* • *A Little Fate*

Moon Shadows
(with Jill Gregory, Ruth Ryan Langan, and Marianne Willman)

The Once Upon Series
(with Jill Gregory, Ruth Ryan Langan, and Marianne Willman)
Once Upon a Castle • *Once Upon a Star* • *Once Upon a
Dream* • *Once Upon a Rose* • *Once Upon a Kiss* • *Once Upon
a Midnight*

Silent Night
(with Susan Plunkett, Dee Holmes, and Claire Cross)

Out of This World
(with Laurell K. Hamilton, Susan Krinard, and Maggie Shayne)

Bump in the Night
(with Mary Blayney, Ruth Ryan Langan, and Mary Kay McComas)

Dead of Night
(with Mary Blayney, Ruth Ryan Langan, and Mary Kay McComas)

Three in Death

Suite 606
(with Mary Blayney, Ruth Ryan Langan, and Mary Kay McComas)

In Death

The Lost
(with Patricia Gaffney, Ruth Ryan Langan, and Mary Blayney)

The Other Side
(with Mary Blayney, Patricia Gaffney, Ruth Ryan Langan,
and Mary Kay McComas)

Time of Death

The Unquiet
(with Mary Blayney, Patricia Gaffney, Ruth Ryan Langan,
and Mary Kay McComas)

Mirror, Mirror
(with Mary Blayney, Elaine Fox, Mary Kay McComas, and
R. C. Ryan)

Down the Rabbit Hole
(with Mary Blayney, Elaine Fox, Mary Kay McComas, and
R. C. Ryan)

ALSO AVAILABLE . . .

The Official Nora Roberts Companion
(edited by Denise Little and Laura Hayden)

HEART OF THE GAME

The Heart's Victory

and

Rules of the Game

TWO NOVELS IN ONE

NORA ROBERTS

St. Martin's Paperbacks

This is a work of fiction. All of the characters, organizations, and events portrayed in this book are either products of the author's imagination or are used fictitiously.

Published in the United States by St. Martin's Paperbacks, an imprint of St. Martin's Publishing Group

For information, address St. Martin's Publishing Group, 120 Broadway, New York, NY 10271.

www.stmartins.com

ISBN: 978-1-250-83186-6

Our books may be purchased in bulk for promotional, educational, or business use. Please contact your local bookseller or the Macmillan Corporate and Premium Sales Department at 1-800-221-7945, ext. 5442, or by email at MacmillanSpecialMarkets@macmillan.com.

Printed in the United States of America

St. Martin's Paperbacks edition / March 2022

10 9 8 7 6 5 4 3 2 1

The Heart's Victory

CHAPTER 1

Foxy stared at the underbelly of the MG. The scent of oil surrounded her as she tightened bolts. "You know, Kirk, I can't tell you how much I appreciate your lending me these coveralls." Her smooth contralto voice was touched with sarcasm.

"What are brothers for?" Foxy heard the grin in his voice though all she could see were the bottoms of his frayed jeans and his grimy sneakers.

"It's wonderful you're so broad-minded." She gritted her teeth on the words as she worked with the ratchet. "Some brothers might have insisted on fixing the transmission themselves."

"I'm no chauvinist," Kirk returned. Foxy watched Kirk's sneakers as he walked across the concrete floor of the garage. She heard the click and clatter of tools being replaced. "If you hadn't decided to be a photographer, I'd have put you on my pit crew."

"Fortunately for me, I prefer developing fluid to motor oil." She wiped the back of her hand over her cheek. "And to think if I hadn't been hired to shoot the photos for Pam Anderson's book, I wouldn't be here right now up to my elbows in car parts."

When Foxy heard his quick, warm laugh, it struck her how much she had missed him. Perhaps it was because their two-year separation had worked no change on him. He was precisely the same, as if she had closed the door and opened it again only minutes later. His face was still weathered and bronzed with creases and dents that promised to grow only deeper and more attractive with age. His hair was still as thickly curled as her own, though his was a dark gold and hers a rich russet. The familiar mustache twitched above his mouth when he smiled. Foxy couldn't remember him ever being without it. She had been six and he sixteen when it had first appeared, and seventeen years later it was a permanent fixture on his face. Foxy had seen, too, that the recklessness was still there. It was in his smile, in his eyes, in his movements.

As a child, she had worshiped him. He had been a tall, golden hero who allowed her to tag behind and pay homage. It had been Kirk who had absently dubbed her Foxy, and the ten-year-old Cynthia Fox had clung to the name as if it were a gift. When Kirk left home to pursue a career in professional racing, Foxy had lived for his occasional visits and short, sporadic letters. In his absence, he grew more golden, more indestructible. He was twenty-three when he won his first major race. Foxy had been thirteen.

This tender, testing, learning year of her life had been one of indescribable pain. It had been late when Foxy had driven home from town with her parents. The road was slick with snow. Foxy watched it hurl itself against the windows of the car while the radio played a Gershwin tune she was too young to either recognize or appreciate. She had stretched out on the backseat, closed her eyes, and begun to hum a tune popular with her own generation. She wished briefly that she were home so that she could put on her records and call her best friend to talk about things that were important—*boys*.

There had been no warning as the car began its skid. It circled wildly, gaining speed as the tires found no grip on the slick, wet snow. There was a blur of white outside the car windows and she heard her father swear as he fought to regain control of the wheel, but her fear never had the chance to materialize. Foxy heard the crunching impact as the car slammed into the telephone pole, felt the jerk and the quick pain. She felt the cold as she was tossed from the car, then the wet swish of snow against her face. Then she felt nothing.

It had been Kirk's face that Foxy saw upon awakening from the two-day coma. Her first wave of joy froze as she remembered the accident. She saw it in his eyes—the weariness, the grief, the acceptance. She shook her head to deny what he had not yet told her. Gently, he bent down to rest his cheek on hers. "We've got each other now, Foxy. I'm going to take care of you."

And so he had, in his fashion. For the next four years, Foxy followed the circuit. She received her education from a series of tutors with varying degrees of success. But during her teenage years, Cynthia Fox learned more than American history or algebra. She learned about piston displacement and turbo engines; she learned how to take an engine apart and how to put it back together; she learned the rules of the pit lane. She grew up in what was predominantly a man's world, with the smell of gasoline and the roar of engines. Supervision at times had been lax, at others, nonexistent.

Kirk Fox was a man with one consuming passion: the race. Foxy knew there were times he forgot her existence completely, and she accepted it. Seeing the dents in his perfection only caused her to love him more. She grew up wild and free and, inconsistently, sheltered.

College had been a shock. Over the next four years, Foxy's

world had expanded. She discovered the eccentricities of living in a dormitory with females. She began to learn more about Cynthia Fox. Having a discerning eye for color, cut, and line, she had developed her own distinctive taste in clothes. She found that clubs and sororities were not for her; her childhood had been too freewheeling to allow her to accept rules and regimentation. It had been easy for Foxy to resist college men because they seemed to her to be foolish, immature boys. She had entered college a gangling, awkward girl and graduated a willow-slim woman with her own innate grace and a passion for photography. For the two years following college, Foxy poured every ounce of her talent and effort into building her career. The assignment with Pam Anderson was a two-fold gift. It allowed her to spend time with her brother while nudging the crack in the door of opportunity yet wider. Foxy knew the first part of the gift was still more important to her than the second.

"I suppose you'd be shocked to learn I haven't seen the underside of a car in over two years." Foxy made the admission as she tightened the last of the bolts.

"What do you do when your transmission needs work?" Kirk demanded as he took a final look under the MG's hood.

"I send it to a mechanic," Foxy muttered.

"With your training?" Kirk was appalled enough to bend down and glare at the top of her head. "You can get twenty years to life for a crime like that."

"I don't have time." Foxy sighed, then continued, as if to make amends, "I did change the points and plugs last month."

"This car is a classic." Kirk closed the hood gently, then wiped the surface with a clean rag. "You're crazy if you let just anybody get their hands on it."

"Well, I can't send it out to Charlie every time it gets the sniffles, and besides . . ." Foxy stopped her justifications at the sound of a car pulling up outside.

"Hey, this ain't no place for a businessman." Foxy heard the smile in her brother's words as she set down the ratchet.

"Just checking on my investment."

Lance Matthews. She recognized the low, drawling voice instantly. Just as instantly her hands clenched into tight balls. Heat bubbled in her throat. Slowly, Foxy forced herself to remain calm. *Ridiculous,* she thought as she flexed her fingers; *resentments shouldn't survive a six-year separation.*

She saw from her vantage point that he, too, wore jeans and sneakers. While his showed no streaks of grease, they were frayed and worn. *He's just slumming,* she thought and suppressed an indignant sniff. Six years is a long time, she reminded herself. He might be almost tolerable by now. But she doubted it.

"I couldn't get here for the practice run this morning. How'd she do?"

"A 200.558." She heard the click and fizz of a beer being opened. "Charlie wants to give her a last going-over, but she's prime, absolutely prime." From the tone of her brother's voice, Foxy knew he had forgotten she was there, forgotten everything but the car and the race.

"He's got his mind fixed on setting a pit record Sunday." There was a faint snap, and a pungent aroma drifted to Foxy. It annoyed her that she recognized it as the scent of the slender cigars Lance habitually smoked. She rubbed her nose with the back of her hand as if to erase the fragrance from her senses. "New toy?" Lance asked, walking over to the MG. Foxy heard the hood lift. "Looks like the little number you bought your sister after she got her license. She still playing with cameras?"

Incensed, Foxy gave a push and rolled out from under the

car. For the instant she lay on the creeper, she saw a look
of surprise cross Lance's face. "It's the same little number,"
she said coldly as she struggled to her feet. "And I don't play
with cameras, I work with them."

Her hair was pulled in a ponytail back from her grease-
smeared face. The coveralls left her shapeless and sloppy.
In one oil-splattered hand, she held the ratchet. Through her
indignation, Foxy noted that Lance Matthews was more attractive than ever. Six years had deepened the creases in his
rawboned face, which, by some odd miracle, just escaped being handsome. *Handsome* was too tame a word for Lance
Matthews. His hair was richly black, curling into the collar
of his shirt and tossed carelessly around his face. His brows
were slightly arched over eyes that could go from stone-gray
to smoke depending on his mood. The classic, aristocratic
features were offset by a small white scar above his left brow.
He was taller than Kirk with a rangier build, and there was
an ease in his manner that Kirk lacked. Foxy knew the indo-
lent exterior covered a keen awareness. Through his twen-
ties he had been one of the top drivers in the racing world.
She had heard it said that Lance Matthews had the hands
of a surgeon, the instincts of a wolf, and the nerve of the
devil. At thirty, he had won the world championship and
abruptly retired. From her brother's less than informative
letters, Foxy knew that for the past three years Lance had
successfully sponsored drivers and cars. She watched as his
mouth formed the half-tilted smile that had always been his
trademark.

"Well, if it isn't the Fox." His eyes ran down the coveralls
and back to her face. "Six years hasn't changed you a bit."

"Nor you," she retorted, furious that their first meeting
would find her so attired. She felt like a foolish, gangling
teenager again. "What a pity."

"Tongue's as sharp as ever." His teeth flashed in a grin.

Apparently the fact that she was still a rude, bad-tempered urchin appealed to him. "Have you missed me?"

"As long as I possibly could," she replied and held the ratchet out to her brother.

"Still hasn't any respect for her elders," Lance told Kirk while his eyes lingered on Foxy's mutinous face. "I'd kiss you hello, but I never cared for the taste of motor oil."

He was teasing her as he had always done and Foxy's chin shot up as it always had. "Fortunately for both of us, Kirk has an unlimited supply."

"If you walk around like that for the rest of the season," Kirk warned as he replaced his tool, "you might as well work in the pits."

"The season?" Lance's look sharpened as he drew on his cigar. "You going to be around for the season? That's some vacation."

"Hardly." Foxy wiped her palms on the legs of the coveralls and tried to look dignified. "I'm here as a photographer, not as a spectator."

"Foxy is working with that writer, Pam Anderson," Kirk put in as he picked up his beer again. "Didn't I tell you?"

"You mentioned something about the writer," Lance murmured. He was studying Foxy's face as if to see beneath the smears of grease. "So, you'll be traveling the circuit again?"

Foxy remembered the intensity of his eyes. There were times when they could stop your breath. There was something raw and deep about the man. Even as an adolescent, Foxy had been aware of his basic sensuality. Then she had found it fascinating; now she knew its dangers. Willpower kept her eyes level with his. "That's right. A pity you won't be along."

"Not a pity," he countered. The intensity disappeared from his eyes and Foxy watched them grow light again. "Kirk's driving my car. I intend to tag along and watch him win." He saw Foxy frown before he turned to her brother. "I suppose I'll meet Pam Anderson at the party you're having tonight. Don't wash the grease off, Foxy." He patted a clean spot on her chin before he walked to the door. "I might not recognize you. We should have a dance for old times' sake."

"Stuff it in your manifold," Foxy called after him, then cursed herself for trading dignity for childish taunts. After shooting Kirk a glare, she stepped out of the coveralls. "Your taste in friends eludes me."

Kirk shrugged, glancing out the window as Lance drove away. "You'd better test-drive the car before you drive to the house. It might need some adjustments."

Foxy sighed and shook her head. "Sure."

* * *

The dress Foxy chose for the evening was made of paper-thin crepe de chine. The muted pastels of lavender and green clung and floated around her slender, curved figure. With a draping skirt and strapless bodice covered by the sheerest of short jackets, it was a romantic dress. It was also very alluring. Foxy thought with grim satisfaction that Lance Matthews was in for a surprise. Cynthia Fox was not a teenager any longer. After placing small gold hoops in her ears, she stood back to judge the results.

Her hair was loose, left to fall below her shoulders in a thick mane of gleaming russet curls. Her face was now clear of black smudges. Her prominent cheekbones added both elegance and delicacy to the piquant quality of her triangular face. Her eyes were almond-shaped, not quite gray, not quite green. Her nose was sharp and aristocratic, her mouth full and just short of being too wide. There was a hint of her brother's recklessness in her eyes, but it was banked and smoldering. There was something reminiscent of the wilds in her, part deer, part tigress. Much more than beauty, she possessed an earthy, untapped sensuality. She was made of contradictions. Her willowy figure and ivory complexion made her appear fragile while the fire in her hair and boldness of her eyes sent out a challenge. Foxy felt the night was ripe for challenge.

Just as she was slipping into her shoes, a knock sounded at her door. "Foxy, can I come in?" Pam Anderson peeked through a crack in the door, then pushed it wider. "Oh, you look marvelous."

Foxy turned with a smile. "So do you."

The dreamy pale blue chiffon suited Pam's china-doll looks perfectly. Studying the petite blond beauty, Foxy wondered again how she had the stamina for as demanding a career as that of a freelance journalist. How does she manage to get such in-depth interviews when she speaks like a magnolia blossom and looks like a hothouse orchid? They had known each other for six months, and though Pam was five years Foxy's senior, the younger woman was developing maternal instincts toward the older.

"Isn't it nice to start off a job with a party?" Pam moved to the bed and sat as Foxy ran a comb through her hair. "Your brother's home is lovely, Foxy. My room's perfect."

"It was our house when we were kids," Foxy told her, frowning over her perfume bottle. "Kirk kept it as sort of a base camp since it's so close to Indianapolis." Her frown turned upward into a smile. "Kirk's always liked to camp near a track."

"He's charming." Pam ran her fingers over her short, smooth page boy. "And very generous to put me up until we start on the circuit."

"Charming he is." Foxy laughed and leaned closer to the mirror as she added color to her lips. "Unless he's plotting track strategy. You'll notice, sometimes he leaves the rest of the world." Foxy stared down at the lipstick tube, then carefully closed it. "Pam . . ." Taking a quick breath, she glanced up and met Pam's eyes in the mirror. "Since we'll be traveling so closely, I think you should understand Kirk a bit. He's . . ." She sighed and moved her shoulders. "He's not always charming. Sometimes he's curt, and short-tempered, and downright unkind. He's very restless, very competitive. Racing is his life, and at times he forgets people aren't as insensitive as cars."

"You love him a lot, don't you?" The clear insight and hint of compassion in the quiet blue eyes were a part of the reason for Pam's success in her field. She was not only able to read people, but to care.

"More than anything." Foxy turned until she met the woman's face rather than the reflection. "More still since I grew up and discovered he was human. Kirk didn't have to take on the responsibility of raising me. I don't think it occurred to me until I was in college that he'd had a choice. He could have put me in a foster home; no one would have criticized him. In fact"—she tossed her head to free her shoulders of her hair, then leaned back against the dresser— "I'm sure he was criticized by some for not doing so. He kept me with him, and that's what I needed. I'll never forget him for that. One day perhaps I'll pay him back." Smiling, Foxy straightened. "I suppose I'd better go down and make sure the caterer has everything set. The guests will be arriving soon."

"I'll come with you." Pam rose and moved to the door. "Now, what about this Lance Matthews you were grumbling about earlier? If I did my homework properly, he's a former driver, a very successful driver, now head of Matthews Corporation, which, among other things, designs racing cars. He's designed and owns several Formula One cars, including the ones your brother will be driving this season. And yes . . . the Indy car, too. Isn't he . . . ?" She made a small cluck of frustration as her inventory of facts grew sketchy. "He's from a very old, wealthy family, isn't he? Boston or New Haven, shipping or import-export. Disgustingly rich."

"Boston, shipping, and disgusting," Foxy affirmed as they moved down to the first floor. "Don't get me started on him tonight or you'll have nightmares."

"Do I detect a smidgeon of dislike?"

"You detect a ton of dislike," Foxy countered. "I've had to rent a room to hold my extra dislike of Lance Matthews."

"Mmm, and rent prices are soaring."

"Which only makes me dislike him more." Foxy moved directly to the dining room and examined the table.

Lacquered wooden dishes were set on an indigo tablecloth. The centerpiece was an earthenware jug filled with sprays of dogwood and daffodils. One look at the setting, at the chunky yellow candles in wooden holders, assured Foxy that the caterer knew his business. "Relaxed informality" was the obvious theme.

"Looks nice." Foxy resisted dipping a finger into a bowl of iced caviar as the caterer bustled in from the kitchen.

He was a small, fussy man, bald but for a thin ring of hair he had dyed a deep black. He walked in quick, shuffling steps. "You're too early." He stood protectively between Foxy and the caviar. "Guests won't be arriving for another fifteen minutes."

"I'm Cynthia Fox, Mr. Fox's sister." She offered a smile as a flag of truce. "I thought perhaps I could help."

"Help? Oh no, good heavens, no." To prove his words, he brushed at her with the back of his hand as though she were an annoying fly threatening his pâté. "You mustn't touch anything. It's all balanced."

"And beautifully, too," Pam soothed as she gave Foxy's

arm a warning squeeze. "Let's go have a drink, Foxy, and wait for the others to arrive."

"Silly, pompous man," Foxy mumbled as Pam urged her into the living room.

"Do you let anyone else set your f-stops?" Pam asked with bland curiosity as she sank into a chair.

Foxy laughed as she surveyed the portable bar. "Point taken. Well, there seems to be enough liquor here to keep an army reeling for a year. Trouble is, I don't know how to fix anything more complicated than the gin and tonic Kirk drinks."

"If there's a bottle of dry sherry, pour some in a very small glass. That shouldn't tax your ingenuity too far. Going to join me?"

"No." Foxy scouted through the bottles. "Drinking makes me just a little too honest. I forget the basic rules of survival—tact and diplomacy. You know the managing editor of *Wedding Day* magazine, Joyce Canfield?" Pam gave an affirmative response as Foxy located and poured sherry. "I ran into her at this cocktail party a few months back. I'd done several layouts for *Wedding Day*. Anyway, she asked me what I thought of her dress. I looked at her over the rim of my second spritzer and told her she should avoid yellow, it made her look sallow." Foxy crossed the room and handed Pam her glass. "Honest but dumb. I haven't taken a picture of a wilted bouquet for *Wedding Day* since."

Pam laughed her quiet, floating laugh and sipped her sherry. "I'll remember not to ask you any dangerous questions when you have a glass in your hand." She watched Foxy run a finger over a high, piecrust table. "Does it feel strange being home?"

Foxy's eyes were dark, the green merely sprinkled over the gray. "It brings back memories. Strange, I really haven't thought of my life here in years, but now . . ." Walking to the window, she pulled back the sheer ivory curtain. Outside, the sun was dipping low in the sky, shooting out sprays of red and gold light. "Do you know, this is really the only place I could define as home. New York doesn't count. Ever since my parents died, I've moved around so much, first with Kirk, then with my career. It's only now that I'm here that it occurs to me how rootless my life has been."

"Do you want roots, Foxy?"

"I don't know." When Foxy turned back to Pam, her face was puzzled. "I don't know," she repeated. "Maybe. But I want something. It's out there." She narrowed her eyes and stared at something she could not yet see.

"What is?"

Foxy jolted as the voice shattered her thoughts. Kirk stood in the doorway studying her with his easy smile, his hands thrust into the pockets of dun-colored slacks. As always, there was an aura of excitement around him.

"Well." Giving him a considering look, Foxy crossed to him. "Silk, huh?" With sisterly prerogative, she fingered the collar of his shirt. "Guess you don't change too many engines in this." Kirk tugged on her hair and kissed her simultaneously.

In her heels, she was nearly as tall as he, and their eyes were level with each other's. As Pam watched she noticed how little family resemblance they shared; only the curling heaviness of their hair was similar. Kirk's eyes were a dark true green, and his face was long and narrow. There was nothing of his sister's elegance or her delicacy about him. Studying his profile, Pam felt a tiny quiver chase up her spine. Quickly she glanced down at her drink. Long-term assignments and quivering spines didn't mix.

"I'll fix you a drink," Foxy offered, drawing away from her brother and moving to the bar. "We don't dare go into the other room for another two and a half minutes. Oops, no ice." She closed the lid on the ice bucket and shrugged. "I'll be heroic and challenge the caterer. Pam's drinking sherry," she called over her shoulder as she left the room.

"Want a refill?" Kirk asked, turning his attention to Pam for the first time.

"No, thanks." She smiled and lifted her glass to her lips. "I haven't had a chance to thank you yet for putting me up. I can't tell you how nice it is not to be sleeping in a hotel."

"I know all about hotels." Kirk grinned and sat across from her. For the first time since they had met the day before, they were alone. Pam felt the quiver again and ignored it. Kirk took a cigarette from the holder on the table and lit it. For those few seconds, he studied her.

Class, he thought. *And brains.* This was no racing groupie. His eyes lingered an instant on the soft pink mouth. *She looks like something in a store window. Beautiful, desirable, and behind a wall of glass.*

"Foxy's spoken of you so often, I feel I know you." Pam immediately cursed herself for the inanity and took another sip of sherry. "I'm looking forward to the race."

"So am I," Kirk answered, then leaned back in his chair and studied her more openly. "You don't look the type to be interested in pit stops and lap speeds."

"No?" Pam countered as she collected her poise. "What type do I look like?"

Kirk smoked in long, deep drags. "The type who likes Chopin and champagne."

Pam swirled the remaining sherry in her glass and held his gaze. "I do," she answered, then relaxed against the cushions of her chair. "But as a journalist, I'm interested in all kinds of things. I hope you'll be generous with your thoughts and feelings and your knowledge."

A smile lifted the corners of his mustache. "I've been known to be generous with all manner of things," he mocked, wondering if the dewy texture of her skin was as soft as it looked. The doorbell broke the silence. Kirk rose, took the drink from Pam's hand, and pulled her to her feet. Though she told herself it was a foolish reaction, her heart thundered. "Are you married?" he asked.

"Why . . . no." She frowned, confused.

"Good. I never like sleeping with married women."

He spoke so matter-of-factly, it took Pam a moment to react. Angry color flooded her porcelain cheeks. "Of all the presumptuous—"

"Listen," Kirk interrupted. "We're bound to sleep together before the season's finished. I'm not much on games, so I don't play."

"And would it shock you very deeply," Pam returned with the coldness only a Southern-bred voice can achieve, "if I decline your generous invitation?"

"Seems like a waste," Kirk concluded with a careless shrug. He took Pam's hand as the doorbell pealed a second time. "We'd better answer it."

CHAPTER 2

Over the next hour, the house filled with people and grew noisy. As the room filled, the patio doors opened to allow guests to spill outside. The night was warm and still.

For Foxy, there were both new faces and old friends. She wandered from group to group, assuming the role of unofficial hostess. The caterer's proud balance had been long since shattered as trays and bowls were scattered throughout the house. People milled in every corner. Still, the breezy informality of the party was linked with a common bond. These were racing people, whether they were drivers, wives, or privileged fans.

Flushed and laughing, Foxy answered the door to admit a late arrival. Her smile of greeting faded instantly. There was some satisfaction to be gained from seeing a look of surprise in Lance's gray eyes. It came and went with the lift and fall of his brow. Slowly he took his gaze over the length of her. There was a look of consideration on his face, which Foxy equated with a man about to purchase a piece of sculpture for his den. Instantly the ease fled from her stance as her chin lifted and her shoulders straightened. Annoyed, she gave him the same casual appraisal he gave her.

Both his turtleneck and slacks were black. The night

apparel lent him a mysterious, dangerous look only accentuated by his leanness and reckless looks. About him was the odd air of calm Foxy remembered. It was an ability to remain absolutely motionless and absorb everything. The true hunter possesses it, and the bullfighter who survives. Now, as she knew he was absorbing her, Foxy challenged him with her eyes though her heart beat erratically. *Anger,* she told herself. *He always makes me so angry.*

"Well, well, well." Lance's voice was quiet and oddly intimate over the hum of the party. He met her eyes, then smiled at her sulky pout. "It seems I was wrong."

"Wrong?" she repeated and reluctantly shut the door behind him rather than in his face.

"You have changed." He took both her hands, ignoring her sharp jerk of protest. Holding her away from him, he let his eyes roam down the length of her again. "You're still ridiculously thin, but you've managed to fill out a bit in a few interesting places."

Her skin trembled as if a cool breeze had caressed it. Furious with the sensation, Foxy tried to snatch her hands away. She failed. "If that's a compliment, you can keep it. I'd like my hands back, Lance."

"Sure, in a minute." Her anger and indignation rolled off him as he continued to study her. "You know," he said conversationally, "I always wondered how that funny little face of yours would turn out. It had an odd appeal, even when it was splattered with transmission fluid."

"I'm surprised you remember how I looked." Resigned that he would not let her go until he was ready, Foxy stopped struggling. She took a long, hard look at him, searching his face for any flaws that might have developed during the past six years. She found none. "You haven't changed a bit."

"Thanks." With a grin, he transferred his hold to her waist and led her toward the sounds of the party.

"That wasn't intended as a compliment." Foxy had a strange reaction to his quick grin and intimate touch. The wariness remained with her, but it was tempered with amusement. Foxy drew firmly away from him as they entered the main room. It was, she reminded herself, always so simple for him to charm her. "I imagine you know just about everyone." She made a quick sweep of the room with the back of her hand. "And I'm certain you can find your way to the bar."

"Gracious to the last," Lance murmured, then gave her another measuring stare. "As I recall, you didn't always dislike me so intensely."

"I was a slow learner."

"Lance, darling!" Honey Blackwell bore down on them. Her hair was short and fluffed and silver blond, her face pretty and painted, her body all curves and dips. She had money and an unquenchable thirst for excitement. She was, in Foxy's opinion, the classic racing leech. As her arms circled Lance's neck he rested his hands on her generous hips. She kissed Lance with single-minded enthusiasm as he watched Foxy's disdainful smirk over Honey's bare shoulder.

"Apparently, you two have met." Inclining her head, she turned and moved to the center of the party. *And apparently,* she added to herself, *you can manage to amuse yourselves without me.* Feeling a hand on her arm, Foxy glanced up.

"Hi. I knew you'd stand still long enough eventually for me to introduce myself. I'm Scott Newman."

"Hello. Cynthia Fox." Her hand was taken in a very proper shake.

"Yes, I know. You're Kirk's sister."

Foxy smiled at him as she completed her study of his features. His face was well formed, just escaping fullness. His eyes were deep brown, his nose straight, his mouth long and curved. He wore his brown hair at a conservative length, neither long nor short. They stood eye to eye, as he was a few inches short of six feet. He was handsomely tanned and trim without being lean. His three-piece suit was well cut, but the jacket had been casually left unbuttoned. He was, Foxy decided, the perfect model for a study of up-and-coming young executives. She thought briefly that it was a pity he hadn't dressed up the beige suit with a deep-toned shirt.

"We'll be seeing a lot of each other over the next few months," he told her, unaware of the trend of her thoughts.

"Oh?" She gave him her full attention as she eased out of the way of someone bearing a tray of crackers and Gouda cheese.

"I'm Kirk's road manager. I see to all the traveling arrangements, accommodations for him and the crew, and so forth." His eyes smiled over to hers while he lifted his glass to his lips.

"I see." Foxy tilted her head, then tossed back her hair. "I haven't been around for a few years." Catching a glimpse of her brother out of the corner of her eye, Foxy focused on him, then smiled. He had the animated look of a knight-on-quest as a brunette hung on his arm and a small tangle of people hung on his words. "We didn't use a road manager when I was on the team," she murmured. Foxy remembered more than once falling asleep in the backseat of a car in a garage that smelled of gasoline and stale cigarettes. Or camping on the infield grass, waiting for the morning and the race. *He's a comet,* she thought, watching her brother. *A brilliant, flaming comet.*

"There've been a number of changes in the past few years," Scott commented. "Kirk began winning more important races. And, of course, with Lance Matthews's sponsorship, his career has come more into focus."

"Yes." She gave a quick laugh and shook her head. "Money talks after all, doesn't it?"

"You haven't got a drink." Scott noticed the lack of glass, but not the sarcasm in her voice. "We'd better fix that."

"Sure." Foxy linked her arm in his and allowed him to lead her to the bar. *I don't care one way or the other about Lance Matthews's money.*

"What would you like?" Scott asked.

Foxy glanced at him, then at the short, graying professional bartender. "A spritzer," she told him.

* * *

Moonlight shone through the young leaves. The flowers in the garden were still new with spring, their colors muted with night. Their fragrance was light and tender, only whispering of the promise of summer.

With a mighty sigh, Foxy dropped on one seat of a white glider and propped her feet up on the other. Dimly over the stretch of lawn, she could hear the sounds of the party ebb and flow. By slipping into the kitchen and out the back door, she had escaped to steal a few moments of quiet and solitude. Inside, the air was thick with smoke and clashing perfumes. Foxy took a long, greedy breath of spring air and pushed with her feet to set the glider into motion.

Scott Newman, she decided, was handsome, polite, intelligent, and interested. And, she admitted, ordinary. Rolling her eyes on a sigh, Foxy stared up at the sky. Wisps of dark clouds were edged in gray. As they passed lazily across the moon the light shifted and swayed. *There I go,* she mused, *being critical again. Does a man have to stand on one foot and juggle for me to consider him entertaining? What am I looking for? A knight?* Foxy frowned and rejected the choice. *No, knights are all polished and shiny and pure. I think my taste runs to something with a bit of tarnish and*

*maybe a few scratches. Someone who can make me laugh
and cry and make me angry and make my knees tremble
when he touches me.* She laughed quietly, wondering how
many men she was looking for. Leaning her head back, she
crossed her ankles. The hem of her dress lifted to tickle her
knee. Tossing up her arms, she gripped the slender poles on
either side of the glider. *I want someone dangerous, someone wild and gentle and strong and smart and foolish.* With
another laugh for her own specifications, she stared up at the
stars. With a hazy blue light, they peeked and glimmered
through the shifting clouds.

"Which star do I wish on?"

"The brightest is usually the best."

With a quick gasp, Foxy dropped her hands and searched
for the owner of the voice. He was only a dark shadow, tall
and lean. As it moved she thought of the steady stalking grace
of a panther. Lance's black attire blended with the night, but
his eyes caught the luminescence of the moon. For a moment,
Foxy felt an eeriness, a displacement of the quiet suburban
garden into a primitive, isolated jungle. Like a large cat of
prey, his eyes glowed with their own light and conquered the
dark. Shadows fell over his face and deepened its chiseled
lines. She thought Lucifer must have looked equally dark and
compelling as he fell from heaven into the flames.

"What are you wishing for?" His voice was so quiet, it
shook the air.

Suddenly Foxy became aware that she was holding her
breath. Carefully she released it. It was only the surprise, she
insisted, that had made her skin quiver. "Oh, all I can get,"
she returned flippantly. "What are you doing out here? I
thought you'd be knee-deep in blondes."

Lance swung onto the glider. "I wanted some air," he told
her as he stood staring down at her, "and some quiet."

Disturbed that his motives mirrored hers, Foxy shrugged and closed her eyes as if to ignore him. "How did you manage to tear yourself away from Miss Lush Bust?"

The sounds of the party penetrated the quiet of the night. Foxy felt his eyes on her face but stubbornly kept hers closed. "So," he murmured, "you've grown claws. You shouldn't sharpen them on someone's back, Foxy. The face is cleaner."

She opened her eyes and met his. Reluctantly she admitted that she had been nasty from the moment she had seen him again. Unprovoked nastiness was out of character for her. Foxy sighed and shrugged. "I'm sorry. I don't usually make a habit of snarling and spitting. Sit down, Lance, I'll try to behave." A small smile accompanied the invitation. He did not, as she had expected, sit across from her. Instead, he dropped down beside her. Foxy stiffened. Either unaware of or unconcerned by her reaction, Lance propped his feet next to hers on the opposite bench.

"I don't mind sparring, Fox, but a rest between rounds is always refreshing." Pulling out his lighter, he flicked it at the end of a long, thin cigar. The flame licked and flared. Strange, she thought as she relaxed her muscles, how clearly I remember that scent.

"Let's see if we can manage to be civilized for a few minutes," Foxy suggested and twisted slightly to face him. A smile hovered on her lips. She was an adult now, she reminded herself, and could meet him on his own terms. "Shall we discuss the weather, the latest best-seller, the political structure of Romania? I know"—she propped her cheek on her palm—"the race. How does it feel to be designing cars instead of racing them? Are you more hopeful for the Indy car you designed, or the Formula One for the Grand Prix races? Kirk's done very well on the GP circuit since the season opened. The car's supposed to be very fast and very reliable."

Lance saw the mischief in her eyes and lifted a brow. "Still reading racing magazines, Foxy?"

"If I didn't keep up to date, Kirk would never forgive me." She laughed, a low, heavy sound.

"I see that hasn't changed," Lance commented. She gave him a puzzled smile. "Even at fifteen, you had the sexiest laugh I'd ever heard. Like something stealing through the fog." He blew out a stream of smoke as she shifted in her seat. Moonlight showered on her hair, shooting out hundreds of tiny flames. She felt just the smallest hint of his power tempting her.

"The main branch of your company is in Boston," Foxy began, navigating to safer ground. "I suppose you live there now."

Lance smiled at her maneuver and tipped off the ash at the end of his cigar. "Most of the time. Ever been there?" He tossed his arm over the back of the seat. The gesture was so casual Foxy was barely aware of it.

"No." The glider's motion continued, slow and soothing. "I'd like to. I know there are fabulous contrasts. Brownstones and ivy, and steel and glass. I've seen some very effective pictures."

"I saw one of yours not too long ago."

"Oh?" Curious, she turned her head toward him and was surprised to find their faces nearly touching. His warm breath touched her lips. The power was stronger this time, and even more tempting. As she inched cautiously away his eyes never flickered from hers.

"It was taken in winter, but there was no snow, only a bit of frost on naked trees. There was a bench, and an old man was sleeping on it wrapped up in a gray and black topcoat. The sun came low through the trees and fell right across him. It was incredibly sad and quite beautiful."

Foxy was for the moment at a total loss. She had not

expected Lance Matthews to possess any sensitivity or appreciation for the fine points of her craft. As they sat in silence something was happening between them, but she knew neither how to resist or encourage it. It was something as elemental as man and woman and as complex as emotion. His eyes continued to hold hers as his fingers tangled in the tips of her hair.

"I was very impressed," he went on as she remained silent and perplexed. "I noticed your name under it. I thought at first it couldn't be you. The Cynthia Fox I remembered didn't have the ability to take a picture with that much depth, that much feeling. I still knew you as a wide-eyed adolescent with a vile temper." When Lance broke the look to flick away the stub of his cigar, Foxy let out a quiet, shaky breath.

Relax, she ordered herself. *Stop being an idiot.*

"In any case, I was curious enough to do some checking. When I found it was you, I was doubly impressed." As he turned back to her one brow lifted and disappeared under the tousled front of his hair. "Obviously you're very good at what you do."

"What? Play with cameras?" But she smiled with the question. The evening air had mellowed her mood.

His grin was quick. "I've always thought a person should enjoy their work. I've been playing with cars for years."

"You can afford to play," she reminded him. Her voice cooled without her being aware of it.

"You've never forgiven me for having money, have you?" There was a light amusement in his voice that made her feel foolish.

"No." She shrugged. "I suppose not. Ten million always seemed so ostentatious."

He laughed, a low rumble, then tugged on her hair until she faced him again. "Only new money is ostentatious in Boston, Foxy. Old money is discreet."

"What constitutes 'old,' financially speaking?" Foxy found she enjoyed his laugh and the friendly hand on her hair.

"Oh, I'd say three generations would be the bare minimum. Anything less would be suspect. You know, Fox, I much prefer the lily of the valley to the gasoline you used to wear."

"Thanks. I do wear unleaded now and again, but only when I'm feeling reckless." She rose with a sigh. It surprised her that she would have preferred sitting with him to rejoining the party. "I'd better get back in. Are you coming?"

"Not yet." He took her hand and with a swift jerk spun her around until she tumbled into his lap.

"Lance!" With a surprised laugh, she pushed against his chest. "What are you doing?" Her struggles were halfhearted, though his hands were still firm on her waist. Foxy's mood was still mellow.

"I never kissed you hello."

Laughter died on her lips as she sensed danger. Quickly she jerked back, but he cupped his hand around the base of her neck. She managed a startled "no!" before his mouth closed over hers.

The kiss began light and teasing. Indeed, she could feel the curve of a small smile on the lips that touched hers. Perhaps if she had struggled, perhaps if her protest had continued, it would have stopped at a careless brush of lips. But as their mouths met, Foxy froze. It seemed her heart stopped pumping, her lungs stopped drawing and releasing air, her pulse stopped beating as her blood lay still. Then, in a sudden wild fury, her blood began to swim again.

Who deepened the kiss first she would never know. It seemed instantaneous. Hot and hungry, their mouths took from each other in a moist, depthless, endless kiss. The muffled groan that touched the air might have come from either of them or both. Her breasts were soft and yielding against his chest as she used tongue and teeth and lips to take the kiss still deeper. He explored all the intimate recesses of her mouth while she wallowed in his flavor, his scent, in the feel of his skin against hers. His hand moved once in a long, bruising stroke down her back and waist and over her hip and thigh. The thin material of her dress was little more than air between them. At the rough caress, Foxy strained closer, nipping his lip to provoke more heat. His answer was to crush her mouth savagely, desperately, until her senses tangled into ecstatic confusion. With a quiet sound of pleasure, she went limp in his arms. Their lips clung for an instant longer as he drew her away.

Her eyes seemed as gray as his as they watched each other in silence. Her arms were still locked around his neck. Foxy could no longer smell the flowers but only his warm male aroma, she could no longer hear the laughter of the party for the quiet sound of his breathing, she could no longer feel the breeze, but only the spreading heat of his hands. Only he existed. An owl swooped from the tree behind them and hooted three times. Instantly the spell was shattered. Foxy shuddered, swallowed, and struggled to her feet.

"You shouldn't have done that." As tingles continued to race along her skin she avoided his eyes and brushed distractedly at the skirt of her dress.

"No? Why not?" Lance's voice was as calm as a shrug. "You're a big girl now." He stood, and she was forced to tilt her head to see his face. "You enjoyed that as much as I did. It's a little late to play the flustered maiden."

"I'm not playing the flustered maiden," Foxy denied hotly as her eyes shot back to his. "Whether I enjoyed it or not is beside the point." Realizing she was fitting his description precisely, she tossed her hair behind her back in annoyance. She planned to make a dignified exit as she stepped from the glider, but Lance stopped her with a hand on her arm before she had taken two steps across the grass.

"What is the point, Fox?" He no longer sounded amused or calm but irritated.

"The point is," she said between her teeth, "don't do it again."

"Orders?" he murmured softly. "I don't take orders very well."

"I'm not asking for a ham on rye," she countered. "I was off guard." Foxy tried to reason out her response to him while justifying it. "And—and tired and perhaps a bit curious. I overreacted."

"Curious?" His laugh was male and again amused. "Did I satisfy your curiosity, Foxy? Maybe like Alice, you'll find it 'curiouser and curiouser.' " He trailed his fingers lightly up her arm. Foxy shied away as her skin trembled.

"You're impossible!" She pushed the hair from her face in impatient fury. "You've always been impossible." With this, she whirled and ran toward the safety of the party. Lance watched her dress float and swirl around her.

CHAPTER 3

The Indianapolis 500 is an event that transforms Indianapolis from an ordinary midwestern city into the focus of the racing world. More people watch this one race than any other single sporting event in the country. It is for car racing what Wimbledon is for tennis, what the Kentucky Derby is for horse racing, what the World Series is for baseball—prestige, honor, excitement.

Foxy was relieved that the sky was empty of clouds. There was not even the smallest wisp to hint of rain. The mixture of rain and racing always made her uneasy. A breeze teased the ends of the ribbon that held her hair in a ponytail. Her jeans were old friends, nearly white with wear at the knees and snug at the hips. A baseball-style shirt in red and white pinstripes was tucked neatly into the waist. Around her neck hung the secondhand Nikon she had purchased while in college. Foxy would not have traded it for a chest of gold. From her vantage point in the pits, she could see that the grandstands were empty. Reporters, television crews, drivers, mechanics all milled about attending to business or drinking coffee from foam cups. The air was quiet enough to allow an occasional birdsong to carry, but it was not calm. A current ran through the air, stirring up waves of tension and excitement. In less than two hours, the stands and infield would be swarming with people. When the green flag was waved, Indianapolis Motor Speedway would hold four hundred thousand people, a number that rivaled the population of some American cities. The noise would explode like one long roar of thunder.

During the hours that followed, there would be a continuous drone of engines. The pits would grow steamy with heat and thick with the smell of fuel and sweat. Eyes would be glued to the small, low-slung cars as they tore around the two-and-a-half-mile oval. Some would think only of the thrill of the race.

Foxy's feelings were more complicated. It had been two years since she had stood near a racetrack and six since she had been a part of the racing world. But it was, she discovered as she stared around her, like yesterday. The feelings, the emotions inside her, had not been altered by her absence. There was anticipation, excitement. She was almost lightheaded with it, and she knew it would grow only more intense after the race began. There was a wonder and pride at knowing her brother's skill, a talent that seemed more innate than learned. But underlying all was a deep-rooted fear, a terror so rich and sharp, it never dulled with the years. All the sensations scrambled inside her, and she knew when the green flag was waved, they would all merge together into one heady, indescribable emotion. Nothing had changed.

Foxy knew the ropes. There were some drivers who would grant interviews and speak cheerfully, casually, about the race to come. Others would be technical or abstract, some belligerent. She knew Kirk would grant early interviews, answering questions with his patented brand of appealing arrogance. To Kirk each race was the same and each race was unique. It was the same because he drove each to win, unique because each race presented problems unlike any before or after. Foxy knew after the interviews that he would disappear and remain alone until it was time to be strapped into the cockpit. From long experience, she knew how to be unobtrusive. She moved among drivers and timers and mechanics and the dozens of other photographers, letting her camera record the prerace routine.

"What are you poking around here with that thing for?"

Foxy recognized the grumble but finished her shot before turning. "Hiya, Charlie." With a grin, she tossed her arms around his neck and nuzzled his grizzled cheek. She knew he would protest and grumble as well as she knew the hug pleased him.

"Just like a female," he muttered, but Foxy felt the slight squeeze of his hands on her back before he pulled away.

For the next few minutes, they studied each other openly. She saw little change. There was a bit more gray in his beard, a bit less hair on his head, but his eyes were the same clear blue she had first seen ten years before. He had been fifty then, and she had thought him ancient. As Lance Matthews's chief mechanic, Charlie Dunning had ruled the pits like a despot. He continued to do so now as the head of Kirk's team.

"Still skinny," he said in disgust. "I should've known a few years wouldn't put any weight on you. Don't you make enough money to eat by taking pictures?"

"No one's been leaving chocolate bars lying around for me lately." She pinched his cheek as she spoke, knowing he would suffer torture and death before admitting he had planted chocolate bars for a skinny kid to find. "I missed you at Kirk's party the other night," she added as he shuffled and grumbled.

"I don't go to kids' parties. So you and the fancy lady are going to take in the Indy and the rest of the Grand Prix races this season." He sniffled and set his mouth in a disapproving line.

"If you mean Pam, then yes, we are." Foxy decided Charlie had nearly perfected irascibility. "And she's a journalist."

"You just mind that neither of you gets in the way."

"Yes, Charlie," Foxy said demurely, but his eyes narrowed at the gleam in hers.

"Still sassy, too. If you hadn't been so puny, I'd have taken a strap to you years ago."

Grinning, Foxy lifted the camera and shot a full-faced picture. "Smile," she suggested.

"Sassy," Charlie repeated. As his lips started to twitch he turned and lumbered away.

Foxy watched until he had disappeared into the crowd before she turned around. She gave a small gasp as she bumped into Lance. He rested his hands briefly on her shoulders as his eyes locked with hers. She had managed to completely block out the interlude on the glider, but now it all came flooding back in full force. The mouth, which had been hungry on hers, twitched in a half smile.

"He always did have a soft spot for you."

Foxy had forgotten everything but the dark gray eyes that watched her. As his smile grew, touched now with arrogance, she jerked out of his hold. He was dressed in much the same manner as she was, in jeans and a T-shirt. His hair danced on his forehead as the breeze caught it. Mentally she cursed him for being so wickedly attractive.

"Hello, Lance." Her voice was marginally friendly with overtones of aloofness. Foxy was pleased with it. "No reporters dogging your footsteps?"

"Hello, Foxy," he returned equally. "Taking a few snapshots?"

"Touché," Foxy muttered. Turning away, she lifted the Nikon to her face and became absorbed in setting the aperture.

She thought she must have gained an extra sense where Lance Matthews was concerned. His presence could be felt on the surface of her skin. It was both uncomfortable and arousing.

"Looking forward to the race, Foxy, or has it lost its charm?" As he spoke Lance tangled his fingers in the thick softness of her ponytail. Foxy wasted four shots.

"I heard Kirk won the pole position in the time trials. He knows how to cash in on that kind of advantage." When she turned back to him, her face was calm, her eyes cool. One kiss, she told herself, was nothing to be concerned about. They were still the same people. "I imagine as the owner, you're pleased." His smile was not the answer Foxy was looking for. "I've seen the car. It's very impressive." When he still did not reply, Foxy let out a frustrated breath and squinted up at him. "This conversation is fascinating, Lance, but I really must get back to work."

His hand curled firmly around her upper arm as she turned to go. He watched her in silence, and she was forced to toss up a hand to shield her eyes from the sun. "I'm having a small party tonight." His voice was quiet. "In my suite at the hotel."

"Oh?" Foxy employed the arched-brow look she had perfected in college.

"Seven o'clock. We'll have dinner."

"How small a party?" Foxy met his eyes steadily, though hers were shadowed by her hand.

"Very small, as in you and me."

"Smaller," she corrected evenly, "as in just you." Two mechanics, clad in the vivid red shirts of Kirk's team, moved past them. Lance's gaze never wandered from hers. "I have a date with Scott Newman."

"Break it."

"No."

"Afraid?" he taunted, bringing her an inch closer with a slight movement of his hand.

"No, I'm not afraid," Foxy retorted. The green in her eyes shimmered against the gray in his. "But I'm not stupid either. Maybe you've forgotten, I'm not a newcomer where you're concerned. I've already seen your string of—ah—ladies," she said with a dash of scorn. "It was quite a boost to my education, watching you pick and shuffle and discard. I do my own picking," she added, growing angrier as he remained silent. "And I do my own discarding. Go find someone else to feed your voracious ego."

Abruptly Lance smiled. His voice was light and amused. "You still have a vile temper, Foxy. You've also got a bright, inquiring mind and energy in every cell. You'll outdistance Newman in an hour, and he'll bore you to distraction."

"That's my problem," Foxy snapped, then remembered to jerk her arm free.

"That it is," Lance agreed cheerfully. He deprived her of having the last word by walking away.

Infuriated, Foxy whirled around, prepared to stomp off in the opposite direction. With a small shock, she saw that the grandstands were filling with people. Time was moving quickly. Annoyed, she swiftly walked down into the pit area.

As she interviewed a rookie driver Pam watched the entire scene between Lance and Foxy. It wasn't possible for her to hear what passed between them, but she had clearly seen the variety of emotions take possession of Foxy's face. She watched them with the objectivity and curiosity peculiar to her trade. There was something physical between them; she had only to see them together to be certain. She was certain, too, that Foxy was kicking out against it like an ill-tempered mule and that she had come out second best in the battle that had just taken place.

Pam had liked Lance Matthews immediately. She was

prone to judge people quickly, then calculate the most direct
and productive approach to them. The consistent accuracy of
her judgment had helped her climb to success in her profession. She had judged Lance Matthews as a man who did not
so much shun convention as make his own. He would at-
tract both men and women simply because he had so much
to offer. He had strength and arrogance and a rich sensuality. Pam thought he would be indispensable as a friend and
terrifying as a lover.

The rookie, blissfully unaware of her preoccupation, continued to answer her questions as she wound up the interview. With one eye cocked on Lance's back, Pam thanked
him graciously, wished him luck, and hurried off.

"Mr. Matthews!"

Lance turned. He watched a small, delicate-faced blonde
dressed impeccably in gray slacks and a blazer running toward him. A tape recorder was slung over one shoulder, a
purse over the other. Curious, he waited until she caught up
with him. Pam paused and offered Lance a breathless smile.

"Mr. Matthews, I'm Pam Anderson." She held out a hand
whose nails were polished a baby-pink. "I'm doing a series
of articles on racing. Perhaps Foxy mentioned me."

"Hello." Lance held her hand a moment as he studied her.
He had expected someone sturdier. "I suppose we missed
each other at Kirk's party the other night."

"You were pointed out to me," Pam told him, deciding to
use flat-out honesty as her approach. "But you disappeared
before I could wrangle my way over to you. Foxy disappeared, too."

"You're very observant." Though the annoyance in his
voice was only slight, Pam recognized it and was pleased.
She knew she had his full attention.

"Our friendship is still at the apprentice stage, but I'm very
fond of Foxy. I also know how to mind my own business."

She brushed absently at her hair as the wind teased it into her eyes. "Professionally, I'm only interested in the race and any and all aspects thereof. I'm hoping you'll help me. Not only do you know what it's like to design and own a Formula One, you know what it's like to compete in one. You also know this track and the specifics of an Indy car. The fact that you're a well-known figure not only in racing circles but in society will add tremendous readability to the series."

Sometime during Pam's speech, Lance had stuck his hands in his pockets. He waited for a full ten seconds to see if she was finished before he started to chuckle. "A few minutes ago, I was trying to figure out how you could be the same Pam Anderson who wrote that blistering series on foul-ups in the penal system." He inclined his head in a gesture she took as a seal of approval. "Now I know. We'll have plenty of time to talk over the next few months." Pam watched his gaze shift and focus to where Foxy leaned against a fence and fiddled with lenses. She saw the birth of his patented smile. "Plenty of time." When his attention darted back to Pam, his grin widened and settled. "What do you know about the 500?"

"The first 500 was in 1911, and the winning car had an average speed of 74.59 miles per hour. The track was originally paved in brick, hence the nickname the Old Brickyard. It's a full-throttle race where a driver moves to high gear and stays there. It's not a Grand Prix race because no points are given, but there are many similarities between the Formula One car and the Indy car. There are also a number of drivers who have competed in both the 500 and the Grand Prix circuit . . . like Kirk Fox. The cars here are fueled by alcohol. An alcohol fire is particularly dangerous because there's no flame."

"You've done your homework." Lance grinned at the computerlike flow of information.

"Oh, I have the facts," she agreed, liking the directness of his gaze. "But they don't tell the whole story. Forty-six people have died at this race, but only three in the last ten years. Why?"

"Cars are safer," Lance answered. "They used to be built like battleships, and in a crash they stayed solid and the driver absorbed all the power. Now it's the fragility of the cars that saves lives. Cars self-destruct around a driver, diffusing the power away from him. The restraint systems have been improved, and the drivers wear fire-resistant clothes from the shoes up." Sensing that the starting time was drawing near, Lance led her back toward the start-finish line.

"So racing has become fairly safe?" Pam asked. Her look was as candid as her voice was soft.

Again Lance gave her his full attention. She was a very sharp lady. "I didn't say that. It's safer, but there will always be the element of risk. Without it, a race like the Indy would just be some cars going in a circle."

"But a crash doesn't bring the fear it once did?"

He grinned again and shook his head. "I doubt if many drivers think about crashing. If they did, they wouldn't get into a cockpit. It's never going to happen to you, always to someone else. When you do think about it, you accept it as part of the rules. A crash is never the worst fear in any case. It's fire. There isn't a driver alive who doesn't have a gut fear of fire."

"What about when you're driving and another driver crashes? What do you feel then?"

"You don't," he answered simply. "You can't. There isn't room in the cockpit for emotion."

"No." She nodded. "I can understand that. But there is one thing I don't understand. I don't understand why."

"Why?"

"Why do people strap themselves into a car and whirl

around a circuit at earth-shattering speeds. Why do they risk injury or death? What's the motivation?"

Lance turned and frowned at the track. "It varies. I imagine there're as many motivations as there are drivers—the thrill, the competition, the challenge, the money, the prestige, the speed. Speed can be addictive. There's the need to prove your own capabilities, to test your own endurance. And, of course, there's the ego that goes with any sport." As he turned back to Pam he saw Kirk step out into the sunlight. "Drivers all have different degrees of need, but they all need to win."

Foxy moved around the car, crouching and snapping as Kirk was strapped into the cockpit. He pulled the balaclava over his head, and for the moments before he fixed the helmet over it, he looked like an Arthurian knight preparing to joust. He answered Charlie's questions with short words or moves of his head. Already, his concentration was consumed by the race. Beneath his helmet visor, his eyes were unfathomable, his expression neither relaxed nor tense. There was an air about him of being separate, not only from the people crowded around the car, but from himself. Foxy could sense his detachment, and her camera captured it. As she straightened she watched Lance walk over and bend close to her brother's head.

"I got a case of scotch says you won't break the track record."

She saw Kirk's imperceptible nod and knew he had accepted the challenge. He would thrive on it. From the opposite side of the car, Foxy studied Lance, realizing he knew Kirk better than she had imagined. His eyes lifted and met hers as the engine roared to life between them. As Kirk cruised onto the track to take his pole position Foxy disappeared inside the garage area.

As the last strands of "Back Home Again in Indiana" floated on the air, the crowd roared with approval at the release of the thousands of colored balloons. For miles, those who were not at the Motor Speedway would see the drifting orbs and know that the 500 was under way. The order was official, ringing out over the rumble of the crowd. "Gentlemen, start your engines." On the starting grid, tension revved as high as the engines.

The stands were a wave of color and noise as the cars began their pace lap. The speed seemed minimal. The cars themselves, low splashes of color and lettering, were in formation and well behaved. They shone clean and bright in the streaming light of the sun. No longer could bird songs be heard. Suddenly the pace car pulled away and sped off the track.

"This is it," Foxy murmured, and Pam jumped slightly.

"I thought I'd lost you." She pushed her sunglasses more firmly on her nose.

"You don't think I'd miss the start, do you?" There was a long sports lens on her camera now, and she had it trained on the track. "They'll get the green flag any second now." Pam noticed that she seemed a bit pale, but as she opened her mouth to comment, the air exploded with noise. With professional ease, Foxy drew a bead on the white flash of Kirk's racer.

"How can they do it?" Pam spoke to herself, but Foxy lowered her camera and turned to her. "How can they keep up that pace for five hundred miles?"

"To win," Foxy said simply.

The afternoon wore on. The noise never abated. The heat in the pits was layered with the smell of fuel, oil, and sweat. Out of a field of thirty, ten cars were already out of the running due to mechanical failure or minor crashes. A broken gearbox, a failed clutch, a split-second error in judgment brought the curtain down on hope. Pam had discarded her blazer, rolled up the sleeves of her white lawn blouse, and now stalked the pit area with her tape recorder. Trickles of dampness worked their way down Foxy's back. Her shirt clung to her skin, and her hair curled damply around her face. But there was another tickle between her shoulder blades, one that had her stiffening and turning away from the track. Lance stood directly behind her. He spoke first but looked beyond her. The track was a valley cupped inside the mountains of the grandstands.

"He's going into lap 85." He had a cold drink in his hand and held it out to her without shifting his gaze. Foxy took it and drank, though his thoughtfulness confused her. "Yes, I know. He's got nearly a full lap on Johnston. Have you timed his average speed?"

"Just over 190."

Foxy watched Kirk maneuver through a tight cluster of cars. She held her breath as he passed a racer in the short chute between turns three and four. She stared down into floating chunks of ice, then drank again. "You've set up a tremendous pit crew. I timed the last fuel stop at under twelve seconds. They've given Kirk an edge. And it's obvious the car's fast and handles magnificently."

Slowly Lance lowered his eyes and looked down at her. "We both know racing is a matter of teamwork."

"All but this part," Foxy countered. "Out there it's really up to Kirk, isn't it?"

"You've been standing a long time." The softness of Lance's voice brought Foxy's attention back to him. "Why don't you sit down for a while." He could nearly see the headache that was drumming inside her skull. Surprising them both, he lifted a hand to her cheek in a rare gesture of tenderness. "You look tired." He dropped his hand, then stuck it in his pocket.

"No, no, I can't." Foxy turned away, oddly moved by the lingering warmth on her cheek. "Not until it's over. You're going to lose that scotch, you know."

"I'm counting on it." He swore suddenly, causing her to turn back to him. "I don't like the way number 15 handles turn one. He gets closer to the wall every time."

"Fifteen?" Foxy narrowed her eyes as she searched the streaking stream of cars. "That's one of the rookies, isn't it? The kid from Long Beach."

"The *kid*'s a year older than you are," Lance muttered. "But he hasn't the experience to go that high in the groove. He's going to lose it."

Seconds later, number 15 approached turn one again, only to challenge the unforgiving wall too closely. Sparks flew as the rear wheels slammed into the solid force, then were sheared off and tossed into the air as the car began to spin out of control. Pieces of fiberglass began to spray the air as three cars swerved, maneuvering like snakes around the wounded racer. One nearly lost control, its wheels skidding wildly before gripping the asphalt. The yellow flag came down as number 15 flipped into the infield and lay still. Instantly it was surrounded by emergency crews and fire extinguishers.

As always when she witnessed a crash, a frozen calm descended over Foxy. She did not think or feel. From the instant the car connected with the wall, she had lifted her camera and recorded each step of the crash. Dispassionately she focused, set speed and depth of field. One of her shots would be a classic study of a car in distress. She felt only a shudder of relief when she saw the driver crawl from the wreckage and give the traditional wave to assure the crowd he was unharmed.

"My God. How can a man walk away from a wreck like that?" Foxy heard Pam's voice behind her but continued to shoot the routine of the emergency crew in the infield.

"As I told you before, the very fragility of the racer and the improved restraints have saved more than one life on the grid." Lance answered Pam but his attention was on Foxy. Her face was without color or expression as she lowered her camera.

"But not all of them," she stated as she caught the blur of Kirk's car as it whizzed by. "And not every time." She felt the cold passing as warmth seeped back under her skin. "You'd better go interview that driver. He'll be able to give you a firsthand report on what it's like to see your life pass before your eyes at two hundred miles an hour."

"Yes, I will." Pam gave her a searching look but said nothing more before she moved away.

Foxy pushed a stray hair from her face, allowing her camera to dangle by its strap. "I suppose number 15 will have more respect for turn one the next time."

"You're very professional and unflappable these days, aren't you, Fox?" Lance's eyes were cold as steel under his lowered brows. Foxy remembered the look and felt an inward tremor.

"Photographers have to have good nerves." She met his look of annoyance without flinching. She knew if annoyance turned to genuine anger, he could be brutal.

"But feelings aren't necessary," he countered. He gathered the strap of her camera in one hand and pulled her closer. "There was a man in number 15. You never missed a frame."

"What did you expect me to do?" she tossed back. "Get hysterical? Cover my eyes with my hands? I've seen crashes before. I've seen them when they haven't walked away, when there hasn't been anything to see but a sheet of fire. I've watched both you and Kirk being dragged out by the epaulettes. You want emotion?" Her voice rose in a sudden torrent of fury. "Go find someone who didn't grow up on the smell of death and gasoline!"

Lance studied her in silence. Color had shot back into her face. Her eyes were like a raging sea under a haze of clouds. "Tough lady, aren't you?" His tone was touched with amusement and scorn, a combination Foxy found intolerable.

"Damn right," she agreed and tossed her chin out further. "Now, take your hands off my camera."

At first, the only thing that moved was his left brow. It rose in an arch that might have indicated humor or acceptance. In an exaggerated gesture, he lifted both hands, holding them aloft, empty palms toward her. Still, he did not back off, and they stood toe to toe. "Sorry, Fox." She knew him well enough to detect the dregs of temper in his voice. Her own anger forced her to ignore it.

"Just leave me alone," she ordered and started to brush by him. To her fury, he stepped neatly in her path and blocked her exit.

"I'll just be another minute," he told her. Before she had grasped his motive, Lance had shifted the camera to her back and pulled her into his arms.

As she opened her mouth to protest he closed his over it and plundered its depths. She was caught fast. Instead of pushing against him, her hands gripped desperately on his upper arms. They would not obey the command her brain shot out to them. Her mouth answered his even as she ordered it to be cold and still. The flame sparked and burned just as quickly, just as intensely, as it had the night on the glider. She could not deny that even if her mind and her heart were her own, her body was his. Never had she known such perfection in a touch, such intimacy, such hunger. She lifted her arms to lock them around his neck as her body melted into his. The whine of finely tuned engines whirled in her brain, then was lost in a flood of need and desire. The people who milled around them faded, then disappeared from her world as she strained closer. She demanded more of him even as she gave all of herself. Ultimately it was Lance who drew away. They were still tangled in each other's arms, their faces close, their bodies molded. With his quiet, probing intensity, he stared down at her.

"I suppose you'll tell me I shouldn't have done that."

"Would it make any difference if I did?" Her knees wanted badly to tremble, but Foxy forced them to be still.

"No," he answered. "It wouldn't."

"Will you let me go now?" Foxy was pleased at the cool, impersonal timbre of her voice. Inside her stomach dozens of bats were waging war.

"For now," he agreed. Though he loosened his grip, he kept his hands light on her hips. "I can always pick up where I left off."

"Your conceit is threatening to outweigh your arrogance these days, Lance." Firmly Foxy drew his hands from her hips. "I don't know which is more unappealing."

Lance grinned at the insult and tweaked her nose in a brotherly fashion. "You're cute when you're dignified, Foxy." His glance wandered over her head as he saw Kirk veer off the track and onto the pit lane. "Kirk's coming in. With any luck, the second half of the race will run as smoothly as the first."

Refusing to dignify any of his comments with an answer, Foxy dragged her camera back in front of her and walked away. Tucking his hands in his pockets, Lance rocked gently on his heels and watched her.

Only half of the starters finished the race. Foxy had known Kirk would win. She had studied his face during his brief, final pit stop and had seen the confidence mixed with the strain and tension. Cars no longer looked shiny in the sun but were dull with grime. After the checkered flag came down, Foxy watched Kirk take his victory lap as the roars of the crowd and the crew washed over her. She knew he would come into the pits ready for adulation. His eyes would no longer be opaque. His mouth would be lifted in that easy boyish grin, and all the lines of strain would have magically vanished. Tirelessly he would grant interviews, sign autographs, accept congratulations. The layers of sweat and grime that covered him were his badge of success. He would take it all in, recharging his system. Then it would be over for him, a thing of the past. In two days, they would be on their way to Monaco for the qualifying races. The Indianapolis 500 would be to Kirk no more than a newspaper clipping. For him, it was always the next race.

CHAPTER 4

Monte Carlo is cupped between the high, forested peaks of the Maritime Alps and the brilliant blue waters of the Mediterranean Sea. Buildings are packed together, a dense pattern of skyscrapers and elegant old homes. It has the feel and look, if not the size, of a great city while maintaining a fairy-tale aura.

It was the colors that appealed to Foxy. The whites and pastels that dominated the buildings, the rich, ripe greens and browns of the mountains, and the perfect blue of the sea. Lush flowers and palms added a taste of paradise. It was a country of culture and castles, warm sea breezes, and barren peaks. The romantic in Foxy instantly fell in love with it.

With Kirk immersed in qualifying races and practice sessions and Pam involved with interviews and local color, Foxy often found herself thrown together with Scott Newman. She found him kind, considerate, intelligent, and—though she detested Lance for being right—dull. He planned too thoroughly, considered too carefully, and followed through too accurately for Foxy's taste. Each of their dates, no matter how casual, was given an itinerary. He dressed perfectly, even elegantly, and his manners were identical. With Scott, Foxy knew there would be no disasters, no dangers, no surprises. More than once, she felt a twinge of guilt, knowing her character would never be as untarnished as his. He was a knight on a white charger who rescued his quota of damsels in distress each day, then polished his armor.

Restlessly Foxy wandered from window to window mulling over her analysis. There was a light staccato clicking from Pam's typewriter. She could see boats of all sizes and descriptions docked in the Bay of Monaco or moving out to sea. She recalled that during one of the qualifying races, a car had taken a turn badly and joined the boats in the water. Foxy turned from the window and watched Pam's fingers fly over the keys. The table where she worked was strewn with notes and paper and cassettes. There was a unique organization to it all, but only Pam had the solution.

"Are you going to the casino tonight?" Foxy asked. She felt restless and dissatisfied.

"Mmm, no . . . I want to finish this segment." Pam's rhythm never altered. "You going with Scott?"

Frowning, Foxy threw herself into a chair and draped her feet over the arm. "Yes, I suppose."

At the sulky tone, Pam sighed and stopped typing. Foxy's long mouth was pursed in a pout, and her brows were drawn together over moody eyes. Russet curls tumbled without design over her shoulders. All at once, Pam felt very old.

"All right." She propped her elbows on her table and laid her chin on her laced hands. "Tell Momma." Quite purposely, her tone was mild and patronizing. Foxy's chin shot out. Met with Pam's amused, affectionate smile, however, her defiance melted.

"I'm being an idiot," Foxy confessed with a self-deprecating laugh. "And I don't know why. I'm absolutely crazy about Monte Carlo. It has to be one of the most romantic and perfect spots in the universe. More, I'm getting paid to be here. I even have a terrific-looking man dancing attendance on me, and I'm . . ." She drew a deep breath and swept her arms in a huge circle.

"Bored," Pam supplied. She lifted her cup, sipped cold coffee, and grimaced. "You've been left almost entirely in Scott's company. Though he is nice, he isn't the most stimulating companion. Kirk's not available, I'm tied up, Lance is—"

"I don't need Lance's company," Foxy said too quickly. Her frown became more pronounced. Not having Lance Matthews to contend with was a blessing, not a problem.

Pam said nothing for a moment, recalling the tempestuous kiss she had seen them exchange at the Indianapolis Speedway. "In any case," she said carefully, "you've been deserted."

"Scott really is very nice." Somehow, Foxy felt the statement defended both Scott and herself. "And he's not pushy. I made it clear from the beginning that I wasn't interested in a serious relationship and he accepted it. He didn't argue." Foxy swung herself out of the chair and began to pace. "He hasn't tried to lure me into the bedroom, he doesn't lose his temper, he doesn't forget the time, he doesn't do anything outrageous." Foxy remembered that both times Lance had kissed her, it had been over her protests. "He makes me feel comfortable," she added tersely. She glared at Pam, daring her to comment.

"My fuzzy blue slippers do the same thing for me."

Foxy wanted badly to be angry, but a gurgle of laughter escaped. "That's terrible."

"You're not built to be satisfied with comfortable relationships." Pam twirled a pencil between her fingers and frowned at the eraser. "Like your brother, you thrive on challenges of one sort or another." Shaking off a quick moodiness, she lifted her eyes and smiled. "Now, Lance Matthews . . ."

"Oh no," Foxy interrupted, holding her hand up like a traffic cop. "Stop right there. I might not be looking for comfort, but I'm not looking for a bed of nails either."

"Just a thought," Pam said mildly. "I seriously doubt he would ever make you feel bored or comfortable."

"Comfortable boredom begins to sound more appealing," Foxy commented. "In fact," she added as she headed for the door, "I'm going to thoroughly enjoy myself tonight. In all probability I'll win a fortune at roulette. I'll buy you a hot dog out of my winnings at the race tomorrow." With a wink, she shut the door behind her.

Alone, Pam allowed her smile to dissolve. For the next few minutes, she stared down at the typewritten page in her machine. *Kirk Fox,* she decided, *is becoming a problem. Not that he has made even the slightest advance since his arrogant declaration the night of his party,* she mused. *He's been much too involved with the races to do any more than vaguely acknowledge my presence.* Pam ignored the annoyance the fact brought her and straightened a pile of blank typing paper. *And of course, he's had all those women hanging around him.* Pam sniffed and shrugged and went back to her typing. *With any luck,* she thought as she attacked the keys, *he'll be just as busy throughout the entire season.*

Feeling guilty over her discussion of Scott, Foxy dressed with special care for the evening. Her dress was a stretchy black jersey that clung to her curves and left her shoulders bare. The neckline was cut straight, secured with elastic just above the subtle swell of her breasts. She swept her hair off her neck into a chignon, letting loose tendrils fall over her brow and cheeks. With the addition of a thin silver chain around her neck and a quick spray of cologne, she felt ready for the elegance of the Monte Carlo casino.

Just as she was transferring the bare necessities into a small silver evening bag, a knock sounded on her door. With one quick glance around the hotel room, Foxy went to admit Scott. She found herself face-to-face with Lance Matthews.

"Oh," she said foolishly as she recalled her success in avoiding him since Indiana. Abruptly it occurred to her that she had never seen him in evening dress before. His suit was impeccably cut, fitting over his broad shoulders without a wrinkle. He looked different, if no less dangerous. He was, for a moment, a stranger: the Harvard graduate, the longtime resident of Beacon Hill, the heir to the Matthews fortune.

"Hello, Fox. Going to let me in or do I have to stand out in the hall?" The tone, and the ironic lift of his mouth made him Lance again. Foxy straightened her shoulders.

"Sorry, Lance, I'm practically on my way out."

"Prompt as well as beautiful?" There was an amused light in his eyes. "The two rarely go together." He stepped forward and cupped her chin in his hand before she had time to start evasive action. "We'll have to have a cocktail before dinner. The reservation isn't until eight."

Foxy backed up, then noted with disgust that the action only brought Lance farther into the room. "You'll have to run that by me again." She lifted a hand to the one on her chin but found it unbudgeable.

"We've nearly an hour before dinner," Lance stated simply. His eyes roamed her face with a hint of a smile. "Perhaps you've an idea how we might pass the time."

"You might try a few hands of solitaire," Foxy suggested evenly. "In your *own* room. Now, I'd like my face back."

"Would you?" Amusement was smooth and male in his tone. "Pity. I'm quite taken with it." With the barest of pressure, he brought her an inch closer as his gaze dropped and lingered on her mouth. "Newman sends his regrets," Lance said softly as his eyes moved back to hers. "Something—ah—came up. Do you have a wrap?"

"Came up?" Foxy repeated. She found no relief when her

chin was released as his hands moved to her bare shoulders. She felt the temperature of the room rise ten degrees. "What are you talking about?"

"Newman discovered he didn't have the evening free after all. It's a pity to cover up such elegant shoulders, but the nights here can be cool in June." They were closer than they had been a moment before, but Foxy didn't know how he had contrived it. His hands were still light on her shoulders.

"What do you mean, didn't have the evening free?" she demanded. She started to back away but his hands tightened on her shoulders slightly but meaningfully. The mockery in his smile caused her temper to soar along with her heart rate. "What did you do? What did you say to him? He's much too polite to break a date without telling me himself. You intimidated him," she finished hotly, glaring into Lance's smile.

"I certainly hope so since that was my intention." He confessed to the crime so easily, Foxy could only splutter. "Fetch your wrap."

"My—my . . . I certainly will not!" she managed in a choked voice.

"Suit yourself." Lance shrugged and took her hand.

"If you think I'm going out with you," Foxy began as she tugged furiously at her hand, "you're not running on all your cylinders. I'm not going anywhere."

"Fine." Lance's hands spanned her waist. "I find the idea of staying here very appealing." Before she could move away, he lowered his mouth to the gentle incline between her neck and shoulder. Her skin trembled.

"No." Hearing the waver in her voice, Foxy fought to steady it. The room was already swaying. "You can't stay."

"Room service is excellent here," Lance murmured as he caught the lobe of her ear between his teeth. "You smell like the woods in spring, fresh and full of secrets."

"Lance, please." It was becoming very difficult to think

as his mouth roamed over her skin, leaving a soft trail of quick kisses.

"Please what?" he whispered. Lightly he rubbed his lips over hers. His tongue teased the tip of hers before she could answer. Foxy could feel the quicksand sucking and pulling at her legs. Desperately she pushed away from him and filled her lungs with air.

"I'm starving," she said abruptly. She considered the statement a tactical retreat. Hoping to hide her vulnerability, she brushed casually at the curls that rested on her flushed cheeks. "Since you frightened off my escort, I suppose I should make you pay for my dinner. At a restaurant," she added hastily as he cocked a brow. "Then you'll have to take me to the casino as Scott was going to do."

"My pleasure," Lance replied with a faint bow.

"And I," she said, feeling stronger with the distance between them, "shall take pains to lose as much of your money as possible." Lifting a thin silk shawl from the bed, Foxy tossed it over her shoulders and flounced from the room. She managed for nearly an hour to remain cool and aloof.

* * *

Moonlight spilled over the Bay of Monaco. A breeze that had been born far out to sea drifted easily into shore. It carried its own perfume. The terrace of the restaurant was canopied by stars and palm fronds. Music floated by the secluded table, but it was too soft for Foxy to distinguish any words. Only the melody flickered like the lights of the twin white candles on the tablecloth. Between these was a red rose in a slender vase. The murmur of other diners seemed more a backdrop than a reality. Foxy was finding it difficult to maintain an indifference to an ambience that called so strongly to her romantic soul. Above all else, she wanted

Lance to see her as a mature, sophisticated woman and not a silly child who melted at soft music and starlight. Still, she trod carefully with the iced champagne. So far she had managed to keep the conversation impersonal and safe.

"I noticed the car gave Kirk a bit of trouble yesterday." Foxy speared her steamed shrimp and dipped it absently in its sauce. "I hope it's been worked out."

"An engine ring; it's been replaced." As he spoke Lance watched her over the rim of his glass. There was a light in his eyes that had Foxy doubling her guard.

"It's amazing, isn't it? So often it's a tiny thing, a twenty-five-cent part or an overlooked screw that can be the deciding factor in a race where hundreds of thousands of dollars are at stake."

"Amazing," Lance agreed in a somber tone that was belied by his half smile.

"If you're going to laugh at me," Foxy said as her chin tilted, "I'll simply get up and leave."

"I'd just bring you back." With narrowed eyes, she studied Lance for a full minute. Her prolonged examination did not appear to disturb him as he kept his eyes steady on hers. His mouth was still curved in an annoying half smile.

"You would, too," Foxy conceded with grudging admiration. Chivalrousness was simply not one of Lance's qualities, and Foxy knew that she had had enough of chivalrousness for a while. "And if I kicked up a scene that landed us both in a cell, you wouldn't be a bit bothered . . . not as long as you had your way." She sighed and shook her head, then took a sip of wine. "It's hard to gain an edge on a man who's so utterly nerveless. You drove that way. I remember." Her mouth moved in a pout as she looked back in time. "You drove with the same single-minded intensity as Kirk, but there was a smoothness he still lacks. You stalked; he charges. He's all fire and thrust, you were precise and ruthlessly steady. There was an incredible ease in your driving; you made it look simple, so effortless. But then you raced because you enjoyed it." Foxy twirled the stem of her glass between her fingers and watched the starlight play on the swirling wine.

Intrigued, Lance studied her with more care. "And Kirk doesn't?"

"Enjoy it?" Her surprise was evident in both her eyes and her voice. "He lives for it, and that's entirely different. Enjoyment comes much lower on the list." She tilted her head, and her eyes caught the flicker of the candles. "You didn't live for it or you couldn't have given it up at thirty. If Kirk lives to be a hundred, they'll have to carry him to the cockpit, but he'll still race."

"It appears you had more perception as a teenager than I gave you credit for." Lance waited until their steak Diane was served, then thoughtfully broke a roll in half. "You've always hated it, haven't you?"

Foxy met his eyes levelly. "Yes," she agreed and accepted the offered roll. "Always." Her silence grew pensive as she spread butter on the roll. "Lance, how did your family feel about your racing?"

"Embarrassed," he said immediately. Foxy was forced to laugh as she met his eyes again.

"And you enjoyed their embarrassment as much as you enjoyed racing."

"As I said"—he lifted his glass in toast—"you are perceptive."

"Families of drivers all seem to have different ways of dealing with racing. It's more difficult standing in the pits than driving on the grid, you know," she said softly, then sighed and deliberately shook off the mood. "I suppose now that you're in the business end of it, your family's no longer embarrassed." Foxy bit into the crusty roll. "It's more acceptable, though you hardly need the money."

"You took an oath to see that I do after tonight," he reminded her. "You'd better eat all of your steak. Losing money takes more energy than winning it."

Sending him a disdainful smirk, Foxy picked up her knife and fork.

* * *

The evening was still young when they entered the casino. Foxy found her indifferent veneer dissolving. The combination of elegance and excitement was too potent.

"Oh!" She took in the room with a long, sweeping glance and squeezed Lance's arm for emphasis. "It's fabulous."

Clothes in a kaleidoscope of hues and the glitter and gleam of jewels caught her eye. There was a hum of voices in a hodgepodge of languages accented by the quick, precise French of the croupiers. There was a mix of other sounds: the click and clatter of the roulette balls jingling in the wheels, the soft scrape of wood on baize as markers were drawn in, the flutter and whoosh of cards being shuffled, the crackle of new money and the jangle of coin.

With a laugh, Lance tossed an arm around her shoulders. "Foxy, my love, your eyes are enormous and shockingly naive. Haven't you ever been to a den of iniquity before?"

"Stop teasing," she demanded, too impressed to be properly insulted. "It's so beautiful."

"Ah, but gambling's gambling, Fox, whether you do it in a plush chair with a glass of champagne or in a garage with a bottle of beer."

"You should know." Tilting her head, she shifted her eyes

to his and smiled. "I remember the poker games. You would never let me play."

"You were a very precocious brat." He slid his hand up her neck and squeezed.

"You were just afraid that I'd beat you."

His grin was quick and powerful. Guiltily Foxy admitted that she was glad to be there with him instead of with Scott. Lance Matthews exuded an excitement Scott Newman would not even understand.

"What big eyes you have," Lance murmured as his fingers lingered on her skin. "What goes on behind them, Foxy?"

"I was thinking how furious I should be with you because of the maneuvering you did with Scott, and how guilty I am that I'm not."

He laughed, then gave her a hard, brief kiss. "Too guilty to enjoy yourself?"

"No," she said immediately, then shrugged. "I suppose I'm basically selfish and not very nice."

Lance's mouth twisted into a grin. "Then we should suit each other well enough." He laced his fingers with hers, then led her to a roulette table.

Seated, Foxy moved her attention instantly to the wheel as the tiny silver ball bounced and jumped. When it stilled, she watched the croupier scoop in the losing markers and add them to those of the winners. Foxy thought the table a Tower of Babel. As she glanced from face to face she heard lilting Italian, precise London-style English, low, guttural German, and other languages that she could not distinguish. Faces were varied as well; some old, some young, some bored, some animated, many carrying the unmistakable polish of wealth. But it was the face directly across from her that fascinated her.

The older woman was beautiful. Her hair was like white

silk swept around a fine-boned oval face. The lines in her skin were far too much a part of it to detract from the beauty. Rather, they matured and gave character to what had once been a delicate elegance. Her eyes were like sharp green emeralds, but it was diamonds she wore at her throat and ears. They seemed more fire than ice. She wore flaming red silk with absolute confidence. Foxy watched in fascination as she lifted a long, slender black cigarette and drew gently.

"Countess Francesca de Avalon of Venice," Lance whispered in Foxy's ear as he followed her gaze. "Exceptional, isn't she?"

"Fabulous." Turning to Lance, Foxy was vaguely surprised to see him offer her a glass of champagne. As the stem passed from his fingers to hers she noticed the tidy pile of markers in front of her. "Oh, are these the chips?" Tracing a fingernail down the edges, she looked back at Lance. "How much do you bet at a time?"

He shrugged and cupped his hands around the end of his cigarette as he lit it. "I'm just along for the ride."

With a laugh, Foxy shook her head. "I have a hard enough time with plain francs, Lance. I don't even know how much these little things are worth."

"An evening's entertainment," he said easily and lifted his glass.

Sighing, Foxy chose five chips and unwittingly bet five thousand francs on black. "I don't suppose I should lose all your money at once," she said confidentially.

"That's generous of you." Repressing a smile, Lance settled back and watched the wheel spin.

"Vingt-sept, noir."

"Oh!" Foxy said, surprised, then pleased. "We've won." Looking up, she caught the blatant amusement on Lance's face. His eyes, she realized, were more silver than gray. "You needn't look so smug." She shook off her preoccupation and sipped the effervescent wine. "That was just beginner's luck. Besides"—she gave him a wicked grin—"it'll hurt more if I win a bit first." Her gaze shifted to the two stacks of five markers on black, but as she started to reach for them, Lance laid a hand on her arm.

"He's started the wheel, Fox. You've let it ride." Her face was so completely horrified, Lance dissolved into laughter.

"Oh, but I didn't mean . . . that must be over a hundred dollars." A glance at the spinning wheel made her giddy, and she swallowed more wine.

"Must be," Lance agreed gravely.

Foxy watched the ball bounce its capricious way around the wheel. She felt a mixture of fear, guilt, and excitement as the wheel began to slow.

"Cinq, noir."

She closed her eyes on a shudder of relief. Remembering herself, she quickly drew the four stacks of five in front of her. As Lance chuckled she turned and gave him a haughty glare. "It would have served you right if I *had* lost."

"Quite right." Lance signaled for more champagne. "Why don't you bet on one of the columns, Foxy," he suggested as he tapped the ash of his cigarette into an ashtray. "You've got to take more than a fifty-fifty chance in life."

She grinned and tossed her head. "Your loss," she announced as she impulsively pushed five chips to the head of column one.

It was, as it turned out, his gain. With uncanny consistency, the stack of markers in front of Foxy grew. Once, she unknowingly lost twenty thousand francs, then cheerfully gained it back on the following spin. Perhaps it was her complete ignorance of the amounts she wagered, or her random betting pattern, or simply the generosity of Lady Luck, but she won, spin after spin after spin. And she found winning was much to her taste. It was a heady experience that left her nearly as giddy as the seemingly bottomless glass of champagne at her side. Lance sat calmly back and watched the flow and ebb and flow of her winnings. He enjoyed the way she used her eyes to speak to him, letting them widen and glisten on a win or roll and dance on a loss. Her laugh reminded him of the warm mists on Boston's Back Bay. Her pleasure in winning was engagingly simple, her nonchalance in losing charmingly innocent. She was a child and woman at perfect balance.

"Are you sure you wouldn't like to bet some of this?" Foxy asked generously, indicating the stacks of markers.

"You're doing fine." Lance twirled a stray curl of russet around his finger.

"That, young man, is a gross understatement."

Foxy twisted her head quickly and looked into sharp emerald eyes. The Countess de Avalon stood behind her, leaning on a smooth, ivory-handled cane. It shocked Foxy momentarily to see that she was so tiny, no more than five feet. Imperiously she waved Lance to sit as he started to get to his feet. Her English was quick and precise, with only a trace of accent. "You have won resoundingly, signorina, and cleverly."

"Resoundingly, Countess," Foxy returned with a wide smile, "but accidentally rather than cleverly. I came determined to lose."

"Perhaps I will change my strategy and come determined to lose," the countess commented. "Then I, too, might have such an accident." She gave Lance a slow, thorough, and entirely feminine appraisal. Foxy felt a tickle of jealousy and was completely astounded by it. "You appear to know me; might I return the pleasure?"

"Countess de Avalon." Lance gently inclined his head. "Cynthia Fox." Foxy took the extended hand in hers and found it small and fragile. But the quick study the green eyes made of her was full of power.

"You are very lovely," the countess said at length, "very strong." She smiled, showing perfect white teeth. "But even ten years ago, I would have lured him away from you. Never trust a woman of experience." Dismissing Foxy with a mere shifting of the eyes, the countess gave her attention to Lance. "And who are you?"

"Lance Matthews, Countess." He brought the offered hand to his lips with perfect charm. "It's an honor to meet you."

"Matthews," she murmured, and her eyes narrowed. "Of course, I should have seen from the eyes, the 'devil-take-it' look. I knew your grandfather quite well." She laughed. It was a young, sultry sound. "Quite well. You've the look of him, Lancelot Matthews . . . You're named for him. Very appropriate."

"Thank you, Countess." Lance's smile warmed. "He was one of my favorite people."

"And mine. I saw your aunt Phoebe in Martinique two years ago. A singularly boring woman."

"Yes, Countess." The smile became grim. "I'm afraid so."

With a regal sniff, the countess turned to a fascinated Foxy. "Never relax for a moment with this one," she advised. "He is every bit the rake his grandfather was." She laid her hand briefly on Foxy's, and squeezed. "How I envy you." She turned and walked away in a flash of red silk.

"What a magnificent woman," Foxy murmured. Turning back to Lance, she gave him a wistful smile. "Do you suppose your grandfather was in love with her?"

"Yes." With a gesture of his finger, Lance signaled the croupier to cash in his markers. "He had a blistering affair with her, which the family continues to pretend never happened. It was also complicated because they were both married. He wanted her to leave her husband and live with him in the south of France."

"How do you know so much about it?" Intrigued, Foxy made no objection when he drew her to her feet.

"He told me." Lance set her shawl around her shoulders. "He told me once he'd never loved anyone else. He was over seventy when he died, and he would still have left everything to live with her if she had permitted it."

Foxy walked slowly through the casino with Lance unaware of how many pairs of eyes watched them; a russet-haired beauty and the man with the dark, brooding attraction. "It sounds so wonderfully sad," she said after a moment. "But I suppose it was dreadful for your grandmother, knowing he loved someone else all those years."

"My dear, innocent Fox," Lance said dryly. "My grandmother is a Winslow of Boston. She was quite content with the Matthews merger, their two offspring, and her bridge club. Love is untidy and plebeian."

"You're making that up."

"As you like," he said easily.

"Let's not take a cab," she said as they stepped outside. She tossed her head back to the stars. "It's so beautiful." Smiling into his eyes, she tucked her hand in his arm. "Let's walk, it isn't far."

They ignored the light stream of traffic and walked under the warm glow of street lamps. Champagne spun pleasantly in Foxy's head and lifted her feet just an inch from the sidewalk. The countess's warning was forgotten, and she was completely relaxed. The walk under the slice of moon and smattering of stars seemed to occur in a timeless realm, full of the scents and mysteries of night.

"Do you know," Foxy began and spun away from him, "I love palm trees." Giggling, she rested her back against one and smiled at Lance. "I always wanted one when I was little, but they don't do well in Indiana. I had to settle for a pine."

Moving closer, he brushed curls from cheeks flushed with wine and excitement. "I had no idea you were so interested in horticulture."

"I have my secrets." Swirling out of reach, she leaned over a sea wall. "I wanted to be a skin diver when I was eight," she told him as she peered out into the dark sea. "Or a heart surgeon, I could never make up my mind. What do you want to be when you grow up, Lance?" She turned back to him, and the wind caught and pulled at her free curls. Her eyes were speared with laughter.

"Starting pitcher for the Red Sox." His eyes dropped to the elegant curve of her neck as she threw back her head and laughed.

"I bet you've got a whole bagful of pitches." She sighed with the pleasure of laughter. "You never told me how much I won in there."

"Hmm?" Lost in the flicker of moonlight in her hair, he listened with half an ear.

"How much did I win in the casino?" she repeated, pushing dancing curls from her face.

"Oh." He shrugged. "Fifty, fifty-five thousand francs."

"What?" The one syllable was half laugh, half choke. "Fifty-five *thousand?* That's—that's more than ten thousand dollars!"

"At the current rate of exchange," Lance agreed carelessly.

"Oh, good grief!" Her hands flew up to cover her mouth as her eyes grew impossibly wide. "Lance, I might have lost!"

"You did remarkably well." Amusement was back in his eyes and in his voice. "Or remarkably poorly considering your desire to lose."

"I had no idea I was gambling with that kind of money; I never would have tossed it around that way. Why . . . you're crazy!" Helplessly she began to laugh. "You're a lunatic. Certifiable." She dropped her head to his shoulder as her laughter floated warmly on the quiet night. When he brought his arms around her, she made no protest. "I might have lost, you know," she managed between giggles. "And I might easily have fainted cold if I'd have found out how much those chips were worth while the wheel was still spinning." Taking a deep breath, she lifted her brilliant eyes to his. "Now, it seems I've added to your already disgusting fortune."

"The winnings are rightfully yours," he corrected, but Foxy stepped back horrified.

"Oh no, it was your money. In any case . . ." She paused, distracted, and plucked a daisy from a clump of grass at the foot of the sea wall. The champagne was still flowing. "In any case," she repeated as she tucked the flower in her hair, "you wouldn't have expected me to make up your losses." With this logic, she began to walk again, holding out a hand for his. "Of course," she began on a new thought, moving away before Lance could take her hand. "You could buy me something extravagant." She whirled back to him with a smile. "That would be perfectly aboveboard, I believe."

"Is there anything particular you have in mind?"

Her footsteps clicked on the sidewalk as she continued to circle away from him. "Oh, perhaps a pack of Russian wolfhounds." Her laughter drifted. "Or a line of those marvelous horses with the sturdy legs . . . Clydesdales. Or a flock of Albanian goats. I'm almost certain they have goats in Albania."

"Wouldn't you rather have a sable?"

"Oh no," she answered. She wrinkled her nose and, either by accident or design, moved just out of his reach. "I don't care much for dead animals. I know! A pair of black Angus so

I can start my own herd." The decision made, she stopped. Lance slipped his arms around her. "You will be sure to get one male and one female, won't you? It's very important if you want things to move along properly."

"Of course," he agreed as his lips traced her jawline.

"I shouldn't tell you this." Foxy sighed as her arms encircled his neck. "I'm terribly glad you intimidated Scott."

"Are you?" Lance murmured, gently nipping at the pulse in her throat.

"Oh yes," she whispered and drew him closer. "And I'd very much like it if you'd kiss me now. Right now." The last word was muffled as their lips found each other.

They seemed to fuse together in one instant of blinding heat. The instant was an eternity. She tangled her fingers in his hair as if she could bring him yet closer when now even the breeze from the sea could not come between them. Her body had molded to his as if it had no other purpose. She could feel his heart beat at the same speeding rhythm as her own. Unnoticed, her shawl slipped to the ground as he explored the smooth skin of her back. Together, they began to taste more of each other. His lips tarried on her throat, lingering and savoring the sweetness before moving to trace her cheekbone and whisper over her closed lids.

She discovered a dark, male flavor along the column of his neck. She wanted to go on tasting, go on learning, but his mouth demanded that hers return to his. The power of the new kiss pierced her like a spear of lightning, shooting a trembling heat through her every cell. With a moan, she swayed against him. Lance plundered her surrendering mouth, drawing more and more from her until she was limp in his arms. When his lips parted from hers, she murmured his name and rested her head on his shoulder.

"I don't know if it's you or the champagne, but my head's spinning." Foxy shivered once, then snuggled closer. Lance moved his hand to the base of her neck and tilted her face back to his. Her eyes were dark and heavy, her cheeks flushed, her mouth soft and swollen from his.

"Does it matter?" His voice was rough as he tightened his grip to bring her closer. She did not resist, but stepped back into the fire. "Isn't it enough to know that I want you to-night?" he murmured against her ear before his tongue and teeth began to fill her senses again.

"I don't know. I can't think." Drawing away, Foxy took two steps back and shook her head. "Something happens to me when you kiss me. I lose control."

"If you're telling me that so I'll play fair, Foxy, you've mis-calculated." In one quick motion, he closed the distance between them. "I play to win."

"I know," she replied and lifted a hand to his cheek. "I know that very well." Turning, she walked back to the sea wall and breathed deeply to clear her head. She leaned back and lifted her face to the moon. "I always admired your un-swerving determination to come out on top." She lowered her face to look at him, but his was still shadowed by the palm. "I loved you quite desperately when I was fourteen."

He didn't speak for a moment but bent and picked up her wrap. "Did you?" he murmured as he stepped from the shadows.

Moonlight fluttered over her as she tossed windblown curls from her eyes. "Oh yes." Relaxed, Foxy continued with champagne-induced honesty. "It was a wonderfully painful crush, my very first. You were quite impressive and I was quite romantic." Lance was beside her now, and Foxy turned her head to smile at him. "You always looked so in-destructible, and very often you brooded."

"Did I?" He answered her smile as he lay the wrap over her shoulders.

"Oh yes. You had this single-minded intensity about

you . . . You still do a great deal of the time. It's terribly attractive, but it was more pronounced when you were racing. Then, there were your hands."

"My hands?" he repeated and paused in the act of reaching in his pocket for his lighter.

"Yes." Foxy surprised him by taking both his hands in hers and studying them. "They're quite the most beautiful hands I've ever seen. Very lean, very strong, very elegant. I always thought you should've been an artist or a musician. Sometimes I'd pretend you were. I'd set you up in a drafty old garret where I'd take care of you." She released his hands and pulled absently at her wrap as it slipped off her shoulders. "I wanted badly to take care of someone. I suppose I should've had a dog." She laughed lightly but was too involved with her memories to notice that Lance did not laugh with her. "I was snarling jealous of all those women you had. They were always beautiful. I remember Tracy McNeil especially. You probably don't remember her at all."

"No." Lance flicked on his lighter and frowned at the flame. "I don't."

"She had beautiful blond hair. It was clear down to her hips and straight as an arrow. I hated my hair as a child. It was all curly and unmanageable and such an awkward color. I was quite certain the only reason you kissed Tracy McNeil was because she had straight blond hair." The scent from Lance's cigar stung the air, and Foxy breathed it in. "It's amazing how naive I was for someone raised in a man's world. Anyway, I languished over you for the better part of a year. I imagine I was a nuisance around the track, and you were very tolerant for the most part." A yawn escaped her as she grew sleepy in the sea air. "After I turned sixteen, I felt I was quite grown up and ready to be treated as a woman. The crush I'd had on you became very intense. I'd find every opportunity to be around you. Did you notice?"

"Yes." Lance blew out a thin stream of smoke, and it vanished instantly into the breeze. "I noticed."

Foxy gave a rueful laugh. "I thought I was being so clever in my pursuit. You were always so kind to me, I suppose that's why when you stopped being kind, it was all the more devastating. Do you remember that night? It was at Le Mans, the twenty-four-hour race," she went on before he could answer. "The night before the race I couldn't sleep so I walked down to the track. When I saw you going into the garage area, I was certain it was fate." With a sigh, Foxy absently fingered the flower in her hair. "I followed you in. My palms were sweating. I wanted you to notice me." Turning her head, Foxy met Lance's eyes with a gentle smile. "As a woman. A girl's right on the border at sixteen, and I wanted so desperately to get to the other side. And my feelings for you were very adult and very real, even though I had no idea how to handle them.

"I was very nonchalant when I came in, do you remember? 'Hello, how are you, couldn't you sleep?' You were wearing a black sweater; black always suited you. You were very remote, you'd been remote off and on for weeks. It only made you more romantic." With a soft, low laugh, she lifted her palm to his cheek. "Poor Lance. How uncomfortable my adulation must have made you."

"*Uncomfortable* is a mild word for what you were doing to me," he muttered. Turning away, he tossed his cigar over the wall and into the sea.

"I wanted to be sophisticated," she went on, not hearing the annoyance in his tone. "I had no idea how to make you want to kiss me. I tried to remember all the ploys I'd ever seen the heroine use in the movies. It was dark, we were alone. What next? The only thing I could come up with was to keep as close as possible. You were tinkering under the hood of the car, doing your best, I'm sure, to ignore me so that I'd go away and let you get on with it. There was just that one small light on, and the garage smelled of oil and gasoline. I thought it was as romantic as Manderley." Foxy turned and grinned cheerfully while the wine made her remember. "Romance has always been my big weakness. Anyway, I was standing behind you, trying to think of what to do next, and I began to wonder what in the world you were doing to the car. I started to peek over your shoulder just as you turned around, and we collided. I remember you grabbed my arms to steady me, and my knees turned to water instantly. The physical part of it was incredible, probably because I'd never experienced it before. My heart started pounding, and my skin went hot then cold. It seemed as though I'd be swallowed up by your eyes, they'd gotten so dark, so intense. I thought: *This is it.* I was positive you were going to pull me into your arms and kiss me. I *knew* you were. We were Clark Gable and Vivien Leigh and the garage was Tara. Then you were shouting at me, absolutely livid that I was continually in your way. You swore magnificently, giving me a good shake before you pushed me away. You said some really dreadful things; the worst, to me, was that you called me an annoying child. Anything else, I could have passed off, but that crushed my pride and my ego and my fantasies with one blow. I never gave a thought to the tension you must have been under with the race the next day, or to the simple fact that I *was* in your way. I only thought about what you were saying to me and how it hurt. But I've always been a survivor. As soon as it began to hurt too badly, my defenses came up. When I turned and ran out of that garage, I didn't love you anymore, but I hated you almost as obsessively."

"You were better off," Lance murmured. After a moment, he twisted his head and ran a fingertip down her cheek. "Have you forgiven me?"

Foxy gave him an easy smile. "I suppose. It's been years,

and since it cured me of being in love with you, I should be grateful." With another yawn, she rested her head against his shoulder.

"Yes, I suppose you should," he agreed softly. "Come on, I'll get you back before you fall asleep on the sidewalk."

Drowsy but willing, Foxy went with him as he slipped an arm around her waist.

CHAPTER 5

Monaco's Grand Prix is a classic example of a round-the-houses circuit. The course is short, just under two miles, and in the heart of a crowded civic complex. No part of the circuit is straight for more than a few feet, and among its eleven curves are two hairpins. One lap includes seventeen corners. The course is anything but flat; its ups and downs range from sea level to 132 feet above. Its hazards include curbs, sea walls, a three-hundred-foot tunnel, utility poles, and, of course, the sparkling Mediterranean. For the driver, there is not a second's rest in the hundred laps. It is short, slow, and unlike any other Formula One course in the world. It stands as a great test of man and machine as its constant demands make it more fatiguing than longer, faster circuits. Here was a course that tested a car's reliability and a man's endurance. Still, it remains romantic and somehow mystical, like a yearly joust before the prince and princess.

Through quick maneuvering, Pam had managed to corner Kirk for an interview. There were just over two hours before race time, and the pits were crowded and noisy. Monaco's pits stood exposed to the course at the head of the small, picturesque harbor. Behind them, the water was crowded with yachts and sailboats. Pam found herself glancing around for Foxy. Though it annoyed her, she knew she would be more comfortable if she did not interview Kirk alone. Pushing this thought aside, she looked directly into his eyes. This type of contact was as essential to her style as her clean-lined, elegant clothes and her calm, unruffled manner. The sharp, probing, tenacious mind was well camouflaged by the fragility of her appearance.

"I've heard a lot of differing opinions on this course," she began, adding her professional smile. "Some, especially the carmakers I've spoken to, consider Monaco a drawing-room circuit. How do you feel about it?"

Kirk was leaning back against a wall, sipping from a foam cup. Thin wisps of steam rose from it. His eyes squinted against the sun, and he looked completely at ease. Pam felt stiff and formal. It annoyed her that Kirk Fox always caused her to feel stiff and formal and somehow out of place.

"It's a race," he answered simply as he watched her over the rim of his cup. "It's not fast. It's rare a driver goes over a hundred and forty and usual to go less than thirty on the hairpins. But then, it's more a test of stamina and ability than speed."

"The driver's or the car's?" Pam countered.

His eyes crinkled deeper at the corners as he grinned. To her fascination, they seemed to grow greener. "Both. Two thousand or more gear changes in two and a half hours is a strain on a man and a machine. And there's the tunnel. You go from daylight to dim and back to daylight. Do your batteries ever run down?" he asked, taking the tape recorder that hung at her side.

"No," she returned coolly. If he was going to laugh at her, she wasn't going to give him the satisfaction of reacting. She cleared her throat and straightened her shoulders. "You had a crash here two years ago that totaled your car and broke

The Heart's Victory 71

your left shoulder. Will that experience affect your driving today?"

"Why should it?" Kirk countered, then drained his coffee. He was watching her with complete concentration, oblivious to the milling crowds in the pit area.

"Don't you worry about crashing again?" Pam insisted. As the frisky breeze tugged at her hair she tucked it behind her ear with a quick, impatient gesture. There was a tiny turquoise stone on the lobe. "Don't you ever consider that the next time you crash, you might be killed? Doesn't that come home to you, particularly when you pass over the part of the course where you crashed before?"

"No." Kirk crushed the cup between his fingers, then tossed it carelessly aside. "I never think about the next crash, only about the next race."

"Isn't that foolhardy?" Knowing her tone had become argumentative did not prevent her from continuing. She was irritated with him without having a clear reason why. Pam always conducted her interviews craftily, charmingly. Now she knew she had lost the reins but felt no impulse to reach for them again. "Or are you just smug? One instant of miscalculation, one insignificant mechanical flaw, can result in disaster, yet you don't think about it? You've had your share of crashes, been yanked out of wrecks, had your bones broken, and been laid up in hospitals. Tell me," she demanded, "what goes through your mind as you're roasting in the cockpit, hurtling around a track at two hundred miles an hour? What do you think of when they're strapping you into that machine?"

"Winning," Kirk answered without hesitation. The sharpness of her tone apparently bounced off the smooth nonchalance of his. His eyes roamed calmly over her face. The faint pink tint that temper gave her skin emphasized its flawlessness. He wondered how it would feel under his hand. The gold of her hair grew more vibrant as the sun washed over it. Pam watched the journey of his eyes and frowned. His eyes dropped to her lips.

"Is winning really all that important?"

Kirk's gaze shifted from her mouth to her eyes. "Sure. It's all there is."

It was clear from his tone that he was completely sincere. Helplessly Pam shook her head. "I've never known anyone like you." It was unlike her to lose her temper on the job, and she took a long breath to steady it. "Even here among all these other drivers, I haven't met anyone who thinks along the same straight, unswerving line you do. I suppose if you had the choice, you'd like to die on the track in a blaze of glory."

Kirk's grin was quick. "That would suit me, but I'd like to put it off about fifty years, and I'd prefer it to be *after* I'd crossed the finish line."

Pam's lips curved of their own accord. He was outrageous, she thought, but honest. "Are all race-car drivers as mad as you are?"

"Probably." Before she realized his intent, Kirk tangled his fingers in her hair. "I wondered if it was as soft as it looked. It is." The back of his hand brushed her cheek. "Like your skin." Pam's usual aplomb deserted her, leaving her silent and staring. "Your voice is soft, too, and very appealing. I like the way you always look as though you've stepped out of a bandbox. It gives me the urge to muss you up a bit." His voice was as insolent and amused as his grin.

Pam felt her cheeks grow warm and was infuriated. She had thought she had left blushing behind years before. "Is this a pass?" she asked in a scathing voice.

Kirk laughed, and she heard a trace of Foxy in the sound. "No, it's just an observation. When I make a pass, you won't have a chance to ask." Still grinning, he pulled her close and planted a long, hard kiss on her mouth. He thought she tasted like some rich, dangerous dessert and lingered over her longer than he had intended. When he released her, he felt the small whisper of air escape her lips as if she had held it there in surprise. "That," he said easily, "was a pass."

As he turned and sauntered away Pam lifted a finger to trace the place where his mustache had brushed her skin. *A crazy man,* she decided, unwilling to admit how deeply shaken she was. *A truly crazy man.*

* * *

Nearly two hours later, Foxy stood in almost the precise spot where her brother had been. Her mood was just short of grim. All too clearly, she remembered every detail from the evening before. The wine had not been kind enough to dull her memory.

I told him to kiss me, she thought on a wave of self-disgust. I practically ordered him to. It wasn't bad enough that I went out with him when I should've known better, but I made certain he knew I was enjoying myself every minute. Blasted champagne! Letting out her breath in a huff, she crammed the straw hat she wore further down on her head. Then I babble on about the silly crush I had on him when I was a teenager. Oh boy, when I go out to humiliate myself, I don't do it by halves. All that business about being in love with him and fantasizing about him. Closing her eyes, Foxy made a strangled sound in her throat. The breeze blew from the harbor, cooling her skin under her white gauze blouse. She set her teeth and lifted her camera as the parade lap began. I wonder if it's possible to avoid him for the rest of the season? Better, she added as she worked systematically, for the rest of my life.

As the drivers lined up for the green flag Foxy scurried

for a new angle. In a moment, the air thundered with engines, and utilizing the motor drive, she shot each row of cars as the flag set the start. Crouched on one knee, she caught the low, fragile sleekness so unique to the Formula One racer. Her movements were calm and professional, absorbing her concentration, lending her an air of efficiency at odds with the sassy straw hat and thin, faded jeans. The lead car was already rounding the first curve before she rose. As she turned back toward the pits she collided with Lance. His hands came out to steady her, bringing her an uncomfortable sensation of déjà vu. Hastily Foxy disentangled herself from his hold, then made a business of adjusting her camera.

"I'm sorry, I didn't know you were behind me." Realizing she would have to meet his eyes sooner or later, she tossed her hair behind her shoulder and boldly lifted her chin. The amusement she had expected to see on his face was absent. There was no mockery in the dark gray depths of his eyes. She recognized the long, thorough study he was making and backed away from it. "You're looking at me as though I were an engine that wasn't responding properly." Frowning, Foxy busied herself by dragging sunglasses out of her camera case. She felt more at ease once they were in place. A shield was a shield, however slight.

"You might say I found a few surprises when I opened the hood."

Foxy was not certain how to take the quiet quality of his voice. His continued unblinking study was unnerving. She knew he was capable of watching her endlessly without speaking. He could be incredibly, almost unnaturally patient when he chose to be. Knowing she would be outmatched in this sort of contest, Foxy took the initiative. "Lance, I'd like to speak with you about last night." Her sophisticated demeanor was hampered by rising color. The roar of engines cut her off, and she turned away to watch the cars hurtle by.

The pack was still thick after the first lap. Cheeks cool, Foxy took a deep breath and turned back to Lance. His eyes left the track to meet hers, but he said nothing. He was waiting, composed and contained. Foxy could have cheerfully strangled him. "I wasn't really myself last night, you see," she began again. "Wine . . . liquor has a tendency to go straight to my head, that's why I usually avoid it altogether. I don't want you to think, that is, I wouldn't want you to feel . . . I didn't mean to be so . . ." Frustrated, she jammed her hands into her pockets and shut her eyes. "Oh, help," she muttered and turned away again. Lance remained silent as she squirmed and struggled. She wondered how it was possible to cast the line and be the fish at the same time.

That was brilliant, Foxy, she berated herself. Why don't you try again, maybe you can top your own incoherency record. Get it out quick and stop stammering like an idiot. Setting her chin, she turned to face him again, meeting his eyes straight on. "I didn't mean to give you the impression I would sleep with you." Once it was said, Foxy let out a hasty breath and plunged ahead. "I realize I might have given that impression last night, and I don't want you to misunderstand."

Lance waited nearly a full minute before he spoke, all the while watching Foxy steadily. "I don't believe I misunderstood anything." His comment was ambiguous and left her floundering.

"Yes, well . . . I know when you took me back to my room you didn't, well, you didn't . . ."

"Make love to you?" he supplied. In a quick move, he stripped off her sunglasses, leaving her eyes vulnerable. Even as she blinked against the change in light, he closed the slight distance between them. His hand came to her arm, warning her not to back away. "No, I didn't, though we're both perfectly aware that I could have. Let's say I had a whim to play by the rules last night." His smile spread lazily, packed with confidence, while his voice became low and intimate. "I don't need champagne to seduce you, Foxy." His mouth lowered to brush lightly over hers before she could move. It was a kiss that promised more.

Infuriated by his calm arrogance, incensed that her pulses had responded instantly, Foxy snatched the glasses back from him and jerked away. "Stuff your seductions." Her suggestion was drowned out by the noise of the second lap. Foxy threw an annoyed glare over her shoulder at the line of cars. Temper sparked in her eyes when she turned back to face Lance. "Just remember that last night was a lapse of intelligence on my part, that's all. And all that—that stuff I talked about . . ." To her greater fury, she felt her cheeks grow warmer. What had possessed her to confess that foolish crush? "All that business about that night in the garage was just as ridiculous as it sounded."

"How ridiculous was that?" Lance asked with an ease in direct contrast to Foxy's agitation. She barely resisted stomping her foot.

"I was sixteen years old and very naive. I'm sure it's not necessary to go into it any further."

"You're not sixteen anymore," Lance commented with a slight inclination of his head that reminded her of the elegant man of the evening before, "but you're still naive."

"I am not," she blurted out indignantly, then saw his brow lift and disappear under his fall of hair. Knowing her dignity was threadbare, she drew herself straight. "That's hardly relevant and strictly a matter of your own opinion." He smiled at that with quick charm, and Foxy hurried on. "I've got work to do, and I imagine you can find something to keep you busy for the next ninety-eight laps."

"Ninety-seven," Lance corrected as the leaders sped by. "Kirk's in third position," he noted absently before he looked back down at Foxy. "My opinion, Fox, might be to your advantage as it should induce me to continue playing by the rules for a while longer. It makes an interesting change." He grinned, a crooked, challenging half grin, and she was instantly wary. "There's no telling when I'll stop being a nice guy, though."

"Nice guy!" Foxy repeated and rolled her eyes at the thought.

Still grinning, Lance took the sunglasses from her and perched them back on her nose before walking away.

* * *

Over the next three months, Foxy used all her skill to avoid Lance Matthews. From Monaco to Holland to France to England to Germany, she made certain to stay out of his way. Whenever possible, she coupled herself with Pam. She felt if she was not alone, Lance would not find the opportunity to approach her for a personal conversation. Her pleasure with her success was slightly marred by the fact that he did not appear to be fretting for lack of personal conversations. Their schedule since Monaco had been tight. For the racing team there had been little time for anything but work and travel, meals and sleep. It was a hard, demanding circuit, packed with qualifying heats and practice runs and races. Away from the track, the hotels all began to seem the same. But each grid had a separate identity. Each was different, with its own problems, its own dangers.

With the end of summer came Italy and the Monza circuit. The grueling months in Europe had taught Foxy an important lesson. When the season was over, she would never follow the circuit again. Her days of moving from town to town, from pit area to pit area, were over. With each race her nerves had become more highly strung, her composure more difficult to maintain. It became apparent to her that the two years she had spent away from racing had left their mark. She could never be a part of it again. She knew if she ever came back to Italy, it would be to visit Rome or Venice, not Monza.

With night came utter silence. All during the day, the track had vibrated with the practice runs. As Foxy sat alone in the deserted grandstands she thought she could hear ghost cars whiz past, feel their phantom breeze. Sixty years of speed. The sky was faultlessly clear with a white moon and gleaming blue stars. The musky scent of the forest drifted to her, almost crowding the air. Behind her came the quiet chirp of crickets and small insects. It was warm, without the burning heat of the long, sun-filled day. There were no harsh fumes, no screaming tires or thundering engines. It was a night for promises and secrets, a night for romance and soft words. With a sigh, Foxy closed her eyes on the thought of Lance. *More than anything else,* she realized wearily, *I need a little peace.*

A hand on her shoulder brought her quickly back to the present. "Oh, Kirk!" She placed a hand to her drumming heart and smiled up at him. "I didn't hear you."

"What are you doing out here all alone?"

"I wanted some quiet," she told him as he dropped down beside her. "There's too much going on back at the hotel. What are you doing here?"

He shrugged. "I like the track the night before a race." Carelessly he leaned back, then propped his feet on the seat in front of him. She saw he wore his old, reliable sneakers. "This is a fast track. We'll set a record tomorrow." He spoke with the absolute confidence of fact, not speculation.

"Did Charlie fix the exhaust problem?" Foxy studied his profile. Her mind was not on the car, not on the race, but on him. As in the past, she tried to draw on his confidence to soothe her own nerves.

"Yeah. Has Lance been bothering you?"

The question was so abrupt and so unexpected, Foxy took nearly a full minute to react. "What?" The one syllable was spoken with complete incredulity.

"You heard me." She heard the annoyance in Kirk's tone as he shifted in his seat to face her. His features were set and serious. "Is he bothering you?"

"Bothering me," Foxy repeated carefully. She ran the tip of her tongue between her teeth, then lifted her brows. "Maybe you should be more specific."

"Damn it, you know what I mean." Exasperated, Kirk rose and stared out at the track. His hands retreated into his pockets. Foxy could feel his discomfort and marveled at it. She understood Kirk well enough to know he rarely put himself into an uncomfortable position. "I've seen the way he's been looking at you," he muttered, and she heard the scowl in his voice. "If he's been doing more than looking, I want to know about it."

Though Foxy clasped both hands over her mouth, the giggle escaped. When Kirk whirled around, his face was a study in fury. Even in the dark, she could see his eyes glitter with temper. She pressed her lips together firmly, but her laughter burst out of its confines. She could only shake her head and struggle to compose herself as he glared at her.

"What the devil's so funny?" he demanded.

"Kirk, I . . ." She was forced to stop and cough, then take several deep breaths before she could trust herself to speak. "I'm sorry, I just didn't expect you to—to ask me something like that." She swallowed hard as another giggle threatened. "I'm twenty-three years old."

"What does that have to do with anything?" he tossed

back, watching her eyes shine with good-humored affection. He felt like a total fool and scowled more deeply.

"Kirk, when I was sixteen, you never paid a bit of attention to any of the boys who hung around the track, and now you're—"

"Lance isn't a boy." Kirk cut her off furiously, then ran a hand through his hair. The thick locks, sprang back in precisely the same manner Foxy's did. "And you're not sixteen anymore."

"So I've been told," she murmured.

Letting out a frustrated breath, Kirk jammed his hands farther into his pockets. "I should've paid more attention to you when you were."

"Kirk." The humor left her voice as she rose to stand beside him. "It's nice of you to be concerned, but it's unnecessary." Touched both by his caring and his discomposure, Foxy laid her head on his shoulder. *What an odd man he is,* she thought, *with such unexpected scraps of sweetness.*

"It is necessary," he muttered, wishing he didn't feel obligated to pursue the matter. He was closer to Lance than to any other person in his life other than his sister. With Lance, there was the added bond of manhood and shared adventures. It was some of these adventures that prodded Kirk on when he wanted nothing more than to drop the entire subject. "You're still my sister," he added, half to himself. "Even if you have grown up a bit."

"A bit?" Foxy grinned again. A reckless mischief gleamed in her eyes, reminding Kirk uncomfortably of himself. "Kirk, I passed 'a bit' at twenty."

"Look, Foxy," Kirk cut in impatiently. "I know Lance. I know how he . . ." He hesitated and swore.

"Operates?" Foxy supplied and earned a fierce glare. Her laughter was unavoidable, but she tempered it by kissing his cheek. "Stop worrying about me. I learned a little more than photography in college." When Kirk's expression failed to alter, she kissed his other cheek and continued. "If it makes you feel any better, Lance isn't bothering me. If he were, I could handle it quite nicely, I promise you, but he isn't. We hardly speak." She tried to be pleased by the statement, but found herself annoyed.

"He looks," Kirk mumbled. His sister's scent lifted on the faint breeze. Her hair had been soft and fragrant against his cheek. His frown deepened. "He looks a lot."

"You're imagining things," Foxy said firmly, then tried to draw Kirk away from the subject of Lance Matthews. She found speaking of him brought back disturbing memories. "Tell me, Mr. Fox," she began, mimicking the tone of a sports reporter, "are you always so introspective the night before a race?"

He did not answer at once, but simply stared out over the track. Foxy wondered what he saw there that she didn't. "It occurred to me recently that a woman's better off not getting involved with a man like me. She'll only get hurt." Restlessly he shifted, then turned to her. Foxy studied him curiously. There was something in his eyes she could not understand, and it puzzled her that he seemed tense. She sensed it was more than the race that was pulling at his nerves. "Lance is a lot like me," he continued. "I don't want you hurt. He could do that, maybe not meaning to, but he could do it."

"Kirk, I . . ."

"I know him, Foxy." He pushed away the beginnings of her objections and placed his hands on her shoulders. "No woman's ever been more important to him than cars. I don't think it's smart to get mixed up with men like us. There's always going to be another race, Foxy, another car, another track. It pushes everything and everyone else into the backseat. I don't want that for you. I know it's what you've always

had. I've never done the things I should've done for you, and
I . . ."

"No, Kirk." She stopped him by flinging her arms around
his neck. "No, don't." Foxy buried her face in his shoulder
the same way she had years before in her hospital bed. He
had been her rock when her world had crumbled away from
its foundations. "You did everything you could."

"Did I?" Kirk sighed and hugged her tighter. "If I had it
to do again, I know I'd do exactly the same things. But that
doesn't make them right."

"It was right for us." She lifted her face to look at him with
glistening eyes. "It was right for me."

Letting out a long breath, he tousled her hair. "Maybe."
After cupping her face in his hands, he kissed both her
cheeks. His mustache whispered along her skin causing her
to smile at the old familiarity. "I never expected you to grow
up, I guess. And I never thought you'd be beautiful and that
I'd have to worry about men. I should've paid more attention
while it was happening. You never complained."

"What about? I was happy." When he dropped his hands
from her face, she took them in hers. His palms were hard
and she felt the faint line of a scar along the back. She remembered that he had gotten it in Belgium eight years before in a minor crash. "Kirk," she spoke quickly, wanting to
put his mind at ease, "we were both where we needed to be.
I don't regret anything, and I don't want you to. Okay?"

She stood still as he studied her face. His eyes had long
since adjusted to the night, enabling him to see her features
clearly. He realized she had grown up right under his nose.
Somehow the woman who looked back at him roused his
protective instincts profoundly, while the girl had always
seemed somehow indestructible. Perhaps he understood the
pitfalls of womanhood, while those of childhood were a

mystery to him. It was an uncharacteristic gesture when he lifted her fingers to his lips, yet it was a gesture that flooded Foxy's eyes with warm tears. "I love you," he said simply. "Don't do that," he warned as he brushed a tear from her lashes. "I don't have anything to mop them up with. Come on." He slipped an arm around her shoulders and began to walk with her from the grandstands. "I'll buy you a cup of coffee and a hamburger. I'm starved."

"Pizza," she countered. "This is Italy."

"Whatever," he said agreeably as they moved without haste through the moonlight.

"Kirk." Foxy tilted her face, and now her eyes shone with mischief. "If Lance does bother me, will you beat him up?"

"Sure." Kirk grinned and tugged on her hair. "As soon as the season's over."

Foxy laughed. "That's what I figured."

* * *

It was just after eleven when they walked down the hall of the hotel to their rooms. Pam heard Foxy's laugh and the low answering sound of her brother's. Nibbling on her lip, she waited for the sounds of their doors closing. She badly needed to talk to Foxy, to have someone laugh and joke and take her mind off Kirk Fox. For weeks Pam had been able to think of little but him. As they had moved from country to country, from race to race, he had grown remote. He spoke to her rarely, and when he did, he was unmistakably aloof. It became apparent that he had lost interest in the flirtation he had initiated. His coolness might have caused her some minor annoyance or even some amusement under normal circumstances. But Pam had discovered that the circumstances here were far from normal. As Kirk had gradually grown more taciturn she had grown gradually more tense. Sleeping had become a major feat and eating a monumental task. Her tension had come to an unexpected climax when Kirk stepped from his car during the final laps of the race in France. Their eyes met for only one brief instant, but abruptly the realization had come to her that she was in love with him. The very thought had terrified her; he was so different from any of the men she had been attracted to in the past. But this was not mere attraction, and the old rules were insignificant. Briefly Pam had considered chucking the assignment and returning to the States. Professional pride refused to allow her this convenient escape. Personal pride kept her aloof from him. She did not want to be another of his trophies, another victory for Kirk Fox.

Hearing no sound in the hall, Pam drew a thin robe over her nightgown, deciding to slip down to Foxy's room. The instant she opened the door, she froze. Kirk walked silently down the hall. His head was bent but it snapped up immediately as she made a small sound of surprise. Stopping, he surveyed her carefully with eyes that held no expression. Framed in the doorway, Pam felt her breath backing up in her lungs. She seemed to have lost the power to force it out, just as she had lost the power to command her feet to move back into the room. His eyes held hers as he began to walk again, and though her fingers tightened on the knob, she did not retreat. Calm settled over her suddenly. This, she knew, was what she wanted, what she needed. When he stopped in front of her, they stood unsmiling, studying each other. The light from her room bathed them in a pale yellow glow.

"I've walked by your door a hundred times the last few months."

"I know."

"I'm not walking by tonight." There was a challenge in his voice, a hint of anger around his mouth. "I'm coming in."

"I know," Pam said again, then stepped back to allow him to enter. Her calm acceptance caused him to hesitate. She saw doubt flickering in his eyes.

"I'm going to make love to you," he told her in a statement that reflected a rising temper.

"Yes," she agreed with a nod. A smile touched her lips as she recognized the nervousness in his tone. *He's just as terrified as I am,* she realized when, after a brief hesitation, Kirk stalked into the room. Quietly Pam closed the door behind him. They turned to face each other.

"I don't make promises." His voice was rough as he studied her. His hands stayed firmly in his pockets.

"No." Her robe whispered gently as she moved to switch off the light. The room was softened by starlight and moonbeams. In the courtyard below her window someone spoke quickly in Italian, then laughed heartily.

"I'll probably hurt you," he warned in a lowered voice.

"Probably," Pam agreed. She walked to him until they were both silhouetted in the moonlight. He found her perfume quiet, understated, and unforgettable. "But I'm much sturdier than I look."

Unable to resist, he lifted a hand to her hair. It was as soft as a cloud under his palm. "You're making a mistake." In the dim light, he watched the sheen of her eyes.

"No." Pam lifted her arms until they circled his neck. "No, I'm not."

On a low groan, Kirk pulled her against him and took the offered mouth. As she felt him lift her Pam melted against him.

CHAPTER 6

There was the usual crush of people and noise as the starting time approached. The light, insistent drizzle did nothing to hamper attendance. The skies were lead-gray and uncompromising. Slicks were exchanged for rain tires.

Foxy stood before the basin in the empty ladies' room and rinsed the taste of sickness from her mouth. With the absent gestures of habit, she sponged her face and touched up her pallor with makeup. The palms of her hands were still hot and moist, and automatically she ran cool water over them. The drone of the loudspeaker penetrated the walls. Knowing she had only a few minutes until the start, she picked up her camera case and hurried out. The swarming crowd swallowed her instantly. Because she was preoccupied she didn't notice Lance until she was nearly upon him.

"Cutting it a bit closer than usual, Foxy?" She glanced up just as the thrust of the crowd pushed her against him. His grin faded as his hands touched the still clammy skin of her arms. "You're like ice," he muttered, then pulled her free of the throng and into a narrow hallway.

"For heaven's sake, let me go," she protested. Her legs were still a bit rubbery and nearly folded under her at the sudden movement. "They're going to start in a minute."

Ignoring her, Lance put a firm hand under her chin, then jerked her face to his. His eyes were narrowed and probing. Color had not yet returned to her cheeks, and the camouflage of makeup did not deceive him. "You're ill." The statement came partly as an accusation as he propped her against a wall. "You can't go out there while you're sick." Lance slipped an arm around her waist to lead her away, and she struggled against him. The sound of revving engines filled the air.

"For Lord's sake!" Foxy pushed unsuccessfully against him, frustrated by his interference. "I'm sick before every race, but I don't miss the start. Let me go, will you?"

His expression altered rapidly from surprise to disbelief to fury. Trapped between him and the wall, Foxy saw the changes and realized she had made a mistake. "You'll damn well miss this one," he grated, then half dragged, half carried her away from the pits. Feeling his grip, Foxy conceded and went peacefully. In silence, he led her to the restaurant under the main grandstand. "Coffee," he barked to the waiter as he pushed Foxy into a corner booth.

"Listen, Lance," she began, recovered enough to be indignant.

"Shut up." His voice was quiet, but so full of fury, she obeyed instantly. She had seen him angry before, but she decided she would have to go back some years to find a memory of an anger that sharp. His mouth was set in an uncompromising line, his voice vibrated with temper just under control. But it was his eyes, heated to a smoky gray, which kept her silent. Discretion, she reflected, sometimes is the better part of valor.

The restaurant was empty, silent save for the vibrations of the cars outside on the grid. There was a gray wall of gloom beyond the window, broken only by thin, clear rivulets of rain on the glass. Foxy watched one wind its slow, erratic way down the pane. The waiter set a pot of coffee

and two cups on the table between them, then disappeared.
The look in Lance's eyes told him he wanted solitude not service. Picking up the angry vibes Lance transmitted, Foxy
watched as he poured the coffee into each cup. Curiosity
began to temper her annoyance. *What is he so worked up
about?* she wondered.

"Drink your coffee," he ordered in clipped tones.

Her brows arched at the command. "Yes, sir," she said
humbly and lifted her cup.

A flash of trembling fury sparked in his eyes. "Don't push
me, Foxy."

"Lance." She set down her coffee untasted, then leaned
toward him. "What's the matter with you?"

He studied the perplexity on her face before drinking half
his coffee, hot and black. The pallor clung stubbornly to her
cheeks, lending her a look of vulnerability. Her eyes were
young and earnest as her own coffee sat cooling in front of
her. "How do you feel?" he asked as he drew out a cigar and
his lighter.

"I'm fine," she answered cautiously. She noted he didn't
light the cigar but merely twirled it between his fingers. Silence spread again. *This is ridiculous,* Foxy decided, and
opened her mouth to demand an explanation.

"You're sick before every race?" Lance demanded suddenly.

Foxy hesitated over the question and began to stir her coffee. "Listen, Lance—"

"Don't start with me." The sharp order startled her and
she lifted her eyes and encountered dark fury in his. "I asked
you a question." His voice was too controlled. Though never
timid, Foxy respected a temper more volatile than her own.
"Are you ill, physically ill," he repeated in slow, precise tones,
"before every race?"

"Yes."

Though soft, his oath was so violent she shuddered. Her wary eyes settled on his face. "Have you told Kirk?" he demanded.

"No, of course not. Why should I?" His temper flared again at the incredulity in her voice. Sensing danger, Foxy quickly laid her hand on his. "Lance, wait a minute. In the first place, at this point in my life, it's certainly my problem. When I was a kid, if I had told Kirk how I reacted to the start of a race, he would have worried, he would have been concerned, he might even have banned me from the track. All of those things would have made me guilty and miserable." She paused a moment and shook her head. "But he wouldn't have stopped. He couldn't have stopped."

"You know him well." Lance drained his cup, then poured more from the pot. His movements were smooth but Foxy was aware that his temper was just below the surface.

"Yes, I do." Their eyes met again, his heated, hers calm. "Racing's first with Kirk, it always has been. But I've always been second." Foxy made an imploring gesture, wanting him to understand her as badly as she had wanted Kirk to understand the night before. "That was enough. If he had put me first, he would have been a different person altogether. I love Kirk just the way he is . . . maybe because of the way he is. I owe him everything." As Lance opened his mouth to speak Foxy rushed on. "No, please listen, you don't understand. He gave me a home, he gave me a life. I don't know what would have happened to me after the accident if I hadn't had Kirk. How many twenty-three-year-old men would choose to be saddled with a thirteen-year-old girl? He's been good to me. He's given me everything he was capable of giving. I know he's not perfect. He's moody, he's self-absorbed. But, Lance, in all these years, he's never asked for anything except that I be there." She let out a long breath, then stared into her coffee. "It doesn't seem like much to ask."

"That all depends," Lance said quietly. "But in any case, you can't be there forever."

"No, I know that." Her shoulders moved with her sigh. Facing the window again, she watched the rain trickle down the glass without seeing her own ghostly reflection. "I realized this time around that I can't cope with it anymore, not in person anyway. I can't handle watching him get into a car and waiting for him to crash, knowing one day he might not walk away from it." She shifted her eyes back to Lance, and for a moment they were drenched in despair. "I won't watch him die."

"Foxy." Lance leaned over to take her hand. His voice was gentle now, without any sign of temper. "You know better than most that not every driver is killed on the track."

"I don't love every driver," she countered simply. "I've already lost two people in a car. No, no," she said quickly as he began to speak. She pressed her fingers to her eyes, simultaneously shaking her head as if to push the words away. "I don't dwell on it. I don't think about any of this often. You go crazy if you do." After taking a deep breath, Foxy felt more composed and met his eyes. "I'm not morbid about all of this, Lance. I just don't cope with it very well. And it gets harder all the time."

"I know the danger shouldn't be minimized, Foxy," Lance began, frowning at the weariness he saw in her eyes. "But you're aware of the improved safety features. A driver's much more protected than he used to be. Fatalities are the exception, not the rule."

"Statistics are just numbers on paper. They don't mean anything to me." She smiled as his brows drew together, then shook her head. "You can't understand because you're one of them. You're a unique breed. You all say you race for a variety of reasons, but there's really only one. You race because you love it. It's your mother and mistress and best friend. Drivers flirt with death, break their bones, singe their skins, and get back on the grid before the smoke's cleared. In the hospital one day, in the cockpit the next; I've seen you do it. It's like a religion, and I can't condemn it any more than I can comprehend it. Some people call it a science, but that's a lie. I've lived with it all my life, and it never makes any more sense. That's because it's emotional, and emotions rarely make sense." Foxy leaned her head against the cool glass of the window and stared into the rain. "I keep hoping one day he'll have had enough. Someday he'll find something else to take its place." When she looked back at Lance, her eyes were steady and studying. "I always wondered . . . Why did you quit?"

"I didn't love it anymore." With a half smile, he reached over and tucked her hair behind her ear.

"I'm glad," she said simply, smiling back at him. Toying with her coffee, she lapsed into silence a moment. "Lance, you won't say anything about this to Kirk?" Foxy lifted her eyes and used them shamelessly.

"No, I won't say anything." He watched relief flutter over her face before she lifted her cup. "But, Fox." The cup paused at her lips. "I'd like you to skip the last races in the circuit."

"I can't do that." She shook her head as she tasted the coffee. It was strong and cold, causing her to wrinkle her nose and set it back down. "Not only because of Kirk, but because I have a commitment to Pam." Foxy leaned back and watched Lance frown at her through a haze of cheroot smoke. "It's my job to photograph these races, and my work is very important to me."

"And when the season's over?"

It was her turn to frown. Her eyes reflected the gray light coming through the window. "I have my own life, my own work. I have to resolve to myself that I can't be a part of Kirk's life. I'm not equipped for it. My emotions are too near the surface. And I'm a coward," she added briskly, then started to slide from the booth. "I have to get back."

Lance was out of the booth before her and blocking her way. Even as her eyes rose to his in question, his arms came around her. He drew her close, nestling her head against his chest. "Oh, don't," she murmured and shut her eyes. A treacherous warmth flooded through her. "I can't handle you when you're kind." She could feel his lips trail over her hair while his hand moved gently up and down her spine. "Lance, please, if you're not careful, I'll start flooding the place with tears, and you've already terrified the waiter."

"Tears?" He spoke quietly, as if considering. "You know, Foxy, I don't believe I've ever seen you cry, not once in all the years I've known you."

"I have an aversion to humiliating myself in public." She felt cozy and pampered and entirely too right in his arms. "Lance, please don't be nice to me. I could get used to it." She lifted her face, but her smile never materialized. She could read his intent in his eyes. "Oh, help," she murmured as his mouth touched hers.

There was no need to brace herself for the explosion because his lips were gentle. There was no demand, no fire, just a lingering tenderness. Even as she felt her bones melt into submission, she felt oddly protected. The slow, soft embrace confused her, disarmed her, seduced her more successfully than his most ardent demand. His lips were warm, tasting hers without pressure, giving only comfort and pleasure. She had not known he was capable of such poignant tenderness. Because he was not asking, she gave more freely. The kiss lengthened, but remained a quiet gift. Reality slipped away leisurely, leaving Foxy with only Lance inside her world. When her mouth was free, she could not speak. Her eyes asked him questions.

"I'm not quite sure what to do with you," he murmured.

Taking a handful of her hair, he let it run through his fingers. "It was simpler before I found out you had a fragile side. I doubt that I deal very well with frailty."

Nonplussed, Foxy bent to lift her camera gear. She had not felt fragile until he had touched her so gently. Knowing there was no safety in the feeling, she tried to shake it off. "I'm not frail at all," she denied, then stood straight and faced him.

A smile flickered over his face, lifting his mouth and lighting up his eyes. "You don't like to be."

"I'm not," she countered with a quick shake of her head. No one had ever made her feel that way before, and Foxy was afraid he would touch her, making her feel that way again. She knew from experience that only the strong survived intact.

Lance studied her face before he took the camera case from her. "Humor me then," he suggested, then closed his hand over hers to lead her outside.

*   *   *

When the team returned to the States, Kirk led the competition for the world championship by five points. A win at Watkins Glen would give him the title. But through the high spirits and growing confusion, Foxy noticed subtle changes in the people closest to her. She herself had been preoccupied since the race in Italy. Something seemed to be nagging at the outside of her mind. The sensation did not make her uneasy as much as curious. She was accustomed to being in full control of her thoughts and feelings, but now it seemed part of her mind belonged to someone else. She found herself thinking more and more of Lance.

Since their talk over coffee, he had treated her with a strange gentleness. Oddly the gentleness was mixed with an aloofness that only added to Foxy's confusion. Since the kiss he had given her in the restaurant, Lance had not touched or indeed attempted to touch her again. Having never seen him be gentle or diffident before, Foxy began to wonder if she really knew him as well as she had assumed. Unwillingly she was drawn to him.

She noted a change in her brother. He grew more quiet and more withdrawn. Because she had seen him go inside himself before, Foxy accepted it. She attributed his mood to pressure over the championship. In Pam, she saw a growing serenity. Often during the qualifying races and long practice sessions, Foxy wished for a portion of Pam's absolute calm.

The 2.3-mile course climbed and weaved through terrain that was alternately wooded and open. Trees were ablaze with autumn colors, which grew more vibrant with each passing day. Foxy had forgotten that New York possessed such rustic charm. October leaves stretched toward a hard blue sky and swirled and spun to the ground. There was the combination of biting air and heat from the sun so peculiar to fall. Of all the tracks she had seen in a decade of her life, Foxy favored Watkins Glen. There was something simple and basically American about it.

She watched the race begin through the lens of her camera. *The last one,* she thought, and let out a long breath as she straightened. Beside her, Charlie Dunning stared after the cars while he rolled the stub of a fat cigar around in his mouth.

"This'll do it, Charlie." Foxy smiled as he turned to her, squinting against the sun.

"Don't you get tired of taking pictures?" he demanded as he scowled at her camera.

"Don't you get tired of playing with cars and chasing women?" she countered sweetly.

"Those are both worthwhile occupations." He pinched her waist and snorted. "You're getting skinnier."

"You're getting cuter." Foxy rubbed his grizzled beard with her palm and winked. "Wanna get married?"

"You're still a smart-aleck brat," he grumbled as he turned a rosy pink under his whiskers.

Grinning, Foxy dipped in his shirt pocket and pulled out a candy bar. "Let me know if you change your mind," she told him as she unwrapped the chocolate and took a bite. "I'm not getting any younger, you know."

With grumbles and mutters, Charlie moved away to lecture his mechanics.

"That's the first time Charlie's blushed in his life," Lance commented.

Foxy twisted her head and watched him approach. An odd thrill sped up and down her spine before it spread out at the base of her neck. His dark gray turtleneck was snug, showing off his lean torso. His mouth was cocked in a half smile. Abruptly she felt the memory of its pressure on hers. The sensation was so genuine, so vital, she was certain he must feel it too. As she looked at him it was as though a thin veil lifted from her eyes, and she saw him clearly for the first time: the dark gray eyes that saw so much and told so little, the well-shaped mouth that could give such pleasure, the firm chin and rawboned features that were so much more interesting than clean good looks. This was why Scott Newman had seemed so dull, why no boy or man she had ever known had measured up in her eyes. There was only one, had always been only one man in her heart.

I've never stopped loving him, she realized on a wave of alarm. *I never will.*

"You all right?" He reached for her as the color drained from her face. The gesture, coupled with the concern in his voice, snapped her back to reality.

"No . . . yes, yes, I'm fine." Foxy brushed a hand over her eyes as if to clear the mists. "I—I was daydreaming, I suppose."

"About wedded bliss with Charlie?" The careless brush of his hand through her hair sent tremors speeding through her.

"Charlie?" Blankly she glanced down at the chocolate bar in her hand. It was softening in the sunlight. "Oh, yes, Charlie. I was—I was teasing him." She wished desperately for a moment alone to pull herself together. Her mind was whirling with new knowledge. All of her senses seemed to be competing with each other for dominance.

Lance studied her with growing interest. "Are you sure you're all right?" His brow lifted in that habitual gesture and disappeared under his hair. "You look rattled."

Rattled? she thought, nearly giggling at the understatement. I'm going under for the third time. "I'm fine," she lied, then forced herself to smile. "How are you?"

Cars wound around the "Ss" and zoomed past. Absently she wondered how many laps she had missed while she had been in her trance. "Just fine," Lance murmured. There was a faint smile on his lips as he watched her. "Your chocolate's melting."

Dutifully Foxy took a bite of the bar. "What will you do after the race is over?" she asked, hoping she sounded only mildly interested.

"Relax."

"Yes." A portion of the tension slid out of her shoulders as she glanced around. It would be over in a matter of hours. "I guess we all will. It's been a long summer."

"Has it?" Lance retorted. Foxy wore a white Oxford shirt under a navy crew-neck sweater. Carelessly, Lance rubbed the collar between his thumb and forefinger while his eyes rested on hers. There was something proprietary in the casual gesture. "It doesn't seem very long ago that you popped out from under the MG in Kirk's garage."

"It seems like years to me," Foxy murmured as she turned back to the track. Cars hurtled by, and the noise was one continuous demand—roar and whine. She could smell oil and gas and heated rubber. "It doesn't seem to bother Pam at all," Foxy commented as she spotted the small blond figure near the edge of the pits. "I suppose it's easier if you're not personally involved with one of the drivers."

With a quick laugh, Lance took her chin and examined her face. "Do you need glasses or have you been off in space for the past few weeks?"

"What are you talking about?" Foxy was not ready to have him touch her and carefully backed away.

"Foxy, my love, Pam is very personally involved with one of the drivers. Take off your blinders."

Eyes narrowed against the sun, Foxy turned to study Pam's profile. She was watching the race steadily with her delicate hands tucked into the pockets of a spotless ivory blazer. Foxy turned back to Lance's amused face with a sharp glance. "You don't mean Kirk?" *Of course he means Kirk,* she realized even as she spoke. *I'd have seen it myself if I hadn't been so tangled up with Lance.* "Oh dear," she said on a sigh.

"Don't you approve, little sister?" Lance said dryly, then turned her back to face him. His hands remained light on her arms. "Kirk's a big boy now."

"Oh, don't be ridiculous." Foxy pushed her hair behind her back in a quick gesture of annoyance. "It's not a matter of approving, and in any case, Pam's wonderful."

"Then what's the problem?"

Foxy turned and gestured to where Pam stood. Her hair was rolled neatly at the nape of her neck with only a few wisps dancing gently around her composed face. "Just look at her," Foxy ordered impatiently. "That's how Melanie Wilkes would look today. Lord, she even sounds like her, with that quiet, cultured voice. Pam's tiny and fragile and should be serving tea in a drawing room. Kirk will swallow her whole."

"You've forgotten what a strong lady Melanie Wilkes was, Foxy." His fingers trailed lightly over her cheek. "Think about it," he advised before he turned and walked away.

For some moments, Foxy stood still. Being in love with Lance was not a new sensation, but now she loved as a woman and not as a child. This was no fairy-tale crush but a real, encompassing need. She knew now the agonies and joys of being in his arms, knew the heat and pressure of his mouth. She could never, as she had at sixteen, be content with making him the hero of her dreams. And after tomorrow, she remembered and shut her eyes against the painful reality, *I'll very likely never see him again.* Unable to deal with her situation, Foxy pushed it from her mind.

And now, there's Pam and Kirk, she reminded herself. Her loyalties at war, she walked over to the blond woman and stood beside her as the grid vibrated with passing cars.

"He's taken the lead a bit sooner than usual," Pam commented as she followed the flash of Kirk's car. "He wants badly to win this one." With a light laugh, she turned to Foxy. "He wants badly to win every one."

"I know . . . he always has." The calm blue eyes caused Foxy to take a long breath. "Pam, I know it's none of my business, but I'd . . ." With a sound of frustration, she turned back to the track and stuck her hands in her pockets. "Oh, I'm going to make a terrible fool of myself."

"You think I'm wrong for Kirk," Pam supplied gently.

"No!" Foxy's eyes grew wide with distress. "I think Kirk's wrong for you."

"How strangely alike the two of you are," Pam murmured, studying Foxy's earnest face. "He thinks so, too. But it doesn't matter, I know he's exactly right for me."

"Pam . . ." Foxy shook her head as she searched for the right words. "Racing . . ."

"Will always come first," Pam finished, then shrugged her slim shoulders. "Of course I know that. I accept that. The fact is, as much as it surprises even me, it's partly that which attracted me to him—the racing, his absolute determination to come out on top, his almost negligent attitude about danger. It's as exciting as it is frustrating, and I'm hooked. I think I'm going to be terrified, and then when the race starts, I'm not. I want him to win." She turned to Foxy with a brilliant smile. "I think I'm almost as bad as he is. I love him, I love who he is and what he is. Being second in his life is enough for me." Hearing her own words echo back to her, Foxy could do no more than stare out at the track. "I'm not trying to usurp your place with him," Pam began, and Foxy turned back quickly.

"Oh, no. No, it's not that. It's nothing like that. I'm glad for Kirk, he needs someone . . . someone who understands him the way you do." She ran her fingers through her thick mane of hair. It glowed like the russet leaves on the surrounding trees. "But I care about you, too." She made a frustrated gesture with her hands as if that would help her express herself. "He can be cruel by just forgetting."

"I don't bruise easily." Pam laid a hand on Foxy's shoulder. "Not as easily, I think, as you do." At Foxy's confused expression, she smiled. "It's easy for one woman in love to recognize another. No, no, don't start babbling a denial." She laughed as Foxy's mouth opened then closed. "If you need to talk, we will. I feel quite an expert on the subject."

"It's academic," Foxy told her with a restless movement of her shoulders. "Tomorrow we'll go our separate ways."

"You still have today." Pam gave Foxy's shoulder a quick squeeze. "Isn't that really all there is?"

It happened so suddenly. At first Foxy's brain rejected it. Even as Pam spoke, Kirk rounded the turn in front of them. She saw him swerve to avoid the abrupt fishtailing of the racer to his right, then waited for him to regain control. She saw the skid begin, heard its squeal echo through her head as she watched it grow wider and more violent. Part of her brain screamed in panic while still another kept insisting he would pull out of it. He had to pull out of it. The sound of the blowout was like a gunshot and just as lethal. Then there were columns of smoke and shrieking metal as the car slammed into the wall and careened away. Wheels and pieces of fiberglass rained in the air as the racer continued to spin wildly.

"No!" The cry was wrenched from Foxy as she darted toward the track. With one quick jerk, she freed herself from Pam's restraining hand and ran.

Jagged pieces of fiberglass flew with deadly abandon. A fear greater than any she had ever known filled her, blacking out all thoughts, all feelings. Her only reality was the twisting hulk of machine that held her brother in its bowels. Inches from the grid, her breath was cut off by a vise around her waist. The force lifted her off the ground, and she kicked uselessly in the air to free herself. She shook the hair from her eyes in time to see Kirk's car topple into the infield.

"For God's sake, Foxy, you'll kill yourself." Lance's voice was harsh in her ear as she writhed and struggled for freedom. In terror, she waited for the belching smoke to burst into flame.

"Let me go!" she shouted as she realized the vise around her waist was his arm. "It's Kirk, can't you see? I've got to get to him." Her breathing was ragged as she clawed at the imprisoning arm. "Oh God, I've got to get to him!" she shouted again, desperately fighting to free herself.

"There's nothing you can do." Lance jerked her back against him, cutting off her wind for a moment. Over her head, he could see members of the emergency team spraying the wreck with extinguishers while others worked to free Kirk from the cockpit. "There's nothing you can do," he said again. Her struggles ceased abruptly. She went so completely limp, he thought she had fainted until he heard her speak.

"Let me go." Foxy spoke quietly now, so that he barely heard her. "I won't do anything stupid," she added when he did not lessen his grip. "I'm all right, Lance, let me go."

Slowly he lowered her back to the ground and released her. She neither turned to him nor spoke, but watched in silence as they pulled Kirk from the wreckage. She gave no sign that she knew Pam stood beside her. Behind them, the pits were like a tomb. The white flag fluttered in the autumn breeze.

CHAPTER 7

The walls in the hospital waiting room were pale green. The floor was uncarpeted; an inconspicuous beige tile with tiny brown flecks disguised a day's collection of dust and dirt. On the wall opposite Foxy was a print of a Van Gogh still life. It was the sole spot of color in the drab little room. Foxy knew she would never see the print again without remembering the hours of torment and ignorance. Pam sat near the window, framed by drapes just darker than the walls. Occasionally she took sips of cold coffee. Charlie sat on a vinyl sofa and gnawed at the stub of a long-dead cigar. Lance paced. Unceasingly he prowled the small room, sometimes with his hands in his pockets, sometimes smoking. Once or twice, Foxy heard Pam murmur something to him, then caught the low rumble of his response. She did not hear the words, nor did she attempt to. They did not interest her. She felt the same nameless, unspeakable fear she had known in the first moments of consciousness after her own accident. She had been helpless then, and she knew she was helpless now. Lance had been right when he told her there was nothing she could do. Now Foxy accepted it. Anger and panic were buried under the numbing terror of the unthinkable. Her mind drifted and emptied as she stared at the Van Gogh print. Kirk's skid had begun more than three hours before.

"Miss Fox?"

With a jolt, Foxy was pulled back to the present. For a moment, she merely stared at the green-gowned figure in the doorway. "Yes?" she managed in a surprisingly strong voice as she rose to meet him. It floated through her mind that the doctor was very young. His mustache was dark but reminded Foxy of Kirk's. His surgical mask hung by its ties at his throat.

"Your brother's out of surgery." There was a quietness to his voice, which, like his hands, he used for healing. "He's in recovery."

Cautiously Foxy held off relief and kept her gaze steady on his face. "How extensive are his injuries?"

The doctor heard and respected the control in her tone, but saw that her eyes were hurting and afraid. "He had five broken ribs. His lungs collapsed, but they've been reinflated and the concussion's mild. The ribs will be painful, but since there was no puncture, the danger's minimal. His leg . . ." He hesitated a moment, and Foxy felt a fresh thrill of fear.

"He didn't . . ." She swallowed, then forced herself to ask. "He didn't lose it?"

"No." He took her hand for reassurance and found it ice cold but without a tremor. "But it's a complicated injury, we've had to do some reconstructing. It's an open, comminuted fracture, and there's some artery damage. We've realigned the bones, and the outlook is good that he'll have full use of the leg in a few months. Meanwhile, there's a risk of infection." After releasing her hand, the doctor allowed his gaze to sweep the people behind her before returning to Foxy. "He's going to be here for some time."

"I see." Foxy let out a shaky breath. "Is there anything else?"

"Minor burns and abrasions. He's a very lucky man."

"Yes." Foxy's agreement was solemn as she stared down at her hands. She joined them together, not knowing what else to do with them. "Is he conscious?"

"Yes." The doctor grinned and looked younger yet. "He wanted to know who won the race." Foxy bit her bottom lip hard and continued to look straight ahead as he went on. "He'll be in a room in about an hour; you can see him then. Only one visitor tonight," he added firmly, again letting his eyes trail over the people behind Foxy. "The others can see him tomorrow. We're not giving him a phone for twenty-four hours."

Foxy nodded and spoke quickly. "Miss Anderson will stay to see him tonight then."

"Foxy," Pam began, shaking her head as she stepped forward.

"He'll want you," Foxy told her as their eyes met. "He'll be satisfied knowing I was here. You will stay, won't you?"

Feeling tears well up behind her eyes, Pam nodded quickly, then turned away. She had managed with a great deal of willpower to remain composed during the wait. Now, Foxy's simple generosity did what the hours of torture had not. Moving to the window, she stared out and let the tears have their freedom.

"The desk has my number," Foxy told the doctor. "Will you see that I'm called if there's any change before morning?"

"Certainly. Miss Fox," he added, recognizing the signs of shock and fatigue in her eyes. "He's going to be fine."

"Thank you."

"Charlie, wait around and take Pam back after she's seen Kirk," Lance ordered as he took Foxy's arm. "I'll take Foxy now." He turned to the doctor and spoke briskly. "There'll be reporters downstairs in the lobby. I don't want her to have to deal with them tonight."

"Take the service elevator down to the garage level. There's a cabstand near the entrance."

"Thanks." Without waiting for her assent, Lance began to lead Foxy down the corridor.

"You don't have to do this," she said. Her voice held no inflection at all as she allowed herself to be piloted.

"I know what I have to do," he tossed back and jammed the button on the service elevator. Behind them, the crepe soles of nurses' shoes made soft sounds against the tile.

"I didn't thank you before for stopping me from running out on the track." There was a quick ding of a bell before the doors slid open. Foxy made no protest as he pulled her into the empty car. "It was a stupid thing to do."

"Stop it, damn it! Just stop it." He whirled and took her by the shoulders. His fingers pressed tightly into her flesh. "Scream, cry, take a punch at me, but stop acting like this."

Foxy stared up into the furious heat of his eyes. Her emotions refused to surface. Her defenses remained sealed, as if they knew it was still too soon to allow anything to escape. She spoke quietly and her eyes were dry. "I already did all the screaming I'm going to do. I can't cry yet because I'm still numb, and I don't have any reason to take a punch at you."

"It was my car, isn't that enough?" he demanded. The doors opened, and he took her hand before he stalked out. Their footsteps echoed hollowly in the garage as he pulled her toward the entrance.

"Nobody forced Kirk into that car. I'm not blaming you, Lance. I'm not blaming anyone."

"I saw the way you looked at me when they pulled him out."

Fatigue was pouring over Foxy as Lance nudged her into a cab. Turning her head to face him, she made herself speak clearly. "I'm sorry. Maybe I did blame you for a minute.

Maybe I wanted to blame you or anyone else who was handy. I thought he was dead." Because her voice trembled slightly, she paused until she was certain she could continue. "I've tried to be prepared for something like this every day of my life. But I wasn't prepared at all. It doesn't seem to make any difference that I've seen him crash before." Foxy sighed and leaned back against the seat. The streetlights came through the cab window to dance on her closed lids. "I don't blame you for what happened, Lance, any more than I blame Kirk for being who he is. Maybe this time he'll have had enough."

No answer came from Lance but the click and hiss of his lighter. Not having the energy to open her eyes, Foxy kept them closed and took the rest of the brief journey in silence. When they arrived at the motel, they found Scott Newman pacing the corridor in front of Foxy's room. He wore the disheveled look of an executive who has just left a hassle-filled board meeting.

"Cynthia." Giving Lance a quick nod, he held out both hands to her. "The hospital said you were on your way back. How's Kirk? They tell you next to nothing over the phone."

"He's going to be fine," Foxy told him, letting him squeeze her hands. She gave him a shortened version of the doctor's report.

"Everybody's been worried; they'll be glad to hear he's going to be all right. How about you?" He gave her an encouraging smile. "I thought you might need me."

"What she needs is some rest," Lance said shortly.

"It was very considerate of you to wait." Foxy smoothed over Lance's rudeness and added a smile that cost her some concentrated effort. "I'm fine, really, just a bit tired. Pam stayed behind to keep Kirk company for a while."

"The press is itching for the full story," Scott commented as he released her hands and straightened the knot in his tie. "We took a look at the replay. There's no doubt that Kirk had to swerve to avoid a crash with Martell, and that's when he lost it. Defective steering in Martell's racer is the verdict. A bad break for Kirk. Perhaps you'd like to give them a statement or pass one on through me."

"No," Lance answered before Foxy could respond. "Leave it. If you want to be useful, tell the switchboard not to pass any calls through to this room unless it's the hospital." His voice was curt and annoyed. "Give me the key, Foxy," he ordered.

"Of course." Scott nodded as he watched Foxy dig in her bag. "I'm sure I can hold them off at least until morning, but—"

"Come to my room in a couple hours." Lance cut him off and snatched the key from Foxy's hand. "I'll give you enough for a press release. Just see that you keep her out of it. Understand?" Lance jerked open the door.

The fury registered. Scott agreed with another nod before turning to Foxy. "Let me know if there's anything I can do, Cynthia."

"Thank you, Scott. Good night," she managed before Lance shut the door in his face. Bone weary, she moved to a chair and sank into it. "You were very rude," she commented absently as she rubbed at a headache near her temple. "I don't recall that I've ever seen you be quite that rude before."

"Maybe if you took a look in the mirror, you'd understand why." The fury was still in his voice. Foxy watched him calmly from behind the numbing shield of shock and fatigue. "You're standing there getting paler by the minute. I swear the only color in your face right now is in your eyes. And he rambles on like an idiot about press releases." Lance made a gesture of disgust with his hand. "He's got the brains of a soft-boiled egg."

"He's a good manager," Foxy murmured, fighting against the building ache in her head.

"And a great human being," Lance added sarcastically.

"Lance," Foxy began with the first stirrings of curiosity, "were you protecting me?"

When he turned on her, she watched his temper boil in his eyes. Her curiosity increased as she watched him control it. "Maybe," he muttered, then turned to the phone. Foxy heard him mumble a series of instructions but paid no attention to the words.

Odd, she thought, *he seems to be making a habit of protecting me. First in Italy, and now here. It certainly doesn't seem to make him very comfortable, though.* She continued to study him after he had hung up the phone. Instantly he began to pace the room just as he had paced the waiting area in the hospital.

"Lance." He stopped when she quietly said his name. Foxy held out her hand, realizing suddenly how grateful she was that he was there. She wasn't ready to be alone yet. She wasn't feeling strong and capable and indestructible, but tired and vulnerable and afraid. Lance stared at her a moment without moving, then crossed to her to take the offered hand. "Thank you." Her eyes were dark and grave as they clung to his. "It's just occurred to me that I wouldn't have made it through all this without knowing you were there. I didn't even realize that I needed you, but you did. I want you to know how much it means to me."

Something flickered over his face before he raked his free hand through his hair. It was an uncharacteristic gesture of frustration, which reminded Foxy that he was as weary as she. "Fox," he began, but she continued quickly.

"You won't go away tomorrow, will you?" Knowing she was being weak did not prevent her from asking. She needed him, and her hand tightened on his. "If you could just stay for a couple of extra days, just until things settle. I can lie," she continued in a voice that was growing desperate. "I can walk right in that hospital room tomorrow and look at Kirk, look right in his eyes and lie. It's a trick I've learned over the years; and I'm good at it. He'll never have to know how much I hate him being in there. But if you could stay, if I could just know you were there. I know it's a lot to ask, but I . . ." She stopped, then pressed both hands to her eyes. "Oh, Lord, I think the numbness is wearing off." She heard the knock at the door, but took deep steadying breaths, leaving Lance to answer it. In a moment, she heard him move back to her.

"Foxy." He spoke her name gently and took her wrist until she had lowered her hands. Her eyes were young and devastated. "Drink this." He held out a glass filled with the brandy room service had delivered. Though she took it obediently, she only stared down into the amber liquid. Lance watched her for a moment, then crouched down until their eyes were level. "Fox." He waited until she had shifted her gaze from the brandy to him. "Marry me."

"What?" Foxy stared at him, saw the familiar intentness in his eyes, then squeezed her own shut. "What?" she said again, opening them.

Lance urged the brandy toward her lips. "I said, marry me."

Foxy drank the entire contents of the glass in one swallow. Her breath caught on the burn of the brandy, and the small sound thundered in the absolute silence of the room. For several long seconds, she stared into his eyes trying to penetrate the impenetrable. She sensed that under the calm lay a whirlpool of energy, a power that would escape at any instant. He held something, she was unsure what, on a very tight leash. Tension gripped tight in her throat. She tried to swallow it and failed. Her eyes remained steady on his, but her voice was only a whisper. She was afraid. "Why?"

"Why not?" he countered, then took the empty glass from her nerveless fingers.

"Why not?" Foxy repeated. She lifted her hand to make some helpless gesture, but he caught it in his own. Her fingers trembled as he brought them to his lips. Steadily he watched her.

"Yes, why not?"

"I don't know, I . . ." He had succeeded in distracting her with the unconventional proposal. She ran her free hand through her hair and tried to think properly. "There must be a reason, I just can't think."

"Well, if you can't think of any substantial reason against it, marry me and come to Boston."

"Boston?" Foxy echoed him blankly.

"Boston," Lance agreed, and for the first time, a faint smile touched his lips. "I live there, remember?"

"Yes, of course." Foxy rubbed a line between her brows and struggled to concentrate. "Of course I remember."

"We could leave when you were confident that Kirk was settled. More than likely, he'll be staying here for the next couple of months, but there's no need for you to be here." Lance's voice was practical, his face absolutely calm. Frustrated and unsure, Foxy shook her head. *I'm hallucinating. Hallucinations don't hurt,* she reminded herself, then quickly shook off the argument. It was easier to believe it was an illusion than to believe Lance was asking her to marry him in the same tone he might ask her to fetch him a cup of coffee.

"Lance, I . . ." Foxy hesitated, then decided to evade the issue rather than face it head-on. "I don't think I'm taking all this in properly. I'm still a little fuzzy." She swallowed and tried to match his casual tone. "Let me think about it. Give me a day or two."

Lance inclined his head. "That sounds reasonable," he agreed as she rose to move away from him. "No," he said, causing her to turn and gape at him.

"What did you say?"

"I said no, you can't think about it for a day or two." In one quick gesture, he had her firmly by the shoulders and had abolished the distance between them. Foxy saw that his eyes were no longer calm but turbulent. He had held her like this before, she remembered, and had looked at her in precisely the same way. Years ago, she reflected, confused and foolishly disoriented, in the empty garage at Le Mans. Was he going to shout at her again? she wondered. Her brows drew together as she tried to keep the past and present separate.

"What do you want?" she asked, struggling with her feelings for him.

"You." He pulled her yet closer as his eyes burned into hers. "I'm not about to let you walk out of my life, Fox, and I've waited for you long enough." His mouth lowered swiftly but was gentle on hers. Even so, she could feel the imprisoned passion in the grip of his hands. The kiss was thorough, possessive. "Did you really think I'd calmly walk out that door and give you a couple of days to think it over?" His mouth closed over hers again, preventing any response she might have made. Once again, he drew her away, this time to stare down into her bemused eyes. "Do you think I could want you the way that I do, then walk away after you've told me you need me?"

"Lance, I didn't mean to . . ." Foxy shook her head as she searched for some scraps of common sense. "You shouldn't feel obligated, I was grateful . . ."

"The hell with grateful," he declared, then grabbed her hair with both hands. "I'm not interested in some nice, patient emotion like gratitude. That's not what I want from you." Foxy saw the determination in his face, heard the fire in his voice. Her blood began to heat in response. "I don't give a damn if the timing's wrong, or that I'm pressing you when your defenses are down. I'm a selfish man, Foxy, and I've wanted you for longer than I care to think about. I'm going to have you."

Her pulse was beating so quickly, she was giddy. She steadied herself, placing her hands on his arms. "Lance . . ." Her voice would not behave but insisted on coming out in breathless whispers. "What you're talking about isn't what's necessary for marriage. That's a big step, a lifetime commitment, I don't know . . ."

"I love you," he said and stopped her speech cold. Her lips trembled open to form words that would not come. "I want to spend my life with you, and I'm not going back to Boston without you. I can't give you the candlelight and soft words that might smooth the road because I haven't the time or patience for them right now. I'll have to make it up to you later." His hands moved from her hair to her shoulders to her waist, but he brought her no closer. "Foxy, you drive me out of my mind." As she watched, she saw both demand and doubt flicker in his eyes. "You love me, too, I know you do."

"Yes." She rested her cheek against his chest and sighed. "Yes, I love you. Hold me," she murmured, finding again she fit perfectly into his arms. "I need you to hold me." For the next few moments, she allowed herself the incredible luxury of being held and cherished by the man she loved. It's all happening so fast, she thought, then pushed away the fears and listened to the steady drum of Lance's heart. *He loves me.* "Lance." Tilting her head, Foxy brought her lips to his. Instantly his mouth answered hers, passion for passion, wonder for wonder, until their bodies were heated and entwined. Lance loosened his hold as she shivered from spiraling emotions.

"We can be married in a couple of days." He spoke calmly again, but his hands wandered up and down her back before they rested on her hips. "The paperwork will take that long.

Then we'll go to Boston." His eye grew serious on her face. "Pam will be here for Kirk, you understand that, don't you?"

"Yes." Foxy closed her eyes a moment and tried to block out the rushing image of the accident. "Yes, that's for the best. I want to go," she told him as she opened her eyes. "I want to be with you." Her nerves were jumping inside her stomach, refusing to grow steady, and she met his mouth desperately. Foxy felt his hunger and matched it. "Stay with me tonight," she whispered as she buried her face against his neck. "I don't want you to go."

Slowly Lance drew her away and scanned her face. Her cheeks were still pale, her eyes like smoke against her skin. Already there were faint shadows haunting them. "No." He shook his head as he brushed the back of his hand down her cheek. "You're too vulnerable tonight, I've already taken advantage of that. You need sleep." With this, he swept her up in his arms and carried her to the bed. Foxy's body responded to the weightlessness by floating with the fatigue. After he laid her on the mattress, he sat beside her. "Do you want anything?"

"Tell me again."

Lance lifted her hand and turned the palm to his lips. "I love you. Will you sleep?"

"Yes, yes, I'll sleep." Foxy could feel the weariness pressing down on her. She closed her eyes and immediately began to dream. Lance's lips were a soft promise on hers.

"I'll come for you in the morning," he murmured. Dimly she felt the bed shift as he stood. She was asleep before the door closed behind him.

CHAPTER 8

Sunlight fell fresh and brilliant over Foxy's face. She moaned as it began to penetrate her slumber. Her mind gently floated to the surface, noticing small, inconsequential things: the rapid ticking of her travel alarm on the stand beside the bed, the vague itch between her shoulder blades, the uncomfortable warmth of the spread that lay on top of her. She had huddled under it during the night when she awakened cold and frightened in the dark. She did not remember the nightmare yet, the vivid clarity in which she had relived Kirk's crash. She had awakened, panting for breath, cold as ice, with terror ripping away all thought of sleep. She did not remember yet that the tears had finally come in torrents until her eyes were raw and her ribs ached from the strain. She had wept herself numb, then had fallen into a fitful sleep, plagued with doubts about her unconventional engagement to Lance. Perhaps he had proposed out of a sense of duty. Foxy had tried to recapture the feeling she had experienced when he had told her he loved her, but she was cold and miserable. She had huddled under the blanket and wished for morning.

Now that it was here, she found the light annoying and

the spread stifling. She shifted crossly, still half asleep, and wished the spread would disappear without her having to move. As her consciousness swam reluctantly closer to the surface her memory began to merge with it. Her mind clear, she sat up abruptly and rested her face on her knees.

Pull yourself together, Foxy, she ordered, drawing her breath slowly in and out of her lungs. *You had a bad night; now shake it off and get down to business. Lance will be here soon.* Lifting her head, Foxy narrowed her eyes and stared at her left hand, trying to imagine an engagement ring on the third finger.

"I'm going to marry him," she said aloud, just to hear how the words would sound. Her stomach shivered, announcing the state of her nerves. It came to her abruptly that she knew absolutely nothing about the man who lived in Boston and ran a multimillion-dollar business. The Lance Matthews she knew was a cocky ex-driver who played a mean hand of poker and knew how to tear down an engine. The only hint she had seen of the other side of him had been on their date in Monte Carlo. It was, she reflected, not enough. She was going to marry him without knowing the whole man. Did he belong to the country club? Did he play golf on Saturdays? Foxy tried to imagine Lance swinging a nine iron and got nowhere. Shutting her eyes, she let the reckless side of her push away the doubts. *This is no time to sit around thinking,* she told herself. *What does it matter if he plays golf or backgammon or if he's into yoga? What does it matter if he wears a three-piece suit and carries a briefcase or if he wears jeans and sneakers?* Biting down on her lips, Foxy wondered when she had sewn this particular patchwork of thought together. *I've got to get up and put myself together so that I don't look like a zombie when he gets here.*

Throwing off the spread, Foxy rose from the bed and

discovered that every muscle in her body was taking revenge on her for the restless night. *A hot shower,* she reflected, and began to strip off the clothes she had slept in. *I'm not nervous, I'm just groggy.* When Lance knocked at her door thirty minutes later, Foxy was just completing her attempt to camouflage the results of the wakeful night.

She wore a plain yellow shift, with her hair neatly coiled at her neck. Lance studied her face carefully before speaking. Her eyes were freed now from shock but were still haunted by shadows. He took her chin in his hand and frowned. Her fragile looks were intensified by the violet smudges under her eyes. Weeping had left them faintly swollen and weary.

"You've been crying," he accused, making Foxy realize that all her attempts with base and blusher and mascara had been for nothing. His voice was taut, and she could feel the tension in his fingers. It added to her own. "Didn't you sleep?" he demanded.

"Not very well," she admitted and wondered why he seemed so angry. "I woke during the night. It all seemed to hit me at once."

Lance's frown deepened. "I should have stayed."

"No." She shook her head, searching his eyes for the reason for the roughness in his voice. "I needed to be alone to get it out of my system. I'm better now."

Something flickered in his eyes before they became unfathomable. "Have you changed your mind?"

Foxy knew he was speaking of their marriage and felt a quick thrill of alarm. She forced herself to speak calmly. "No."

Lance nodded and released her chin. "Fine. We'll take care of the paperwork before we go by the hospital. Ready?"

Foxy frowned but stepped into the corridor, closing the

door at her back. "When we see Kirk," she began as they walked toward the steps, "I'd like to tell him about our plans myself . . . when the time's right."

Lance's brow lifted and fell. "Fine."

Miffed by his tone and by his cool self-possession, Foxy tilted her face to his and spoke coldly. "Maybe I should've asked if you'd changed your mind."

"I'd have let you know if I had," he returned as they stepped into the sunlight.

"Undoubtedly," she agreed. Saying nothing, Lance led her to the sleek blue Porsche he had rented that morning. For the first time since her screaming fear of the previous afternoon, Foxy began to feel the full emotion of anger. "Are you going to have your lawyers draw up a contract? I want to be certain to read the fine print."

"Save it, Foxy," Lance warned and opened the passenger door.

"No." She stood back and glared. "I don't know why you're acting like this. Maybe you're just a miserable human being in the mornings. I'll get used to it, I suppose. But you'd better get used to the fact that I say what I want when I want. If you don't like it, you can—"

Her tirade was cut off as he slammed the door shut and pulled her roughly into his arms. His mouth came down hard on hers. Angry and dominant, his lips bruised hers while she stood too surprised to protest or respond. He held her, ravishing her mouth until she was breathless. Then, with a suddenness that left her gasping, he set her aside. "And I know how to shut you up when I don't want to hear it."

Foxy managed one indignant huff. "You're a maniac," she told him as he opened her door again.

"All right," he agreed. Then, without giving her a chance for further comment, he nudged her into the car.

For the first time, Foxy noticed two young girls standing on the sidewalk giggling. Furious and embarrassed, she folded her arms and clamped her lips shut. She would not give him the satisfaction of either arguing or submitting herself to his idle conversation. In utter silence, they drove off to secure a marriage license.

A scant two hours later, after speaking only when unavoidable, they walked into Kirk's hospital room. Foxy did her best not to register any shock at the sight of the bandages and plaster. His leg was surrounded by an external fixture rather than a cast. To Foxy's eyes it looked like an erector set built by a clever teenager. Surrounded by white sheets and bandages, tubes and metal, Kirk lay propped up in bed. He was scowling at Pam with the look of a man who has just finished giving a heated speech. Instantly Foxy sensed the tension and glanced from one to the other. She thought it best to employ tact and make no comment. Because she had known Kirk would hate them, she hadn't brought any flowers. Empty-handed, she crossed to the bed and gravely studied him.

"You're a mess," she concluded, making her voice lightly scornful. Her stomach trembled at the number of bandages and the terrifyingly foreign-looking apparatus around his leg. As she had hoped, the scowl faded and a grin took its place.

"You're cute, too. Hi, Lance. I think I might have dented a fender on your car."

"Scraped the paint, too," he said easily as his hands disappeared into his pockets. Watching him, Pam noted that he was uncomfortable in hospital rooms. Foxy, she mused, was putting up a front Kirk would see through if it occurred to him to look. But of course it wouldn't. "I'd keep clear of Charlie for a while," Lance advised as he glanced over to find Pam's eyes on him. Her face was composed, but he could detect the signs of a sleepless night. He had seen the expression she wore before, on wives, parents, and lovers of countless other drivers. A quick, silent understanding passed between them before he looked back at Kirk.

"I heard Betinni took first and hooked the championship." Hampered by the position, Kirk's shrug was awkward. "He's a good driver. We've been passing off the lead all season." He shifted a bit, and Foxy caught the brief wince of pain. Knowing sympathy would only earn her a growl, she turned to Pam.

"Well," she said with a smile a shade too bright, "I don't suppose he's been giving you any trouble."

"On the contrary." Pam glanced at Kirk, then back to his sister. "He's been giving me a great deal."

"Pam." Kirk's irritated tone held a warning. She ignored both.

"He's ordered me back to Manhattan. He's very annoyed because I'm not going."

Unsure what to say, Foxy looked from Pam to Kirk, then to Lance. "Well," she said and cleared her throat.

"He seems to think I'm being quite unreasonable," Pam added in the same mild tone.

"And stupid," Kirk tossed out. His scowl was back, deeper than before.

"Oh yes." Pam smiled gently. "And stupid. I'd forgotten that."

"Look," Kirk began, and Foxy recognized the dangerous pitch in his voice. "You've got no reason to hang around here."

"I've got a hospital fetish," Pam returned.

"Damn it, I don't want you!" Kirk shouted, then cursed at the pain that followed his outburst.

Firmly Lance took Foxy's arm as she started to move forward. "Keep out of it," he ordered quietly.

"Too bad," Pam retorted. Her voice was soft, but she stood

like a general facing the enemy, her shoulders straight. The sun streamed through the window behind her, haloing her hair. "You're not getting rid of me. I love you."

"You're crazy," Kirk threw back, fidgeting in the bed.

"Very likely."

He narrowed his eyes at her careless response. In the strong sunlight, her skin looked like alabaster. He felt the need rise surprisingly fast. "I'm not letting you stay," he ground out in defense.

"What're you going to do?" Pam countered with a shrug. "Kick me back to Manhattan with your good leg?"

"I will as soon as I can get up," Kirk muttered, furious that he had to lie flat on his back to argue with a woman half his size.

"Yeah?" The slang came with elegant ease from Pam's delicately tinted lips. She walked over and gave his mustache a hard tug that brought out a sound of surprised protest. "Remind me to be scared later. Now as I see it I've got three choices. I can murder you, jump off a bridge, or I can cope. I come from a long line of copers. You, on the other hand," she added with a pat on his cheek, "simply have no choice at all. You're stuck with me."

"Think so, huh?" Kirk's mouth twisted into a reluctant grin. "Guess you're pretty tough."

"You guess right," she agreed, then bent to kiss him lightly. Kirk grabbed a handful of her hair and took the kiss deeper.

"We're going to settle this when I can stand up," he muttered, but pulled her back to kiss her again.

"I'm sure we will," Pam said with a smile as she sat on the edge of the bed. Foxy noted that his hand sought hers.

He loves her, she realized suddenly. *He really loves her.* Her eyes fastened on Pam with a look of respect and hope. *Maybe,* she thought rapidly, *maybe she's the answer. Maybe he's finally found an alternative.*

"Well." Pam smiled into Foxy's bemused face. "Is there any news from the outside world?"

"News?" Foxy repeated, trying to reorganize her thoughts.

"Earthquakes, floods, wars, famine," Pam prompted with a laugh. "I feel I've been neatly cut off for the past twenty-four hours."

"There hasn't been any of those that I know of," Foxy answered with a glance at Kirk. *This is the time,* she told herself. *This is the time to tell him.* Suddenly she felt ridiculously nervous and awkward. "Lance and I," she began, then her eyes sought his for reassurance. Taking a deep breath, she looked back at Kirk and spoke quickly. "Lance and I are going to be married." Instantly Foxy saw the surprise and puzzlement cover Kirk's face. His brows drew together as he stared at her.

"Well!" Pam rose quickly and hugged Foxy. "This is news. The best kind." Glancing over Foxy's head, she met Lance's eyes. "You're a very lucky man."

"Yes," he returned, unsmiling. "I know."

"Married?" Kirk interrupted. "What do you mean, married?"

"The usual definition," Foxy told him as she moved to his bedside. "You've heard it before, it's still quite popular."

"When?" he demanded shortly.

"As soon as the blood tests and paperwork are taken care of," Lance put in casually. After strolling over to the bed, he slipped an arm around Foxy's shoulders. Kirk watched the gesture, then lifted his eyes to Lance's face. "What's the matter?" Lance asked him with a grin. "Did you want us to get your permission?"

"No," Kirk mumbled uncomfortably. Looking up into Foxy's face, he remembered the little girl. "Yeah," he admitted with a sigh. "Maybe. I could have used a little warning, anyway."

"You're hardly in any shape to beat him up now," Foxy pointed out. Lance's arm around her eased away her tension, and her eyes laughed down at Kirk.

Kirk studied his best friend and then his sister. When he held out his hand, Foxy slipped hers into it. "You sure?"

Foxy turned her head until she faced Lance. *He's the only man I've ever loved,* she mused. *It's not a fantasy anymore, but real. Am I sure?* she asked herself, keeping both her mind and heart open. She took her time studying his familiar face, then answered the question she thought she saw in his eyes. "Yes," she said and smiled. "I'm sure." Rising on her toes, she met his mouth and felt the morning's nerves drain away. "Very sure." Her hand was still warm in Kirk's. "Don't worry about me," she told Kirk as she turned back to him.

"It's a new habit I've gotten into, but be happy and I won't worry," he countered, foolishly feeling as if something precious was being stolen from him. "I guess you're all grown up."

"I guess so," she said softly and returned the pressure of his hand.

"Give me a kiss," he ordered. After Foxy raised her head again, Kirk fastened his eyes on Lance. An essential male understanding passed between them. They knew each other as well as brothers ever do, but now they were joined deeper by the woman between them. Perhaps if they had not been close, had not been intimate with each other's thoughts over the years, it would have been simpler. The very quality of their friendship made it complex. "Don't hurt her," Kirk warned as he kept possession of Foxy's hand. "Are you going to live in that house in Boston?"

"That's right," Lance answered. Foxy watched them, knowing they said more than she could translate.

Abruptly Kirk's expression softened and a smile appeared. "I'm not going to be in any shape to walk down an aisle to give her away." He squeezed the hand he held in his, lingering over it a moment before he offered it to Lance. "Keep her happy," he commanded as Foxy's hand passed from one man to the other.

CHAPTER 9

Three days later, Foxy sat in Lance's rented Porsche as it ate up the miles between New York and Massachusetts. Her hands lay in her lap but were rarely still. She continued to twist the plain gold band around and around the third finger of her left hand. *Married,* she thought yet again. *We're actually married.* It had been so quick, so lacking in emotion—a few moments in front of a blank-faced judge, a few words spoken. An unruffled fifteen minutes. It had been almost like a play until the ring had slipped onto her finger. That made it real. That made her Mrs. Lancelot Matthews.

Cynthia Matthews, she mused, trying out the sound in her mind. Or perhaps, she reflected, I could try for more elegance with Cynthia Fox-Matthews. She nearly laughed aloud. Elegance needs more than a hyphen. Foxy Matthews, she decided with a mental nod. That'll just have to be good enough.

"You're going to wear a ridge into your finger before we get to Rhode Island." Lance spoke quietly, but Foxy jumped in her seat as if he had shouted. "Nervous?" he asked with a laugh in his voice.

"No." Not wanting to confess what silliness her mind had

been engaged in, she prevaricated. "I was just thinking . . . Kirk looked much better, didn't he?"

"Um-hum." Lance switched on the wipers as a light rain began to fall. "Pam's the best medicine he can get."

"Yes, she is." Foxy shifted in her seat so that she had a clear view of his profile. *My husband,* she thought and nearly lost the thread of the conversation. "I've never known anyone else who could handle Kirk so well. Except you."

"Kirk needs a co-driver who can't be intimidated into backing off," Lance told her, glancing toward her briefly. "You've always handled him in your own way. Even when you were thirteen, you could do it without letting him know he was being handled."

The faintest frown line appeared between Foxy's brows. "I never considered it handling exactly . . . And I didn't realize anyone else noticed."

"There isn't anything about you I haven't noticed over the years." Lance turned to her again with a deep, quiet look. Foxy's pulse hammered erratically.

Will he always be able to do this to me? she wondered. *Even after the novelty of marriage wears off, will he be able just to look at me to turn me into jelly? It hasn't changed in ten years, will it change in ten more?* Lance's voice broke into her thoughts, and she twisted her head to look at him again. "I'm sorry, what?"

"I said it was a nice gesture for you to give Pam your bouquet. Of course, it's rather a shame you don't have some small remembrance."

Foxy started to speak, then flushed and fumbled in her bag for her brush. Buried at the bottom was the white velvet ribbon she had removed from the spray of orchids Lance had given her for a bridal bouquet. The thought that he might think her sentiment foolish held her tongue. She had the brush in her hand before she remembered her hair was pinned up. Hastily she stuffed the brush back in her bag. Rain pattered lightly on the windows and blurred the autumn landscape.

"I suppose it was a bit cut and dried, wasn't it?" Lance commented. "Ten minutes in front of a judge, no friends or traditional trappings, no tears or rice." He glanced at her again, his brow lifted under his hair. "I suppose you're feeling a bit cheated."

"No, of course not." Though her mind had wandered once or twice to the complicated beauty of a traditional wedding, she didn't feel cheated so much as curious. *Would she feel married if the wedding had included veils and organ music? Would she have this awkward sense of it not being quite real if there had been a ceremony ending with old shoes and rice?* "Besides," she said with a shake of her head. "I don't have any Great-aunt Sarah to weep softly in the back pew." The thought of family had her worrying her wedding band again.

"You did specify plain gold with no stones or markings?"

"What?" Foxy followed Lance's brief glance to her hands. "Oh, yes." Guiltily she dropped her right hand to her side. "Yes, it's exactly what I wanted."

"Does it fit?"

"Fit? Why yes, it fits."

"Then why the devil do you keep twisting it on your finger?" The annoyance in his tone was sharp.

Well aware it was justified, Foxy sighed. "I'm sorry, Lance. It all seems to be happening so fast, and going to Boston . . ."

She bit her lip, then confessed. "I'm nervous about meeting your family. I haven't had a great deal of experience with families."

Lance lay his hand on hers a moment. "Don't judge the way of families by mine," he advised dryly. "They're not the type you see on a Christmas card."

"Of course," Foxy concluded with a wry grin, "that's supposed to reassure me."

"Just don't let them bother you," Lance advised with a careless shrug. "I don't."

"Easy for you to say," she retorted, wrinkling her nose at him. "You're one of them."

"So are you." Lifting her hand, Lance ran his thumb over her wedding band. "Remember it."

"Tell me about them."

"I suppose I'll have to sooner or later." With this, he drew out a cigar and punched in the car lighter. "My mother is a Bardett—that's an old Boston family. I believe they gave Paul Revere directions."

"How patriotic."

"The Bardetts are notoriously patriotic," he returned before he touched the glowing lighter to the tip of his cigar. "In any case, my mother enjoys being both a Bardett and a Matthews, but more than anything else, she enjoys committees."

"Committees?" Foxy repeated. "What sorts of committees?"

"All sorts of committees, as long as they're suitable for a Bardett-Matthews. She loves to organize them, attend them, complain about them. She's a snob from the top of her pure white coiffure to the tip of her Italian shoes."

"Lance, how dreadful of you."

"You said you wanted to hear about them," he countered easily. "Mother loves doing charitable work. It reads well in the society pages. She also feels anyone poor enough to require aid should have the good taste not to ask for it until she has a chance to organize the committee. But snob or not, she does a lot of good despite her motives, so it hardly matters."

"You're being very hard on her." Foxy frowned at the tone of his voice as she remembered her own mother: a happy, disorganized, loving woman with Kirk's penchant for ragged sneakers.

Lance gave Foxy a curious, sidelong glance. "Perhaps. She and I have never seen things the same way. My father used to find her committees amusing and harmless. I'm not as tolerant as he was." Foxy's frown deepened, and he gave her his crooked smile. "Don't worry, Fox, you won't see any blood spilled. We don't get along, but we're quite civilized about it. Bardetts, you see, are always civilized."

"And the Matthews?" Foxy asked, becoming intrigued.

"The Matthews have a tendency to produce a black sheep every generation or so. A couple of hundred years back, a Matthews ran off and married a serving wench from a local tavern. Spoiled the blood a bit." He grinned as if pleased with the flaw, then drew on his cigar. "But for the most part, the Matthews are every bit as . . . upstanding as the Bardetts. My grandmother is all dignity. According to the stories that drop from time to time, she never batted an eye when my grandfather had his affair with the countess. As far as she was concerned, it didn't happen. Her daughter, my aunt Phoebe, is exactly as the countess said: dull. She hasn't had an original thought in fifty years. There's an alarming number of aunts, uncles, cousins, and in-laws."

"They don't all live in Boston, do they?"

"No, thank heaven. They're spread over the States and Europe, but a large clutch huddle in Boston and Martha's Vineyard and thereabouts."

"I suppose your mother was surprised when you told her about our getting married." Foxy caught herself before she twisted the ring again.

"I haven't told her."

"What?" Incredulous, she turned to stare at him. "You didn't tell her?"

"No."

Foxy started to demand why, then thought of the reason herself. *He's ashamed of me.* Swallowing, she twisted back to stare at the gray autumn rain. Cynthia Fox of Indiana doesn't measure up to the Bardetts and Matthews of Boston. "I suppose," she said in a tight voice, "you could keep me hidden in an attic room. Or we could forge a pedigree."

"Hmm?" Preoccupied, Lance glanced at her averted head, then back at the road. After passing a slow-moving truck, he tossed his cigar out the window.

For several moments, Foxy tried to hold her tongue and temper. She failed. "We could tell them I'm a deposed princess from some Third World country. I won't speak any English for the first six months." She rounded on him, hurt and furious. "Or I could be the daughter of some English baron who died and left me penniless. After all, it's the lineage that's important, not the money."

Her tone captured Lance's attention. Looking over, he caught the sheen of angry tears in her eyes. Instantly his brows drew together. "What are you babbling about?"

"If you don't think I'm good enough to pass as Mrs. Lancelot Matthews, then you can just . . ." Her suggestion was lost as he whipped the car to the shoulder of the road. Before she could catch her breath, he had her arms in a punishing grip.

"Don't you ever let me hear you say that again, do you understand?" His face was furious, but Foxy tilted her chin and met it levelly.

"No, no, I don't understand. I don't understand anything." To her humiliation, tears began to well up in her eyes and spill out onto her cheeks. The weeping surprised both of them; her because it began so suddenly, not giving her an opportunity to control it, and him because he had never seen her cry before.

"Don't," Lance ordered roughly, then gave her a brisk shake. "Don't do that."

"I will if I want to." Foxy swallowed and let the tears fall.

Lance swore before he let her go. "All right, go ahead. We'll swim back to Boston, but I want to know what brought on the flood."

Foxy fumbled in her purse for a tissue and found none. "I don't have a tissue," she said miserably, then wiped at the tears with the back of her hand. With another well-chosen oath, Lance pulled his handkerchief from his jacket pocket and stuffed it into her hand. "It's silk," she said and tried to give it back to him.

"I'll strangle you with it in a minute." As if to prevent himself from doing so, Lance gripped the steering wheel. "We're not moving," he said in a firm voice, "until you tell me what's gotten into you."

"It's nothing, nothing at all," she claimed as she dampened the white silk. Foxy was thoroughly disgusted with herself, but her temper forced her to continue. "Why should it bother me that you haven't even told your family we're married?"

For a few moments, there was only the sound of the drizzling rain and Foxy's sniffles. The car became still except for the monotonous back-and-forth movement of the windshield wipers. "Do you think," Lance began in even, precise tones, "that I didn't tell my family of our marriage because I'm ashamed of you?"

"What else should I think?" Foxy tossed back. "I don't suppose a Fox from Indiana is very impressive."

"Idiot!" The word vibrated in the small closed car. Foxy's sob was transformed into a gasp. Fascinated, she watched Lance struggle to control what appeared to be a violent surge of temper. When he spoke, it was too soft and too controlled. "I didn't tell my family because I wanted a couple of days of peace before they descend on us. As soon as they know we're married, the whole social merry-go-round gets started. A honeymoon would have been the ideal answer, but I explained to you it's impossible until I straightened out a few things. I've been away from the business for several months. I felt after the circuit and Kirk's accident, we both could use a few days of quiet. It never occurred to me you'd see it as anything else."

With a quick gesture of his hand, Lance put the car in first gear and merged back into the traffic. The silence was complete and unbearable. Foxy crumpled Lance's handkerchief into a tight ball and wished for a way to begin the conversation over again.

The days since Kirk's accident had been jumbled together into a mass of time rather than distinct minutes and hours. She knew she had slept and eaten, but could not have told how many hours her eyes had been closed or what food she had tasted. Her marriage seemed steeped in unreality. *But it is real,* she reminded herself. *And Lance is right. I'm an idiot.*

"I'm sorry, Lance," she murmured, lifting her eyes to his profile.

"Forget it." His answer was curt and unforgiving. Recognizing the dismissal in his tone, she turned back to the view of misty rain.

Are all brides so insecure? she wondered, closing her eyes. *This isn't like me. I'm acting like a different person, I'm thinking like a different person.* Weariness began to close over her, and she let her mind drift. *I'll feel better once we're settled in. A few days of quiet is exactly what I need.* She let the pattering rain lull her to sleep.

* * *

Foxy moaned and stirred. She no longer heard the steady hum of the Porsche beneath her but felt a quiet swaying. She felt a cool spray on her face and turned her head away from it. Her cheek brushed something warm and smooth.

The scent that teased her nostrils was instantly familiar. Opening her eyes, she saw Lance's jawline. Gradually she realized she was being carried. She nuzzled her face into his shoulder as the rain continued to fall halfheartedly. A gloomy dusk was settling, bringing with it a thin fog.

Along with Lance's scent she could detect the fragrance of damp leaves and grass, an autumn smell she would soon begin to associate with New England. His footsteps were nearly soundless, swallowed by the mists swirling close to the ground. There was something eerie and surreal about the dimming light and silence. Disoriented, Foxy shifted in his arms.

"Decide to join the living again?" Lance asked. He stopped, heedless of the drizzle and looked down at her.

"Where are we?" Totally confused, Foxy twisted her head to peer around. Almost at once, she saw the house. A three-story brownstone rose in front of her. Its walls were cloaked in ivy, dark green and glistening in the rain. Wrought-iron balconies circled the second and third stories, and they, too, were tangled with clinging ivy. The windows were tall and narrow. Even in the gloom, the house had an ageless elegance and style. "Is that your house?" Foxy asked. As she spoke she let her head fall back in order to see the roof and chimney.

"It was my grandfather's," Lance answered, studying her reaction. "He left it to me. My grandmother always preferred their house in Martha's Vineyard."

"It's beautiful," Foxy murmured. The rain that washed her face and dampened her hair was forgotten. She felt an immediate affection for the aged brownstone and tenacious ivy. *He had roots in this house,* she thought, and fell in love. "It's really beautiful."

"Yes, it is," Lance agreed as his eyes roamed her face.

Foxy looked up to meet his gaze. She smiled, blinking raindrops from her lashes. "It's raining," she pointed out.

"So it is." He kissed her, lingering for a moment. "Your lips are wet. I like the way the rain clings to your hair. In this light you look very pale and ethereal." His eyes were the color of the mist that grew thicker and seemed to be spun into threads around them. "If I let you go, will you vanish?"

"No," she murmured, then combed her fingers through the damp hair that fell over his forehead. "I won't vanish." A quick surge of need for him throbbed through her, causing her to shiver.

"I suppose you're real enough to catch a chill from standing in the rain." He tightened his grip on her and began to walk again.

"You don't have to carry me," she began.

Lance climbed nimbly up the front steps. "Don't you think we should do something traditional?" he countered as he maneuvered a key into the lock of the door. Pushing it open with his shoulder, he carried Foxy over the threshold and into the darkened house. "Welcome home," he murmured, then captured her lips in a long, quiet kiss.

"Lance," she whispered, incredibly moved. "I love you."

Slowly he set her on her feet. For a moment, they stood close, their faces silhouetted by the darkening sky. Before they closed the door, Foxy decided, there should be nothing between them. "Lance, I'm sorry about making that scene in the car."

"You've already apologized."

"You were angry enough for two apologies."

He laughed and kissed her nose, changed his mind and took her mouth again. It seemed that he could draw from a kiss more than she had known she had to offer. "Anger is the handiest weapon against tears," he told her as he ran his hands up and down her arms. "You threw me, Fox. You always do when you forget to be invincible." He lifted his finger to run it along her jawline, and his eyes were dark as he watched the journey. "Perhaps I should have explained things to you, but I'm simply not used to explaining myself to anyone. We're both going to have some adjustments to make." He took both her hands in his, then lifted them to his lips. "Trust me for a while, will you?"

"All right." She nodded. "I'll try."

After releasing her hands, Lance closed the door, shutting out the damp chill. For an instant, the house was plunged into total darkness, then abruptly the entrance hall streamed with light. Foxy stood in its center and turned around in a slow circle. To her left was a staircase, gleaming and uncarpeted. Its oak banister looked smooth as silk. To her right was a mirrored clothes stand that had once reflected the face of Lance's great-great-grandmother. He watched as she made a study of Revere candlesticks and a gilt-framed Gainsborough. The light from the chandelier showered down on her, catching the glint of rain in her hair. She had a wraithlike quality in the simple green dress she had chosen to wear as a bride. It had long narrow sleeves and a high mandarin collar. Its skirt fell straight and unadorned from a snug waist. Her only jewelry was the plain gold band he had placed on her finger. She looked as untouched as springtime, but the sensuality of autumn was in her movements.

"I wouldn't have pictured you in a place like this," Foxy said after completing her circle.

"Oh?" Lance leaned against the wall and waited for her to elaborate.

"It's beautiful," she went on in a voice touched with wonder. "Really beautiful, but it's so . . . settled," she decided, then looked back at him. "I suppose that's it. I've never thought of you as settled."

"I enjoy being settled now and again," was his careless answer. Foxy thought that in the trim gray suit he looked at ease amid the ivy and brownstone. Yet there was something in his eyes, she realized, that would never quite be tamed. Expert tailoring and priceless antiques would never alter the man he was. Knowing she was mad to prefer the sinner to the saint, Foxy was nevertheless glad.

"But I should be prepared to pack at a moment's notice?" she asked, giving him a smile a great deal like her brother's.

"How fortunate I am to have married a woman who understands me." His grin was crooked and familiar and still managed to send her pulse racing. He moved toward her, then wound one of the curls that framed her face around his finger. "And an exceptional-looking creature as well; quite bright, quick with her tongue, impulsive enough to be fascinating, and with a voice that constantly sounds like she's just been aroused."

Foxy flushed with a mixture of amusement and embarrassment. "Sounds like you made quite a deal."

"Oh, I did," Lance agreed but his grin faded and he studied her with serious eyes. "A smart businessman knows when to make his pitch." As quickly as it had grown grave, his expression lightened. Bemused, Foxy watched the changes. "Hungry?" he asked suddenly.

Intrigued, Foxy shook her head. "No, not really." She remembered the long hours he had spent driving, "I suppose there must be a can or something around I could open."

"I think we might do better." Taking her hand, Lance led her down the hallway. The rooms to the right and left were dark and mysterious. "I called Mrs. Trilby yesterday. She does the housekeeping and so forth. I told her I was coming in and to have things ready. I'm not fond of dustcovers and empty pantries." He passed through a door at the end of the hall. As he turned the switch light spilled into the kitchen.

"Oh, it's wonderful!" Foxy cried as she moved into the room. "Does it work?" she demanded, going immediately to the small arched fireplace that was built into one wall.

"Yes, it works." Lance smiled as she bent closer to peer inside.

"I love it," she said with a laugh as she straightened. "I'll probably want a fire in it in August." She ran her finger over a pine trestle table, which stood in the bow of a bay window. "The only fire I have in my kitchen is when I burn the bacon."

"This is your kitchen," Lance reminded her. He watched her as he loosened the knot in his tie, then slipped it off. There was something intensely intimate in the casual gesture. Foxy felt a quick thrill and turned to walk the room.

"I'm not very domestic," she confessed. "I don't even know where I keep the coffee."

"Try the counter behind you," Lance suggested as he turned to find what Mrs. Trilby had tucked into the refrigerator. "Can you cook?"

"Name it," Foxy challenged, then located the coffee. "I can cook it."

"We'll skip the Beef Wellington due to lack of time and imminent starvation. How about a couple of omelets?"

"Kid stuff." Foxy peeked over her shoulder. "Do you cook?"

"Only if I fall asleep at the beach."

"Get me a skillet," she ordered, trying to look disgusted.

The Lancelot Matthewses enjoyed their wedding supper of omelets and coffee at the kitchen table. Outside, the darkness was complete, with the rain still pattering and the moon a prisoner of the clouds. Time was lost to Foxy. It might have been seven in the evening or three in the morning. The feeling of timelessness was soothing, and wanting to prolong it, she ignored the watch on her wrist. Beneath her light conversation, her nerves were struggling to reach the surface. She chided herself for having them, attempted to ignore them, but they remained, under the veneer of confidence. She toyed with the rest of her eggs as Lance divided the last of the pot of coffee between them.

"That's why you're so thin," he commented. When Foxy looked up blankly, he went on. "You don't take enough interest in food. You lost weight during the season. I watched it slide off you."

Foxy shrugged away the pounds but dutifully applied herself to the rest of her eggs. "I like to eat in restaurants as the exception rather than the rule. I'll gain it back in a couple weeks." She smiled up at him. "I do have a growing interest in a hot bath, though."

"I'll take you up," he said and rose. "Then I'll go out and get the bags. The rest of the luggage should arrive by tomorrow."

Foxy rose, too, and began to stack the dishes. Though she knew it was foolish, she felt her nerves rise with her. "You don't have to take me up, just tell me which bath to use. I'll find it."

He watched her back as she set the dishes in the sink. "The second door on the right's the bedroom, the bath's through there. Leave the dishes," he ordered.

Foxy started to refuse, but his hand on her shoulder gently persuaded her to forget her qualms. She needed a few moments alone to collect her wits. "All right," she agreed, then turned with a nod. "I won't be long. I imagine you'd like a bath after the driving you did today."

"Take your time." They left the kitchen together and walked down the main hall. "I'll use another bath."

"Fine," Foxy said as they parted at the end of the hall. *How polite we are,* she thought as she fled up the stairs. *How terrifyingly married.*

In the bedroom, a pair of French doors opened out onto a balcony. The walls were covered with a rich cream wallpaper with dark trim along the floor and ceiling. The furniture was a mixture of periods and styles; Hepplewhite, Chippendale, Queen Anne, and the result was both exquisite and natural. Set into the far wall was a white brick fireplace with a marble mantel; there were logs waiting to be lit within it. Foxy decided Mrs. Trilby must be efficient. The bed was a high four-poster and was covered with a midnight-blue silk counterpane. An heirloom, she knew instantly, probably priceless. She caught her bottom lip between her teeth. This was the sort of thing she would have to learn to deal with— more, to live with.

I'm being an idiot. I married Lance, not his money, not his family. Bride's nerves. I wouldn't feel so awkward and tense if I'd had more experience. Foxy's gaze strayed to the bed again before she took a deep breath and looked down at her hands. Her wedding band glinted back at her. Ignoring the fluttering in her stomach, she began to undress. In her slip, she walked into the bath and discovered more proof of Mrs. Trilby's efficiency. Fresh towels were laid out along with a collection of fragrant soaps, oils, and bath salts. The tub itself was sunken, large enough for two, and Foxy's skin tingled at the thought of languishing in it.

As the hot water began to run she experimented with scents and oils. The room grew rich with steam and fragrance. She began to enjoy herself. Thirty minutes later, she stepped out of the tub, her muscles loose, her skin pink and scented. Choosing a mint-green towel, she wrapped it like a sarong around her body. Lulled by the bath, she hummed lightly as she pulled the confining pins from her hair. It tumbled in a confused mass past her shoulders, and she ran her fingers through it in a vain attempt to set it to rights. *There'll be a brush and a robe in the bags,* she told her reflection. *Surely*

Lance has brought them up by now. Leaving her hair carelessly tangled, Foxy opened the connecting door and walked into the bedroom.

The room was lit by the warm glow of china lamps and a crackling fire. It was the scent and sound of the burning wood that caused Foxy to glance toward the fireplace. She was halfway into the room before she saw him. With a small sound of surprise, she clutched at the towel that was tucked loosely over her breasts. Dressed in a black kimono-style robe, Lance stood beside a round, glass-topped table. He paused in the act of opening a split of champagne and studied every inch of his wife. With her free hand, Foxy pushed at her steam-dampened curls.

"Enjoy your bath?" he asked, opening the champagne without taking his eyes from her.

"Yes." Making a quick search, Foxy spotted her cases. "I didn't hear you in here," she said, knowing her voice was not quite its normal pitch. "I was just going to get my brush and a robe."

"Why?" Deftly he poured two glasses of the sparkling wine. "I like you in green." Foxy's fingers tightened on the towel as he smiled. It was the wicked, devilish smile that always pulled at her. "And I like your hair when it's not quite tamed. Come." He held out a glass. "Have some champagne."

It was not as Foxy had planned it. She knew she should have been dressed in the peignoir Pam had given her. She should have been alluring and confident and ready for him. It had not been in her plans to greet her husband on their wedding night clad in only a bath towel with her hair flying every which way and a look of stunned surprise on her face. She obeyed him, however, accepting the wine in the hope that it would soothe the sudden dryness in her throat. As she started to lift the glass to her lips, he reached out and took her wrist. Her pulse throbbed desperately under his fingertips.

"No toast, Foxy?" he said softly, the smile still lingering on his lips. His eyes remained on hers as he took a step closer and touched his glass to hers. "To a well-driven race."

She lifted her glass warily, watching him as she sipped. The champagne was ice cold and thrilling on her tongue.

"Only one glass tonight, Fox," Lance murmured. "I don't want your mind clouded."

Her heart hammering, Foxy turned away. "This is a lovely room." She hastily cleared her throat and moistened her lips. "I've never seen so many antiques in one place."

"Are you fond of antiques?"

"I don't know," she answered as she moved around the room. "I've never had any. You must like them." The last word was only a whisper as she turned around and found him directly behind her. There was something eerie about the soundless way he moved. She would have taken a quick step in retreat, but his hand circled her neck.

"It appears there's only one way to get you to hold still." With the merest pressure of his fingers, he brought her to her toes and firmly covered her mouth. Foxy felt the room dip and sway. His tongue teased the tip of hers before it traced her lips. "Would you like to discuss my Hepplewhite collection?" he asked. From her limp fingers, he took the half-filled glass of champagne.

Foxy opened her eyes. "No." Even the short word was difficult to form as her gaze strayed to his mouth. In an instant he was kissing her again, and the passion built, shuddering through her. She was clinging to him without having been aware of moving at all. The towel slipped unnoticed to the floor. With a low sound of pleasure, Lance buried his mouth against the curve of her throat while his hands ran over her heated skin. She felt the pain of desire and pressed closer to him. "Lance," she murmured as the blood drummed in her head. "I want you. Love me. Love me now." The words were lost under his mouth as it returned urgently to hers. "The light," she said breathlessly as he lowered her to the bed.

His eyes were dark and compelling. "I want to see you."

His body fitted itself to hers. He did not love gently. She had not expected gentleness, she had not expected patience. She had expected quick heat and urgent demands, and she was not disappointed. His hands moved roughly over her, exploring before they possessed. From her lips, his mouth trailed down along her throat, hungry always hungry, as it journeyed to her breast. Foxy moaned with trembling pleasure as he flicked his tongue over her nipple. The ache of desire spread from her stomach. His hands were bruising, arousing as they wandered down her rib cage, lingering at her waist and hips as his mouth continued to ravish her breast.

She began to move under him, a woman's instinct making her motions sensual and inviting. Lean and firm, his hands massaged the sensitive skin of her inner thigh, and her muscles went lax, her joints fluid. She learned that he made love as he had raced—with intensity and absorption. There was a ruthless, steady dominance in him, a power that demanded much more than submission. Surrender would have been too tame a response. More, she discovered her own power. He needed her. She could feel it in the urgency of his hands, taste it in the hunger of his mouth. She heard it as he spoke her name. They were tangled together, flesh against flesh, mouth against mouth while it seemed the only reality was dark, moist kisses and heated skin. The faint scent of wood smoke added something ageless and primitive.

As her body tingled under his hands she began to make her own explorations. She discovered the hard, rippling muscles that his leanness had disguised. As she moved her hands to his hips Lance groaned against her mouth and took the kiss deeper. His hands grew wild, desperate, and she tumbled with him into a world ruled by sensation. The pleasure was acute, so sharp it brought with it a hint of pain. There seemed to be no part of her that he did not wish to know, to enjoy, to conquer. She locked her arms tightly around his neck, burying her mouth against his throat. His taste filled her until champagne seemed a poor substitute. Here was something dark and male she had yet to learn, and she traced the tip of her tongue over his skin, exploring, discovering. Passion was building beyond anything she had imagined possible. Both emotionally and physically, her response was absolute. She was his.

Her breath was clogging in her lungs, passing through her lips as moans and sighs. Desire reached a turbulent peak when she whispered his name. "Lance." His mouth took hers with fresh desperation, cutting off her words. He shifted on top of her, urging her legs apart with the movement.

The pleasure she had thought already at its summit, increased. Passion came in hot, irresistible waves, overpowering her with its tumultuous journey until all need, all sensation focused into one.

The dawn approached slowly. She was still wrapped tightly in his arms when the hiss of rain lulled her to sleep.

CHAPTER 10

Foxy felt content. A dull red mist behind her lids told her the sun was falling on her face. With a small sigh, she allowed sleep to drift slowly away. She remembered the ease of Saturday mornings when she had been a young girl. Then she would lie in bed, dozing blissfully, knowing there was nothing but pleasure in the day ahead. There would be no worries, no time schedules, no responsibilities. School and Monday morning were centuries away. Foxy drifted on the edge of consciousness with the sensation of being both protected and free—a combination of feeling that had not been hers for a decade. She inched closer to it and clung.

There was a weight around her waist that added to her sense of security. Beside her was warmth. She snuggled yet closer to it. Lazily her lids fluttered open, and she looked directly into Lance's eyes. The past was whisked away as the present took over, but the sensation she woke with remained. Neither she nor Lance spoke. She saw by the clearness of his gaze that he had been awake for some time. There was no hint of sleep in his eyes. They were as sharp and focused as hers were soft and heavy. His hair was tousled around his head, reminding her that it had been her fingers that had disturbed it short hours before. They continued to watch each other as their mouths moved closer to linger in a whisper of a kiss. The thought that they were naked and tangled together seeped through Foxy's drowsy contentment. The arm around her waist was firm in its possession.

"You looked like a child as you slept," he murmured as his mouth journeyed over her face. "Very young and untouched."

Foxy did not want to tell him that her thoughts had been childlike as well. As his fingers traced her spine she began to feel more and more as a woman. "How long have you been awake?"

His hand roamed with absentminded intimacy over her hip and thigh. Reminded that his touch the night before had not been absentminded, she felt her drowsiness swiftly abating. "Awhile," he said as he tightened his arm to bring her yet closer. "I considered waking you." His eyes roamed to her sleep-flushed cheeks, to the rich confusion of her hair against the pillowcase, to the full softness of her untinted mouth. "I rather enjoyed watching you sleep. There aren't many women who can manage to be both soothing and exciting the first thing in the morning."

Foxy arched her brows deliberately. "You know a great deal about women first thing in the morning?"

He grinned, then nuzzled the white curve of her neck. "I'm an early riser."

"A likely story," Foxy murmured, feeling her contentment mixing with a more demanding sensation. "I suppose you're hungry." She felt the tip of his tongue flick over her skin.

"Oh yes, I have quite an appetite this morning." He caught her bottom lip between his teeth. Desire quickened in Foxy's stomach. "You have the most appealing taste," he told her as he teased her lips apart. "I'm finding it habit forming. Your skin's amazingly soft," he went on as his hand moved to cup her breast. "Especially for someone who appears to be mostly bone and nerve." He ran his thumb over its peak and watched her eyes cloud. "I don't think I'm going to get enough of you anytime soon."

He was leading her quickly into passion with quiet words and experienced hands. His touch was no longer that of a stranger and was all the more arousing for its familiarity. She knew now what waited for her when all the doors were opened. She learned and enjoyed and shared. The morning grew late.

It was past noon when Foxy moved down the staircase toward the main floor. She moved slowly, telling herself that the day would last forever if she didn't hurry it. She wanted to explore the house, but firmly turned toward the kitchen. The other rooms would wait until Lance was with her. She had only taken two steps down the hall when the doorbell rang. Glancing up the stairs, Foxy concluded that Lance could hardly be finished showering and decided to answer the bell herself.

There were two women standing on the sheltered white porch. One look told Foxy that they were not door-to-door salespeople. The first was young, around Foxy's age, with warm brunette hair and a rosy complexion. She had a youthful beauty and frank, curious brown eyes. Her clothes were casual but expensive: a tweed suit with a fitted jacket and flared skirt softened by a silk blouse. Supreme confidence was in her every move.

The second woman was more mature but no less striking. Her hair was white and short, brushed back from a delicately pale face. She had few lines or wrinkles, and her not inconsiderable beauty depended more on her superb bone structure and cameo coloring than on the prodigal application of makeup. Her ice-blue suit matched her eyes; its simplicity cunningly announced its price. It occurred to Foxy in the instant they studied each other that her face was quite lovely but expressionless—like a painting of a lovely landscape executed without imagination.

"Hello." Foxy shifted her smile from one woman to the other. "May I help you?"

"Perhaps you'd be good enough to let us in." Foxy heard the distinct Boston cadence in the older woman's voice before she breezed into the hallway. More curious than annoyed, Foxy stepped aside to allow the younger woman to cross the threshold. Standing in the center of the hall, the matron stripped off her white kid gloves and surveyed Foxy's straight-leg jeans and loose chenille sweater. The air was suddenly redolent with French perfume. "And where," she demanded imperiously, "is my son?"

I should have known, Foxy thought as the cool blue eyes examined her. *But how totally unlike her he is. There's not even a shade of resemblance.* "Lance is upstairs, Mrs. Matthews," Foxy explained and tried a fresh smile. "I'm—"

"Well, fetch him then," she interrupted with an imperious movement of her hand. "And tell him I'm here."

It was not the rudeness as much as the tone of contempt that fanned Foxy's temper. Careful to guard her tongue, she spoke precisely. "I'm afraid he's in the shower at the moment. Would you care to wait?" She employed the tone of a receptionist in a dentist's office. From the corner of her eye, she caught the look of amusement in the younger woman's face.

"Come, Melissa." Mrs. Matthews flapped her gloves against her palm in annoyance. "We'll wait in the living room."

"Yes, Aunt Catherine." Her tone was agreeable but she flashed Foxy a look of mischief over her shoulder as she obeyed.

Taking a long breath, Foxy followed. She took care not to search the room like a newcomer, deciding that Catherine Matthews need not know she had seen little more than the bedroom of Lance's house. Her eyes fluttered over a baby grand piano, a Persian carpet, and a Tiffany lamp before moving back to the queenly figure that had settled into a ladder-back chair. "Perhaps you'd like something while you wait," Foxy offered. Hoping her tone was more polite than her thoughts, she tried the smile again. She was aware of the fact that an introduction was in order, but Catherine's air of scorn persuaded her to hold back her identity. "Some tea perhaps," she suggested. "Or some coffee."

"No." Catherine set her leather envelope bag on the table beside her. "Is Lancelot in the habit of having strange young women entertain his guests?"

"I wouldn't know," Foxy returned equably. Her backbone stiffened in automatic defense. "We haven't spent a great deal of time discussing strange young women."

"I'm quite certain that conversation is not why my son enjoys your companionship." Placing both hands on the ends of the chair's arms, she tapped a manicured finger against the polished wood. "Lancelot rarely chooses to dally with a young lady because of the prodigiousness of her vocabulary. His taste generally eludes me, but I must say, this time I'm astounded." With an arch of her brow, she gave Foxy a calculated look. "Where *did* he find you?"

"Selling matchbooks in Indianapolis," Foxy tossed out before she could prevent herself. "He's going to rehabilitate me."

"I wouldn't dream of it," Lance stated as he walked into the room. Foxy was instantly grateful to see that he was dressed much as herself: jeans, T-shirt, and bare feet. He gave Foxy a brief kiss as he moved past her to greet his mother. Bending down, he brushed the offered cheek with his lips. "Hello, Mother, you're looking well. Cousin Melissa." He smiled and kissed her cheek in turn. "I see you're lovelier than the last time."

"It's good to see you, Lance." Smiling, Melissa made a flirtatious sweep with her lashes. "Things are never dull when you're around."

"The highest of compliments," he replied, then turned back to his mother. "I imagine Mrs. Trilby told you I was coming in."

"Yes." She crossed surprisingly slender, youthful-looking legs. "I find it quite annoying to hear of my son's whereabouts from a servant."

"Don't be too annoyed with Mrs. Trilby," Lance countered carelessly. "She probably thought you knew. I intended to call you at the end of the week."

Catherine bristled at his deliberate misunderstanding of her meaning. When she spoke, however, her voice was cool and expressionless. Watching her, Foxy recalled Lance saying how the Bardetts were always civilized. *In their own fashion,* Foxy mused, thinking of her initial encounter. "I suppose I should be grateful that you intended to call me at all since you appear to be involved with your"—her eyes drifted to fasten briefly on Foxy—"guest." She lifted her brow, arching it into a smooth, high forehead. "Perhaps you would send her along so that we might have a private conversation. Since Trilby isn't here, she might make a pot of tea."

Foxy, knowing she would explode if she stayed, turned with the intention of locking herself into the bedroom until she could be trusted again.

"Foxy." Lance spoke her name mildly, but she recognized the underlying tone of command. Eyes flaming, she turned back. Lance casually crossed the room and slipped his arm over her shoulders. "I don't believe you've been introduced."

"Introductions," his mother cut in, "are hardly necessary or appropriate."

Lance inclined his head. "If you've finished insulting her, Mother, I'd like you to meet my wife."

There was total silence. Catherine Matthews did not gasp in alarm or surprise but merely stared at Foxy as if she were a strange piece of artwork in a gallery. "Your wife?" she repeated. Her voice remained calm, her face devoid of emotion. Folding her hands in her lap, she turned her eyes to her son. "When did this happen?"

"Yesterday. Foxy and I were married in the morning in New York. We drove up directly afterward for"—the grin flickered in his eyes as he kept them on his mother—"an informal honeymoon."

He's enjoying this, Foxy realized as she heard the amusement lace his voice. She knew, too, by the ice in Catherine's that she was not.

"One hopes Foxy is not her given name."

"Cynthia," Foxy put in distinctly as she grew weary of being referred to as an absent participant.

"Cynthia," Catherine murmured thoughtfully. She did not offer her hand or cheek for a token embrace or kiss; instead she carefully studied Foxy's face for the first time, obviously considering what could be done to salvage the situation. *I'm the situation,* Foxy realized with a quick flash of humor. "And your maiden name?" Catherine demanded with an inclination of her head.

"Fox," she told her with a mimicking nod.

"Fox," Catherine repeated, tapping her finger on the arm of the chair again. "Fox. The name is vaguely familiar."

"The race driver Lance sponsors," Melissa supplied helpfully. She stared at Foxy with undisguised fascination. "I suppose you're his sister or something, aren't you?"

"Yes, I'm his sister." The bold curiosity in her voice made Foxy smile. "Hello."

Mischief streaked swiftly over Melissa's face. Like Lance, Foxy noted, she was enjoying the encounter. "Hello."

"You met her on a—a . . ." Catherine's fingers waved as she searched for the proper term. "A race-car track?" The first hint of fury whispered through the words. Foxy stiffened again at the expression of contempt that was turned on her.

"I could do with some coffee, Fox, would you mind?" At Lance's calm request, she tossed her head back to flame at him. "Melissa will give you a hand," he continued, nearly cutting off her explosion. "Won't you, Melissa?" He addressed his cousin, but never took his eyes from his wife.

"Of course." Melissa rose obediently and crossed the room. Trapped, Foxy fought down the surge of temper. She turned, leaving Lance and his mother without another word. "Did you really meet Lance on a racetrack?" Melissa asked as the kitchen door swung behind them. There was no guile in the question, simply curiosity.

"Yes." Struggling with fury, Foxy managed to keep her tone level. "Ten years ago."

"Ten years? You had to have been a child." Melissa settled down at the table while Foxy scooped out coffee. Sunlight poured through the windows, making the drizzling rain of the day before only a memory. "Now, ten years later, he marries you." Elbows on the table, Melissa made a cradle out of her hands and set her chin on it. "It's terribly romantic."

As she felt her anger taper off Foxy blew out a long breath. "Yes, I suppose it is."

"I wouldn't worry too much about Aunt Catherine," Melissa advised, studying Foxy's profile. "She wouldn't have approved of anyone she hadn't handpicked."

"That's comforting," Foxy replied. Wanting to keep busy, she began to brew a pot of tea as well.

"There'll also be a large contingent of women between twenty and forty who'll want to murder you," Melissa added as she crossed her silk-covered legs. "There hasn't been a shortage of hopefuls for the title of Mrs. Lancelot Matthews."

"Marvelous." Foxy turned to Melissa and leaned back against the counter. "Just marvelous."

"You'll meet the bulk of them socially in the first few weeks," Melissa told her cheerfully. Foxy noted that like Catherine's, Melissa's nails were perfectly tended. "Of course, Lance will be there to guard against unsheathed claws at parties and dances, but you'll have to be alert during charity functions and those lovely luncheon meetings."

"I won't have time for much of that sort of thing," Foxy told her with undisguised relief. Turning away, she managed to locate an appropriate cream and sugar set. "I have my work."

"Work? Do you have a job?" The utter incredulity in her voice caused Foxy to turn back again and laugh.

"Yes, I have a job. Isn't it allowed?"

"Yes, of course, depending . . ." The tip of Melissa's tongue ran slowly along her teeth as she considered. "What do you do?"

"I'm a freelance photographer." Leaving the kettle on to heat, Foxy joined her at the table.

"That might do well enough," Melissa said with a thoughtful nod.

"What do you do?" Foxy countered, growing intrigued.

"Do? I . . ." Melissa searched for a word, then smiled with a gesture of her hand. "I circulate." Her eyes danced with such blatant good humor, Foxy was forced to laugh again. "I graduated from Radcliffe three years ago, then I took the obligatory Grand Tour. My French is flawless. I know who's tolerable and who's not in Boston society, how to get the best table at the Charles, where to be seen and with whom, where to buy shoes and where to buy lingerie, how to order creamed chicken for fifty Boston matrons, and where the skeletons are buried in the majority of closets. I've been mad about Lance since I was two, and if I wasn't his cousin and ineligible, I should certainly despise you. But I couldn't have married him in any case, so I'm going to like you very well and enjoy watching you twist a few noses out of shape."

She paused to catch her breath but not long enough for Foxy to get a word in. "You're fabulously attractive, particularly your hair, and I would imagine when you're suited up, you're devastating. Lance would never have chosen anyone with ordinary good looks. And of course, there's your tongue. You certainly set Aunt Catherine down a peg. You'll have to keep it sharp to get through the next weeks unscarred. But I'll help you. I enjoy watching people do things I haven't the courage to do. There now, your kettle's boiling."

Slightly dazed, Foxy rose to take it from the burner. "Are all Lance's relatives like you?"

"Heavens no. I'm quite unique." Melissa smiled with perfect charm. "I know a great number of the people in my circle are bores and snobs, and I haven't any illusions about myself." She shrugged as Foxy began to steep the tea in a porcelain pot. "I'm simply too comfortable to give them a black eye now and again as Lance does. I admire him tremendously, but I haven't the inclination to emulate him." Melissa tossed her hair casually behind her shoulder, and Foxy saw an emerald flash on her hand. "There are times Lance does things strictly to annoy the family's sensibilities. I believe he might have started racing with that in mind. Of course, he became quite obsessed with it for a while. And still, he's involved with designing and building cars rather than driving them . . ." Melissa trailed off, studying Foxy with thoughtful brown eyes.

Hearing the speculation in her voice, Foxy met the stare

and spoke without inflection. "You're thinking perhaps he married me to again annoy the family's sensibilities."

Melissa smiled and shrugged her tweed-clad shoulders. "Would it matter? You took first prize. Enjoy it."

Both women turned as the prize strolled into the room. His eyes flickered over Foxy, then settled on his cousin. "Mother's anxious to get along, Melissa."

"Pooh." She wrinkled her nose as she rose. "I'd hoped all this would make her forget about the meetings she's dragging me to. I suppose she told you there's a party at Uncle Paul's tomorrow night. They'll expect you now."

"Yes, she told me." There was no enthusiasm in his voice, and Melissa grinned.

"I'm looking forward to it now. I expect Grandmother might even put in an appearance . . . under the circumstances. You really know how to keep them off balance, don't you?" Melissa winked at Foxy before she crossed over to Lance. "I haven't congratulated you yet."

"No," he agreed and lifted a brow. "You haven't."

"Congratulations," she said formally, then rose on her toes to peck both of his cheeks. "I like your wife, cousin. I shall come back soon whether you invite me or not."

"You're one of the few I don't draw the bolt against." Lance gave her a quick pinch on the chin. "She'll need a friend."

"Don't we all?" Melissa countered dryly. "We'll go shopping soon," she decided as she turned back to face Foxy. "That's a quick way to get to know each other. I'll see you tomorrow night," she continued before she moved to the door, "for your trial by fire."

Foxy watched the door swing to and fro after Melissa. "I'm feeling a bit singed already," she muttered.

Lance crossed the room and cupped her chin in his hand. "You seemed to hold your own well enough." His eyes grew serious as he studied her face. "Shall I apologize for my mother?"

"No." Foxy closed her eyes for a moment, then shook her head. "No, it isn't necessary. And as I think back you did try to warn me." She opened her eyes and shrugged. "I suppose you knew she wouldn't approve."

"There's very little I do my mother approves of," he countered. He traced his thumb over her jawline while his eyes remained on hers. "I don't base anything I do on her approval, Foxy, least of all my marriage to you. Our lives are our own." His brows lowered into a frown, and he kissed her, hard and quick. "I asked you before," he reminded her, "to trust me."

With a sigh, Foxy turned away. The air seemed suddenly thick with the scents of coffee and tea. "It appears we didn't manage our few days of peace." Picking up the teapot, she poured the contents down the sink. She felt his hands on her shoulders and straightened them automatically. Nothing was going to mar her first full day as his wife. Whirling, Foxy threw her arms around his neck. "We still have today." All the anger melted along with her bones as Lance covered her offered mouth with his. "I don't think I want any coffee now," she whispered as their lips parted and met again. "Do you?"

For an answer, he grinned and drew away. Before she realized his intent, Foxy was slung over his shoulder. Laughing, she pushed the hair from her eyes. "Lance," she said with a mock shiver as he swung through the kitchen door. "You're so romantic."

CHAPTER 11

Foxy considered dressing for her first social evening as Mrs. Lancelot Matthews equal to dressing for battle. Her armor consisted of a slim tube top and loosely pleated evening pants in pale green. Standing in front of the full-length mirror, she adjusted the vivid emerald hip-length jacket and fastened it with a thin gold belt. Deliberately she set about arranging a more dramatic style for her hair.

"If they're going to stare and whisper," she muttered as she pinned up the back of her hair, "we'll give them something to stare and whisper about." Using her brush lightly, she persuaded her curls to fall in soft disorder around her face. "I wish I was built," she complained with a glare at her willowy reflection.

"I'm rather fond of your construction," Lance stated from the doorway. Startled, Foxy turned and dropped the brush. Looking casually elegant in a black suit of the thinnest wool, he leaned against the jamb. His eyes trailed over her in a lazy arch before returning to lock on hers. "Going to give them their money's worth, are you, Foxy?"

She shrugged carelessly, then stooped to retrieve her brush. As she turned away to place it on her dresser she felt his hands descend to her shoulders. "My mother got under your skin, didn't she?"

Foxy toyed with the collection of bottles and jars on the dresser's surface. "It's only fair," she parried. "I got under hers." She heard him sigh, then felt his chin rest atop her head. She kept her eyes lowered on her own restless fingers.

"I suppose I should have apologized for her after all."

Foxy turned, shaking her head. "No." With her own sigh, she offered an apologetic smile. "I'm pouting, aren't I? I'm sorry." Determined to change the mood, she stepped back a bit and held out her hands, palms up. "How do I look?" Below the fall of curls, her eyes were saucy and teasing.

Catching her wrist, Lance spun her into his arms. "Fantastic. I'm tempted to forgo dear Uncle Paul's little party. I'm very possessive of what's mine." His mouth lowered to rub against hers. "Shall we play truant, Foxy, and lock the door?"

She wanted badly to agree; his mouth promised such delights. To keep the scales balanced, she drew her face away from the warmth of his lips. "I think I'd like to get it over with. I'd rather meet a cluster of them at one time than meet them in dribbles."

He brushed his fingers through her hair. "Pity," he murmured. "But then you always have been a brave soul. I believe you should have a reward for valor before the fact." He slipped his hand into his pocket, then held out a small black box.

"What is it?" Foxy demanded, giving him a curious look as she accepted it.

"A box."

"Clever," she muttered. After opening it, Foxy stared down at two shimmering diamonds shaped like exquisite tears of ice. "Lance, they're diamonds," she managed as she lifted wide eyes to his.

"So I was told," he agreed. The familiar crooked grin claimed his mouth. "You suggested once I buy you something extravagant. I thought these more appropriate than Russian wolfhounds."

"Oh, but I didn't mean for you to actually . . ."

"Not all women can wear diamonds," he said, moving lightly over her protest. "It takes a certain finesse or they look overdone or tawdry." As he spoke, he took the gems from the box and fastened them to her ears. His touch was smooth and practiced. Lifting her chin with his fingers, he critically studied the result. "Yes, it's as I thought, you're well suited. Diamonds need a great deal of warmth." He turned her so that she looked into the mirror. "A lovely woman, Mrs. Matthews. And all mine." Lance stood behind her, his hands on her shoulders.

The mirror reflected a pose of natural affection between husband and wife. Foxy's throat clogged with emotion. I'd trade a dozen diamonds, she thought, for a moment such as this. When her eyes met his in the mirror, her heart and soul were in them. "I love you," she told him in a voice that trembled with her feelings. "So much that sometimes it scares me." Her hands reached up to grasp his with a sudden desperation she neither understood nor expected. "I never realized love could scare you, making you think of all the what-ifs there are in life. This has all happened so fast that when I wake up in the mornings, I still expect to be alone. Oh, Lance." Her eyes clung to his. "I wish we could have been an island a little while longer. What are they going to do to us? All these people who aren't you and me."

Lance turned her until she was facing him and not his reflection. "They can't do anything to us unless we let them." Gently his mouth lowered to hers, but her head fell back, inviting more. His arms tightened as the kiss grew lengthy and intimate. "I think we'll be a bit late for Uncle Paul's party,"

Lance murmured as he changed the angle of the kiss, then teased the tip of her tongue with his.

Foxy pushed the jacket from Lance's shoulders, working it down his arms until it dropped to the floor. Slowly she moved her hands up the silk front of his shirt while her mouth answered his. She felt his response in the tensing of his muscles, in the strength of his hands as they moved to her hips. Locking her arms around his neck, she strained closer. His lips moved to her hair, then her temple, until they burrowed at her throat. His warm musky scent mingled with hers, creating a fragrance Foxy thought uniquely their own. She slipped out of her shoes. "Let's be very late for Uncle Paul's party," she murmured and sought his mouth again.

* * *

Foxy found her imagination had not been sufficiently extravagant in its picture of Paul Bardett's party. Her first misconception had been the number of people. In attendance were more than double her most generous estimate. The elegant old brownstone on Beacon Hill was packed with them. They thronged the tiny, elegant parlor with the Louis XVI furniture, strolled on the terrace under the Chinese lanterns, moved up and down the carpeted staircase. Foxy was certain that every exclusive designer from either side of the Atlantic was represented, from the most conservative sheath to the most flamboyant evening pajamas. During her seemingly endless introductions to the vast Matthews-Bardett clan, she was treated to smiles, handshakes, pecks on the cheek, and speculation. The speculation, as the kisses and the smiles, came in varying degrees. Sometimes it was vague, almost offhand, and other times it was frank, direct, and merciless.

Such was the case with the senior Mrs. Matthews, Lance's grandmother. Even as Lance introduced them, Foxy saw the faded blue eyes narrow in appraisal.

Edith Matthews was not a flamboyant countess from Venice. Her sturdy, matronly figure was clad decently in a tasteful black brocade relieved only by a small ruching of white lace at the throat. Her hair was more silver than white, waved carefully away from a strong-boned face. Foxy studied her in turn, wondering if there had once been beauty there, masquerading now behind the mask of age. With the countess, she had been certain, the beauty was still very much alive in the vibrant green eyes. The clasp of Mrs. Matthews's hand was quick, firm enough though the skin was thin, and the eyes told Foxy only that she was being considered: acceptance was being withheld.

"It appears you've cheated us out of a wedding, Lancelot," she said in a quiet voice, raspy with age.

"There seems to be no shortage of them each year," he countered. "One shouldn't be missed very much."

She shot him a look under brows Foxy noticed were thin and beautifully arched. "There are those who have been rather looking forward to yours. Well, never mind," she went on, waving him away with a queenly flick of her fingers. "You will do things your own way. You'll live in the house your grandfather left you?"

Lance was smiling at the gesture she had used. It had been employed in exactly the same way for as long as he could remember. "Yes, Grandmother."

If she recognized the teasing lilt to his voice, she ignored it. "He would like that." She shifted her eyes to Foxy. "I have no doubt he would have liked you as well."

Accepting this as the highest form of approval she would receive, Foxy took the initiative. "Thank you, Mrs. Matthews."

Impulsively she bent and brushed the wrinkled cheek with her lips. There were soft scents of lavender and talc.

The beautifully arched brows drew together, then relaxed. "I'm old," she said and sighed as if the thought were not unpleasant so much as unexpected. "You may call me Grandmother."

"Thank you, Grandmother," Foxy replied obediently and smiled.

"Good evening, Lancelot." Foxy's pleasure faded as she heard Catherine Matthews's greeting. "Good evening, Cynthia. You look lovely."

Foxy turned to face her and saw the practiced social smile. "Thank you, Mrs. Matthews." *Manners at ten paces,* Foxy reflected, and thought pistols might be preferable. She watched Catherine's eyes flicker, as dozens of others had that evening, over the diamonds on her ears.

"I don't believe you met my sister-in-law, Phoebe," she said smoothly. "Phoebe Matthews-White, Lancelot's wife, Cynthia."

A small, pale woman with a nondescript face and hair the color of a lead pencil held out her hand. "How do you do?" She pushed her gray-framed glasses more securely on her nose and squinted her birdlike eyes. "I don't believe we've met before."

"No, Mrs. Matthews-White, we haven't."

"How odd," Phoebe said with mild curiosity.

"Lancelot and Cynthia summered in Europe," Catherine put in as she gave Lance an arched look.

"Henry and I stayed at the Cape this year," Phoebe confided, easily distracted from her curiosity. "I simply hadn't the energy for a trip to Europe this season. Perhaps we'll spend the holidays in St. Croix."

"Hello, Lance!"

Foxy turned to see a woman in delicate pink embrace her husband. Her photographer's eye detected a perfect model. She had what Foxy labeled the Helen of Troy look—classic delicacy with a sculptured, oval face. Her eyes were deep blue, round, and striking, the nose small and straight over a Cupid's bow mouth. Her figure was as classic as her face, richly curved and enticing in a simple silk sheath. Foxy saw the face in soft focus against the background of white satin—a study of feminine perfection. She knew the woman would photograph magnificently.

"I just learned you were back in town." The Cupid's bow brushed over Lance's cheek. "How bad of you not to have let me know yourself."

"Hello, Gwen. You're lovelier than ever. Hello, Jonathan."

Foxy glanced just beyond Gwen's right shoulder and saw the masculine version of her classic looks. These eyes, however, were not on Lance, but on her. His profile was magnificent, and her fingers itched for her camera.

"Catherine," Gwen said as she tucked her arm in Lance's. "You simply must persuade him to stay this time."

"I'm afraid I could never persuade Lancelot to do anything," Catherine returned dryly.

"Foxy." Lazily, Lance circled his fingers around her wrist. "I'd like you to meet Gwen Fitzpatrick and her brother Jonathan, old family friends."

"What a perfectly dreadful introduction," Gwen complained as her sapphire eyes roamed Foxy's face. "You must be Lance's surprise."

Foxy recognized the cool speculation and responded to it. "Must I?" She sipped at her glass of champagne. Still, she thought, the face is lovely regardless of the woman within. It has so many possibilities. "Have you ever modeled?" she asked, already formulating angles and lighting.

Gwen's brows arched. "Certainly not."

"No?" Foxy smiled, amused at the chipped ice in Gwen's tone. "What a pity."

"Foxy's a photographer," Lance put in and cast her a knowing glance.

"Oh, how interesting." Skillfully, she drenched the words in boredom before turning her attention back to Lance. "We were all simply stunned to hear you were married, and so suddenly. But then, you always were impulsive." Foxy struggled to remain amused. Again the round blue eyes shifted to her. "You must share your secret with those of us who tried and failed."

"You only have to look at her to learn the secret," Jonathan Fitzpatrick stated. Taking Foxy's fingers, he lifted them to his lips, watching her over her own knuckles. "A pleasure, Mrs. Matthews." His eyes were appealing and insolent. Foxy grinned, liking him instantly.

"How charming," Gwen murmured as she sent her brother a frosty glance.

"Hello, everyone." Stunning in red silk, Melissa popped up beside Foxy. "Lance, I simply must borrow your wife a moment. Jonathan, you haven't flirted with me once tonight. I'm terribly annoyed. You'll have to see if you can charm me out of the sulks as soon as I get back. Excuse us, won't you?" Beaming smiles in all directions, Melissa maneuvered Foxy through the crowd and onto a shadowed section of the terrace. "I thought you might like a breather," she commented as she adjusted the cuff of her sleeve.

"You really are unique," Foxy managed when she caught her breath. "You're also right." As she set the glass of champagne down on a white iron table, she heard the wind whispering through drying leaves. The approaching winter was in the air. Still, she preferred the light chill of fresh air to the growing stuffiness inside.

"I also thought a little road mapping might help you." Melissa carefully checked the cushion of a chair for dampness before sitting.

"Road mapping?"

"Or who's who in the Matthews-Bardett circle," Melissa explained and daintily lit a cigarette. "Now." She paused again as she blew out a stream of smoke and crossed her legs. "Phoebe, Lance's aunt on his father's side—relatively harmless. Her husband is in banking. His main interest is the Boston Symphony, hers is 'doing what's proper.' Paul Bardett, Lance's uncle on his mother's side—very shrewd, occasionally witty, but his life revolves around his law practice. Corporate stuff, very dry and very boring if he corners you. You met my parents, Lance's cousins by marriage on his father's side." Melissa sighed and tapped the ash of her cigarette on the terrace floor. "They're very sweet really. Daddy collects rare stamps and Mother raises Yorkshire terriers. Both of them are obsessive about their respective hobbies. Now, about the Fitzpatricks." She paused and ran the tip of her tongue over her upper lip. "It's best if you know Gwen was the front-runner in the 'Who Will Finally Bag Lance Matthews Contest.' "

"She must be very annoyed," Foxy murmured. She walked to the edge of the terrace where the shadows deepened. With sudden clarity, she was reminded of the night of Kirk's party when she had sought out the scent of spring; the first time Lance had kissed her, on the glider in the moonlight. "Were they . . ." Foxy shut her eyes and bit her lip. "Were they . . ."

"Lovers?" Melissa supplied helpfully, taking a sip of Foxy's wine. "I imagine. Lance seems quite the physical sort to me." Glancing over, she studied Foxy's back. "You're not the jealous type, are you?"

"Yes," Foxy murmured without turning around. "Yes, I think I am."

"Oh dear," Melissa said into the champagne. "That's too bad. In any case, that was Chapter One, this is Chapter Two. Oh, and as for Jonathan." Melissa finished the wine and gently crushed her cigarette under her heel. "He's a dangerous flirt and hopelessly charming and insincere. I've decided to marry him."

"Oh." Foxy turned back now and stared at her strange fountain of information. "Well, congratulations."

"Oh, not yet, darling." After rising, Melissa carefully brushed out her skirts. The pearls at her throat gleamed white in the moonlight. "He doesn't know he's going to ask me yet. I shouldn't think the idea will occur to him until around Christmastime."

"Oh," Foxy said blankly, then frowned at the empty glass Melissa handed her.

"You're perfectly free to flirt with him," she added generously. "I'm not the jealous type at all. I believe I'd like a spring wedding, perhaps May. A four-month engagement is perfectly long enough, don't you think? We'd best go back in," she said, linking her arm with Foxy's before she could answer. "I have to begin enchanting him."

CHAPTER 12

During the next week, Foxy established a routine. On a search through the house, she had located the perfect site for her darkroom. Her time was absorbed with the clearing out of a basement storage room, arranging for her equipment to be shipped from New York and altering the room to suit its new function. Lance's days were spent in his Boston office while Foxy spent hers relocating her career base. Before she could continue with the creative aspects of her work, there were practicalities to be seen to. There was cleaning, plumbing to be installed, equipment to be set up. During the transition, Foxy was grateful that Mrs. Trilby proved to be efficient indeed, and quite proprietary about the top three stories of the house. She left the basement to Foxy without a murmur of protest. But there was no doubt in Foxy's mind that the tiny, prim lady in crepe-soled shoes would have snarled like a tiger if she had interfered with the working routine of the living quarters. Foxy left the polishing of the Georgian silver to Mrs. Trilby while she set up her enlarger and bathing tanks. The arrangement suited them both.

Foxy alternated work in her darkroom with solitary explorations of the city. She shot roll after roll of film, recording her impressions and feelings with her camera. She became reacquainted with loneliness. It surprised her that after so many years of thoughtless independence, she should so strongly need another's company. Knowing Lance's business needed careful attention after his months on the road helped her to keep any complaints to herself. Complaints, in any case, were something she rarely uttered. Problems were made to be worked out, and she was accustomed to doing so for herself. The loneliness itself was fleeting, forgotten when she and Lance were together, dulled by her fascination with the city that was now her home. When loneliness threatened, she fought it. Work was her panacea, and Foxy indulged in it lavishly. Within a week, her darkroom was operable, and the prints of the racing season were half completed.

As she studied a set of drying work prints Kirk jumped into her mind. Had it only been three weeks since the accident? she mused as she brushed her hair away from her eyes. It seemed like a lifetime. Wasn't it, in essence? In some strange way, Kirk's accident had been the catalyst that had altered her life. The world she existed in now was far removed from the one she had known as Cynthia Fox. With an unconscious gesture, she fingered her wedding ring.

Hanging wet and glossy, a print of the white racer as it would never be again caught Foxy's attention. She had highlighted it, muting the background into a smudge of varied colors without shape. It had been an unconscious tribute to her brother as she had once thought of him—indestructible. Abruptly a flood of homesickness overwhelmed her. It was an odd sensation and a new one. There had been no truly consistent home in her life in over ten years. But there had been Kirk. Impulsively Foxy left her work in the darkroom and rushed up the steps to the first floor. Hearing the hum of the vacuum in the upstairs hall, she ducked into Lance's study.

Closing herself in the room, she dropped into the chair

behind Lance's walnut desk and picked up the phone. In moments, the lines were clicking between Massachusetts and New York.

"Pam!" Foxy felt a quick rush of pleasure the instant she heard the quiet, Southern voice. "It's Foxy."

"Well, if it isn't Mrs. Matthews. How are things in Boston?"

"Fine," Foxy replied automatically. "Yes, fine," she repeated, unconsciously adding a nod for emphasis. "Well." She sighed and settled back in the chair with a laugh. "Different certainly. How's Kirk?"

"He's doing very well," Pam's voice continued lightly. "Impatient, naturally, to get out of the hospital. I'm afraid you've missed him just now. He's down in X-ray."

"Oh." Her disappointment was clear, but Foxy pushed it away. "Well, how are you? Are you managing to keep Kirk in line and maintain your sanity?"

"Just barely." Pam's laugh was easy and familiar. Foxy smiled with the pleasure of hearing it. "He'll be sorry he missed your call."

"I missed him all of a sudden," Foxy confessed with a small shake of her head. "Everything's moved so fast in the past few weeks, sometimes I almost feel like someone else. I think I needed him to remind me I was still the same person." She stopped and laughed again. "Am I rambling?"

"Only a tad. Kirk's not only reconciled to your marriage now, but quite pleased about it. I think he's talked himself into believing he arranged the entire thing between races." Pam waited a beat, then continued in the same tone. "Are you happy, Foxy?"

Knowing Pam had meant the question seriously and not as casual conversation, Foxy took a moment to answer. She thought of Lance, and a smile coaxed her lips upward. "Yes, I'm happy. I love Lance, and on top of that, I'm lucky enough to love the house and Boston. I suppose I've been a bit lost, especially since Lance is back at his office. Everything here is so different, at times I feel I've stepped through the looking glass."

"Boston society can be a wonderland of sorts, I imagine," Pam replied. "Have you been spending your time chasing white rabbits?"

"I've been working, my friend," Foxy countered in a tone that reflected her raised brows. "My darkroom here is now fully operable. I'll be sending you the prints in a week or so. I'll send you numbered work prints. If you need more copies, or want something enlarged or reduced, give me the number."

"Sounds good. How many prints do you have so far?"

"Finished?" Foxy's brow furrowed as she considered. "A couple hundred if you count the ones I have drying."

"My, my," Pam remarked. "You have been a busy one, haven't you?"

"Photography has become not only my career but my salvation. It saves me from luncheons." There was a smile in her voice now as she settled back into the deep cushion of the chair. "I went to my first, and my last, earlier this week. Nothing and no one will induce me to go through that again. I'm simply not cut out for *functions*."

"Ah well," Pam comforted with a cluck of her tongue. "They will probably carry on without you. I take it you've met Lance's family by now."

"Yes. He has a cousin, Melissa, who's really a character. I like her. His grandmother was rather sweet to me. For the rest"—Foxy paused and wrinkled her nose—"there's been everything from casual friendliness to rank disapproval." Pam could all but hear the shrug in her voice. "I'm looking at this first round of social obligations and introductions as kind of a pledge week. After it's done, I'll know them, and they'll know me, and that will be that." She grinned. "I hope."

"Lance's mother is a . . . formidable lady," Pam commented.

"Yes," Foxy agreed, surprised. "How did you know?"

"My mother and she are slightly acquainted," she answered. Foxy was reminded that Pam had been born and bred in the world she had found herself thrust into by marriage. "I met her myself once when I was covering a story on art patrons." Pam recalled her impression of an elegant, aristocratic woman with cool eyes and beautiful skin. She remembered no warmth at all. "Just keep your feet planted, Foxy. It'll all settle in a few months."

Toying with the brass model of a Formula One that served as a paperweight, Foxy sighed. "I'm trying, Pam, but I do wish Lance and I could just lock the doors for a while. Our honeymoon was interrupted before it had really begun. I'm selfish enough to want a week or two alone with him while I'm getting used to being a wife."

"That sounds more reasonable than selfish," Pam corrected. "Maybe you'll be able to get away once he's finished designing this new car for Kirk. From what I gather, it's a bit complicated because of some new safety features Lance is working on."

"What car?" Foxy demanded softly as she felt her blood turn cold.

"The new Formula One Lance is designing for Kirk. Hasn't he told you about it?"

"No, no he hasn't." Foxy's voice was normal but her eyes were dull and lifeless as she stared down at the polished surface of Lance's desk. "I suppose it's for next season."

"That's why they're pushing to move it along," Pam agreed. "It's practically all Kirk can talk about. He's hoping to fly into Boston as soon as he's out of here so that he can be in on it before it's a finished project. The doctors seem to feel his avid interest in the car is a good motivation for getting him back on his feet quickly." Pam rambled on while Foxy stared without seeing anything. "There's no doubt he's cooperating so well with his therapist because he wants to walk out of here by the first of the year."

"If he's not on his feet," Foxy put in slowly, "they can lift him out of his wheelchair and strap him into the cockpit." Though it cost her some effort, she managed to keep her voice carefully level. "I'm sure Lance would have no objections."

"I wouldn't be surprised if Kirk tried to arrange it." Pam made a sound that was half laugh, half sigh. "Ah, well. What I would like, if you can do it, are some shots of the new car. Seeing as you have an in with the head man, you should be able to get close enough to take a shot or two. I'd especially like a few at the test track when it's progressed that far."

Foxy shut her eyes on the headache that was beginning to throb. "I'll do what I can." *Will I never get away from it?* she wondered and squeezed her eyes tighter. *Never?* "I have to get back to work, Pam. Give Kirk my love, will you? And take care of yourself."

"Be happy, Foxy, and give our best to Lance."

"Yes, I will. Bye." With studied care, Foxy replaced the phone on its cradle. The cold shield over her skin remained, stretching out to extend to her brain. There was a void where her emotions might have been. Anger hovered on the edge of her consciousness, but failed to penetrate. Kirk's accident replayed in her head, not with the smooth motion of a movie, but with the quick, staccato succession of a slide show. Each frame was distinct and horrible.

There were countless grids in her memory, countless wrecks. They came back to her in a montage of cars and drivers and pit crews all jumbled together in a throbbing mass of speed. She sat, swamped by the largeness of Lance's chair, and remembered all of ten years as the light shifted with evening. Outside, the temperature began to drop with the sun. When the door to the study opened, Foxy turned her eyes to it with little interest.

"Here you are." Lance strolled into the room, leaving the door open behind him. "Why are you sitting in the dark, Fox? Don't you get enough of that in your fortress in the basement?" Moving to her, he cupped her chin in his hand and kissed her. The gesture was casual and somehow possessive. When he received no response, he narrowed his eyes and studied her face. "What is it?"

Foxy looked up at him, but her eyes were shadowed in the dimming light. "I just talked to Pam."

"Is it Kirk?" The quick concern in his voice melted the shield that covered her. Under it was the boiling fury of betrayal. She struggled to remain objective until she understood. "Are you concerned about his health?" she asked, but drops of anger burned through the words.

Frowning at the tone, Lance traced her jaw with his finger and felt the tension. "Of course I am. Has there been a complication?"

"Complication," she repeated tonelessly as her nails bit into her palms. "That depends on your viewpoint, I suppose. Pam told me about the car."

"What car?"

The blatant curiosity and puzzlement in his voice snapped her control. Knocking his hand from her face, Foxy rose, putting the chair and her temper between them. "How could you begin designs on a car while he's still in the hospital? Couldn't you even wait until he can walk again?"

Understanding replaced the puzzlement on Lance's face. He made no attempt to close the distance between them, but when he spoke, his voice was patient. "Fox, it takes time to design and build a car. Work was begun on this months ago."

"Why didn't you tell me?" She tossed the words at him,

more annoyed than soothed by the patience in his tone. "Why were you keeping it from me?"

"In the first place," he began, frowning as he watched her, "designing cars is my business, and you're aware of it. I've designed cars for Kirk before, you're aware of that, too. Why is this different?"

"He was nearly killed less than a month ago." Foxy gripped the supple leather of Lance's chair.

"He crashed," Lance said calmly. "He's crashed before. You and I both know that there's always the chance he'll crash again. It's a professional risk."

"A professional risk," she repeated while fresh fury grew in her eyes. "Oh, how like you! That makes it all neat and tidy. How marvelous it must be to be so impersonally logical."

"Be careful, Foxy," Lance said evenly.

"Why are you encouraging him to go back to it?" she demanded, ignoring his warning. "He might have had enough this time. He has Pam now, he might . . ."

"Wait a minute." Though shadows washed the room, Foxy had no need to see his face clearly to recognize his anger. "Kirk doesn't need any encouraging. Accident or no accident, he'll be back on the grid next season. It's no use trying to delude yourself, Foxy. Neither a wreck nor a woman is going to keep Kirk out of a cockpit for long."

"We'll never be sure of that now, will we?" she countered furiously. "You'll have one all ready for him. Custom fit. How can he resist?"

"If I didn't, someone else would." Lance's hands slipped into his pockets as his voice became dangerously quiet. "I thought you understood him . . . and me."

"All I understand is that you're planning to put him into another car, and he's not even able to stand up yet." Her voice became desperate and she dragged an impatient hand through her hair. "I understand that you might have used your influence to persuade him to retire, and instead—"

"No." Lance interrupted her flatly. "I won't be held responsible for what your brother chooses to do with his life."

Foxy swallowed hard, struggling not to cry. "No, you don't want the responsibility, I can understand that, too." Bitterness spilled over and colored her words. In the dimming light, her eyes glittered both with anger and despair. "All you have to do is draw some lines on paper, balance some equations, order some parts. You don't have to risk your life, just your money. You've plenty of that to spare." Her mind began to spin with a cascade of thoughts and accusations. "On a different level, it's a bit like the casino in Monte Carlo." Foxy raked her hands through her hair again, then gripped them together, furious that they were trembling. "You could just sit back and watch the action, like some . . . some overlord. Money doesn't mean very much to someone who's always had it. Is that how you get your satisfaction?" she demanded, too incensed to realize that his very silence was ominous. "By paying someone to take the risks while you sit back in safety and watch?"

"That's enough!" He moved like lightning, giving her no chance to evade him. In an instant, he had pulled her from behind the chair until he towered over her. "I don't have to take that from you. I did my time on the grid and quit because it was what I wanted to do." Temper was sharp in his voice, hard in the fingers that gripped her arms. "I retired because I chose to retire. I'll race again if I choose to race again. I don't justify my life to anyone. I pay no one to take risks for me."

Fear over the thought of Lance taking the wheel again coated her anger. Her voice trembled as she fought to suppress even the possibility from her brain. "But you're not going to race again. You're not—"

"Don't tell me what I'm going to do." The words were clipped and final.

Foxy swallowed her terror and spoke with a desolate calm. Once again, she felt herself being shifted to the backseat. With Kirk, she had accepted the position without thought, but now, waves of anger, frustration, and pain spilled through her. "How foolish of me to have thought my feelings would be important enough to matter to you." She started to move past him, but he stopped her by placing his hands on her shoulders. The gesture itself was familiar enough to bring an ache to the pit of her stomach.

"Foxy, listen to me." There were hints of patience in Lance's voice again, but they were strained. "Kirk is a grown man, he makes his own decisions. Your brother's profession has nothing to do with you anymore. My profession has nothing to do with us."

"No." Calmly she lifted her eyes to meet his. "That's simply not true, Lance. But regardless of that, Kirk will drive your car next season, and you'll do precisely what you want to do. There's nothing I can do to change any of it. There never has been with Kirk, and now my position's been made clear with you. I'm going upstairs now," she told him quietly. "I'm tired."

The room was dark now. For some moments he studied her in complete silence before taking his hands from her shoulders. Without speaking, she took a step back, then moved around him and walked from the room. Her footsteps were soundless as she climbed the stairs.

CHAPTER 13

Morning came as a surprise to Foxy. She had lain awake for hours, alone and unhappy. Her conversation with Pam played over in her mind, and the argument with Lance came back to haunt her. Now she awoke, unaware of having fallen asleep, and the morning sun was streaming onto the bed. Lance's side of the bed was empty. Foxy's hand automatically reached out to touch the sheets where he would have slept. Some warmth still lingered on the spot, but it brought her no comfort. For the first time since their wedding night, they might have slept in separate beds. They had not woken tangled together, to drift into morning as they had drifted into night.

The heaviness that lay on Foxy did not come from sleep but from dejection. Arguing with Lance was certainly not a novel occupation to her, but this time Foxy felt the effects more deeply. *Perhaps,* she thought as she stared at the ceiling, *it's because now that I have more, I have more to lose. He's probably still downstairs. I could go down and . . . No.* Foxy interrupted her own train of thought with a shake of her head. No, there was too much here to be resolved over morning coffee with Mrs. Trilby hanging over his shoulder. *In any case, I could use the day to sort things out.*

Mechanically Foxy rose and showered. She took her time dressing, though her choice of cords and a rag sweater were simple. As she dressed, she mentally outlined her schedule. She would work on the racing prints until eleven, then she would walk to the public gardens and continue on her new project. Satisfied with her agenda, she moved downstairs. There was no sign of Lance, and though she told herself it was for the best, she lingered by the hall phone a moment, undecided. No, she told herself firmly. *I will not call him. We can't discuss anything rationally over the telephone. Is there anything to discuss?* she wondered and frowned at the phone as if it annoyed her. Lance seemed clear enough on his opinion of our positions last night. *I won't accept it,* she told herself staunchly, still staring at the phone. *I will not accept it. He can't go back to racing.* She swallowed the iron taste of fear that had risen to her throat. He couldn't have meant that. Squeezing her eyes tight, Foxy shook her head. *Don't think about it now. Go to work and don't think about it.* She took a deep breath and turned her back on the phone.

After confiscating a cup of coffee from the kitchen, Foxy closeted herself in her darkroom. The prints still hung on the line as she had left them. Without consciously planning to do so, she pulled the print of Kirk's racer down and studied it. *A comet,* she thought, remembering. *Yes, he is a comet, but doesn't even a comet have to burn out sometime? There'll be other pictures of him next year, but someone else will have to take them. Maybe Lance will arrange for that, too.* A sharp, frustrated sound escaped her. *I can't think about all of this anymore.* She pulled down the dry prints, then began to work on a fresh roll of film. Time passed swiftly and in such absolute silence that she was jolted when a knock sounded on the door. Foxy frowned as she went to answer it. Mrs. Trilby had never ventured into her territory.

"Melissa!" she exclaimed as her frown flew into a smile. "What a nice surprise."

"It's not dark," Melissa said with a small pout as she moved past Foxy and into the room. "Why is it called a darkroom if it isn't dark? I'm disillusioned."

"You came at the wrong time," Foxy explained. "I promise it was quite dark in here a couple of hours ago."

"I suppose I'll have to take your word for it." Melissa slowly walked down the line of new prints Foxy had hanging. "My, my, you really are a professional, aren't you?"

"I like to think so," Foxy answered wryly.

"All so technical," Melissa mused as she wandered around the room and scowled at bottles and timers. "I suppose this is what you studied in college."

"I majored in photography at USC. Not Smith," she added with a lift of brow. "Not Radcliffe, not Vassar, but at that little-known institution, the state college."

"Oh, dear." Melissa bit her lip but a small portion of the smile escaped. "Some of the ladies have been giving you a bad time, I take it."

"You take it right," Foxy agreed, then wrinkled her nose. "Well, I suppose I'm just a nine-days wonder. They'll forget about me soon enough."

"Such sweet naivete," Melissa murmured as she patted Foxy's cheek. "I'll let you hold on to that little dream for a while. In any case," she continued, briskly brushing a speck from her pale blue angora sweater, "there's a dance at the country club Saturday. You and Lance are coming, aren't you?"

"Yes." Foxy didn't bother to suppress her sigh. "We'll be there."

"Buck up, darling. The obligations will taper off in a few months. Lance had never been one to socialize more than is absolutely necessary. And"—she smiled her singularly charming smile—"it's such a marvelous excuse to go shopping." Melissa gave the room another sweeping glance. "Are you all done in here?"

"Yes, I've just finished." Foxy glanced at her watch and gave a satisfied nod. "And right on schedule."

"Well then, let's go shopping and buy something fabulous to wear Saturday night." She linked her arm with Foxy's and began to lead her from the room.

"Oh no." She stopped long enough to close the darkroom door behind her. "I went on one of your little shopping safaris last week. You invaded every shop on Newbury Street. I haven't taken my vitamins today, and anyway, I have a dress for Saturday. I don't need anything."

"Good grief, do you have to *need* it before you buy it?" Melissa turned back from her journey to the stairs and gaped. "You only bought one little blouse when we went shopping before. What do you think Lance has all that lovely money for?"

"For a multitude of things, I'm sure," Foxy replied gravely. Still, a smile tugged at the corners of her mouth. "But hardly for me to spend on clothes I have no need for. In any case, I use my own money for personal things."

Melissa folded her arms and studied Foxy with care. "Why, you're serious, aren't you, pet?" She looked puzzled as she lifted her shoulders. "But Lance has simply hordes of money."

"I know that. I often wish he didn't." As she started to climb the stairs to the first floor Melissa took her arm.

"Wait a minute." Her voice had altered from its brisk good humor. It was quiet now, and serious. "They really are giving you a bad time, aren't they?"

"It doesn't matter," Foxy began, using a shrug to toss off the question.

"Oh, but I think it does." Melissa's hand was surprisingly

firm on Foxy's arm. She kept Foxy facing her on the narrow stairway. "Listen to me a minute now. I'm going to be perfectly serious for a change. This business about you marrying Lance for his money is just typical nonsense, Foxy. It doesn't mean anything. And not everyone is saying it or thinking it. There are some morons who carry on about status and bloodlines, of course, but I never pay much attention to morons." She smiled when she paused for breath, but her eyes remained grave. "You've already won over a great many people, people like Grandmother, who's no pushover. And you've done that by simply being yourself. Surely Lance has told you how many people are pleased with his taste in wives."

"We don't discuss it." Foxy dragged her hand through her hair with a sound of frustration. "That is, to be more exact, I haven't said anything about his less friendly relations. It hardly seems fair to hound him with complaints."

"Is it fair for you to stand quiet while a scattered few toss rocks at you?" Melissa countered, lifting a brow uncannily as Lance did. "Martyrdom is depressing, Foxy."

Foxy grimaced at the title. "I don't think I care much for that." Shaking her head, she gave Melissa a rueful smile. "I suppose I'm being too sensitive. There've been so many changes all at once, and I'm having a hard time juggling everything."

Melissa linked her arm with Foxy's again as they mounted the stairs. "Now, what else is there?"

"Does it show?"

"I'm very perceptive," Melissa told her carelessly. "Didn't you know? My guess is that you and Lance had a tiff."

"Your term is a bit mild," Foxy murmured as she pushed open the door to the first floor. "But we'll go with it."

"Whose fault was it?"

Foxy opened her mouth to blame Lance, closed it again

on the thought of blaming herself. She gave up with a sigh. "No one's, I suppose."

"That's the usual kind," Melissa said briskly. "The best cure is to go out and buy something fabulous to boost your ego. Then, if you want to make him suffer, you can be coolly polite when he gets home. Or"—she gestured fluidly with her hand—"if you want to make up, you send Mrs. Trilby home early and have on as little as possible when he gets here."

"Melissa." Foxy laughed as she watched her retrieve her coat and purse from the hall stand. "What a lovely way you have of simplifying things."

"It's a gift," she said modestly, studying her reflection in the antique mirror. "Are you going to be fun and come shopping with me, or are you going to be horribly industrious?"

"I think," Foxy mused thoughtfully, "I've just been insulted." On impulse, she leaned over and kissed Melissa's cheek. "You tempt me, but I'm very strong-willed."

"You're actually going to work this afternoon?" The look she gave Foxy was filled with both admiration and puzzlement. "But you even worked this morning."

"People have often been known to work an entire day," Foxy pointed out, then grinned. "It can get to be a habit . . . like potato chips. I'm starting a series of photographs on children, so I'm off to the park."

Melissa frowned as she slipped into her short fur jacket. "You make me feel quite the derelict."

"You'll get over it," Foxy comforted as she ran a curious finger down the soft white pelt.

"Of course." Melissa swirled around and kissed both of Foxy's cheeks. "But for a moment, I feel guilty. Have a nice time, Foxy," she said as she swung out the door.

"You, too," Foxy called over the quick slam. With a laugh, she pulled her own suede jacket from the closet. In a lighter frame of mind, she swung her purse over one shoulder and her camera case over the other. As she turned she all but collided with Mrs. Trilby. "Oh, I'm sorry." *Crepe-soled shoes,* Foxy thought with an inward sigh, *should be outlawed.*

"Are you going out, Mrs. Matthews?" Mrs. Trilby stood stiffly in her gray uniform and white apron.

"Yes, I have some work planned this afternoon. I should be back around three."

"Very good, ma'am." Mrs. Trilby stood expressionless in the archway as Foxy moved to the front door.

"Mrs. Trilby, if Lance . . . if Mr. Matthews should call, tell him I . . ." Foxy hesitated, and for a moment the unhappiness and indecision was reflected on her face.

"Yes, ma'am?" Mrs. Trilby prompted with the slightest softening of her tone.

"No," Foxy shook her head, annoyed with herself. "No, nothing. Never mind." She straightened her shoulders and sent the housekeeper a smile. "Goodbye, Mrs. Trilby."

"Good day, Mrs. Matthews."

Foxy stepped outside and breathed in the crisp autumn air. Though her MG had been shipped from Indiana and now sat waiting in the garage, Foxy opted to walk. The sky was piercingly blue, empty of clouds. Against the unrelieved color, the bare trees rose in stark supplication. Dry leaves whirled along the sidewalk and clung to the curbs. Now and then, the wind would whip them around Foxy's ankles until they fell again to be crunched underfoot. The crisp perfection of the day lifted her spirits higher, and she began to formulate an outline for the project she had in mind.

Mums were still stubbornly beautiful throughout the public gardens. There were flashes of rich color along the paths where rosy-cheeked children darted and played. The afternoon was fresh and sharp. Babies were rolled along in carriages or strollers by their mothers or uniformed nannies. Toddlers practiced the art of walking on the leaf-carpeted grass.

Foxy moved among them, sometimes shooting pictures, sometimes striking up a conversation with a parent, then charming her way into the shot she wanted. She had learned from experience that photography was more than knowing the workings of a camera or the speed of film. It was the ability to read and portray an image. It was patience, it was tenacity, it was luck.

She lay on her stomach on the cool grass, aiming her Nikon at a two-year-old girl who wrestled with a delighted bull terrier puppy. The child's blond, rosy beauty was the perfect foil for the dog's unabashed homeliness. A pool of sunlight surrounded them as they tussled, finding each other far more interesting than the woman who crawled and scooted around them snapping a camera. The dog yapped and rushed in circles, the child giggled and captured him. He escaped to be cheerfully captured again. At length, Foxy sat back on her heels and grinned at her models. After a quick exchange with the girl's mother, she stood, prepared to load a fresh roll of film.

"That was a fascinating performance."

Glancing up, Foxy found herself facing Jonathan Fitzpatrick. "Oh, hello." She tossed her hair behind her back, then brushed a stray leaf from her jacket.

"Hello, Mrs. Matthews. A lovely day for rolling in the grass."

His smile was so blatantly charming, Foxy laughed. "Yes, it is. Nice to see you again, Mr. Fitzpatrick."

"Jonathan," he corrected and plucked another leaf from her hair. "And I'll call you Foxy as Melissa does. It suits you. Now, may I ask what it is you're doing, or is it a government secret?"

"I'm taking pictures, of course." With a grin, Foxy continued to load her camera. "I make a habit of it, that's why I'm a photographer."

"Ah yes, I did hear that." As she bent her head over her work, the sunlight shot small flames through her hair. With admiration, Jonathan watched them flare. "Professional, are you?"

"That's what I tell the publishers." Finished, she closed the camera and gave Jonathan her attention again. The resemblance to his sister was striking, yet she felt no discomfort with him as she had with Gwen. He was, she thought on another quick study, an exact opposite of Lance: fair and smooth and harmless. Instantly annoyed with her habitual comparisons, she gave him her best smile. "I'm working on a project with children at the moment."

Jonathan studied her, taking in the easy smile, the large gray-green eyes, the face that became more intriguing each time it was seen. He completed his examination in a matter of seconds and decided Lance had won again. This was no ordinary lady. "May I watch awhile?" he asked, surprising them both. "I have the afternoon free. I was just crossing to my car when I spotted you."

"Of course." She bent to retrieve her camera case. "But I'm afraid you might find it boring." Turning, she began to walk in the direction of the Mill Pond.

"I doubt that. I rarely find beautiful women boring in any circumstances." Jonathan fell into step beside her. Foxy cast him a sidelong look. He had the smile of the boy next door and the profile of an Adonis. Melissa, Foxy mused, is going to have her hands full.

"What do you do, Jonathan?"

"As I please," he answered as he slipped his hands into the pockets of his leather jacket. "Theoretically, I'm an executive in the family business. Import-export. In reality, I'm a paper shuffler who charms wives when necessary and escorts daughters."

Humor sparkled in Foxy's eyes. "Do you enjoy your work?"

"Immensely." When he looked down with his easy grin, she decided he and Melissa were ideally suited for each other.

"I enjoy mine as well," she told him. "Now stand out of the way while I do some."

There was a bench by the pond where a willow dipped into the mirrorlike water. A woman sat reading while a chubby toddler in a bright red jacket tossed crackers to paddling ducks. Nearby, an infant snoozed in a stroller in a square of sunshine. A forgotten rattle hung limply in the curled fingers. After exchanging a quiet word with the woman on the bench, Foxy set to work. Taking care not to disturb him, she captured the delight of the toddler as he threw his crumbs high in the air. Ducks scrambled for the free meal. The boy squealed with pleasure and tossed again, sometimes sampling a cracker himself while the ducks vied for the soggy offering. She translated the sound of his laughter onto film.

Using sun and shade, she expressed the peace and innocence of the fat-cheeked infant. Changing angles, speeds and filters, she altered moods and heightened emotions, until, satisfied, she stopped and let the camera hang by its strap.

"You're very intense while you work," Jonathan commented as he moved up to join her. "You look very competent."

"Is that a compliment or an observation?" Foxy asked him, then snapped on her lens cover.

"A complimentary observation," Jonathan countered. He continued to study her profile as she secured her equipment. "You fascinate me, Foxy Matthews. I find you one more reason to envy Lance."

"Do you?" She looked up, revealing a guileless interest that surprised him. "And are there many others?"

"Scores," he said promptly, then took her hand. "But you're at the top of the list. Is it true your brother's Kirk Fox and that Lance snatched you from the racing world?"

"Yes." Foxy was immediately on guard. Her tone cooled. "I grew up at the racetrack."

Jonathan lifted a brow. "I've struck a nerve. I'm sorry." He ran his thumb absently across her knuckles. "Would it help if I said I'm curious, not critical? Lance's racing career also fascinates me, and I've followed your brother's as well. I thought you might have some interesting stories to tell." His voice, Foxy noted, was not like Gwen's; it was far too honest.

"I'm sorry." She sighed and moved her shoulders. "That's the second time today I've been overly sensitive. It's a bit difficult being the new kid on the block."

"You were a bit of a surprise." His touch was so light that Foxy had forgotten he still held her hand. "There are those who require everything well planned and predictable. Lance seems to prefer the unique."

"Unique," Foxy murmured, then shot Jonathan a direct, uncompromising stare. "I don't have any money, I haven't a pedigree. I spent my adolescent years around garages and mechanics. I didn't go to an exclusive college, and all I've seen of Europe is what I could squeeze in between time trials and races."

Watching her, Jonathan observed the tiny flecks of unhappiness in her eyes. Sunlight flickered through the willow leaves to catch the highlights of her hair. "Would you like to have an affair?" he asked casually.

Stunned, Foxy stepped back, her eyes huge. "No!"

"Have you ever ridden on the swan boat?" he inquired just as easily.

Her mouth opened and closed twice in utter confusion. "No," she managed cautiously.

"Good." He took her hand again. "We'll do that instead."
He smiled, keeping her fingers tightly in his. "All right?"

Warily Foxy studied his face. Before she realized it, a
smile began to tug at the corners of her mouth. "All right,"
she agreed. *Melissa will never be bored,* she decided as she
let Jonathan lead her away.

"Would you care for a balloon?" His voice took on a formal note.

"Yes, thank you," she returned in a matching tone. "A blue
one."

The next two hours were the most carefree Foxy had spent
since she had begun her social duties as Mrs. Lance Matthews. With Jonathan, she glided on the Mill Pond, tucked
in a swan boat with tourists and sticky-fingered preschoolers. They walked through the gardens eating ice cream with
Foxy's balloon trailing on its string at their backs. She found
him undemanding, easy to talk to, a tonic for depression.

When Jonathan pulled up in front of the brownstone,
Foxy's mood was still light. "Would you like to come in?"
She shifted the strap of her case onto her shoulder. "Perhaps
you could stay for dinner."

"Another time. I have a dinner engagement with Melissa."

"Tell her hello for me." With a smile, Foxy opened her
door. "Thank you, Jonathan." On impulse, she leaned across
the seat and kissed his cheek. "I'm sure it was much more
fun than an affair, and so much simpler."

"Simpler anyway," he agreed, then brushed a finger down
her nose. "I'll see you and Lance on Saturday."

"Oh, yes." Foxy made a face before she slid from the car.
"Oh, tell Melissa I totally approve of her plans for May." She
laughed at his puzzled face, then waved him away. "She'll
know what I mean." Slamming the door, she shivered once
in the cooling air before moving up the path to the house. The
front door opened as she reached for the knob.

"Hello, Foxy." Lance stood in the doorway. With a quick scan, he took in her smile, bright eyes, and blue balloon. "Apparently you've had an enjoyable afternoon."

Her buoyant mood left no place for remnants of anger from yesterday's argument. They could talk and be serious later, now she wanted to share her pleasure. "Lance, you're home early." She was glad to find him waiting and smiled again.

"Actually, I believe you're home late," he countered as he shut the door behind her.

"Oh?" A look at her watch told her it was nearly five. "I didn't realize. I suppose I lost track of the time." With the balloon tied jauntily to its strap, Foxy set down the camera case. "Have you been home long?"

"Long enough." He studied her autumn-kissed cheeks. "Want a drink?" he said as he turned and walked back into the drawing room.

"No, thank you." His coolness had seeped through Foxy's elated spirits. She followed him, calculating the best way to bridge the gap before it widened further. "We didn't have any plans for this evening, did we?"

"No." Lance poured a generous helping of scotch into a glass before he turned back to her. "Do you intend to go out again?"

"No, I . . ." She stopped, paralyzed by the ice in his eyes. "No."

He drank, watching her over the rim. The tension that had flown from her during the afternoon returned. Still, she could not yet bring herself to speak of Kirk or racing. "I ran into Jonathan Fitzpatrick in the public gardens," she began, unbuttoning her jacket in order to keep her hands busy. "He brought me home."

"So I noticed." Lance stood with his back to the wide stone fireplace. His face was cool and impassive.

"It was beautiful out today," Foxy hurried on, fretting for

a way out of the polite, meaningless exchange. Warily, she watched Lance pour another glass of scotch. "There seem to be a lot of tourists still, but Jonathan said they slack off during the winter."

"I had no idea Jonathan was interested in the tourist population."

"I was interested," she corrected, then pulled off her jacket with a frown. "It was crowded in the swan boats."

"Did Jonathan take you?" Lance asked mildly before he tossed back the contents of his glass. "How charming."

"Well, I hadn't been before so he—"

"It appears I've been neglecting you," he interrupted. Foxy's frown deepened as he lifted the bottle of scotch again.

"You're being ridiculous," Foxy stated as her temper began to rise. "And you're drinking too much."

"My dear child, I haven't begun to drink too much." He poured another glass. "And as for being ridiculous, there are some men who would cheerfully beat a wife who spends afternoons with other men."

"That's a Neanderthal attitude," she snapped. She tossed her jacket into a chair and glared at him. "It was perfectly harmless. We were in a public place."

"Yes, buying balloons and riding on swans."

"We had an ice cream cone as well," she supplied and jammed her hands into her pockets.

"Your tastes are amazingly simple." Lance glanced briefly into his glass before lifting it and swallowing. "For someone in your current position."

Her shocked gasp was trapped by the obstruction in her throat. Absolutely still, she stood while all color drained from her face. Against the pallor, her eyes were dark with hurt. Swearing richly, Lance set down his glass.

"That was below the belt, Fox, I'm sorry." He started

toward her, but she backed away, throwing out her hands to ward him off.

"No, don't touch me." She took quick, deep breaths to control the tremor in her voice. "I've had to listen to the innuendos, I've had to put up with the knowing smirks and tolerate the sniping, but I never expected it from you. I'd rather you had beat me than said that to me." Turning quickly, she fled up the stairs. Before she could slam the bedroom door, Lance caught her wrist.

"Don't turn away from me," he warned in a low, even voice. "Don't ever turn away from me."

"Let go of me!" she shouted, trying to pull away from him. Before she thought about what she was doing, she swung out with her free hand and slapped him.

"All right," he said between his teeth as he locked both her arms behind her back. "I had that coming, now calm down."

"Just take your hands off me and leave me alone."

"Not until we settle this. There are some things that have to be explained."

"I don't need to explain anything." She tossed her head to free her eyes from her hair. "Now take your hands off me. I can't bear it."

"Don't push me too far, Foxy." Lance's voice was as dark and dangerous as his eyes. "I'm running low on self-control, particularly after last night. Now calm down, and we'll talk."

"I don't have anything to say to you." Cold with fury, she stopped struggling and stared up at him. "I had my say yesterday, and you've had yours tonight. It looks like we understand each other well enough."

"Then we won't talk," Lance said harshly before his mouth came down on hers. With an iron grip, he handcuffed her wrists so that her frantic movements were useless. There was something calculating as well as brutal in the kiss. She recognized the same ruthlessness she knew him to be capable of in racing. Knowing her struggles were futile, she forced her body to go limp and her mouth to remain passive. "Ice won't work," Lance muttered and lifted her off her feet. "I know how to melt it."

As he began to carry her to the bed Foxy's passive acceptance disappeared. She pushed hard against his chest and felt herself falling. Her small cry of alarm was knocked from her as she hit the mattress. Before she could roll away, he was on top of her.

His body molded itself to hers as his mouth took hers again. Foxy's body heated to his touch. Her sweater and jeans were tossed carelessly to the floor and the thin chemise she wore was no barrier against his hands. Her nipples were taut against the silk as he sought the sensitive hollow of her throat with his lips and tongue. She continued to struggle even as his hand moved down the silk to the flatness of her stomach. His fingers moved over the top of her leg where the chemise ended.

Desire surged through her, weighing on her limbs as she pushed and twisted. She knew she needed to escape not only from him but from herself. Her movements brought only more arousal. With his tongue, he traced the peak of her breast through the chemise, catching it then between his teeth as her fingers dug into his shoulders. He exploited her weaknesses, explored the secrets only he knew until the fire kindled and flared. She responded. She arched against him now not in protest, but in answer. Hungrily her mouth sought his as her fingers fumbled with the buttons of his shirt. His skin was hot against her palms, his muscles tight.

Abruptly, his mood altered. His cool control vanished as a thunderous urgency took its place. Hooking his hands in the bodice, he ripped the chemise down the front in one sharp gesture. Foxy heard him curse her as his breathing grew as labored as hers. His hands were wild now, bruising over her naked skin while his mouth was hard and demanding. Control was lost for both of them. There was only sensation, only need, only the dark pleasure of damp flesh and deep kisses. But even as he took her, even as she gave herself without reservation, Foxy knew neither of them had won.

CHAPTER 14

It started raining early Saturday morning. Then the cold arrived and turned the rain to snow before afternoon. Alone, with the house rattling around her, Foxy watched it fall in thin sheets. The ground was still warm, and the snow melted even as it landed. It poured down quickly enough, but left no trace. *There'll be no snowmen built today,* Foxy mused and hugged her elbows. *I wonder where he could have gone.*

Lance had already left when she awakened, and the house was empty. Foxy knew that what had passed between them the night before had cost them both dearly. In the end, he hadn't taken her in anger, and she had given herself willingly. Desire had won over both of them but misunderstanding remained in its wake. Discovering herself alone in a cold bed had shot a shaft of gloom over her, which grew only sharper as the hours passed. The morning hours spent in her darkroom had been productive but had done nothing to alleviate her dilemma.

What's happening to my marriage? she asked herself as she stared out at the stubbornly falling snow. *It's barely begun, and it seems to be going nowhere. Like the snow out there,* she mused, and lay her fingers on the windowpane.

It just keeps disappearing. Could it be as fragile as an early snow, and as fleeting? Foxy shook her head and cradled her elbows. *I won't let it be.* The sound of the phone had her whirling around. *Lance,* she thought instantly and raced to answer it.

"Hello," she said with anticipation ripe in her voice.

"Hiya, Foxy. How are things in the real world?"

"Kirk." Her disappointment was outweighed by her pleasure. She dropped down on an ottoman and pushed the disappointment aside. "It's good to hear your voice." Even as she said the words, she realized how true they were. Her pleasure increased and turned to happiness. "How are you?" she demanded. "Have you talked them into letting you out? Where's Pam?"

"I think marriage has slowed you down," he commented gravely. "Can't you think of anything to say?"

Laughing, Foxy tucked her feet under her. "Just answer any or all of the above questions, but start with the first one. How are you?"

"Pretty good. Healing. They might be persuaded to let me out in a couple weeks if Pam's willing to cart me back and forth for therapy." She could tell from the sound of his voice that his injuries were hardly uppermost in his mind. *Professional risks.* She remembered Lance's words and bit down hard on her bottom lip.

"I imagine she could be persuaded," Foxy managed to say naturally. "I'm glad you're better." *I worry about you,* she told him silently, then smiled and shook her head. *He wouldn't like to hear that.* "I suppose you're getting bored."

"I passed bored last week," he returned dryly. "I'm getting so good at the *Times* crossword puzzles, I've started doing them in ink to show off."

"You were always cocky. Shall I send you some paste and

colored paper to keep you busy?" She kept her tongue in her cheek as she heard him snarl.

"I'll let that pass because I'm good-natured." Kirk ignored her laughter and continued. "So, tell me about Boston. Do you like it there?"

"It's beautiful." As she answered, Foxy glanced out the window. Flakes were falling in a white curtain and vanishing. "It's snowing now, and I suppose it'll turn cold, but I've done a lot of exploring. I'm rather anxious to see how Boston looks in the winter."

"How about Lance's family?" Kirk demanded. "I can get a weather report from the newspaper."

"Well, they're . . ." She fumbled for words, hesitated, and ultimately laughed. "They're different. I feel a bit like Gulliver, finding himself an oddity in a world where the rules are all different. We're getting used to each other, and I've made a couple of friends." She smiled, thinking of Melissa and Jonathan. Remembering Catherine, she felt the smile slip a bit, and with a shrug began to trace a pattern on the ottoman with her fingernail. "I'm afraid his mother doesn't care for me."

"You didn't marry his mother," Kirk pointed out logically. "I can't imagine my sister letting herself get pushed around by a few Boston bluebloods." He spoke with such easy confidence that Foxy was forced to smile again.

"Who me?" she countered, accepting the strange compliment. "They grow 'em tough in the Midwest, you know."

"Yeah, you're a real Amazon." The rough affection in his tone made her smile sweeten. "How's Lance?"

"He's fine," she answered automatically. Nibbling on her lips, she added, "He's been busy."

"I imagine the plans for the new car have him pretty tied up just now." She heard the excitement creep into Kirk's voice and schooled herself to accept it. "It sounds like a beauty.

I'm itching to get up there and see how it's going. Lance is a damn genius at a drawing board."

"Is he?" Foxy asked with a curious frown.

"It's one thing to come up with ideas, Fox. I have a few of those myself. It's another to be able to put them to practical use." He spoke with a hint of envious amusement, causing Foxy to consider another aspect of her husband.

"Strange, he doesn't seem the type for drawing boards and calculators, does he?"

"Lance isn't any type at all," Kirk corrected. "You should know that better than anyone."

Foxy paused a moment in thought. Her frown deepened, then softened into a smile. "Yes, of course, you're right. And I do know it. I've needed someone to remind me though. It's also nice to hear from my brother that my husband is a genius."

"He was always more interested in the mechanics than the race," Kirk added absently. "So, how are you?"

"Me?" Foxy shook her head to bring her attention back to Kirk. "Oh, fine. You can tell Pam I have the prints finished and I'll be sending them up to her."

"Are you happy?"

She heard the same seriousness in his tone she had heard when Pam had asked the identical question. "What sort of question is that to ask a woman who's only been married a few weeks," she countered lightly. "You're not supposed to come down to happy for at least a month."

"Foxy," Kirk began.

"I love him, Kirk," she interrupted, voicing some of her thoughts for the first time. "It's not always easy and it's not always perfect, but it's the only place for me. I'm happy and I'm sad, and I'm a hundred other things I wouldn't be if I didn't have Lance."

"Okay." She could almost see his nod of acceptance. "As

long as you have what you want. Listen, I really called to let you know. Well, I thought I should tell you first . . ."

Foxy waited a full ten seconds. "What?" she demanded on an exasperated laugh.

"I asked Pam to marry me."

"Thank goodness."

"You don't sound surprised," he complained.

A grin of pure pleasure spread over Foxy's face. "Only that such a nifty driver could be so slow. When are you getting married?"

"An hour ago."

"What?"

"Now you sound surprised," Kirk stated, satisfied. "Pam wouldn't wait until I could stand up, so we got married right here in the hospital. I tried to call you before, but nobody answered."

"I was down in my darkroom." With a sigh, she drew her knees up to her chest. "Oh, Kirk, I'm happy for you. I'm not sure I believe it."

"I'm not sure I do either. She's not like anyone else in the world." Foxy heard the tone, recognized it, and blinked tears from her lashes.

"Yes, I know what you mean. Can I talk to her?"

"She's not here, she's out making arrangements for this place we're going to rent while I'm having my leg prodded. We're hoping to be in Boston by the first of the year so that I can keep an eye on Lance and my car, but we'll stay near the hospital till then."

"I see." *He'll never change,* she told herself and shut her eyes briefly. *I was a fool to think differently.* Everything Lance said the other night was true. Kirk will race as long as he's capable of racing. Nothing and no one could stop him. She clearly remembered the things she had said to Lance in the dimming light of the library. Guilt all but smothered her.

Foxy switched the phone to her other ear and swallowed. "I'll be glad to have you and Pam here, even if it's only until the season starts." Understanding made acceptance easier.

"Will you be coming to Europe?"

"No." Foxy shook her head and made the break. "No, I won't be coming."

"Pam said she didn't think you would. Listen, they're coming in to poke at me again. Tell Lance that Pam and I expect him to break out some champagne when we get into town. The French stuff."

"I'll do that," she promised, relieved that he had let her go without a second thought. "Take care of yourself."

"Sure. Hey, I love you, Foxy."

"I love you, too." After cradling the phone, Foxy drew her knees closer and wrapped her arms around them. As she watched, the snow grew thinner until it was little more than a fine mist.

He doesn't need me anymore, she reflected before she realized the thought had been in her mind. It struck her as odd that she had not fully understood Kirk's need for her until it no longer existed. Their need for each other had been mutual, even when she had been a child. The link between them was strong, perhaps because of the tragedy that had left them only each other. *There'll always be something special between us,* Foxy brooded. *But he has Pam now, and I have Lance.* Resting her chin on her knees, Foxy wondered if Lance needed her. Loved her, yes, wanted her, but did Lance Matthews with his casual self-sufficiency, his easy wealth and supreme confidence *need* her? Was there something special about her that completed his life, or was she simply overly romantic and foolish in wanting to believe it was true? She found, to her surprise, that the answer mattered very much.

Abruptly Foxy's senses tingled. Lifting her head, she

looked up to see Lance standing in the doorway. Moving quickly, she unfolded herself from the ottoman and stood. As she met his eyes every speech she had rehearsed, edited, and re-rehearsed that morning vanished from her mind. Foolishly she tugged her sweatshirt over the hips of her jeans and wished she had worn something more dignified.

"I didn't hear you come in," she said, then cursed herself for the inanity.

"You were on the phone." It was his quiet, measuring look. He stood watching her without a flicker in his eyes to hint at his thoughts. Nerves began to dance in her stomach.

"Yes, I . . . It was Kirk." She tugged her fingers through her hair, unable to keep them still, and inadvertently betrayed her tension.

In silence, Lance continued to scan her face. He came no further into the room when he spoke again. "How is he?"

"Fine. He sounds wonderful actually. He and Pam were married this morning." While making the announcement, Foxy began to wander around the room. She fiddled with priceless pieces of bric-a-brac and toyed with Mrs. Trilby's careful arrangement of fall flowers.

"That pleases you?" Lance asked, studying her restless movements before he crossed to the bar. He lifted a bottle of scotch, then set it down again without pouring any.

"Yes. Yes, very much." Taking a deep breath, she prepared to plunge into an apology for blaming him for Kirk's decision to continue racing. "Lance, I . . . Oh." As she turned, she found him directly in front of her. She backed up a step, surprised, and his brow lifted at her action. While Foxy dealt with feeling awkward and unsettled, Lance slipped his hands in his pockets.

"Apologies aren't my strong suit," he stated as she searched for a way to begin again. "In this case, however, I don't think it's possible to avoid the need for one." His face was closed against her searching gaze. His eyes were on hers, but they did not speak to her. "I apologize both for the things I said to you and for what happened. That hardly makes up for it, but you have my word, nothing like that will happen again."

His stilted formality only added to Foxy's strain. She knew nothing she had planned to say could be said to the polite stranger who stood before her. Dropping her eyes, she studied the pattern in the Aubusson rug. "No absolution, Foxy?" Hearing the softness in his voice, she lifted her eyes again.

The strain, she noted, was not all on her side. She saw the signs of a restless night in his face and was compelled to offer comfort. She lifted a hand to his cheek. "Please, Lance, let's forget about it. We've both said things these past couple of days that shouldn't have been said." Her eyes and mouth were grave as her palm brushed over his cheek. "I don't like apologies either."

Lance lifted his fingers and twined the tip of a curl around them. "You always were a strange mixture of tiger and kitten. I think I'd forgotten how disarmingly sweet you can be." His eyes were no longer silent as he looked at her. "I love you, Foxy."

"Lance." Foxy flung her arms around him and burrowed her face into his neck. At last, the tension inside her uncurled. "I've missed you," she murmured against his neck. "I didn't know where you'd gone, and the house seemed so empty."

"I went into the office," he told her as he slipped his hands under her shirt to caress the warm length of her back. "You should have called if you were lonely."

"I almost did, but I thought . . ." She sighed and closed her eyes, wonderfully content. "I didn't want it to seem as if I was checking on you."

"Idiot," he muttered, then tilted her head back and kissed her briefly. "You're my wife, remember?"

"You have to keep reminding me," she suggested and smiled. "I don't feel like a wife yet, and I don't know the rules."

"We make our own." This time when he kissed her, it was long and lingering. In instant response, her bones liquified. Her mouth clung to his, avid and sweet while his quiet moan of pleasure warmed her skin.

"I want champagne tonight," she murmured against his ear. "I feel like a celebration."

"For Pam and Kirk?" Lance questioned before he came back to her mouth.

"For us first," Foxy countered, drawing away far enough to smile at him. "Then for Pam and Kirk."

"All right. But tomorrow I want to go to the movies and eat popcorn."

"Oh yes!" Her face lit with pleasure. Her eyes danced. "Yes, something either terribly sad or terribly funny. And I want a pizza afterward with pepperoni."

"A very demanding woman." Lance laughed as he took her hand and lifted it to his lips. Suddenly his fingers tightened on hers. Sensing a dramatic change of mood, Foxy stared down at their joined hands. Slowly Lance turned hers to the side and examined the light trail of mauve shadows on her wrist. "It seems I owe you yet another apology."

Distressed that the stiffness was back in his manner, Foxy moved toward him. "Lance, don't. It's nothing."

"On the contrary." The coldness in his voice halted her. "It's quite a lot."

"Don't! I can't stand it when you're like this." Filled with frustration, Foxy paced around the room. "I can't deal with you when you're formal and polite." She whirled to face him, then whirled back to roam the room again. "If you're going to be angry, then at least be angry in a way I can understand. Shout, swear, break something," she invited with an inclusive sweep of her hand. "But don't stand there like a pillar of the community. I don't understand pillars."

"Foxy." A reluctant grin teased Lance's mouth as he watched her storm around the room. "If you knew how difficult you make things."

"I'm not trying to make things difficult." She lifted a pillow from the couch and hurled it across the room. "I'm trying to make thing simple. *I'm* simple, don't you understand?"

"You are," Lance corrected, "infinitely complex."

"No, no, no!" Foxy stomped her foot, furious that they were talking in circles again. "You don't understand anything!" Angrily she tossed her hair behind her back. "I'm going upstairs," she announced and marched from the room.

Going directly to the bath, Foxy turned on the water and let it steam. Carelessly she tossed a mixture of powders and scents into the tub and stripped. *He's an idiot,* she decided as she plopped into the oversized tub. Bubbles rose and frothed around her. *And so am I.* Seething with impotence, Foxy picked up a sponge and began to scrub.

I could probably stop loving him if I really put my mind to it. She scowled at the sponge then squeezed it mercilessly. *I'm going to stop loving him and work on hating him. Once I start hating him,* she concluded, *I won't be an idiot anymore.* As the door opened she glanced up sharply.

"Mind if I shave?" Lance asked casually as he strolled into the room. He had slipped out of his jacket and now wore only his shirt and slacks. Ignoring her glare and not waiting for her assent, he opened the medicine chest.

"I've decided to hate you," Foxy informed him after he had removed the shaving lotion and begun to lather his face.

"Oh?" She watched his eyes shift in the mirror until they met hers. It infuriated her that they were amused. "Again?"

"I was good at it once," she reminded him. "I'm going to be even better at it this time."

"No doubt." The razor stroked clean over his cheek. "Most things improve with age."

"I'm going to hate you perfectly."

"Good for you," Lance told her as he continued to shave. "One should always aim high."

Beyond control, Foxy hurled the wet sponge and hit Lance between the shoulder blades. She felt a surge of satisfaction almost immediately followed by a surge of alarm. *He won't,* she decided grimly, *let me get away with that one.* Still, her eyes challenged his. Slowly Lance set down the razor and bent to pick up the sponge. Foxy's trepidation grew as he turned and walked to the tub. *He wouldn't drown me,* she thought, fending off a few pricks of doubt. Even as she debated the matter, Lance sat on the edge of the tub. She realized with some disgust that she had backed herself neatly into a corner.

Lance made no comment, only dropped the sponge back into the water with a plop. Distracted, Foxy glanced down. Before she realized his intent, his hand was on her head and she was sliding under the hot, fragrant water. Sputtering, she surfaced. Her hair dripped and frothed over her shoulders and into her face as she wiped the bubbles from her eyes.

"I do hate you!" she choked, pushing at her sopping hair. "I'm going to thrive on hating you! I'm going to invent new ways to hate you!"

Lance gave her a calm nod. "Everybody should have a hobby."

"Oh!" Incoherent with fury, Foxy tossed as much water into his face as she could manage. She braced herself for another dunking. To her utter amazement, Lance rolled into the tub in one smooth, unexpected motion. Bubbles spewed over the side. Her shock was transformed into hysterical giggles. "You're crazy," she concluded as she tried to keep herself from submerging under the rocking water. "How can I hate you properly if you're crazy?" Their bodies tangled together effortlessly. Her skin was slick and fragrant from the oil, and his hands slid over it, bringing her closer. His wet clothes were little more than nothing between them. "You're drowning me," Foxy protested as he shifted her. She swallowed bubbles and giggled again. "I knew you were going to drown me."

"I'm not going to drown you," Lance corrected. "I'm going to make love with you." He gripped her waist and nudged her up until her chin cleared the water. His fingers lingered, spreading over her stomach while his hand cupped her breast. There was a gentleness in his touch he rarely used. "Since you were sharing your sponge and water, I figured you wanted me to join you." He grinned as Foxy pushed dripping hair from his eyes. "I didn't want to be accused of being stuffy."

"You're not stuffy," she said softly. Her eyes reflected regret as they met his. "Lance . . ."

"No more apologies tonight." He closed his mouth over hers to shut it off before it could be formed. He took his hands on a slow, easy journey of her body, pausing and lingering, seducing with a quiet touch.

"We should talk," Foxy murmured, but the words were faint and without conviction. Her sigh was more eloquent.

"Tomorrow. Tomorrow we'll be sensible and talk and sort things through." As he spoke, his lips roamed over her face. His hands sought and touched and enticed. "I want you tonight. I want to make love with my wife." He moved his lips to her neck, tasting, before he caught the lobe of her ear between his teeth. Foxy shuddered and drew him closer. "Then I want to take her out and get her a little drunk before I bring her home and make love with her all over again."

His mouth returned to hers, demanding, then possessing, then demanding again. All sensible thoughts floated from Foxy's mind.

CHAPTER 15

Foxy began her workday much later in the morning than was her habit. It was nearly eleven before she had finished sorting and cataloging the prints. As she slid them into a thick envelope for mailing she thought over the last few months. For a moment, as she brought it all back into her mind, she could almost smell the hot scent of fuel, hear the high squeal of tires and roaring engines. Shaking her head, she began to seal the envelope. *I'm finished with all that now. It's behind me.*

Briskly she began to develop the film she had taken of children in the park and around Boston. In the back of her mind, the idea for a book was germinating, a collection of photographs of children. Instinct told her that some of the shots were exceptional. *More time,* she mused, *more variety. I'll have to haunt a few more playgrounds.* Patiently she worked through the morning and early afternoon, letting her fingers act as her eyes when the room was dark. Still, her mind continued to drift to Lance.

Foxy knew the night spent in lovemaking had not solved any of their true problems. Again and again, her thoughts returned to the possibility of Lance going back to racing. Again and again, she closed off the idea. *Coward,* she accused herself as she stood in the dark. *You have to think about it, you have to deal with it. I don't know if I can.* She pressed her fingers against her eyes and took a deep breath. *I have to talk to him. Sensibly. Isn't that what he said? Tonight we'll talk sensibly.* She reflected that they had done little of that since he had asked her to marry him in her motel room near Watkins Glen. It was time, she decided, to find out what each of them wanted from the other, and what each was willing to give.

Locked in the darkroom with a red bulb casting its pale light, Foxy discovered one of the answers for herself. As she moved prints from tray to tray and images formed on the paper, she began to understand fully what she had been looking for. The faces of children looked back at her, some smiling, some caught in temper tantrums or tears. There were sleeping infants, moon-faced toddlers, sharp-eyed preschoolers. Foxy hung the prints with a growing sense of serenity. She wanted children. She wanted a family and all that went with it. The home, the normality, the commitment of a structured family was something she found she wanted and perhaps had been afraid to ask for. A permanent home with the man she loved . . . Lance's children . . . family traditions. *Her* family's traditions.

Would Lance feel the same way? Foxy pushed the hair from her face and tried to think of the answer. She discovered that as long as she had known him, as intimate as they had been, she did not know. *We will have to talk about it,* she told herself as she studied the drying prints. *We will have to talk about a number of things.*

A glance at her watch told her she still had a few afternoon hours left. It was time, she thought, to finish her commitment to Pam and the racing shots. After gathering up her gear, she went upstairs to put a call through to Lance's office. The quick, efficient voice of his secretary answered.

"Hello, Linda, it's Mrs. Matthews. Is Lance busy?"

"I'm sorry, Mrs. Matthews, he's not in. Would you like to leave a message or is there something I could do for you?"

"Well, no, I . . . Yes, actually," Foxy decided with another glance at her watch. She wanted to get this done today. "He's working on a new car, a new Formula One for next season."

"Yes, the one your brother will drive."

"That's right. I'd like to get some pictures if I can."

"That shouldn't be a problem, Mrs. Matthews, if you don't mind a bit of a drive. Mr. Matthews and the crew have the car out at the track today for some testing."

"That's perfect." Foxy picked up the pad and pencil by the phone. "You'll have to give me directions. I haven't been out there yet."

Thirty minutes later, Foxy pulled up near the familiar sight of the oval track. As she stepped from the car the brisk breeze caught at her hair and blew open her unbuttoned jacket. The roaring sound of the engine reached her ears. Shielding her eyes with her hand, she watched the low red blur whiz around the track. The smell of hot rubber and fuel filled the air. *It never changes,* she thought and slipped the strap of her camera around her neck. She recognized Charlie with a group of men, wondered fleetingly where Lance might be, then set to work.

Foxy moved quickly. After choosing the best position for the shots, she selected a lens and set the camera. With quick turns of the controls and shifts of her own body, she snapped shot after shot. It was, she observed, a fast one. The car seemed like a ball of flame as it rounded a curve and sped down the straightaway. *It will suit Kirk,* she mused, easily able to picture him in the cockpit. *And Kirk will suit it.* Foxy straightened, pushing her hair behind her ears as she stood.

"Can't keep you away from the track, huh, kid?"

Turning, Foxy grinned into Charlie's scowling face. "I

can't keep away from you, Charlie," she corrected. She plucked the smoldering cigar from his mouth and gave him a loud, smacking kiss. He shuffled his feet as she handed it back to him.

"Got no respect," he grumbled. He cleared his throat, then squinted at her. "You getting along all right?"

"I'm getting along just fine," she told him. Moving with an old habit, she rubbed her palm over his grizzled beard. "How about you?"

"Busy," he growled, but colored under his fierce frown. "Between your brother and your husband I got no time."

"Price you pay for being the best."

Charlie sniffed, accepting the truth. "Kirk'll be ready for the car when it's ready for him," he prophesied. "Shame we don't have two," he mused as he shifted his narrowed eyes back to the track. "Lance knows how to handle a machine."

Foxy started to make some comment when the full meaning of Charlie's statement sunk in. Her eyes flew to the track and locked on the speeding car. Lance. The iron taste of fear rose in her throat. She shook her head, trying to deny what her mind screamed was the truth. "Lance is driving?" she heard herself ask. Her voice sounded thin and hollow to her ears, as if it had traveled down a long tunnel.

"Yeah, regular test driver's sick." Charlie's answer was casual before he shuffled off. Foxy was left alone as the roaring sound of the engine droned on.

As she watched, the car did a quick fishtail on a curve, then straightened without any slackening of speed. Foxy's brow felt like ice. Queasiness knotted her stomach, and for a moment the bright sunlight dimmed. She chewed on her bottom lip and let the pain overwhelm the faintness. She stood helplessly while dozens of the crashes she remembered passed vividly in front of her mind's eye. *Not again,* she thought in desperation. *Oh God, not again.* He drove as he had always driven, with complete control and determination, not a comet, but a ruthless, cunning tyrant. Foxy began to shiver uncontrollably in the quick autumn breeze. *It'll be hot in the cockpit,* she thought as her fingers went numb on the strap of her camera. *Desperately hot, and all he sees is the track, all he hears is the engine. And the speed's like a drug that keeps pulling him back.*

Fear kept her frozen even after she heard the whine of the slowing engine. She stood straight and still as Lance pulled up near the group of men. Unstrapped, he unfolded himself from the cockpit, pulling off his helmet as he stood. He peeled off the balaclava, then ran a hand through his hair. She had seen him make the same gestures after countless races on countless grids. Pain began to work its way through the cold fear. Her breath became irregular. Lance was grinning down at Charlie, and his laughter carried to her. His brow lifted at something Charlie said, and his eyes followed the careless gesture of the older man until they found Foxy.

For a moment, they only watched each other; husband and wife, man and woman, two people who had known each other for a decade. She saw his expression change, but took no time to decipher it. Tears were coming too quickly for her to prevent them. *I've lost,* she thought, and pressed her hands against the sides of her face. As Lance pushed his way through the group of men Foxy turned and ran toward her car. He called her name, but she wrenched open the door and tumbled inside. The only coherent thought in her mind as she turned the key was escape. Seconds later, she was racing away from the track.

It was nearly dark when Foxy turned down the street toward the brownstone. Streetlights flickered on. Lance's car sat at the curb rather than in the garage, and she pulled her MG behind it. Foxy turned off the engine, and rested her forehead for a moment against the wheel. The two hours she had spent driving had calmed her but left her enervated. She took this time to gain back some strength. With slow, careful movements, she stepped from the car and moved up the walk. Even as she reached for the knob, the door opened. From either side of the threshold, they watched each other.

Lance studied her as if seeing her for the first time—thoroughly, carefully, with no smile to interfere with his concentration. His eyes were guarded but searching. The familiar stillness was on him. She was reminded of the first night, at Kirk's party, when she had opened the door to find him outside. He had looked at her in precisely the same way. *Will I ever get over him?* she wondered almost dispassionately as she met him look for look. *No,* she answered her own question. *Never.*

"Fox." Lance held out a hand to bring her inside, but she ignored it, moving around him. Carefully she set down her camera case but did not remove her jacket before she walked into the parlor. Without speaking, she moved to the bar and poured a snifter of brandy. Her decision had been made during her two-hour drive, but following through now was not going to be easy. Foxy swallowed brandy, shut her eyes as it burned her throat, then swallowed more. Lance stood in the doorway and watched her.

"I've been down to your darkroom looking for you." He frowned at the absence of color in her cheeks and dipped his hands in his pockets. "I saw the pictures you had drying. They're extraordinary, Foxy. You're extraordinary. Every time I think I know who you are, I find another part of you." When she turned to face him fully, he came into the room. "I owe you an explanation for this afternoon."

"No." Foxy shook her head as she set the snifter down on a table. "You told me before your profession had nothing to do with me." Her eyes lifted and held steady on his. "I don't want an explanation."

He took a step closer. The shadows in the room shifted with the movement. "Well then, Foxy, what do you want?"

"A divorce," she said simply. Feeling the pressure of emotions rising in her throat, she spoke quickly. "We made a mistake, Lance, and the sooner we fix it, the easier it should be for both of us."

"You think so?" he countered. His eyes were level with hers.

"It should be easy enough to arrange," she returned, evading the question. "I'd like you to do it since you have lawyers and I don't. I don't want any settlement."

"Another drink?" Lance asked, and turned to the bar.

His casual tone had her eyeing him warily. "Yes," she answered, wanting to appear as composed as he. The room grew quiet save for the clink of glass against glass. With the decanter in hand, Lance crossed to Foxy and filled the snifter again. The sun slanted low in the window and fell at their feet. Foxy sipped, wondering with a flash of giddyness if they should toast their divorce plans.

"No," Lance said, then drank.

"No?" Foxy repeated, wondering now if he had seen into her mind.

"No, Foxy, you can't have a divorce. Can I interest you in something else?"

Her eyes widened, then narrowed at his arrogance. "I'll have a divorce. I'll get a lawyer of my own and sue you for one." She slammed down her glass. "You can't stop me."

"I'll fight you, Fox," he countered with easy assurance as he placed his glass beside hers. "And I'll win." Reaching out, he stroked her hair. "I'm not going to let you go. Not now, not ever. I told you before, I'm a selfish man." Giving her hair a tug, he tumbled her into his arms. "I love you and have no intentions of doing without you."

"How dare you?" Furious, Foxy pushed against him. "How

dare you think so much of yourself that you give no thought to my feelings? You don't know anything about love." She kicked out in frustration as her struggles got her nowhere.

"Foxy, you're going to hurt yourself." Lance locked his arms around her and lifted her off her feet. For a moment, she fought against him, then subsided. She shut her eyes, infuriated that she had to surrender on any level.

"Let go of me." Her voice came from between her teeth, but was quiet and even.

"Will you listen to me now?"

She jerked back her head, wanting to refuse. Her eyes were bright with anger and hurt. "I don't have much choice, do I?"

"Please."

The one simple word knocked her off balance. The word was in his eyes as well. Defeated, Foxy nodded. When Lance released her, she stepped away, moving to the window. The early moon was white and full and promising. Its light fell in showers over the naked trees and glittered over scattered leaves. Foxy thought nothing had ever seemed so lonely.

"I had no idea you were coming out to the track today."

Foxy gave a quick laugh, then rested her forehead against the glass. "Did you think what I didn't know wouldn't hurt me?"

"Fox." The tone of his voice persuaded her to turn and face him. "I didn't think at all, that's the point." He made a quick, uncharacteristic gesture of frustration. "I test the cars from time to time, it's a habit of mine. It didn't occur to me until I turned and saw you standing there how it would affect you."

"Would it have made a difference?"

"Damn it, Foxy!" His voice was hard and impatient.

"Is that an unreasonable question?" she returned. She began to wander about the room as she found standing still was impossible. "It doesn't seem like one to me. It seems perfectly justified. I've discovered something about myself in the past month. I can't be second with you." Foxy paused, taking a deep breath. "I have to be first, I can't ride in the backseat with you the way I've always done with Kirk. It's not at all the same thing. I want—need something solid, something permanent. I've been waiting for it my whole life. This house . . ." She made a helpless gesture as her thoughts came almost too quickly for the words to keep pace. "I want what it stands for. It doesn't matter if we leave it a dozen times a year to go to a dozen different places, as long as it's here to come back to. I want stability, I want commitment, I want a home, children. Your children." Her voice quivered with her feelings, but she turned, dry-eyed, to look up at him. "I want it all, everything."

Foxy turned away again and swallowed. She took two long breaths, hoping they would steady her. "When I saw you in that car this afternoon . . ." Emotions swamped her, and she shook her head before she could continue. "I can't explain what it does to me. Perhaps it's unreasonable, but I can't control it." Pressing the heel of her hand between her eyes, Foxy tried to speak calmly. "I can't live like that again. I love you, and sometimes I can't quite believe that we're together. I don't want you to be anything but what you are. And I know the things I want might not be what's important to you. But when I think about you going back to racing, I . . ."

"Why should I go back to racing?" The question was calm and curious.

Foxy moved her shoulders hopelessly. "You said you might the day I found out about Kirk's new car. I know it's important to you."

"Do you think I would do that to you?" This time the tone of his voice brought Foxy's eyes to his. "Have you been thinking that all this time?" He moved to her, then placed both hands on her shoulders. "I'm not interested in racing again. But if I were, I'd manage to do without it. I'm more interested in my wife, Fox." He shook her, but the gesture was more caress than punishment. "How could I consider racing when I know what it does to you? Can't you see you are first in my life?"

She opened her mouth to speak, but only managed to shake her head before he continued. "No, you probably don't. I don't suppose I've made things very clear. It's time that I did." He rubbed her shoulders lightly before he dropped his hands. "In the first place, I pressured you into marriage, taking advantage of Kirk's accident. I've had some bad moments because of that. Let me finish," he told her as she started to protest. "I wanted you, and that night you looked so lost. I snatched you into marriage and rushed you up to Boston without giving you any of the frills you were entitled to. The truth is, I was afraid you might get away, and I told myself I'd make it up to you after we were married."

"Lance," Foxy interrupted and lifted a hand to his cheek. "I don't need frills."

"Is this the woman who once compared a garage to Manderley?" he countered. He took her fingers to his lips, then let them go. "Maybe I need to give them to you, Foxy. Maybe that's why I was devoured with jealousy at the thought of you spending the afternoon in the park with Jonathan. I should have been with you. I rushed you into being my wife and never bothered to discuss the finer points." With his hands in his pockets, he turned away and roamed about the room. "It's difficult to be patient when you've been in love for nearly ten years."

"What?" Foxy stared at him, then slowly lowered herself to the arm of the sofa. "What did you say about ten years?"

Lance turned to her with his tilted smile. "Maybe if I had explained myself in the beginning, we could have avoided some of these problems. I don't know when I started loving you. It's hard to remember a time when I didn't. You were an adolescent with fabulous eyes and a woman's laugh. You nearly drove me out of my mind."

"Why . . . why didn't you tell me?"

"Fox, you were little more than a child. I was a grown man." With a laugh, he ran his hand through his hair. "Kirk was my best friend. If I had touched you, he would have killed me with perfect justification. No, I couldn't sleep that night at Le Mans because this sixteen-year-old girl was making me crazy. In the garage when I turned around and you all but fell into my arms, I wanted you so badly it hurt. Badly enough that I took my defense in cruelty. Driving you away from me was the only decent thing to do. God, you terrified me."

Shaking his head, he lifted Foxy's neglected drink. "I knew I had to give you time to grow up, time to form your own life. The six years I didn't see you were incredibly long. It was during that time that I started building cars and moved into this house." He turned and looked at her again. "I always pictured you here. It seemed right somehow. You belonged here with me, I felt it. I've never made love to another woman in this house." He set down the glass, and his eyes grew dark and intense. "There's never been anyone but you. Shadows, substitutes at best. I've wanted other women, but I've never loved anyone else. I've never needed anyone else."

Foxy swallowed, not certain she could trust her voice. "Lance, do you need me?"

"Only for day-to-day living." He moved to her, then ran a hand down her hair. "I've learned a few things in the past weeks. You can hurt me." He traced a finger down the side of her throat as his eyes met hers. "I'd never considered that possibility. What you think of me matters. I've never given a damn what anyone thought of me before. You become more important to me in dozens of ways every day. And my need for you doesn't soften." He smiled slowly. "And you still terrify me."

Foxy returned his smile, feeling the blanketing warmth of contentment. "I suppose this sort of marriage will never be completely smooth and settled."

"I shouldn't think so."

"I suppose it'll always be somewhat tempestuous and demanding."

"And interesting," Lance added.

"I suppose when two people have been in love for as long as we have, they can be quite stubborn about it." She lifted her arms. "I've always loved you, you know, even through all the years I tried not to. Coming back to you was coming home. I want you to kiss me until I can't breathe."

Even as she spoke, Lance's mouth claimed hers. "Foxy," he murmured at length and rested his cheek against hers.

"No, no, I'm still breathing." Thirsty, her mouth sought his until he abandoned his gentle caress. Wild, turbulent, electric, their lips met over and over as the room grew soft with dusk. "Oh, Lance." Foxy held him tightly a moment, then lifted his face and combed her fingers through his hair. "How could we both be such idiots and not tell each other what we were feeling?"

"We're both new at marriage, Fox." He rubbed his nose against hers. "We just have to practice more."

"I feel like a wife." She wrapped her arms around his neck and pulled him close. "I feel very much like a wife. I like it."

"I think a wife should have a honeymoon," Lance murmured as he began to enjoy the privileges of a husband. "I should have told you that I've been spending a great deal of extra time at the office so that I could manage a couple of weeks away. Starting now. Where would you like to go?"

"Anywhere?" she asked, floating under the drugging power of his hands.

"Anywhere."

"Nowhere," she decided as she slipped her hands under his

sweater. His back was taut and warm under her palms. "I've heard the service is great here." She smiled up at him when he lifted his face. "And I love the view." Reaching up and behind, Foxy found the phone and tugged it over her head. "Here, call Mrs. Trilby and tell her we've gone to . . . Fiji for two weeks. Give her a vacation. We'll lock the door and take the phone off the hook and disappear."

"I married a very smart woman," Lance concluded. He took the phone, dropping it on the floor with the receiver off. "I'll call her later . . . much later." Lowering his mouth, he rubbed it gently over Foxy's. "You did say something about children, didn't you?"

The eyes that were beginning to close opened again. "Yes, I did."

"How many did you have in mind?" he asked as he kissed the lids closed again.

"I hadn't thought of a number," Foxy murmured.

"Why don't we start with one and work from there?" Lance suggested. "An important project like this should be started immediately, don't you think?"

"Absolutely," Foxy agreed. Dusk became night as their mouths met again.

Rules of the Game

CHAPTER 1

A jock. Terrific." Brooke took a long swallow of strong black coffee, tipped back in her glove-soft leather chair and scowled. "I love it."

"No need to be sarcastic," Claire returned mildly. "If de Marco wants to use an athlete for promotion, why should you object?" She gazed absently at the chunky gold ring on her right hand. "After all," Claire continued in her dry voice, "you'll be making quite a bit directing the commercials."

Brooke sent Claire a characteristic look. Direct, uncompromising gray eyes bored into the soft blue of the older woman's. One of Brooke's greatest talents, and her greatest weapons, was her ability to stare down anyone from a corporate president to a temperamental actor. She'd developed the knack early as a defense against her own insecurity and had since refined it to an art. It was an art, however, that didn't impress Claire Thorton. At forty-nine, she was the head of a multimillion-dollar company that she'd started with brains and guts. For nearly a quarter of a century, she had run things her way, and she intended to keep right on doing so.

She'd known Brooke for ten years—since Brooke had been an eighteen-year-old upstart who had wheedled her way into a job with Thorton Productions. Then she'd watched Brooke work her way up from gofer to gaffer, from gaffer to assistant cameraman and from there to director. Claire had never regretted the impulse that had led her to give Brooke her first fifteen-second commercial.

Intuition had been the basis for Claire's success with Thorton Productions, and intuitively she had sensed sharp talent in Brooke Gordon. In addition, Claire knew her, understood her, as few others did. Perhaps it was because they shared two basic traits—ambition and independence.

After a moment, Brooke gave up with a sigh. "A jock," she muttered again as she gazed around her office.

It was one small room, the pale amber walls lined with prints of stills from dozens of her commercials. There was a two-cushion sofa—reupholstered in chocolate-colored corduroy—not comfortable enough to encourage long visits. The chair with a tufted back had been picked up at a yard sale along with a coffee table that leaned slightly to the left.

Brooke sat behind an old, scarred desk that had a drawer that wouldn't quite close. On it were piles of papers, a gooseneck lamp and assorted disposable pens and broken pencils. The pens and pencils were jammed in a Sevres vase. Behind her at the window, a dieffenbachia was slowly dying in an exquisitely worked pottery bowl.

"Damn, Claire, why can't they get an actor?" Brooke tossed up her hands in her one theatrical gesture, then dropped her chin on them. "Do you know what it's like to try to coax ballplayers and rock stars to say a line without freezing or hamming it up?" With a disgusted mutter that gave no room for comment, she pushed the pile of papers into a semiordered heap. "One call to a casting agent and I could have a hundred qualified actors parading through here itching for the job."

Patiently, Claire brushed a speck of lint from the sleeve

of her rose linen suit. "You know it increases sales if a production's hyped by a recognizable name or familiar face."

"Recognizable name?" Brooke tossed back. "Who's ever heard of Parks Jones? *Stupid* name," she muttered to herself.

"Every baseball fan in the country." The mild smile told Brooke it was useless to argue. Therefore, she prepared to argue further.

"We're selling clothes, not Louisville Sluggers."

"Eight Golden Gloves," Claire went on. "A lifetime batting average of three twenty-five. He's leading the league in RBIs this season. Jones has been at third base in the All-Star game for eight consecutive seasons."

Brooke narrowed her eyes. "How do you know so much? You don't follow baseball."

"I do my homework." A cool smile touched Claire's round, pampered face. She'd never had a face-lift but was religious about her visits to Elizabeth Arden. "That's why I'm a successful producer. Now you'd better do yours." She rose languidly. "Don't make any plans, I've got tickets for the game tonight. Kings against the Valiants."

"Who?"

"Do your homework," Claire advised before she closed the office door behind her.

With an exasperated oath, Brooke swiveled her chair around so that she faced her view of Los Angeles—tall buildings, glittering glass and clogged traffic. She'd had other views of L.A. during the rise in her career, but they'd been closer to street level. Now, she looked out on the city from the twentieth floor. The distance meant success, but Brooke didn't dwell on it. To do that would have encouraged thinking of the past—something Brooke meticulously avoided.

Leaning back in the oversized chair, Brooke toyed with the end of her braid. Her hair was the warm soft red shot with gold that painters attempted to immortalize. It was long and thick and unruly. Brooke was feminine enough not to want it cut to a more manageable length and practical enough to subdue it into a fat braid during working hours. It hung down the back of a thin silk blouse past the waistband of overworked blue jeans.

Her eyes as she mulled over Claire's words were thoughtful. They had misty gray irises, long lids and were surrounded by lashes in the same fragile shade as her hair. She rarely thought to darken them. Her skin was the delicate ivory-rose her hair demanded but the frailty stopped there. Her nose was small and sharp, her mouth wide, her chin aggressive. It was an unsettling face—beautiful one moment, austere the next, but always demanding. She wore a hasty dab of rose lipstick, enameled dimestore earrings and a splash of two-hundred-dollar-an-ounce perfume.

She thought about the de Marco account—designer jeans, exclusive sportswear and soft Italian leather. Since they'd decided to move their advertising beyond the glossy pages of fashion magazines and into television, they had come to Thorton Productions, and so to her. It was a fat two-year contract with a budget that would give Brooke all the artistic room she could want. She told herself she deserved it. There were three Clios on the corner shelf to her right.

Not bad, she mused, for a twenty-eight-year-old woman who had walked into Thorton Productions with a high school diploma, a glib tongue and sweaty palms. And twelve dollars and fifty-three cents in her pocket, Brooke remembered; then she pushed the thought aside. If she wanted the de Marco account—and she did—she would simply have to make the ballplayer work. Grimly, she swung her chair back to face her desk. Picking up the phone, Brooke punched two buttons.

"Get me everything we have on Parks Jones," she ordered as she shuffled papers out of her way. "And ask Ms. Thorton what time I'm to pick her up tonight."

Less than six blocks away, Parks Jones stuck his hands in his pockets and scowled at his agent. "How did I ever let you talk me into this?"

Lee Dutton gave a smile that revealed slightly crooked teeth and a lot of charm. "You trust me."

"My first mistake." Parks studied Lee, a not quite homely, avuncular figure with a receding hairline, puckish face and unnerving black eyes. Yes, he trusted him, Parks thought, he even liked the shrewd little devil, but . . . "I'm not a damn model, Lee. I'm a third baseman."

"You're not modeling," Lee countered. As he folded his hands, the sun glinted on the band of his thin Swiss watch. "You're endorsing. Ballplayers have been doing it since the first razor blade."

Parks snorted then walked around the tidy, Oriental-designed office. "This isn't a shaving commercial, and I'm not endorsing a mitt. It's clothes, for God's sake. I'm going to feel like an idiot."

But you won't look like one, Lee thought as he drew out a fragrant, slim cigar. Lighting it, he studied Parks over the flame. The long, lanky body was perfect for de Marco's—as was the blond, unmistakably California look. Parks's tanned, lean face, navy-blue eyes and tousled curling hair had already made him a favorite with the female fans, while his friendly, laid-back charm had won over the men. He was talented, easy to look at and personable. In short, Lee concluded, he was a natural. The fact that he was intelligent was at times as much a disadvantage as an advantage.

"Parks, you're hot." Lee said it with a sigh that they both knew was calculated. "You're also thirty-three. How much longer are you going to play ball?"

Parks answered with a glare. Lee knew of his vow to retire at thirty-five. "What does that have to do with it?"

"There are a lot of ballplayers, exceptional ballplayers, who slip into oblivion when they walk off the diamond for the last time. You have to think of the future."

"I *have* thought of the future," Parks reminded him. "Maui—fishing, sleeping in the sun, ogling women."

That would last about six weeks, Lee calculated, but he wisely kept silent.

"Lee." Parks flopped into a deep red chair and stretched out his legs. "I don't need the money. So why am I going to be working this winter instead of lying on the beach?"

"Because it's going to be good for you," Lee began. "It's good for the game. The campaign will enhance the image of baseball. And," he added with one of his puckish smiles, "because you signed a contract."

"I'm going to get in some extra batting practice," Parks muttered as he rose. When he reached the door, he turned back with a suspiciously friendly smile. "One thing. If I make a fool of myself, I'm going to break the legs on your Tang horse."

Brooke screeched through the electronically controlled gates then swerved up the rhododendron-lined drive that led to Claire's mansion. Privately, Brooke considered it a beautiful anachronism. It was huge, white, multileveled and pillared. Brooke liked to imagine two black-helmeted guards, rifles on shoulders, flanking the carved double doors. The estate had originally belonged to a silent movie idol who had supposedly decked out the rooms in pastel silks and satins.

Fifteen years before, Claire had purchased it from a perfume baron and had proceeded to redecorate it with her own passion for Asian art.

Brooke stomped on the brake of her Datsun, screaming to a halt in front of the white marble steps. She drove at two speeds: stop and go. Stepping out of the car, she breathed in the exotic garden scents of vanilla and jasmine before striding up the stairs in the loose-limbed gait that came from a combination of long legs and preoccupation. In a crowd, her walk would cause men's heads to turn but Brooke neither noticed nor cared.

She knocked briskly on the door, then impatiently turned the handle. Finding it unlocked, she walked into the spacious mint-green hall and shouted.

"Claire! Are you ready? I'm starving." A neat little woman in a tailored gray uniform came through a doorway to the left. "Hello, Billings." Brooke smiled at her and tossed her braid over her shoulder. "Where's Claire? I haven't the energy to search through this labyrinth for her."

"She's dressing, Ms. Gordon." The housekeeper spoke in modulated British tones, responding to Brooke's smile with a nod. "She'll be down shortly. Would you care for a drink?"

"Just some Perrier, it's muggy out." Brooke followed the housekeeper into the drawing room then slumped down on a divan. "Did she tell you where we're going?"

"To a baseball game, miss?" Billings set ice in a glass and added sparkling water. "Some lime?"

"Just a squirt. Come on, Billings." Brooke's smoky contralto became conspiratorial. "What do you think?"

Billings meticulously squeezed lime into the bubbly water. She'd been housekeeper for Lord and Lady Westbrook in Devon before being prized away by Claire Thorton. On accepting the position, she had vowed never to become Americanized. Edna Billings had her standards. But she'd never quite been able to resist responding to Brooke. A naughty young girl, she'd thought a decade before, and the opinion remained unchanged. Perhaps that was why Billings was so fond of her.

"I much prefer cricket," she said blandly. "A more civilized game." She handed Brooke the glass.

"Can you see Claire sitting in the bleachers?" Brooke demanded. "Surrounded by screaming, sweaty fans, watching a bunch of grown men swing at a little ball and run around in circles?"

"If I'm not mistaken," Billings said slowly, "there's a bit more to it than that."

"Sure, RBIs and ERAs and putouts and shutouts." Brooke heaved a long breath. "What the hell is a squeeze play?"

"I'm sure I have no idea."

"Doesn't matter." Brooke shrugged and gulped down some Perrier. "Claire has it in her head that watching this guy in action will give me some inspiration." She ran a fingertip down a shocking-orange ginger jar. "What I really need is a meal."

"You can get a hot dog and some beer in the park," Claire announced from the doorway.

Glancing up, Brooke gave a hoot of laughter. Claire was immaculately dressed in buff-colored linen slacks and a tailored print blouse with low alligator pumps. "You're going to a ball game," Brooke reminded her, "not a museum. And I hate beer."

"A pity." Opening her alligator bag, Claire checked the contents before snapping it shut again. "Let's be on our way, then, we don't want to miss anything. Good night, Billings."

Gulping down the rest of her drink, Brooke bolted to her feet and raced after Claire. "Let's stop to eat on the way," she suggested. "It's not like missing the first act of the opera, and I had to skip lunch." She tried her forlorn orphan's look. "You know how cranky I get if I miss a meal."

"We're going to have to start putting you in front of the camera, Brooke; you're getting better all the time." With a slight frown at the low-slung Datsun, Claire maneuvered herself inside. She also knew Brooke's obsession with regular meals sprang from her lean adolescence. "Two hot dogs," she suggested, wisely buckling her seat belt. "It takes forty-five minutes to get to the stadium." Claire fluffed her silver-frosted brunette hair. "That means you should get us there in about twenty-five."

Brooke swore and rammed the car into first. In just over thirty minutes, she was hunting for a parking space outside of Kings Stadium. ". . . and the kid got it perfect on the first take," Brooke continued blithely, swerving around cars with a bullfighter's determination. "The two adult actors messed up, and the table collapsed so that it took fourteen takes, but the kid had it cold every time." She gave a loud war whoop as she spotted an empty space, swung into it, barely nosing out another car, then stopped with a jaw-snapping jerk. "I want you to take a look at the film before it's edited."

"What have you got in mind?" With some difficulty, Claire climbed out of the door, squeezing herself between the Datsun and the car parked inches beside it.

"You're casting for that TV movie, *Family in Decline*." Brooke slammed her door then leaned over the hood. "I don't think you're going to want to look any further for the part of Buddy. The kid's good, really, really good."

"I'll take a look."

Together, they followed the crowd swarming toward the stadium. There was a scent of heated asphalt, heavy air and damp humanity—Los Angeles in August. Above them the sky was darkening so that the stadium lights sent up a white misty glow. Inside, they walked past the stands that hawked pennants and pictures and programs. Brooke could smell popcorn and grilled meat, the tang of beer. Her stomach responded accordingly.

"Do you know where you're going?" she demanded.

"I always know where I'm going," Claire replied, turning into an aisle that sloped downward.

They emerged to find the stadium bright as daylight and crammed with bodies. There was the continual buzz of thousands of voices over piped-in, soft-rock music. Walking vendors carried trays of food and drink strapped over their shoulders. Excitement. Brooke could feel the electricity of it coming in waves. Instantly, her own apathy vanished to be replaced by an avid curiosity. People were her obsession, and here they were, thousands of them, packed together in a circle around a field of green grass and brown dirt.

Something other than hunger began to stir in her.

"Look at them all, Claire," she murmured. "Is it always like this? I wonder."

"The Kings are having a winning season. They're leading their division by three games, have two potential twenty-game-winning pitchers and a third baseman who's batting three seventy-eight for the year." She sent Brooke a lifted-brow look. "I told you to do your homework."

"Mmm-hmm." But Brooke was too caught up in the people. Who were they? Where did they come from? Where did they go after the game was over?

There were two old men, perched on chairs, their hands between their knees as they argued over the game that hadn't yet started. Oh, for a cameraman, Brooke thought, spotting a five-year-old in a Kings fielder's cap gazing up at the two gnarled fans. She followed Claire down the steps slowly, letting her eyes record everything. She liked the size of it, the noise, the smell of damp, crowded bodies, the color.

Navy-blue-and-white Kings pennants were waved; children crammed pink cotton candy into their mouths. A teenager was making a play for a cute little blonde in front of him who pretended she wasn't interested.

Abruptly Brooke stopped, dropping her hand on Claire's shoulder. "Isn't that Brighton Boyd?"

Claire glanced to the left to see the Oscar-winning actor munching peanuts from a white paper bag. "Yes. Let's see now, this is our box." She scooted in, then lifted a friendly hand to the actor before she sat. "This should do very well," Claire observed with a satisfied nod. "We're quite close to third base here."

Still looking at everything at once, Brooke dropped into her chair. The Colosseum in Rome, she thought, must have had the same feel before the gladiators trooped out. If she were to do a commercial on baseball, it wouldn't be of the game, but of the crowd. A pan, with the sound low—then gradually increase it as the camera closed in. Then, *bam!* Full volume, full effect. Clichéd or not, it was quintessentially American.

"Here you go, dear." Claire disrupted her thoughts by handing her a hot dog. "My treat."

"Thanks." After taking a healthy bite, Brooke continued with her mouth full. "Who does the advertising for the team, Claire?"

"Just concentrate on third base," Claire advised as she sipped at a beer.

"Yes, but—" The crowd roared as the home team took the field. Brooke watched the men move to their positions, dressed in dazzling white with navy-blue caps and baseball socks. They didn't look foolish, she mused as the fans continued to cheer. They looked rather heroic. She focused on the man on third.

Parks's back was to her as he kicked up a bit of dust around the base. But Brooke didn't strain to see his face. At the moment, she didn't need it—his build was enough. Six-one, she estimated, a bit surprised by his height. No more than a hundred and sixty pounds—but not thin. She leaned her elbows on the rail, resting her chin on her hands.

He's lanky, she thought. He'll show off clothes well. Parks dipped for a grounder then returned it to short. For an instant, Brooke's thoughts scattered. Something intruded on her professional survey that she quickly brushed aside. The way he moved, she thought. Catlike? No. She shook her head. No, he was all man.

She waited, unconsciously holding her breath as he fielded another grounder. He moved loosely, apparently effortlessly, but she sensed a tight control as he stepped, bent, pivoted. It was a fluid action—feet, legs, hips, arm. A dancer had the same sort of nonchalant perfection after practicing a basic routine for years. If she could keep him moving, Brooke mused, it wouldn't matter if the man couldn't say his own name on camera.

There was an unexpected sexuality in every gesture. It was there even when he stood, idly wanting to field another practice ball. It might just work after all, Brooke reflected as her eyes roamed up his body, brushing over the blond curls that sprang around the sides and back of his cap. It might just . . .

Then he turned. Brooke found herself staring full into his face. It was long and lean like his body, a bit reminiscent of the gladiators she'd been thinking about earlier. Because he was concentrating, his full, passionate mouth was unsmiling; the eyes, almost the same shade as the navy hat that shaded them, were brooding. He looked fierce, almost warlike, definitely dangerous. Whatever Brooke had been expecting, it hadn't been this tough, uncompromisingly sexy face or her own reaction to it.

Someone called out to him from the stands. Abruptly, he grinned, transforming into a friendly, approachable man with an aura of easy charm. Brooke's muscles relaxed.

"What do you think of him?"

A bit dazed, Brooke leaned back in her chair and absently munched on her hot dog. "He might work," she murmured. "He moves well."

"From what I've been told," Claire said dryly, "you haven't seen anything yet."

As usual, Claire was right. In the first inning, Parks made a diving catch along the baseline at third for the final out. He batted fourth, lining a long single to left field that he stretched into a double. He played, Brooke thought, with the enthusiasm of a kid and the diabolical determination of a veteran. She didn't have to know anything about the game to know the combination was unstoppable.

In motion, he was a pleasure to watch. Relaxed now, the first staggering impression behind her, Brooke began to consider the angles. If his voice was as good as the rest of him, she mused. Well . . . that was yet to be seen. After polishing off another hot dog, she resumed her position leaning against the rail. The Kings were ahead 2-1 in the fifth inning. The crowd was frantic. Brooke decided she would use some action shots of Parks in slow motion.

It was hot and still on the diamond. A fitful breeze fluttered the flag and cooled the spectators high up in the stands, but below, under the lights, the air was thick. Parks felt the sweat run down his back as he stood on the infield grass. Hernandez, the pitcher, was falling behind on the batter. Parks knew Rathers to be a power hitter who pulled to the left. He planted himself behind the bag and waited. He saw the pitch—a waist-high fast ball—heard the crack of the bat. In that one millisecond, he had two choices: catch the ball that was lined hard at him or end up with a hole in his chest. He caught it, and felt the vibration of power sing through his body before he heard the screams of the crowd.

A routine catch, most would say. Parks was surprised the ball hadn't carried him out of the stadium. "Got any leather left on your glove?" the shortstop called to him as they headed back to the dugout. Parks shot him a grin before he let his eyes drift up to the stands. His eyes locked on Brooke's, surprising them both.

In reaction, Parks slowed a bit. Now there was a face, he thought, a man wouldn't see every day. She looked a bit like a ravished eighteenth-century aristocrat with her wild mane of hair and English rose skin. He felt an immediate tightening in his stomach. The face exuded cool, forbidden sex. But the eyes . . . His never left them as he approached the dugout. The eyes were soft-gray and direct as an arrow. She stared back at him without a blink or a blush, not smiling as most fans would do if they were bold, or looking away if they were shy. She just stared, Parks thought, as if she were dissecting him. With simultaneous twinges of annoyance and curiosity, he stepped into the dugout.

He thought about her as he sat on the bench. Here, the atmosphere was subdued and tense. Every game was important now if they were to maintain their lead and win the division pennant. Parks had the personal pressure of having a shot at a four hundred batting average for the year. It was something he struggled not to think about and was constantly reminded of by the press. He watched the leadoff batter ground out and thought of the redhead in the box behind third base.

Why had she looked at him like that? As if she wondered how he would look on a trophy case. With a soft oath, Parks rose and put on his batting helmet. He'd better get his mind off the little number in the stands and on the game. Hernandez was slowing down, and the Kings needed some insurance runs.

The second batter bounced one to shallow right and beat out the ball. Parks went to stand on deck. He stretched his arms over his head, one hand on the grip, the other on the barrel. He felt loose and warm and ready. Irresistibly, his eyes were drawn to his left. He couldn't see Brooke clearly from this distance, but he sensed she watched him still. Fresh annoyance broke through him. When the batter flied out, Parks approached the box.

What was her problem, anyway? he demanded as he took a testing swing. It would have been simpler if he could have characterized her as a typical Baseball Annie, but there was nothing typical about that face—or about those eyes. Planting his feet, he crouched into position and waited for the pitch. It came in high and sweet. Parks took a cut at it just before the ball dropped.

Coolly, he stepped out of the box and adjusted his helmet before he took his batting stance again. The next ball missed the corner and evened the count. Patience was the core of Parks's talent. He could wait, even when the pressure was on, for the pitch he wanted. So he waited, taking another ball and an inside strike. The crowd was screaming, begging for a hit, but he concentrated on the pitcher.

The ball came at him, at ninety miles an hour, but he had it judged. This was the one he wanted. Parks swung, getting the meat of the bat on the ball. He knew it was gone the moment he heard the crack. So did the pitcher, who watched his two-strike pitch sail out of the park.

Parks jogged around the bases while the crowd roared. He acknowledged the slap of the first base coach with a quick grin. He'd never lost his childlike pleasure in hitting the long

ball. As he rounded second, he automatically looked over at
Brooke. She was sitting, chin on the rail, while the crowd
jumped and screamed around her. There was the same quiet
intensity in her eyes—no light of congratulations, no pleasure. Irritated, Parks tried to outstare her as he rounded third.
Her eyes never faltered as he turned for home. He crossed
the plate, exhilarated by the homer and furious with an unknown woman.

"Isn't that marvelous?" Claire beamed over at Brooke.
"That's his thirty-sixth home run this season. A very talented
young man." She signaled a roving concessionaire for another
drink. "He was staring at you."

"Mmm-hmm." Brooke wasn't willing to admit that her
pulse rate had soared with each eye contact. She knew his
type—good-looking, successful and heartless. She met them
every day. "He'll look good on camera."

Claire laughed with the comfortable pleasure of a woman
approaching fifty. "He'd look good anywhere."

Brooke's answer was a shrug as the game went into its seventh inning. She paid no attention to the score or to the other
players as she watched Parks steadily. She remained, arms
over the rail, chin on hands, booted feet crossed. There was
something about him, she mused, something beyond the obvious attraction, the basic sexuality. It was that looseness of
movement overlying the discipline. That's what she wanted
to capture. The combination would do more than sell de
Marco's clothes, it would typify them. All she had to do was
guide Parks Jones through the steps.

She'd have him swinging a bat in immaculately sophisticated sports clothes—maybe riding through the surf in de
Marco jeans. Athletic shots—that's what he was built for.
And if she could get any humor out of him, something with
women. She didn't want the usual adoring stares or knowing looks, but something fanciful and funny. If the script

writers could pull it off and Jones could take any sort of direction. Refusing to look at the ifs, Brooke told herself she would make it work. Within the year, every woman would want Parks Jones and every man would envy him.

The ball was hit high and was curving foul. Parks chased after it, racing all the way to the seats before it dropped into the crowd four rows back. Brooke found herself face-to-face with him, close enough to smell the faint muskiness of his sweat and to see it run down the side of his face. Their eyes met again, but she didn't move, partly because she was interested, partly because she was paralyzed. The only thing that showed in her eyes was mild curiosity. Behind them there were shouts of triumph as someone snagged the foul as a trophy.

Enraged, Parks stared back at her. "Your name?" he demanded in undertones.

He had that fierce, dangerous look on his face again. Brooke schooled her voice to calmness. "Brooke."

"All of it, damn it," Parks muttered, pressed for time and furious with himself. He watched one thin eyebrow lift and found himself wanting to yank her out of the stands.

"Gordon," Brooke told him smoothly. "Is the game over?"

Parks narrowed his eyes before he moved away. Brooke heard him speak softly. "It's just beginning."

CHAPTER 2

Brooke had been expecting the call—after all, he had her name, and her name was in the book. But she hadn't been expecting it at six-fifteen on a Sunday morning.

Groggily, she groped for the phone as it shrilled, managing to grip the receiver as the cradle fell heavily to the floor. "'Lo," she mumbled without opening her eyes.

"Brooke Gordon?"

"Mmm." She snuggled back into the pillow. "Yeah."

"It's Parks Jones."

Instantly alert, Brooke opened her eyes. The light was soft and dim with dawn, early birds just beginning to chirp. She fumbled for the dented windup alarm beside her bed, then scowled at the time. Biting back a torrent of abuse, she kept her voice soft and sulky. "Who?"

Parks shifted the receiver to his other hand and scowled. "Parks Jones, third base. The Kings game the other night."

Brooke yawned, taking her time about fluffing up her pillow. "Oh," was all she said, but a smile flashed wickedly.

"Look, I want to see you. We're flying back after the game in New York this afternoon. How about a late dinner?" Why was he doing this? he asked himself as he paced the small hotel room. And why, in God's name, wasn't he doing it with a bit more style?

"Dinner," Brooke repeated languidly while her mind worked fast. Wasn't it just like his type to expect a woman to have no plans that couldn't be altered to suit him? Her first instinct was to give him a cold refusal, then her sense of the ridiculous got the better of her. "Well . . ." She drew out the word. "Maybe. What time?"

"I'll pick you up at nine," Parks told her, ignoring the maybe. When he couldn't get a woman out of his head for three days, he was going to find out why. "I've got the address."

"All right, Sparks, nine o'clock."

"Parks," he corrected tersely and broke the connection.

Falling back on the pillow, Brooke started to laugh.

She was still in high good humor when she dressed that evening. Still, she thought it was too bad that the file she had read on Parks hadn't contained a bit more than all those baseball statistics. A few personal details would have given her more of an edge. What would Parks Jones have to say if he knew he was taking his future director to dinner? she wondered. Somehow Brooke didn't think he'd be too pleased when he learned she'd left out that little piece of information. But the whole scenario was too good to miss. And there was the fact that he'd touched off something in her that she wanted to get out of her system before they started to work together.

Wrapped in a bath towel, Brooke pondered her wardrobe. She didn't date often—her choice. Early experience had influenced her attitude toward men. If they were good-looking and charming, Brooke steered clear of them.

She'd been only seventeen when she'd met her first good-looking charmer. He'd been twenty-two and fresh out of college. When he'd come into the diner where she

had worked, Clark had been quick with a joke and generous
with a tip. It had started with a late movie once or twice a
week, then an afternoon picnic in the park. It hadn't bothered Brooke that he wasn't working. He'd told her he was
taking the summer off before he settled down to a job.

His family was well connected, genteel and Bostonian.
The genteel, Clark had explained with an acerbic humor that
had fascinated her, meant there were plenty of heirlooms
and little ready cash. They had plans for him that he was
consistently vague about with the carelessness of the young.
He'd mentioned his family now and again—grandparents,
sisters—with a humor that spoke of an intimacy she envied
almost painfully. Clark could make fun of them, Brooke realized, because he *was* one of them.

He'd needed a bit of freedom, he'd claimed, a few months
to flow after the regimentation of college. He wanted to be in
touch with the *real* world before he chose the perfect career.

Young and starved for affection, Brooke had soaked up
everything he'd told her, believed every line. He had daz-
zled her with an education she had wished for but had never
been able to have. He'd told her she was beautiful and sweet,
then had kissed her as though he meant it. There had been
afternoons at the beach with rented surfboards she'd hardly
noticed that she'd paid for. And when she'd given him her innocence in a kind of panicked, shamed excitement, he had
seemed pleased with her. He'd laughed at her naive embar-
rassments and had been gentle. Brooke had thought she'd
never been happier.

When he'd suggested they live together, she'd agreed eagerly, wanting to cook and clean for him, longing to wake
and sleep with him. The fact that her meager salary and tips
now supported both of them had never crossed her mind.
Clark had talked of marriage the same way he had talked
of his work—vaguely. They were something for the future,

something practical that people in love shouldn't dwell on. Brooke had agreed, rosily happy with what she'd thought was her first real home. One day they would have children, she had thought. Boys with Clark's handsome face, girls with his huge brown eyes. Children with grandparents in Boston who would always know who their parents were and where their home was.

For three months she'd worked like a Trojan, setting aside part of her small salary for the future Clark always talked of while he pursued what he called his studies and systematically rejected all the jobs in the want ads as unsuitable. Brooke could only agree. To her, Clark was much too smart for any manual labor, much too important for any ordinary position. When the right job came along, she knew he would simply stride into it then zoom to the top.

At times he'd seemed restless, moody. Because she had always had to steal her own privacy, Brooke had left him to his. And when he snapped out of it, he'd always been bursting with energy and plans. Let's go here, let's go there. Now, today. Tomorrow was always years away to Clark. To Brooke, for the first time in seventeen years, today was special. She had something—*someone*—who belonged to her.

In the meantime, she'd worked long hours, cooked his meals and hoarded her tips in a small apothecary jar on a shelf in the kitchen.

One night Brooke had come home from a late shift to find that Clark had gone, taking with him her small black-and-white television set, her record collection and her apothecary jar. A note was in its place.

Brooke,
    Got a call from home. My parents are putting on the pressure—I didn't know it would start so soon. I should have told you before, but I guess I kept thinking it would

just go away. An old family tradition—a merger with my third cousin, as in matrimony. Hell, it sounds archaic, but it's the way my people work. Shelley's a nice girl, her dad's a connection of my dad's. I've been more or less engaged to her for a couple of years, but she was still at Smith, so it didn't seem important. Anyway, I'll slip into her family's business. Junior executive with a shot at the V.P. in five years or so. I guess I hoped I'd tell them to take a leap when the time came, but I can't. I'm sorry.

There's no fighting a wall of family and old money and stiff New England practicality, babe, especially when they keep reminding you that you're the heir apparent. I want you to know that these last couple of months I've had more breathing space than I've had in a long time, and I suppose than I'll have in an even longer time.

I'm sorry about the TV and stuff, but I didn't have the cash for the plane fare and the time wasn't right to tell my folks I'd already blown my savings. I'll pay you back as soon as I can.

I kept hoping it wouldn't have to be this way, but I'm backed into a corner. You've been great, Brooke, really great. Be happy.

                                                                    Clark

Brooke had read the note twice before all the words registered. He'd gone. Her things hadn't mattered but he had. Clark was gone and she was alone—again—because she hadn't graduated from Smith or had a family in Boston or a father who could offer someone she loved a comfortable job so he'd choose her. No one had ever chosen her.

Brooke had wept until she was drained, unable to believe

that her dreams, her trust and her future had been destroyed all in one instant.

Then she had grown up fast, pushing her idealism behind her. She wasn't going to be used ever again. She wasn't going to compete ever again with women who had all the advantages. And she wasn't going to slave in a steamy little diner for enough money to keep herself in a one-room apartment with dingy paint.

She had torn the note into tiny pieces, then had washed her face with icy water until all the traces of all the tears were gone.

Walking the pavement with all the money she had left in her pocket, she had found herself in front of Thorton Productions. She had gone in aggressively, belligerently, talking her way past the receptionist and into the personnel office. She'd come out with a new job, making hardly more than she had waiting tables, but with fresh ambition. She was going places. The one thing her betrayal by Clark had taught her was that she could depend on only one person: herself. No one was ever going to make her believe, or make her cry again.

Ten years later, Brooke drew a narrow black dress from her closet. It was a severely sophisticated outfit she had bought mainly for the cocktail circuit that went hand in hand with her profession. She fingered the silk, then nodded. It should do very well for her evening with Parks Jones.

As Parks drove through the hills above L.A. he considered his actions. For the first time in his career he had allowed a woman to distract him during a game—and this one hadn't even tried. For the first time, he had called a virtual stranger from three thousand miles away to make a date, and she didn't even know who the hell he was. For the first time, he was planning on taking out a woman who made him absolutely furious without having said more than a handful of words. And if it hadn't been for the road series that had followed that night game at Kings Stadium, he would have called her before this. He'd looked up her number at the airport on his way to catch a plane to New York.

He downshifted for the incline as he swung around a curve. All during the flight home, he had thought of Brooke Gordon, trying to pigeonhole her. A model or an actress, he had concluded. She had the face for it—not really beautiful, but certainly unique. Her voice was like something whispering through layers of smoke. And she hadn't sounded overly bright on the phone that morning, he reminded himself with a grimace as he stepped on the gas. There was no law that said brains had to go with intriguing looks, but something in her eyes that night . . . Parks shook off the feeling that he'd been studied, weighed and measured.

A rabbit darted out in front of him then stopped, hypnotized by his beams. Parks braked, swerved and swore as it raced back to the side of the road. He had a weakness for small animals that his father had never understood. Then, his father had understood little about a boy who chose to play ball rather than assume a lucrative position of power in Parkinson Chemicals.

Parks slowed to check his direction, then turned down the darkened back road that led to Brooke's tidy wooded property. He liked it instantly—the remoteness, the melodious sound of crickets. It was a small slice of country thirty-five minutes from L.A. Perhaps she wasn't so slow-witted after all. He pulled his MG behind her Datsun and looked around him.

Her grass needed trimming, but it only added to the rural charm of the house. It was a small, A-frame structure with lots of glass and a circular porch. He heard the tinkle of water from the narrow stream that ran behind the house. There was a scent of summer—hot, heavy blossoms he couldn't identify, and an inexplicable aura of peacefulness. He found himself wishing he didn't have to drive back down to a crowded restaurant and bright lights. In the distance a dog began to bark frantically, sending out echos to emphasize the openness. Parks climbed out of the car, wondering what sort of woman would choose a house so far from city comforts.

There was an old brass knocker in the shape of a hog's head at the right of the door. It made him grin as he let it bang. When she opened the door, Parks forgot all the doubts that had plagued him on his drive through the hills. This time he thought she looked like a seductive witch—fair skin against a black dress, a heavy silver amulet between her breasts. Her hair was pulled back at the temples with two combs, then left to fall wildly down to her hips. Her eyes were as misty as hellsmoke, the lids darkened by some subtle, glittering shadow. Her mouth was naked. He caught a drift of scent that brought him a picture of East Indian harems, white silk and dusky female laughter.

"Hello." Brooke extended her hand. It took every ounce of willpower to complete the casual gesture. How was she to have known her heart would start thudding at the sight of him? It was foolish, because she had already imagined what he would look like in sophisticated clothes. She'd had to if she was to plan how to film him. But somehow his body looked rangier, even more male in a suit coat and slacks—and somehow his face was even more attractive in the shadowed half-light of her front porch. Her plans to ask him in for a drink were aborted. The sooner they were in a crowd the better. "I'm starving," she said as his fingers closed over hers. "Shall we go?" Without waiting for his answer, she shut the door at her back.

Parks led her to the car then turned. In heels, she was nearly eye level with him. "Want me to put the top up?"

"No." Brooke opened the door herself. "I like the air."

She leaned back and shut her eyes as he started back down toward the city. He drove fast, but with the studied control she had sensed in him from the beginning. Since speed was one of her weaknesses, she relaxed and enjoyed.

"What were you doing at the game the other night?"

Brooke felt the smile tug at her mouth but answered smoothly, "A friend had some tickets. She thought I might find it interesting."

"Interesting?" Parks shook his head at the word. "And did you?"

"Oh, yes, though I'd expected to be bored."

"I didn't notice any particular enthusiasm in you," Parks commented, remembering her calm, direct stare. "As I recall, you didn't move through nine innings."

"I didn't need to," she returned. "You did enough of that."

Parks shot her a quick look. "Why were you staring at me?"

Brooke considered for a moment, then opted for the truth. "I was admiring your build." She turned to him with a half smile. The wind blew the hair into her face, but she didn't bother to brush it aside. "It's a very good one."

"Thanks." She saw a flash of humor in his eyes that pleased her. "Is that why you agreed to have dinner with me?"

Brooke smiled more fully. "No. I just like to eat. Why did you ask me?"

"I liked your face. And it's not every day I have a woman stare at me as if she were going to frame me and hang me on her wall."

"Really?" She gave him an innocent blink. "I'd think that pretty typical in your profession."

"Maybe." He took his eyes off the road long enough to meet hers. "But then you're not typical, are you?"

Brooke lifted a brow. Did he know he'd given her what she considered the highest compliment? "Perhaps not," she murmured. "Why don't you think so?"

"Because, Brooke Gordon, I'm not typical either." He burst out of the woods and onto the highway. Brooke decided that she'd better tread carefully.

The restaurant was Greek, with pungent foods, spicy scents and violins. While Parks poured her a second glass of ouzo, Brooke listened to a waiter in a grease-splattered apron sing lustily as he served souvlaki. As always, atmosphere pulled at her. Caught up, she watched and absorbed while managing to put away a healthy meal.

"What are you thinking?" Parks demanded. Her eyes shifted to his, disconcerting in their directness, seducing in their softness.

"That this is a happy place," she told him. "The sort you imagine a big family running. Momma and Poppa in the kitchen fussing over sauces, a pregnant daughter chopping vegetables while her husband tends bar. Uncle Stefos waits tables."

The image made him smile. "Do you come from a large family?"

Immediately the light went out of her eyes. "No."

Sensing a boundary, Parks skirted around it. "What happens when the daughter has her baby?"

"She pops it in a cradle in the corner and chops more vegetables." Brooke broke a hunk of bread in half and nibbled.

"Very efficient."

"A successful woman has to be."

Leaning back, Parks swirled his drink. "Are you a successful woman?"

"Yes."

He tilted his head, watching the candlelight play on her skin. "At what?"

Brooke sipped, enjoying the game. "At what I do. Are you a successful man?"

"At the moment." Parks flashed a grin—the one that gave his face a young, rather affable charm. "Baseball's a fickle profession. A ball takes a bad hop—a pitcher blows a few by you. You can't predict when a slump will start or stop—or worse, why."

It seemed a bit like life to her. "And do you have many?"

"One's too many." With a shrug, he set his drink back on the table. "I've had more than one."

With her first genuine curiosity, Brooke leaned forward. "What do you do to get out of one?"

"Change bats, change batting stances." He shrugged again. "Change your diet, pray. Try celibacy."

She laughed, a warm, liquid sound. "What works best?"

"A good pitch." He, too, leaned forward. "Wanna hear one?"

When her brow rose again, he lifted a finger to trace it. Brooke felt the jolt shiver down to her toes. "I think I'll pass."

"Where do you come from?" he murmured. His fingertip drifted down her cheek, then traced her jawline. He'd known her skin would feel like that. Milkmaid soft.

"No place in particular." Brooke reached for her glass, but his hand closed over hers.

"Everyone comes from somewhere."

"No," she disagreed. His palm was harder than she had imagined, his fingers stronger. And his touch was gentler. "Not everyone."

From her tone, Parks realized she was speaking the truth as she saw it. He brushed a thumb over her wrist, finding her pulse fast but steady. "Tell me about yourself."

"What do you want to know?"

"Everything."

Brooke laughed but spoke with perfect truth. "I don't tell anyone everything."

"What do you do?"

"About what?"

He should have been exasperated, but found himself grinning. "About a job, for starters."

"Oh, I make commercials," she said lightly, knowing he would conclude she worked in front of the cameras. The game had a certain mischievous appeal for her.

"I'll be doing that myself soon," he said with a quick grimace. "Do you like it?"

"I wouldn't do it if I didn't."

He sent her a narrowed look, then nodded. "No, you wouldn't."

"You don't sound as though you're looking forward to trying it," Brooke commented, slipping her hand from his. Prolonged contact with him, she discovered, made it difficult to concentrate, and concentration was vital to her.

"Not when I have to spout some silly lines and wear somebody else's clothes." Idly, he toyed with a lock of her hair, wrapping it around his finger while his eyes remained on hers. "You've a fascinating face; more alluring than beautiful. When I saw you in the stands, I thought you looked like a woman out of the eighteenth century. The sort who had a string of anxious lovers."

With a low sound of humor, Brooke leaned closer. "Was that the first pitch, Mr. Jones?"

Her scent seemed intensified by the warmth of the candle. He wondered that every man in the room wasn't aware of it, and of her. "No." His fingers tightened briefly, almost warningly, on her hair. "When I make my first one, you won't have to ask."

Instinctively, Brooke retreated, but her eyes remained calm, her voice smooth. "Fair enough." She would definitely

put him on film with women, she decided. Sultry brunettes
for contrast. "Do you ride?" she asked abruptly.

"Ride?"

"Horses."

"Yeah," he answered with a curious laugh. "Why?"

"Just wondered. What about hang gliding?"

Parks's expression became more puzzled than amused.
"It's against my contract, like skiing or racing." He didn't
trust the light of humor in her eyes. "Should I know what
game you're playing?"

"No. Can we have dessert?" She flashed him a brilliant
smile he trusted less.

"Sure." Watching her, Parks signaled the waiter.

Thirty minutes later, they walked across the parking lot
to his car. "Do you always eat like that?" Parks demanded.

"Whenever I get the chance." Brooke dropped into the
passenger seat then stretched her arms over her head in a
lazy, unconsciously sensual movement. No one who hadn't
worked in a restaurant could fully appreciate eating in one.
She'd enjoyed the food . . . and the evening. Perhaps, she
mused, she'd enjoyed being with Parks because they'd spent
three hours together and still didn't know each other. The
mystery added a touch of spice.

In a few months, they would know each other well. A
director had no choice but to get to the inside of an actor—
which is what Parks would be, whether he liked it or not. For
now, Brooke chose to enjoy the moment, the mystery and the
brief companionship of an attractive man.

When Parks sat beside her, he reached over to cup her chin
in his hand. She met his eyes serenely and with that touch of
humor that was beginning to frustrate him. "Are you going
to let me know who you are?"

Odd, Brooke mused, that he would have the same understanding of the evening she did. "I haven't decided," she said candidly.

"I'm going to see you again."

She gave him an enigmatic smile. "Yes."

Wary of the smile, and her easy agreement, Parks started the engine.

He didn't like knowing that she was playing him . . . any more than he liked knowing he'd have to come back for more. He'd known a variety of women—from icy sophisticates to bubbly groupies. There were infinite shadings in between, but Brooke Gordon seemed to fit none of them. She had both a haughty sexuality and a soft vulnerability. Though his first instinct had been to get her to bed, he now discovered he wanted more. He wanted to peel off the layers of her character and study each one until he understood the full woman. Making love to her would only be part of the discovery.

They drove in silence while an old, soft ballad crooned on the radio. Brooke had her head thrown back, face to the stars, knowing it was the first time in months she'd fully relaxed on a date and not wanting to analyze why. Parks didn't find it necessary to break a comfortable silence with conversation, nor had he found it necessary to slip in those predictable hints about how he'd like to end the evening. She knew there wouldn't be a wrestling match on the side of the road or an embarrassing, infuriating argument when they reached the front door. He was safe, Brooke decided, and closed her eyes. It seemed things were going to work very well after all. Her thoughts began to drift toward her schedule for the next day.

The motion of the car woke her, or rather the lack of motion. Brooke opened her eyes to find the MG parked in her drive, the engine quiet. Turning her head, she saw Parks sprawled in his seat, watching her.

"You drive very well," she murmured. "I don't usually trust anyone enough to fall asleep in a car."

He'd enjoyed the moments of quiet while he'd watched her sleep. Her skin looked ethereal in the moonlight, ghostly pale with a hint of flush in her cheeks. The wind had tossed her hair so that Parks knew how it would look spread on a pillow after a wild night of loving. Sooner or later he'd see it that way, he determined. After his hands had tangled it.

"This time you're staring," Brooke pointed out.

And he smiled—not the quick grin she'd come to expect, but a slow, unsettling smile that left his eyes dark and dangerous. "I guess we'll both have to get used to it."

Leaning over, he opened her door. Brooke didn't stiffen or shift away from the brush of his body against hers; she simply watched. As if, Parks mused, she were considering his words very carefully. Good, he thought as he stepped from the car. This time she'd have something to think about.

"I like this place." He didn't touch her as they walked up the path to her house, though Brooke had expected him to take her hand or her arm. "I had a house in Malibu once."

"Not anymore?"

"Got too crowded." He shrugged as they walked up the porch steps. Their footsteps echoed into the night. "If I'm going to live out of the city, I want a place where I'm not forever stumbling over my neighbor."

"I don't have that problem here." Around them the woods were dark and quiet. There was only the bubbling sound of the stream and the music of tireless crickets. "There's a couple who live about a quarter mile that way." Brooke gestured to the east. "Newlyweds who met on a television series that folded." Leaning back against the door, she smiled. "We don't have any trouble keeping out of each other's way." She sighed, comfortably sleepy and relaxed. "Thanks for dinner." When she offered her hand, she wondered if he would take it or ignore it and kiss her. Brooke expected the latter, even wondered with a drowsy curiosity what the pressure of his lips on hers would be like.

Parks knew what she expected, and her lips, as they had from the first, tempted him. But he thought it was time this woman had something unexpected. Taking her hand, Parks leaned toward her. He saw from her eyes that she would accept his kiss with her own sultry reserve. Instead, he touched his lips to her cheek.

At the brush of his open mouth on her skin, Brooke's fingers tightened in his. Usually she viewed a kiss or embrace distantly, as from behind a camera, wondering dispassionately how it would appear on film. Now she saw nothing, but felt. Low, turbulent waves of sensation swept through her, making her tense. Something seemed to ripple along her skin, though he never touched her—just his hand over hers, just his lips on her cheek.

Slowly, watching her stunned eyes, Parks journeyed to her other cheek, moving his lips with the same featherlightness. Brooke felt the waves rise until there was an echoing in her head. She heard a soft moan, unaware that it was her own. As hunger swept over her, Brooke turned her mouth toward his, but he glided up her skin, whispering over her eyelids so that they fluttered down. Drugged, she allowed him to roam over her face, leaving her lips trembling with anticipation, and unfulfilled. She tasted his breath on them, felt the warm flutter as they passed close, but his mouth dropped to her chin to give her a teasing touch of his tongue.

Her fingers went limp in his. Surrender was unknown to her, so she didn't recognize it. Parks did as he caught the lobe of her ear between his teeth. His body was throbbing, aching to press against hers and feel the yielding softness that came only from woman. Against his cheek, her hair was as silky as her skin, and as fragrant. It took every ounce of control to prevent his hands from diving into it, to keep himself from plundering the mouth that waited, warm and naked, for his. He traced her ear with his tongue and felt her shudder. Slowly, he brushed kisses up her temple and over her brow on his way to her other ear. He nibbled gently, letting his tongue slide over her skin until he heard her moan again.

Still he avoided her mouth, pressing his lips to the pulse in her throat, fighting the urge to move lower, to feel, to taste the subtle sweep of her breast beneath the black silk. Her pulse was jerky, like the sound of her breathing. High up in the mountains, a coyote called to the moon.

A dizzying excitement raced through him. He could have her now—feel that long, willowy body beneath his, tangle himself in that wild mane of hair. But he wouldn't have all of her. He needed more time for that.

"Parks." His name came throatily through her lips, arousing him further. "Kiss me."

Gently, he pressed his lips to her shoulder. "I am."

Her mouth felt as though it were on fire. She had thought she understood hunger, having felt it too often in the past. But she'd never known a hunger like this. "Really kiss me."

He drew away far enough to see her eyes. There was no light in them now; they were opaque with desire. Her lips were parted in invitation, her breath shuddering through them. He bent close, but kept his lips an aching whisper from hers. "Next time," he said softly.

Turning, he left her stunned and wanting.

CHAPTER 3

"Okay, Linda, try to look like you're enjoying this." Brooke cast a look at her lighting director and got a nod. "E.J., sweep up, starting at her toes—take your time on the legs."

E.J. gave her a blinding white grin from his smooth mahogany face. "My pleasure," he said affably and focused his camera on the actress's pink painted toenails.

"It's so hot," Linda complained, fussing with the strap of her tiny bikini. She was stretched out on a towel in the sand—long, blond and beautiful, with a rich golden tan that would hawk a popular suntan lotion. All Linda had to do was to look lush and lazy and purr that she had an *Eden* tan. The bikini would do the rest.

"Don't sweat," Brooke ordered. "You're supposed to be glowing, not wet. When we roll, count to six, then bring up your right knee—slow. At twelve, take a deep breath, pass your right hand through your hair. Say your line looking straight at the camera and think sex."

"The hell with sex, I'm roasting."

"Then let's get it in one take. All right. Speed. Roll film, and . . . action."

E.J. moved up from the manicured toenails, up the long, slender legs, over a rounded hip, golden midriff and barely confined bosom. He closed in on Linda's face—sulky mouth, pearly teeth and baby blues—then went back for a full shot.

"I've got an *Eden* tan," Linda claimed.

"Cut." Brooke swiped a hand over her brow. Though it was still morning, the beach was baking. She thought she could feel the sand burning through the soles of her sneakers. "Let's pump a little life into it," she suggested. "We've got to sell this stuff on one line and your body."

"Why don't you try it?" Linda demanded, falling onto her back.

"Because you're getting paid to and I'm not," Brooke snapped, then clicked her teeth together. She knew better than to lose her temper, especially with this one. The trouble was that since her evening with Parks, she'd been on a perpetual short fuse. Taking a deep breath, Brooke reminded herself that her personal life, if that's what Parks Jones was, couldn't interfere with her work. She walked over and crouched beside the pouting model. "Linda, I know it's miserable out here today, but a job's a job. You're a pro or you wouldn't be here."

"Do you know how hard I worked on this tan to get this lousy thirty-second spot?"

Brooke patted her shoulder, conveying sympathy, understanding and authority all at once. "Well then, let's make it a classic."

It was past noon before they were able to load up their equipment. E.J. reached in the back of the station wagon he used and pulled two iced drinks out of a chest cooler. "Here ya go, boss."

"Thanks." Brooke pressed the cold bottle against her forehead before she twisted off the top. "What was with her today?" she demanded. "She can be a problem, but I've never had to drag one line out of her like that before."

"Broke up with her man last week," E.J. informed Brooke before he took a greedy swallow of grape soda.

Grinning, Brooke sat on the tailgate. "Anything you don't know, E.J.?"

"Not a thing." He propped himself beside her, one of the few on the Thorton staff who wasn't leery of the Tiger-lady, as Brooke had been dubbed. "You're going to that fancy de Marco party tonight."

"Yeah." Brooke gave a slow, narrow-eyed smile that had nothing to do with the brilliance of the sun. The party would be her chance to cut Parks Jones down a few pegs. She could still remember how she had stood shaking on her porch in the moonlight after the echo of his engine had died away.

"It's going to be a kick working with Parks Jones." E.J. downed the rest of his soda in one swallow. "The man's got the best glove in the league and a bat that won't quit smoking. Knocked in two more RBIs last night."

Brooke leaned against the door frame and scowled. "Good for him."

"Don't you like baseball?" E.J. grinned, tossing his empty bottle into the back of the wagon.

"No."

"Ought to have some team spirit," he mused and gave her knee a friendly squeeze. "The better he does, the more punch the campaign'll have. And if he gets into the series—"

"If he gets into the series," Brooke interrupted, "we have to wait until the end of October before we can start shooting."

"Well." E.J. stroked his chin. "That's show biz."

Brooke tried to glare, then chuckled. "Let's get back. I've got a shoot in the studio this afternoon. Want me to drive?"

"Naw." E.J. slammed the tailgate then headed for the driver's seat. "I like living."

"You're such a wimp, E.J."

"I know," he agreed cheerfully. "I've got this thing about traveling at the speed of light." After adjusting mirror-lensed sunglasses on his face he coaxed the station wagon's engine into life. It sputtered and groaned temperamentally while he crooned to it.

"Why don't you buy a new car?" Brooke demanded. "You get paid enough."

He patted the wagon's dash when the engine caught. "Loyalty. I've been cruising in this little darling for seven years. She'll be around when that flashy machine of yours is nuts and bolts."

Brooke shrugged, then tilted back her head to drain the bottle. E.J. was the only one who worked under her who dared any intimacy, which was probably the reason she not only allowed it but liked him for it. She also considered him one of the best men with a camera on the West Coast. He came from San Francisco where his father was a high school principal and his mother owned and operated a popular beauty salon. She had met them once and wondered how two such meticulous people could have produced a freewheeling, loose-living man with a penchant for voluptuous women and B movies.

But then, Brooke mused, she'd never been able to understand families. Always she viewed them with perplexity and longing, as only one on the outside could fully understand. Settling back on the carefully patched seat, she began to plot out her strategy for her afternoon session.

"Heard you took in a Kings game the other night." E.J. caught her swift, piercing look and began to whistle tunelessly.

"So?"

"I saw Brighton Boyd at a party a couple of nights ago. Worked with him on a TV special last year. Nice guy."

Brooke remembered seeing the actor in the box next to hers and Claire's. She dropped her empty bottle on the already littered floor. "So?" she repeated coolly.

"Big Kings fan," E.J. went on, turning the radio up loud so that he had to shout over the top 40 rock. "Raved about Jones's homer—on a two-out, two-strike pitch. The man's a hell of a clutch hitter." While Brooke remained silent, E.J. tapped out the beat from the radio on the steering wheel. There was the glint of gold from a ring on his long dark fingers. "Brighton said Jones stared at you like a man who'd been hit with a blunt instrument. That Brighton, he sure does turn a phrase."

"Hmm." Brooke began to find the passing scenery fascinating.

"Said he came right over to your box chasing a foul. Had a few words to say."

Brooke turned her head and stared into E.J.'s mirrored glasses. "Are you pumping me, E.J.?"

"Hot damn! Can't pull anything over on you, Brooke; you're one sharp lady."

Despite herself she laughed. She knew a "no comment" would only cause speculation she'd like to avoid. Instead she stretched her legs out on the seat and treated it lightly. "He just wanted my name."

"And?"

"And nothing."

"Where'd you go with him?"

The faintest frown creased her brow. "I didn't say I went anywhere with him."

"He didn't ask your name because he was taking a census."

Brooke gave him a cool, haughty look that would have discouraged anyone else. "You're a gossipy old woman, E.J."

"Yep. You go to dinner with him?"

"Yes," she said on a sigh of surrender. "And that's all."

"Not as bright as he looks, then." He patted her sneakered foot. "Or maybe he felt funny about starting something up with the lady who'll be directing him."

"He didn't know," Brooke heard herself say before she could stop herself.

"Oh?"

"I didn't tell him."

"Oh." This time the syllable was drawn out and knowing.

"I didn't think it was necessary," Brooke said heatedly. "It was strictly a social meeting, and it gave me the opportunity to plan how best to film him."

"Mmm-hmm."

She turned back in her seat and folded her arms. "Shut up and drive, E.J."

"Sure thing, boss."

"As far as I'm concerned he can take his golden glove and smoking bat and sit on them."

E.J. nodded wisely, enjoying himself. "You know best."

"He's conceited and cold and inconsiderate."

"Must have been some evening," E.J. observed.

"I don't want to talk about it." Brooke kicked at the empty bottle on the floor.

"Okay," he said affably.

"He's the kind of man," she went on, "who thinks a woman's just waiting to fall all over him just because he's moderately attractive and successful and has an average mind."

"For a Rhodes scholar," E.J. mused as he slowed down for his exit.

"A what?"

"He's a Rhodes scholar."

Brooke's mouth fell open, then shut with a bang. "He is not."

E.J. shrugged agreeably. "Well, that's what it said in *Sports View.* That was supposed to be the main reason he didn't start playing professional ball until he was twenty-two."

"Probably just a publicity hype," she muttered, but she knew better. She rode the rest of the way to the studio in frowning silence.

The de Marco California villa was an eyeful. Brooke decided that it had the dubious ability of making Claire's mansion look simple and discreet. It was huge, E-shaped and dazzling white with two inner courtyards. One held a grottolike pool complete with miniature waterfall, the other a sheltered garden rich with exotic scents.

When Brooke arrived, she could hear the high liquid sounds of harps and mixed conversation. People were ranged through the house, spilling outdoors and clustered in corners. Passing through the gold-toned parlor, she caught the mingling, heady scents of expensive perfumes and spiced food. There was the glitter of diamonds, swirl of silks and flash of tanned, pampered skin.

Brooke caught snatches of conversations as she strolled through, searching for the main buffet.

"But darling, he simply can't carry a series anymore. Did you see him at Ma Maison last week?"

"She'll sign. After that fiasco in England, she's itching to come back to Hollywood."

"Can't remember a line if you feed it to him intravenously."

"Left her for the wardrobe mistress."

"My dear, have you ever seen *such* a dress!"

Hollywood, Brooke thought with halfhearted affection as she pounced on the remains of the pâté.

"I knew I'd find you here."

Brooke turned her head as she speared a chunk of smoked

beef. "Hello, Claire," she managed over a mouthful of cracker. "Nice party."

"I suppose, as you always judge them by the menu." Claire gave her a long, appraising look. Brooke wore a buckskin jumpsuit, soft and smooth as cream, with a thick pewter belt cinched at her waist. She'd braided the hair at her temples and clipped it back over the flowing tousled mane, letting heavy pewter links dangle at her ears. Because she'd been distracted while applying it, she'd neglected her makeup and had only remembered to darken her eyes. As a result, they dominated her pale, sharp-featured face. "Why is it you can wear the most outlandish outfits and still look marvelous?"

Brooke grinned and swallowed. "I like yours, too," she said, noting that Claire was, as always, stylishly neat in pale blue voile. "What have they got to drink in this place?"

With a sigh, Claire motioned to a roving, red-suited waiter and chose two tulip glasses of champagne. "Try to behave yourself. The de Marcos are very old-fashioned."

"I'll be a credit to the company," Brooke promised and lifted her hand in acknowledgment of a wave from a stand-up comic she'd directed in a car commercial. "Do you think I could get a plate?"

"Gorge later. Mr. Jones's agent is here, I want you to meet him."

"I hate talking to agents on an empty stomach. Oh, damn, there's Vera. I should have known she'd be here."

Brooke answered the icy smile from the slim honey-haired model who was the current embodiment of the American look. Their paths had crossed more than once, professionally and socially, and the women had taken an instant, lasting dislike to each other. "Keep your claws sheathed," Claire warned. "De Marco's going to be using her."

"Not with me," Brooke said instantly. "I'll take the ball-player, Claire, but someone else is going to hold the leash on that one. I don't like my poison in small doses."

"We'll discuss it," Claire muttered then beamed a smile. "Lee, we were just looking for you. Lee Dutton, Brooke Gordon. She's going to be directing Parks." She placed a maternal hand on Brooke's arm. "My very best."

Brooke lifted an ironic brow. Claire was always lavish with praise in public and miserly with it behind closed doors. "Hello, Mr. Dutton."

Her hand was grabbed hard and pumped briskly. Discreetly, Brooke flexed her fingers while she made a swift survey. He was shorter than she was and rather round with thinning hair and startling black eyes. A creature of first impressions, she liked him on the spot.

"Here's to a long, successful relationship," he announced and banged his glass exuberantly against hers. "Parks is eager to begin."

"Is he?" Brooke smiled, remembering Parks's description of his venture into commercials. "We're just as eager to have him."

Claire sent her a brief warning look as she tucked her arm through Lee's. "And where is he? Brooke and I are both anxious to meet him."

"He has a hard time getting away from the ladies." Lee gave the proud, apologetic smile of a doting uncle. But the eyes on Brooke were shrewd.

"How awkward for him," she murmured into her glass. "But I suppose he manages to live with it."

"Brooke, you really must try the pâté." Claire sent her a teeth-clenched smile.

"I did," Brooke returned easily. "Tell me more about Parks, Mr. Dutton. I can't tell you what a fan I am."

"Oh, you follow baseball?"

Brooke tilted her glass again. "Why, we were in the park only a few weeks ago, weren't we, Claire?"

"As a matter of fact." Claire didn't bother to try to outstare Brooke this time but turned to Lee. "Do you get to many games?"

"Not enough," he admitted, knowing a game was afoot and willing to play. "But I happen to have a few tickets for Sunday's game," he said, making a mental note to arrange for some. "I'd love to escort both you ladies."

Before Brooke could open her mouth, Claire doled out subtle punishment. "There's nothing we'd like better."

He caught Brooke's quick scowl before she smoothed her features. "Well, there's Parks now." Lee bellowed for him, causing heads to turn before conversation buzzed again.

Parks's first reaction was surprise when he saw Brooke standing beside his agent and the woman he knew was head of Thorton Productions. Then he experienced the same flare of reluctant desire he had felt on the other two occasions he'd seen her. He'd purposely let the days pass before he contacted her again, hoping the power of need would lessen. One glance at her told him it hadn't worked.

Apparently without hurry, he weaved through the crowd, stopping to exchange a few words when someone touched his arm, then gently disentangling himself. He'd learned, at an early age, how to keep from being cornered at a social occasion. In less than two minutes, Parks stood in front of Brooke.

Well done, Brooke thought. She answered Parks's smile cautiously, wondering what his reaction would be when they were introduced. She felt a jab of uneasiness then pushed it aside. After all, he'd been the one to wake her up at dawn and ask for a date.

"Parks, I want you to meet Claire Thorton, the lady who'll

be producing your commercials." Lee laid his hand over Claire's in an unconsciously possessive gesture noticed only by Parks and Brooke. Parks was amused, Brooke annoyed.

"A pleasure, Ms. Thorton." He wanted to say he had expected a dragon from what he'd read of her professionally, not this soft-faced attractive woman with faded blue eyes. Instead, Parks smiled and accepted her hand.

"We're looking forward to working with you. I was just telling Mr. Dutton how much Brooke and I enjoyed your game against the Valiants a few weeks ago." Remembering his muttered demand for Brooke's name at the rail, Claire waited for the reaction.

"Oh?" So this was her friend, he thought, turning to Brooke. With her face, he concluded she must be a regular for Thorton's commercials. "Hello again."

"Hello." Brooke found her hand claimed and held. Taking a hasty sip of champagne, she waited for the bomb to drop.

"Claire tells me Ms. Gordon is her best," Lee told Parks. "Since you'll be working together closely, you'll want to get to know each other."

"Will we?" Parks ran his thumb along Brooke's palm.

"Only my best director for a project this important," Claire put in, watching them closely.

Brooke felt his thumb stop its casual caress, then his fingers tightened. There was no change in his face. To prevent a quick gasp of pain, she swallowed the rest of her champagne. "So you direct commercials," he said smoothly.

"Yes." She tugged once to free her hand, but he only increased his grip.

"Fascinating." Casually, he plucked the empty glass from her other hand. "Excuse us." Brooke found herself being dragged through the crowd of jewels and silks. Immediately, she quickened her pace so that it appeared she was walking with him rather than being led.

"Let go of me," she hissed, giving a nodding smile to another director. "You're breaking my hand."

"Consider it a preview of things to come." Parks pulled her through the open French doors, hoping to find a quiet spot. There was a three-piece band in the garden playing soft, dancing music. At least a dozen couples were taking advantage of it. Parks swore, but before he could maneuver her through the garden to a more private spot, he heard someone call her name. Immediately, he dragged her into his arms.

The hard contact with his chest stole her breath, the arm tight around her waist prevented her from finding any more. Ignoring the choking sound she made, Parks began to sway to the music. "Just wave to him," he ordered against her ear. "I'm not about to be interrupted with small talk."

Wanting to breathe again, Brooke obeyed. She was already planning revenge. When his grip lessened slightly, she drew in a sharp breath of air, letting it out on a string of abuse. "You overgrown bully, don't think you can drag me around just because you're this year's American hero. I'll only take it once, and I'll only warn you once. Don't you *ever* grab me again." Brooke stomped hard on his foot and was rewarded by having her air cut off again.

"You dance beautifully, Ms. Gordon," Parks whispered in her ear. He bit none too gently on the lobe. Between the fury and pain, Brooke felt a stir deep in her stomach. Oh, no, she thought, stiffening. Not again. The band switched to an up-tempo number but he continued to hold her close and sway.

"You're going to have a lot of explaining to do when I faint from lack of oxygen," she managed. Who would have thought that lanky body would be so hard, or the limber arms so strong?

"You won't faint," he muttered, slowly maneuvering her toward the edge of the garden. "And you're the one with the explaining to do."

She was released abruptly, but before Brooke could take a breath, he was pulling her through a clump of azalea. "Look, you jerk . . ." Then she was back inside, dazed by bright lights and laughter. Without pausing, Parks dragged her through the center patio and into the adjoining courtyard.

There was no music here, except the liquid sound of the water falling into the grotto, and only a few couples more intent on themselves than on a man pulling a furious woman in his wake. Parks drew her close to the pool and into the shadows behind the high wall. Brooke was effectively sandwiched between him and the smooth rocks.

"So you like to play games," he murmured.

For the first time she was able to lift her face and stare into his. Her eyes glittered in the moonlight. "I don't know what you're talking about."

"No?"

She had expected him to be annoyed, but she hadn't expected this smoldering fury. It was in his eyes, in the hard lines of his face, in the poised readiness of his body. When she felt her heart begin to thud uncomfortably, she became only more defensive. "You made all the moves," she tossed out. "You *demanded* that I give you my name. You called *me* at six o'clock in the morning for a date. All I did was let Claire drag me to a ball game."

She made an attempt to push by him and found herself pressed back against the wall by a firm hand on her chest. "You were sizing me up," he said slowly. "At the game, at dinner. Tell me, how did I come out?"

Brooke put her hand to his wrist, but was surprised when he let her push his hand away. She began a careless recital she knew would infuriate him. "You move more like a dancer than an athlete—it'll be a plus on film. Your build is good, it'll sell clothes. You can be charming at times, and your face is attractive without being handsome. That could sell anything.

You have a certain sexuality that should appeal to women who'd like their men to have it, too. They're the primary target, as women still do the bulk of buying in ready-to-wear."

Her tone had been schooled to annoy. Even so, Parks couldn't prevent his temper from rising. "Do I get a rating?"

"Naturally." The bitten-off words pleased her enormously. It was a small payment for the scene on her porch, but it was payment. "Your popularity quotient is fair at the moment. It should get higher after the first commercial is aired. Claire seems to think if you could get into the World Series and do something outstanding, it would help."

"I'll see what I can do," he said dryly. "Now, why didn't you tell me who you were?"

"I did."

He leaned closer. She caught a trace of sharp cologne over the smell of wet summer leaves. "No, you didn't."

"I told you I make commercials."

"Knowing I'd conclude you were an actress."

"Your conclusions are your own problem," Brooke told him with a shrug. "I never said I was an actress." She heard a woman's laugh muffled in the distance and the rush of water into the pool beside her. The odds, she mused, were not in her favor at the moment. "I don't see what difference it makes."

"I don't like games," Parks said precisely, "unless I know the players."

"Then we won't play," Brooke countered. "Your job is to do what I tell you—no more, no less."

Parks controlled a wave of fury and nodded. "On the set." He caught the hair at her waist, then let it slide through his hands. "And off?"

"And off, nothing." She'd put more emphasis on the last word than she had intended to. It showed a weakness she could only hope he didn't notice.

"No." Parks stepped closer so that she had to tilt back her head to keep her eyes level with his. "I don't think I like those rules. Let's try mine."

Brooke was ready this time for the sneak attack on her senses. He wouldn't be permitted to seduce her, make her tremble with those featherlight teasing kisses on her skin. With a cool, hard stare, she dared him to try.

He returned the look as seconds dragged on. She caught the glint of challenge in his eyes but didn't see the slow curve of his lips. No man had ever been able to meet her stare so directly or for so long. For the first time in years, Brooke felt a weakness in her primary defense.

Then he did what he had wanted to do from the first moment he had seen her. Parks dove his hands into the lushness of her hair, letting them sink into the softness before he dragged her against him. Their eyes clashed a moment longer, even as he lowered his lips and savaged hers.

Brooke's vision blurred. She struggled to bring it back into sharp focus, to concentrate on that one sense to prevent her others from being overpowered. She fought not to taste the hot, demanding flavor of his lips, to feel the quick, almost brutal nip of his teeth that would tempt her lips to part. She didn't want to hear her own helpless moan. Then his tongue was plundering, enticing hers to answer in a seduction totally different from the teasing gentleness of his first embrace. She struggled against him, but her movements only caused more heat to flare from the friction of her body on his.

Gradually, the kiss altered. The hard pressure became sweet. He nibbled at her mouth, as if savoring the flavor, sucking gently, though his arms kept her pinned tight. She lost even her blurred vision, and her will to resist went with it.

Parks felt the change, her sudden pliancy. Her surrender excited him. She wasn't a woman to relinquish control easily, yet both times he had held her, he'd prized it from her.

With gentleness, he realized, suddenly aware that the anger had fled from his body and his mouth. It was gentleness that won her, whereas force would only be met with force. Now he didn't want to think—not for a moment. He wanted only to lose himself in the soft give of her body, the white-silk scent that poured from her and the dusky flavor of her mouth. They were all the seduction of woman, only intensi-fied by her surrender.

Brooke felt the liquid weight in her limbs, the slow in-sistent tug in her thighs before the muscles went lax. Her mouth clung to his, yearning for more of the magic it could bring with the gentle play of tongue and teeth. His hands began a slow exploration of her body, kneading over the soft material. When she felt him loosen the narrow zipper that ran from her throat to her waist, she roused herself to protest.

"No." The words came on a gasp of breath as his fingers slid along her skin.

Parks gathered her hair in one hand, drawing her head back so that his eyes met hers again. "I have to touch you." Watching her, he glided his fingers over her breast, pausing briefly on the taut point before he roamed down to her flat, quivering stomach. "One day I'll touch all of you," he mur-mured. "Inch by inch. I'm going to feel your skin heat under my hands." His fingers trailed back to her breast, leaving a path of awakened flesh in their wake. "I'm going to watch your face when I make love to you."

Bending, he touched his lips to hers again, tasting her breath as it shuddered into his mouth. Very slowly, he drew up the zipper, letting his knuckles graze along her skin. Then he ran his hands up her back until their bodies fit together again.

"Kiss me, Brooke." He rubbed his nose lightly against hers. "Really kiss me."

Tingling from his touch, aroused by the whispered words, she pressed her open mouth to his. Her tongue sought his, hungry for the moist dark tastes that had already seeped inside of her. He waited for her demands, her aggressions, feeling them build as her body strained against his. With a groan of pleasure, Brooke tangled her fingers in his hair, wanting to drag him closer. When he knew his chain of control was on its last link, Parks drew her away. He'd learned more of her, but not enough. Not yet. And he wasn't going to forget that he had a small score to settle with her.

"When the camera's rolling, it's your game and your rules." He cupped her chin in his hand, wondering how many times he'd be able to walk away from her when his body was aching to have her. "When it's not," he continued quietly, "the rules are mine."

Brooke took a shaky breath. "I don't play games."

Parks smiled, running a fingertip over her swollen mouth. "Everyone does," he corrected. "Some make a career out of it, and they aren't all on ball fields." Dropping his hand, he stepped back from her. "We both have a job to do. Maybe we're not too thrilled about it at the moment, but I have a feeling that won't make any difference in how well you work."

"No," Brooke agreed shortly. "It won't. I can detest you and still make you look fantastic on the screen."

He grinned. "Or make me look like an idiot if it suited you."

She couldn't prevent a small smile from forming. "You're very perceptive."

"But you won't, because you're a pro. Whatever happens between us personally won't make you direct any differently."

"I'll do my job," Brooke stated as she stepped around him. "And nothing's going to happen between us personally." She looked up sharply when a friendly arm was dropped over her shoulder.

"I guess we'll just wait and see about that." Parks sent her another amiable grin. "Have you eaten?"

Brooke frowned at him dubiously. "No."

He gave her shoulder a fraternal pat. "I'll get you a plate."

CHAPTER 4

Brooke couldn't believe she was spending a perfectly beautiful Sunday afternoon at a ball game. What was more peculiar was that she was enjoying it. She was well aware that she was being punished for the few veiled sarcastic remarks she had tossed off at the de Marco party, but after the first few innings, she found that Billings was right. There was a bit more to it than swinging a bat and running around in circles.

During her first game, Brooke had been too caught up in the atmosphere, the people, then in her initial impressions of Parks. Now she opened her mind to the game itself and enjoyed. Being a survivor, whenever she was faced with doing something she didn't want to do, Brooke simply conditioned herself to *want* to do it. She had no patience with people who allowed themselves to be miserable when it was so simple to turn a situation around to your advantage. If it wasn't always possible to enjoy, she could learn. It pleased her to be doing both.

The game had more subtlety than she had first realized, and more strategy. Brooke never ceased to be intrigued by strategy. It became obvious that there were variables to the contest, dozens of ifs, slices of chance counterbalancing skill.

In a game of inches, luck couldn't be overlooked. This had an appeal for her because she had always considered luck every bit as vital as talent in winning, no matter what the game.

And there were certain aspects of the afternoon, beyond the balls and strikes, that fanned her interest.

The crowd was no less enthusiastic or vocal than it had been on her first visit to Kings Stadium. If anything, Brooke reflected, the people were more enthusiastic—even slightly wild. She wondered if their chants and screams and whistles took on a tone of delirium because the score was tied 1-1, and had been since the first inning. Lee called it an example of a superior defensive game.

Lee Dutton was another aspect of the afternoon that intrigued her. He seemed—on the surface—a genial, rather unkempt sort of man with a faint Brooklyn accent that lingered from his youth. He wore a golf shirt and checked pants, which only accented his tubbiness. Brooke might have passed him off as a cute middle-aged man had it not been for the sharp black eyes. She liked him . . . with a minor reservation—he seemed inordinately attentive to Claire.

It occurred to Brooke that he found a great many occasions to touch—Claire's soft manicured hands, her round shoulder, even her gabardine-clad knee. What was more intriguing to Brooke was that Claire didn't, as was her habit, freeze Lee's tentative advances with an icy smile or a stingingly polite word. As far as Brooke could tell, Claire seemed to be enjoying them—or perhaps she was overlooking them because of the importance of the de Marco account and Parks Jones. In either case, Brooke determined to keep an eye on her friend, and the agent. It wasn't unheard-of for a woman approaching fifty to be naive of men and therefore susceptible.

If she were to be truthful, Brooke would have to admit

she enjoyed watching Parks. There was no doubt he was in his element in the field, eyes shaded by a cap, glove in his hand. Just as he had been in his element, she remembered, at the glossy party at the de Marco villa. He hadn't seemed out of place in the midst of ostentatious wealth, sipping vintage champagne or handling cocktail party conversation. And why should he? she mused. After their last encounter, Brooke had made it her business to find out more about him.

He'd come from money. Big money. Parkinson Chemicals was a third-generation, multimillion-dollar conglomerate that dealt in everything from aspirin to rocket fuel. He'd been born with a silver spoon in one hand and a fat portfolio in the other. His two sisters had married well, one to a restauranteur who had been her business partner before he became her husband, the other to a vice president of Parkinson attached to the Dallas branch. But the heir to Parkinson, the man who carried the old family name in front of the less unique Jones, had had a love affair with baseball.

The love affair hadn't diminished during his studies at Oxford under a Rhodes scholarship; it had simply been postponed. When Parks had graduated, he'd gone straight to the Kings' training camp—Brooke had to wonder how his family had felt about that—and there had been drafted. After less than a year on the Kings' farm team, he'd been brought up to the majors. There he had remained, for a decade.

So he didn't play for the money, Brooke mused, but because he enjoyed the game. Perhaps that was why he played with such style and steadiness.

She remembered, too, her impressions of him at the de Marcoses'—charming, then ruthless, then casually friendly. And none of it, Brooke concluded, was an act. Above all else, Parks Jones was in complete control, on or off the diamond. Brooke respected that, related to it, while she couldn't help wondering how the two of them would juggle their need to be in charge when they began to work together. If nothing else, she mused as she crunched down on a piece of ice, it would be an interesting association.

Brooke watched him now as he stood on the bag at second while the opposing team brought out a relief pitcher. Parks had started off the seventh inning with a leadoff single, then had advanced to second when the next batter walked. Brooke could feel the adrenaline of the crowd pulsing while Parks talked idly with the second baseman.

"If they take this one," Lee was saying, "the Kings lock up the division." He slipped his hand over Claire's. "We need these runs."

"Why did they change pitchers?" Brooke demanded. She thought of how furious she would be if someone pulled her off a job before it was finished.

"There's two on and nobody out." Lee gave her an easy paternal smile. "Mitchell was slowing down—he'd walked two last inning and was only saved from having runs score by that rifle shot the center fielder sent home." Reaching in his shirt pocket, he brought out a cigar in a thin protective tube. "I think you'll see the Kings going to the bullpen in the eighth."

"I wouldn't switch cameramen in the middle of a shoot," Brooke mumbled.

"You would if he couldn't focus the lens anymore," Lee countered, grinning at her.

With a laugh, Brooke dove her hand into the bag of peanuts he offered her. "Yeah, I guess I would."

The strategy proved successful, as the relief man shut down the next three batters, leaving Parks and his teammate stranded on base. The crowds groaned, swore at the umpire and berated the batters.

"Now there's sportsmanship," Brooke observed, casting a

look over her shoulder when someone called the batter, who struck out to end the inning, a bum—and other less kind names.

Lee gave a snort of laughter as he draped his arm casually over Claire's shoulders. "You should hear them when we're losing, kid."

The lifted-brow look Brooke gave Claire at the gesture was returned blandly. "Enthusiasm comes in all forms," Claire observed. With a smile for Lee, she settled back against his arm to watch the top of the next inning.

Definitely an odd couple, Brooke mused; then she assumed her habitual position of elbows on rail. Parks didn't glance her way. He had only once—at the beginning of the game when he took the field. The look had been long and direct before he had turned away, and since then it was as though he wasn't even aware of her. She hated to admit it irked her, hated to admit that she would have liked to engage in that silent battle of eye to eye. He was the first man she *wanted* to spar with, though she had sparred with many since her first naive encounter ten years before. There was something exciting in the mind game, particularly since Parks had a mind she both envied and admired.

Lee was on target, as the Kings went to the bullpen when the starting pitcher walked two with one man out. Brooke shifted closer to the edge of her seat to watch Parks during the transition. What does he think about out there? she wondered.

God, what I wouldn't give for a cold shower and a gallon of beer, Parks thought as the sun beat down on the back of his neck. He'd been expecting the change of pitchers and was pleased with the choice. Ripley did well what a reliever was there to do—throw hard and fast. He gave a seemingly idle glance toward the runner at second. That could be trouble, he reflected, doing a quick mental recall of his

opponent's statistics. The ability to retain and call out facts
had always come naturally to Parks. And not just batting
averages and stolen bases. Basically, he only forgot what
he wanted to forget. The rest was stockpiled, waiting until he needed it. The trick had alternately fascinated and
infuriated his family and friends, so that he generally kept
it to himself. At the moment, he could remember Ripley's
earned-run average, his win-loss ratio, the batting average of
the man waiting to step into the batter's box and the scent of
Brooke's perfume.

He hadn't forgotten that she was sitting a few yards away.
The awareness of her kindled inside of him—a not quite
pleasant sensation. It was more of an insistent pressure, like
the heat of the sun on the back of his neck. It was another
reason he longed for a cool shower. Watching Ripley throw
his warm-up pitches to the catcher, Parks allowed himself to
imagine what it would be like to undress her—slowly—in
the daylight, just before her body went from limp surrender
to throbbing excitement. Soon, he promised himself; then he
forced Brooke to the back of his mind as the batter stepped
up to the plate.

Ripley blew the first one by the batter—hard and straight.
Parks knew that Ripley didn't throw any fancy pitches, just
the fast ball and the curve. He was either going to overpower
the hitters, or with the lineup of right-handers coming up,
Parks was going to be very busy. He positioned himself
another step back on the grass, going by instinct. He noted
the base runner had a fat lead as the batter chipped the next
pitch off. The runner was nearly at third before the foul was
called. Ripley looked back over his shoulder at second, slid
his eyes to first, then fired the next pitch.

It was hit hard, smashing into the dirt in front of third then
bouncing high. There was never any opportunity to think,

only to act. Parks leaped, just managing to snag the ball. The runner was coming into third in a headfirst slide. Parks didn't have the time to admire his guts before he tagged the base seconds before the runner's hand grabbed it. He heard the third base ump bellow, "Out!" as he vaulted over the runner and fired the ball at the first baseman.

While the crowd went into a frenzy, Brooke remained seated and watched. She didn't even notice that Lee had given Claire a resounding, exuberant kiss. The double play had taken only seconds—that impressed her. It also disconcerted her to discover that her pulse was racing. If she closed her eyes, she could still hear the cheers from the fans, smell the scent of sun-warmed beer and see, in slow motion, the strong, sweeping moves of Parks's body. She didn't need an instant replay to visualize the leap and stretch, the shifting of muscle. She knew a ballplayer had to be agile and quick, but how many of them had that dancerlike grace? Brooke caught herself making a mental note to bring a camera to the next game, then realized she had already decided to come back again. Was it Parks, she brooded, or baseball that was luring her back?

"He's something, isn't he?" Lee leaned over Claire to give Brooke a slap on the back.

"Something," Brooke murmured. She turned her head enough to look at him. "Was that a routine play?"

Lee snorted. "If you've got ice water for blood."

"Does he?"

As he drew on a cigar, Lee seemed to consider it. He gave Brooke a long, steady look. "On the field," he stated with a nod. "Parks is one of the most controlled, disciplined men I know. Of course—" the look broke with his quick smile "—I handle a lot of actors."

"Bless them," Claire said and crossed her short, slim legs.

"I believe we all agree that we hope Parks takes to this, ah, alternate career with as much energy as he shows in his baseball."

"If he has ten percent of this skill—" Brooke gestured toward the field "—in front of the camera, I'll be able to work with him."

"I think you'll be surprised," Lee commented dryly, "at just what Parks is capable of."

With a shrug, Brooke leaned on the rail again. "We'll see if he can take direction."

Brooke waited, with the tension of the crowd seeping into her, as the game went into the bottom of the ninth inning. Still tied 1-1, neither team seemed able to break through the defensive skill of the other. It should have been boring, she mused, even tedious. But she was on the edge of her seat and her pulse was still humming. She wanted them to win. With a kind of guilty surprise, Brooke caught herself just before she shouted at the plate umpire for calling strike three on the leadoff batter. It's just the atmosphere, she told herself with a frown. She'd always been a sucker for atmosphere. But when the second batter came up, she found herself gripping the rail, willing him to get a hit.

"This might go into extra innings," Lee commented.

"There's only one out," Brooke snapped, not bothering to turn around. She didn't see the quick grin Lee cast at Claire.

On a three-and-two pitch, the batter hit a bloop single to center. Around Brooke, the fans went berserk. He might have hit a home run from the way they're reacting, she thought, trying to ignore the fast pumping of her own blood. This time Brooke said nothing as the pitcher was pulled. How do they stand the tension? she wondered, watching the apparently relaxed players as the new relief warmed up. Base runners talked idly with the opposition. She thought that if she were in competition, she wouldn't be so friendly with the enemy.

The crowd settled down to a hum that became a communal shout with every pitch thrown. The batter hit one deep, so deep Brooke was amazed at the speed with which the right fielder returned it to the infield.

The batter was content with a single, but the base runner had eaten up the distance to third with the kind of gritty speed Brooke admired.

Now the crowd didn't quiet, but kept up a continual howl that echoed and reverberated as Parks came to bat. The pressure, Brooke thought, must be almost unbearable. Yet nothing showed in his face but that dangerous kind of concentration she'd seen once or twice before. She swallowed, aware that her heart was hammering in her throat. Ridiculous, she told herself once, then surrendered.

"Come on, damn it," she muttered, "smack one out of here."

He took the first pitch, a slow curve that just missed the corner. The breath that she'd been holding trembled out. The next he cut at, fouling it back hard against the window of the press box. Brooke clamped down on her bottom lip and mentally uttered a stream of curses. Parks coolly held up a hand for time, then bent to tie his shoe. The stadium echoed with his name. As if deaf to the yells, he stepped back into the box to take up his stance.

He hit it high and deep. Brooke was certain it was a repeat of his performance in her first game, then she saw the ball begin to drop just short of the fence.

"He's going to tag up. He'll tag up!" she heard Lee shouting as the center fielder caught Parks's fly at the warning track. Before Brooke could swear, the fans were shouting, not in fury but in delight. The moment the runner crossed the plate, players from the Kings' dugout swarmed out on the field.

"But Parks is out," Brooke said indignantly.

"The sacrifice fly scored the run," Lee explained.

Brooke gave him a haughty look. "I realize that—" only because she had crammed a few basic rules into her head "—but it hardly seems fair that Parks is out."

Chuckling, Lee patted her head. "He earned another RBI and the fleeting gratitude of a stadium full of Kings fans. He was one for three today, so his average won't suffer much."

"Brooke doesn't think much of rules," Claire put in, rising.

"Because they're usually made up by people who don't have the least idea what they're doing." A little annoyed with herself for becoming so involved, she stood, swinging her canvas bag over her shoulder.

"I don't know if Parks would agree with you," Lee told her. "He's lived by the rules for most of his life. Gets to be a habit."

"To each his own," she said casually. She wondered if Lee was aware that Parks was also a man who could seduce and half undress a woman behind the fragile covering of a rock wall in the middle of a crowded, glitzy Hollywood party. It seemed to her Parks was more a man who made up his own rules.

"Why don't we go down to the locker room and congratulate him?" Genially, he hooked his arms through Claire's and Brooke's, steamrolling them through the still cheering crowd.

Lee worked his way into the stadium's inner sanctum with a combination of panache and clout. Reporters were swarming, carrying microphones, cameras or notepads. Each one was badgering or flattering a sweaty athlete in the attempt to get a quote. In the closed-in area, Brooke considered the noise level to be every bit as high as it had been in the open stadium. Lockers slammed, shouts reverberated, laughter flowed in a kind of giddy relief. Each man knew the tension would return soon enough during the play-offs. They were going to enjoy the victory of the moment to its fullest.

"Yeah, if I hadn't saved Biggs from an error in the seventh inning," the first baseman told a reporter, deadpan, "it might have been a whole different ball game."

Biggs, the shortstop, retaliated by heaving a damp towel at his teammate. "Snyder can't catch a ball unless it drops into his mitt. The rest of us make him look good."

"I've saved Parks from fifty-three errors this season," Snyder went on blandly, drawing the sweaty towel from his face. "Guess his arm must be going. Thing is, some of the hitters are so good they just keep smacking the ball right into Parks's mitt. If you watch the replay of today's game, you'll see what fantastic aim they have." Someone dumped a bucket of water on his head, but Snyder continued without breaking rhythm. "You might notice how well I place the ball in the right fielder's mitt. That takes more practice."

Brooke spotted Parks, surrounded by reporters. His uniform was filthy, streaked with dirt, while his face fared little better. The smudges of black under his eyes gave him a slightly wicked look. Without the cap his hair curled freely, darkened with sweat. But his face and body were relaxed. A smile lingered on his lips as he spoke. That battlefield intensity was gone from his eyes, she noted, as if it had never existed. If she hadn't seen it, hadn't experienced it from him, Brooke would have sworn the man wasn't capable of any form of ruthlessness. Yet he was, she reminded herself, and it wouldn't be smart to forget it.

"With only four games left in the regular season," Parks stated, "I'll be satisfied to end up with a three eighty-seven average for the year."

"If you bat five hundred in those last games—"

Parks shot the reporter a mild grin. "We'll have to see about that."

"A little wind out there today and that game-winning sacrifice fly would've been a game-winning home run."

"That's the breaks."

"What was the pitch?"

"Inside curve," he responded easily. "A little high."

"Were you trying for a four-bagger, Parks?"

He grinned again, his expression altering only slightly
when he spotted Brooke. "With one out and runners on the
corners, I just wanted to keep the ball off the ground. Anything deep, and Kinjinsky scores . . . unless he wants the
Lead Foot Award."

"Lead Foot Award?"

"Ask Snyder," Parks suggested. "He's the current holder."
With another smile, Parks effectively eased himself away.
"Lee." He nodded to his agent while running a casual finger
down Brooke's arm. She felt the shock waves race through
her, and only barely managed not to jerk away. "Ms. Thorton. Nice to see you again." His only greeting to Brooke
was a slow smile as he caught the tip of her hair between his
thumb and forefinger. She thought again it was wise to remember he wasn't as safe as he appeared.

"Hell of a game, Parks," Lee announced. "You gave us an
entertaining afternoon."

"We aim to please," he murmured, still looking at Brooke.

"Claire and I are going out to dinner. Perhaps you and
Brooke would like to join us?"

Before Brooke could register surprise at Claire having a
date with Lee Dutton, or formulate an excuse against making it a foursome, Parks spoke up. "Sorry, Brooke and I have
plans."

Turning her head, she shot Parks a narrowed look. "I don't
recall our making any plans."

Smiling, he gave her a brief tug. "You'll have to learn to
write things down. Why don't you just wait in your box? I'll

be out in half an hour." Without giving her a chance to protest, Parks strolled off toward the showers.

"What incredible nerve," Brooke grumbled, only to be given a sharp but discreet elbow in the ribs by Claire.

"Sorry you can't join us, dear," she said sweetly. "But then you're not fond of Chinese food in any case. And Lee's going to show me his collection first."

"Collection?" Brooke repeated blankly as she was steered into the narrow corridor.

"We've a mutual passion." Claire gave Lee a quick and surprisingly flirtatious smile. "For Oriental art. Can you find your way back to the seats?"

"I'm not a complete dolt," Brooke muttered, while giving Lee a skeptical stare.

"Well then." Casually, Claire tucked her hand into Lee's beefy arm. "I'll see you Monday."

"Have a good time, kid," Lee called over his shoulder as Claire propelled him away.

"Thanks a lot." Stuffing her hands in her pockets, Brooke worked her way up, then out to the lower level, third-base box. "Thanks a hell of a lot," she repeated and stared out at the empty diamond.

There were a few maintenance workers scooping up the debris in the stands with humming heavy-duty cleaners, but other than that the huge open area was deserted. Finding it strangely appealing, Brooke discovered her annoyance waning. An hour before, the air had been alive, throbbing with the pulse of thousands. Now it was serene, with only the faintest trace of the crowd—the lingering odor of humanity, a whiff of salted popcorn, a few discarded cardboard containers. She leaned back against the rail, more interested in the empty stadium than the empty field.

When had it been built? she wondered. How many generations had crammed themselves into the seats and aisles to watch the games? How many thousands of gallons of beer had traveled along the rows of seats? She laughed a little, amused by her own whimsy. When a player stopped playing, did he come here to watch and remember? She thought Parks would. The game, she concluded, would get into your blood. Even she hadn't been immune to it . . . or, she thought wryly, to him.

Brooke tossed her head back, letting her hair fall behind her. The shadows were lengthening, but the heat still had the sticky, sweltering capacity of high afternoon. She didn't mind—she hated being cold. Habitually, she narrowed her eyes and let herself visualize how she would approach the stadium on film. Empty, she thought, with the echo of cheers, the sound of a ball cracking off a bat, a banner left behind to flutter in the breeze. She'd use the maintenance workers, sucking up the boxes and cups and bags. She might title it *Afterthought*, and there'd be no telling if the home team had left the field vanquished or victorious. What mattered would be the perpetuity of the game, the people who played it and the people who watched.

Brooke sensed him before she heard him—only an instant, but the instant was enough to scatter her thoughts and to bring her eyes swerving toward him. Immediately, all sense of the scene she had been setting vanished from her mind. No one else had ever had the power to do that to her. The fact that Parks did baffled her nearly as much as it infuriated her. For Brooke, her work was the one stability in her life—nothing and no one was allowed to tamper with it. Defensively, she straightened, meeting his stare head-on as he walked down to her in the loose, rangy stride that masked over a decade of training.

She expected him to greet her with some smart remark. Brooke was prepared for that. She considered he might greet her casually, as if his lie in the locker room had been perfect truth. She was prepared for that, too.

She wasn't prepared for him to walk directly to her, bury his hands in her hair and crush her against him in a long, hotly possessive kiss. Searing flashes of pleasure rocketed through her. Molten waves of desire overpowered surprise before it truly had time to register. His mouth pressed against hers in an absolute command that barely hid a trace of desperation. It was that desperation, more than the authority, that Brooke found herself responding to. The need to be needed was strong in her—she had always considered it her greatest weakness. And she was weak now, with the sharp scent of his skin in her senses, the dark taste of his mouth on her tongue, the feel of his shower-damp hair on her fingers.

Slowly, Parks drew away, waiting for her heavy lids to lift. Though his eyes never left hers, Brooke felt as though he looked at all of her once, thoroughly. "I want you." He said it calmly, though the fierce look was back on his face.

"I know."

Parks ran a hand through her hair again, from the crown to the tips. "I'm going to have you."

Steadying a bit, Brooke stepped out of his arms. "That I don't know."

Smiling, Parks continued to caress her hair. "Don't you?"

"No," Brooke returned with such firmness that Parks lifted a brow.

"Well," he considered, "I suppose it could be a very pleasant experience to convince you."

Brooke tossed her head to free her hair of his seeking fingers. "Why did you lie to Lee about our having plans tonight?"

"Because I'd spent nine long, hot innings thinking about making love to you."

Again he said it calmly, with just a hint of a smile on his lips, but Brooke realized he was quite serious. "Well, that's direct and to the point."

"You prefer things that way, don't you?"

"Yes," she agreed, settling back against the rail again. "So let me do the same for you. We're going to be working together for several months on a very big project that involves a number of people. I'm very good at my job and I intend to see that you're very good at yours."

"So?"

Her eyes flashed at his amused tone, but Brooke continued. "So personal involvements interfere with professional judgment. As your director, I have no intention of becoming your lover, however briefly."

"Briefly?" Parks repeated, studying her. "Do you always anticipate the length of your relationships beforehand? I think," he continued slowly, "you're more of a romantic than that."

"I don't care what you think," she snapped, "as long as you understand."

"I understand," Parks agreed, beginning to. "You're evading the issue."

"I certainly am not!" Temper flared, reflecting in her stance and her eyes as well as her voice. "I'm telling you straight out that I'm not interested. If that bruises your ego, too bad."

Parks grabbed her arm when she would have swept by him. "You know," he began in a careful tone that warned of simmering anger, "you infuriate me. I can't remember the last time a woman affected me that way."

"I'm not surprised." Brooke jerked her arm out of his hold. "You've been too busy devastating them with your charm."

"And you're too worried about being dumped to have any kind of a relationship."

She made a quick, involuntary sound, as if she'd been

struck. Cheeks pale, eyes dark, she stared at him before she shoved him aside to race up the stairs. Parks caught her before she'd made it halfway. Though he turned her back to face him firmly, his touch was gentle.

"Raw nerve?" he murmured, feeling both sympathy and guilt. It wasn't often he lost control enough to say something he'd have to apologize for. Eyes dry and hurting, Brooke glared at him. "I'm sorry."

"Just let me go."

"Brooke." He wanted to pull her into his arms and comfort, but knew she wouldn't accept it. "I am sorry. I don't make a habit of punching women."

It wasn't charm, but sincerity. After a moment, Brooke let out a long breath. "All right. I usually take a punch better than that."

"Can we take off the gloves—at least for the rest of the day?" How deep was the hurt? Parks wondered. And how long would it take to win her trust?

"Maybe," Brooke returned cautiously.

"How about dinner?"

She responded to the smile before she realized it. "My weakness."

"We'll start there, then. How do you feel about tacos?"

She allowed him to take her hand. "Who's buying?"

They sat outdoors at a busy fast-food franchise with tiny metal tables and hard stools. Sounds of traffic and blaring car radios rolled over them. Brooke relaxed when she ate, Parks noted, wondering if she were consciously aware of the dropping of guards. He didn't think so. The relaxation was the same when she sat in an elegant restaurant with wine and exotic food as it was in a greasy little takeout with sloppy tacos and watered-down sodas in paper cups.

After handing her another napkin, Parks decided to do some casual probing.

"Did you grow up in California?"

"No." Brooke drew more soda through her straw. "You did."

"More or less." Remembering how skilled she was in evading or changing the subject, Parks persisted. "Why did you move to L.A.?"

"It's warm," she said immediately. "It's crowded."

"But you live miles out of town in the middle of nowhere."

"I like my privacy. How did your family feel about you choosing baseball over Parkinson Chemicals?"

He smiled a little, enjoying the battle for control. "Stunned. Though I'd told them for years what I intended to do. My father thought, still thinks, it's a phase. What does your family think about you directing commercials?"

Brooke set down her cup. "I don't have any family."

Something in her tone warned him this was a tender area. "Where did you grow up?"

"Here and there." Quickly, she began to stuff used napkins into the empty cups. Parks caught her hand before she could rise.

"Foster homes?"

Eyes darkening with anger, Brooke stared at him. "Why are you pressing?"

"Because I want to know who you are," he said softly. "We could be friends before we're lovers."

"Let go of my hand."

Instead of obliging, Parks gave her a curious look. "Do I make you nervous?"

"You make me furious," she tossed back, evading one truth with another. "I can't be around you for more than ten minutes without getting mad."

Parks grinned. "I know the feeling. Still, it's stimulating."

"I don't want to be stimulated," Brooke said evenly. "I want to be comfortable."

With a half laugh, Parks turned her hand over, brushing his lips lightly over the palm. "I don't think so," he murmured, watching her reaction over their joined hands. "You're much too alive to settle for comfortable."

"You don't know me."

"Exactly my point." He leaned a bit closer. "Who are you?"

"What I've made myself."

Parks nodded. "I see a strong, independent woman with lots of drive and ambition. I also see a woman who chooses a quiet, isolated spot for her home, who knows how to laugh and mean it, who forgives just as quickly as she angers." As he spoke Parks watched her brows lower. She wasn't angry now, but thoughtful and wary. He felt a bit like a man trying to gain the confidence of a dove who might fly away at any time or choose to nestle in the palm of his hand. "She interests me."

After a moment, Brooke let out a long breath. Perhaps if she told him a little, she considered, he'd leave it at that. "My mother wasn't married," she began briskly. "I'm told that after six months she got tired of lugging a baby around and dumped me on her sister. I don't remember a great deal about my aunt. I was six when she turned me over to social services. What I do remember is being hungry and not very warm. I went into my first foster home." She shrugged then pushed away the debris that littered the table. "It wasn't too bad. I was there for little more than a year before I got shuffled to the next one. I was in five altogether from the age of six to seventeen. Some were better than others, but I never belonged. A lot of that may have been my fault."

Brooke sighed, not pleased to remember. "Not all foster parents take in children for the money. Some of them— most of them," she amended, "are very kind, loving people.

I just never felt a part, because I always knew it would be temporary, that my sister or brother of the moment was real and I was . . . transient. As a result I was difficult. Maybe I challenged the people whose home I was placed in to want me—for me, not out of pity or social obligation or the extra dollars my living with them would bring in.

"My last two years in high school I lived on a farm in Ohio with a nice couple who had an angelic son who would yank my hair when his mother's back was turned." A quick grimace. "I left as soon as I graduated from high school, worked my way cross-country waiting tables. It only took me four months to get to L.A." She met Parks's quiet, steady look and suddenly flared. "Don't feel sorry for me."

The ultimate insult, he mused, taking her rigid hand in his. "I wasn't. I was wondering how many people would have had the guts to try to make their own life at seventeen, and how many would have had the strength to really do it. At the same age I wanted to head for the Florida training camps. Instead I was on a plane heading for college."

"Because you had an obligation," Brooke countered. "I didn't. If I had had the chance to go to college . . ." She trailed off. "In any case, we've both had a decade in our careers."

"And you can have several more if you like," Parks pointed out. "I can't. One more season."

"Why?" she demanded. "You'll only be . . ."

"Thirty-five," he finished with a wry smile. "I promised myself ten years ago that's when I'd stop. There aren't many of us who can play past forty like Mays."

"Yes, it's obvious you play like an old man," she returned dryly.

"I intend to stop before I do."

Taking a straw, she began to pleat it while she studied him. "Quit while you're ahead?"

"That's the idea."

That she could understand. "Does giving it up with half your life ahead of you bother you?"

"I intend to do something with the second half, but at times it does. Other times I think about all those summer evenings I'll have free. Do you like the beach?"

"I don't get there often, but yes." She thought about the long, hot commercial she'd just filmed. "With occasional exceptions," she added.

"I have a place on Maui." Unexpectedly he leaned over, caressing her cheek with fingers that were whisper soft and undeniably possessive. "I'm going to take you there one day." He shook his head as Brooke started to speak. "Don't argue, we do that too much. Let's go for a drive."

"Parks," Brooke began as they rose, "I meant what I said about not getting involved."

"Yeah, I know." Then he kissed her long and lingeringly while she stood with her hands filled with paper plates and cups.

CHAPTER 5

It was three days before Brooke heard from Parks. She was aware that the last four-game series in the regular season would be played out of town. She knew, too, from what she told herself was simply a casual glimpse at the sports section, that Parks had knocked in three more RBIs in the first two games. In the meantime, she was busy looking over the storyboard for his first block of commercials.

The word had come down that the first thirty-second spot would be filmed before the league play-offs, in order to capitalize on Parks's exposure in the competition. That left Brooke little time to prepare, with an already demanding schedule of studio and location shoots, editing and preproduction meetings. But challenge, like food, was vital to her.

Closed off in her office, with a half an hour's leeway before she was due at the studio, Brooke ran over the final script for the initial de Marco commercial. Casually slick, she thought, approving. It had minimal dialogue and soft sell— Parks at the plate, swinging away while dressed in de Marco's elegant sports clothes, then a slow dissolve to the next scene with him dressed in the same suit, stepping out of a Rolls with a slinky brunette on her arm.

"Clothes for anytime—anywhere," Brooke muttered. The timing had been checked and rechecked. The audio, except for Parks's one-line voice-over, was already being recorded. All she had to do was to guide Parks through the paces. The salesmanship hinged on her skill and his charm. Fair enough, she thought and reached for her half cup of cold coffee as a knock sounded at her door. "Yeah?" Brooke turned the script back to page one, running through the camera angles.

"Delivery for you, Brooke." The receptionist dropped a long white florist's box on her cluttered desk. "Jenkins said to let you know the Lardner job's been edited. You might want to check it out."

"Okay, thanks." Curiously, Brooke frowned over the top of the script at the flower box. Occasionally, she received a grateful phone call or letter from a client when they were particularly pleased with a commercial—but not flowers. Then there'd been that actor in the car spot last year, Brooke remembered. The one who was on his third wife. He'd alternately amused and annoyed Brooke by sending her batches of red roses every week. But six months had passed since she had convinced him that he was wasting her time and his money.

More likely it was one of E.J.'s practical jokes, she considered. She'd probably find a few dozen frog legs inside. Not one to spoil someone's fun, Brooke pulled off the ribbon and lifted the lid.

There were masses of hibiscus. Fragrant, dew-soft pink-and-white petals filled the box almost to overflowing. After the first gasp of surprise, Brooke dove her hands into them, captivated by their purely feminine scent and feel. Her office suddenly smelled like a tropical island: heady, exotic, richly romantic. With a sound of pleasure, she filled her hands with the blooms, bringing them up to her face to inhale. In contrast to the sultry scent, the petals seemed impossibly fragile. A small white card fluttered down to her littered desk.

Letting the flowers drift back into the box, Brooke reached for the envelope and tore it open.

I thought of your skin.

There was nothing else, but she knew. She shuddered, then chided herself for acting like a mooning teenager. But she read the line three times. No one had ever been able to affect her so deeply with such simplicity. Though Parks was a thousand miles away, she could all but feel those lean, strong fingers trace down her cheek. The flood of warmth, the flash of desire told her she wasn't going to escape him—had never truly wanted to. Without giving herself any time for doubts or fears, Brooke picked up the phone.

"Get me Parks Jones," she said quickly. "Try Lee Dutton, he'll have the number." Before she could change her mind, Brooke hung up, burying her hands in the flowers again.

How was it he knew just what buttons to push? she wondered, then discovered at that moment she didn't care. It was enough to be romanced—and romanced in style. Lifting a single bloom, she trailed it down her cheek. It was smooth and moist against her skin—as Parks's first kiss had been. The ringing phone caught her dreaming.

"Yes?"

"Parks Jones on line two. You've got ten minutes before they need you in the studio."

"All right. Hunt me up a vase and some water, will you?" She glanced at the box again. "Make that two vases." Still standing with the blossom in her hand, Brooke punched the button for line two. "Parks?"

"Yes. Hello, Brooke."

"Thank you."

"You're welcome."

She hesitated, then let herself speak her first thought. "I feel like a teenager who just got her first corsage."

Dropping flat on his back on the bed, he laughed. "I'd like to see you with some of them in your hair."

Experimentally she held one up over her ear. Unprofessional, she thought with a sigh, and contented herself with the scent of them. "I've a shoot in the studio in a few minutes; I don't think the lights would do them much good."

"You have your practical side, don't you, Brooke?" Parks flexed the slight ache in his shoulder and closed his eyes.

"It's necessary," she muttered but couldn't quite bring herself to drop the blossom back in the box. "How are you? I wasn't sure you'd be in."

"I got in about half an hour ago. They cut us down five to two. I went oh for three."

"Oh." She frowned, not quite sure what she was supposed to say. "I'm sorry."

"I didn't seem to have any rhythm—it'll pass." Before the play-offs, he added silently. "I thought of you, maybe too much."

Brooke felt an odd twist of pleasure that was difficult to pass off. "I wouldn't want to be responsible for a slump, particularly when I remember some of the remedies." His chuckle sounded faint and weary. "Are you tired?"

"A bit. You'd think with the division wrapped up we'd glide through this last series. Last night we went eleven innings."

"I know." She could have bitten off her tongue. "I caught the highlights on the late news," she said breezily. "I'll let you sleep, then. I just wanted to thank you."

Her inadvertent admission had his lips twitching, but he

didn't bother to open his eyes. With them closed, he had no trouble bringing her face into focus. "Will I see you when I get back?"

"Of course. We'll be shooting the first segment on Friday, so—"

"Brooke," he interrupted firmly, quietly. "Will I see you when I get back?"

She hesitated, then looked down at the mass of pink-and-white hibiscus on her desk. "Yes," she heard herself saying. Pressing the flower to her cheek, she sighed. "I think I'm going to make a very big mistake."

"Good. I'll see you Friday."

The trick to being a good director, Brooke had always thought, was to be precise without being too technical, brisk without losing sympathy, then to split yourself up into several small parts so that you could be everywhere at once. It was a knack she had developed early on—on the job— without the formalized training of many of her colleagues. Perhaps because she had worked so many of the other aspects of filming, from timing a script to setting the lights to mixing sound, she was fiercely precise. Nothing escaped her eye. Because she knew actors were often overworked and insecure, she had never quite lost her sympathy for them even when she was ready to rage at a consistently flubbed line. Her early experience at waiting tables had taught her the trick of moving fast enough to all but be in two places at once.

On a set or in a studio, she had complete self-confidence. Her control was usually unquestioned because it came naturally. She never thought about being in charge or felt the need to remind others of it; she simply *was* in charge.

With a copy of the script in one hand, she supervised the

final adjustments on the lights and reflectors. The ball diamond, she had noted immediately, had an entirely different feel at home plate than it had from the stands. It was like being on an island, cupped amid the high mountain of seats, with the tall green wall skirting the back. The distance from plate to fence seemed even more formidable from this perspective. Brooke wondered how men with sticks in their hands could continually hit a moving ball over that last obstacle.

She could smell the grass, freshly trimmed, the dusty scent of dirt that had dried in the sun and a whiff of E.J.'s blatantly macho cologne. "Give me a reading," she ordered the lighting director as she glanced up at the thick clouds in the sky. "I want a sunny afternoon."

"You got it." The lights were focused as Brooke stepped behind camera one to check for shadows on the plate.

Parks loitered at the tunnel entrance a moment, watching her. This was a different woman from the one who he had treated to tacos—different still from the one he had held in his arms at the de Marco party. Her hair was trained back in one long braid, nothing like the flowing mane he was used to seeing. She wore jeans that were white at the stress points, a plain T-shirt the color of scrambled eggs, dusty tennis shoes and winking sapphires at her ears.

But it wasn't her hairstyle or the apparel that denoted the difference. It was the assurance. He'd seen it before, but each time it had been underlying. Now she sparked with it, gesturing, ordering while men and women set about giving her exactly what she demanded. No one questioned her. And, he considered, it was patently obvious that she wouldn't have permitted it.

Grimacing, he tugged at the sleeve of the thin silk shirt he wore. Who the hell would play ball in an outfit like this? he wondered with a glance at the creaseless cream slacks.

The rules of this game were hers, he reminded himself, then stepped into the light.

"Bigelow, get these cables secure before somebody breaks a leg. Libby, see if you can scrounge up some ice water, we're going to need it. Okay, where's . . ." Turning at that moment, Brooke spotted Parks. "Oh, there you are." If she felt any personal pleasure at seeing him, she hid it well, Parks thought wryly as she turned to shout an order at her assistant. "I'm going to want you to stand at the plate so we can check the lighting and camera angles."

Without a word, Parks complied. You might as well get used to it, he told himself. You've got yourself locked into hawking somebody else's clothes for the next two years. He stuffed his hands in his pockets, cursed Lee briefly and stood in the batter's box. Someone stuck a light meter next to his face.

"You gonna wipe out the Valiants in the play-offs?" the technician demanded.

"That's the plan," Parks returned easily.

"I've got fifty bucks on it."

This time Parks grinned. "I'll try to keep that in mind."

"Detrick." Brooke gave the technician a jerk of her head to send him on his way as she approached Parks. "Okay, this is the easy part," she began. "No dialogue, and you're doing what you're best at."

"What's that?"

Brooke lifted a brow at the loaded question but continued smoothly. "Swinging a bat. Since the pitching coach has agreed to throw you a few, you should feel comfortable."

"Ever stood in the box without a helmet?" he countered.

"It wouldn't go with your outfit," she said mildly. She gave him a deliberately slow study—eyes sweeping up, then down, then back up again. "And it looks good."

"I like yours, too." His smile was quick and dangerous. "I'm going to like unbinding your hair."

"Makeup!" she called abruptly. "Give him a dusting, he's going to glow."

"Wait a minute," Parks began, deftly catching the wrist of the woman with the powder.

"No sweating on camera," Brooke drawled, pleased with his reaction. "All I want you to do is what you usually do when you're in uniform. Take your regular stance," she continued. "A couple of those test swings. After you hit the ball, I want one of those grins before you toss the bat aside."

"What grins?" Reluctantly, Parks released the makeup artist's wrist and suffered the powder.

With humor dancing in her eyes, Brooke gave him a singularly sweet smile. "One of those boy-on-the-beach grins. Quick, lots of teeth, crinkles at the corners of the eyes."

He narrowed them dangerously. "I'm going to get you for this."

"Try to keep the strikes to a minimum," she went on blithely. "Every strike's a take. You don't have to hit it out of the park, just *look* like you have. Got it?"

"Yeah, I got it." Annoyed, he nodded to the pitching coach as he walked by.

"You look real cute, Jones."

"Just try to get it near the plate," Parks retorted. "Do I get a bat?" he demanded of Brooke. "Or do I just pretend?"

For an answer, Brooke turned and shouted to her assistant. "Let's have the bat, E.J., are you set? Just roll the film—no sweeps, no pans, no close-ups. Remember, we're selling the clothes."

"This is aluminum."

Distracted, Brooke turned back to Parks. "What?"

"This bat is aluminum."

When he held it out, Brooke automatically took it from

him. "Yes, it appears to be." As she started to pass it back to him, Parks shook his head.

"I use wood. A two seventy-seven A."

She started to come back with a curt remark, then stopped herself. If she was accustomed to anything, it was temperament. "Get Mr. Jones the bat he prefers," she told her assistant, tossing the first one to him. "Anything else?"

For a moment, he regarded her keenly. "Does everybody jump when you say?"

"Damn right. Keep that in mind for the next couple of hours, and we shouldn't have any problems."

His look sharpened fractionally. "While the cameras are on," he returned in a voice only she could hear.

Turning, she walked to stand behind the camera. Automatically, E.J. stepped back so that she could check the angle herself. Brows drawn together, Brooke stared at Parks through the lens as her assistant handed him another bat. "Okay, Parks, would you take your stance?" Her frown deepened as he leaned slightly over the plate, feet planted, knees bent, shoulders lined toward the mound. The frown vanished. "Good," she decided, moving back so that E.J. could take her place.

"Ten bucks says he pulls one to left center."

A brief nod was Brooke's acceptance of the bet. "Parks, when I say action, I want you to take your stance again, then those testing swings. Keep your eye on the mound—*don't* look at the camera. Just forget we're here." With the first smile Parks had seen that morning, Brooke turned to the pitching coach. "Are you all set, Mr. Friedman?"

"All set, sweetheart. I'll try not to blow it by you, Jones."

Parks gave a snort of laughter. "Just see if you can make it to the plate." He gestured to his uncovered head. "And keep it low."

Brooke took a last glance around, assuring herself everyone was in position. "Let's do one for time. Set?" She held up her hand, waiting for absolute silence. "Roll film, and . . . action."

She watched Parks crouch into position, then take two loose swings. The deep blue silk of his shirt caught the light, accenting the play of muscles beneath. Hands on her hips, Brooke counted off the seconds and waited. Parks shifted his weight as the ball came toward him, tensed his muscles then checked his swing. The ball smashed into the pads behind him.

Just barely, Brooke controlled the need to swear. "Cut." Battling her annoyance, she walked to him. "Is there a problem, Parks?"

"Pitch was outside."

"Like hell," Friedman called from the mound. "It caught the corner."

Immediately the crew split themselves up, arguing in favor of the batter or the pitcher. Ignoring them for the moment, Brooke gave her attention to Parks. "This isn't the bottom of the ninth, you're just supposed to hit the ball. You'll notice," she continued, gesturing behind her, "there aren't any fielders, no fans, no press."

Parks set the bat, barrel down in the dirt, and leaned on the handle. "You want me to swing at a bad pitch?"

Brooke met the amused blue eyes levelly. "The quality of the pitch is immaterial," she countered as the argument raged behind them. "Just hit the ball."

With a shrug, he hefted the bat again. "You're the boss . . . at the moment."

The look held, long and challenging, before Brooke turned back to the crew. "Take two," she announced, effectively cutting off the debate.

This time Parks didn't check his swing but drilled the ball up the foul line at third. Without looking at E.J., Brooke held

out her hand. "Time," she requested as a ten-dollar bill was
stuffed in her palm.

Parks noticed a tiny brunette with a stopwatch and clip-
board. "Twelve and a half seconds, Brooke."

"Good. All right, let's go for it."

"This one's going over the fence," E.J. pronounced in an
undertone to Brooke. "Bet ten?"

"Take three," she called out with a nod of assent. "Roll
film, and . . . action!" A satisfied smile touched her lips as she
studied Parks. He was either getting into the spirit of things,
or his own competitive spirit was driving him. Either way,
it was working for her. The look on his face as he crouched
over the plate was exactly what she wanted—the steady intensity that bordered on fierceness. A pity she couldn't work
in a close-up, she mused, then lost the thought as Parks took
a full swing at the pitch.

Power. The word rippled through her as he connected
with the ball. She saw the instant the shirt strained over
his shoulders, was aware of the bunching of muscles in his
thighs beneath the soft, expensive material. It wasn't necessary to follow the path of the ball to know where it had
gone. She knew the flash of grin on Parks's face had nothing to do with her direction. It was sheer pleasure. Brooke
kept the film rolling as his eyes followed the ball out of the
park. Still grinning, he turned to her, then gave a deprecatory shrug.

She should have been angry that he had looked at the camera against her directions, but the movement, the expression
was perfect. Even as she dug in her pocket for E.J.'s ten dollars, she decided to keep it in.

"Cut."

Spontaneous applause broke out, along with a few whistles. "Nice pitch, Friedman," Parks commented.

The coach tossed another ball in the air. "Just making

you look good, Jones. The Valiants' pitchers won't be so friendly."

Brooke swiped the back of her wrist across her damp brow. "I'd like a couple more please. What was the time on that?"

"Fourteen seconds."

"Okay. The light's shifting, check the reading. Mr. Friedman, I'd like to get a couple more."

"Anything you say, sweetheart."

"Parks, I need a full swing like last time. No matter where the ball goes, look up and out—don't forget the grin."

Laying the bat on his shoulder, he drawled, "No, ma'am."

Brooke ignored him and turned away. "Lights?"

The technician finished the adjustments, then nodded. "Set."

Although she considered the third take close to perfect, Brooke ran through another three. Edited, this segment of the commercial would run twelve and a half seconds. That it took only three hours to set up and film showed that she ran a tight schedule.

"It's a wrap. Thanks," she added as she accepted the cup of ice water from her assistant. "We'll set up in front of the restaurant in . . ." She glanced at her watch. "Two hours, Fred, double-check on the Rolls and the actress. E.J., I'll take the film into editing myself." Even as she spoke, Brooke walked over to the mound. "Mr. Friedman." With a smile, she held out her hand. "Thank you."

He found her grip firm and her eyes soft. "My pleasure." With a chuckle, he tossed a spare ball into his mitt. "You know, in my day ballplayers plugged razor blades or beer. We endorsed bats and gloves." He cast a glance at Parks, who was signing a baseball for a technician. "No fancy designers would have asked us to sport his clothes."

Brooke shifted her eyes to Parks. He was laughing now, shaking his head at E.J. as the cameraman ticked off some point on his fingers. The casually elegant clothes suited him, as did the dark wood bat in his hand. "I'd hate to have him know I said it, Mr. Friedman," Brooke commented as she turned back to the coach, "but Parks is a natural."

With a shout of laughter, Friedman patted her on the back. "He won't hear it from me, sweetheart. Last thing my pitchers need is a third baseman with a big head. One more thing," he added before Brooke turned away. "I watched the way you run things." He gave her an expansive grin that revealed good dentures. "You'd make a hell of a coach."

"Thanks." Pleased with the compliment, Brooke made her way toward the plate, and Parks. "You did very well."

He regarded her extended hand with amusement, but accepted it. "For a rookie?" he countered.

When she started to remove her hand, Parks held it firmly, running a light fingertip over the inside of her wrist. He had the satisfaction of feeling her pulse jump then speed up. "I didn't anticipate any problems, as you were simply playing yourself." Behind her, technicians were taking down lights and coiling cable. She heard E.J. describing the new lady he was seeing in glowing, if exaggerated, terms. Using all her willpower, Brooke concentrated on the background noises instead of the feel of Parks's finger tracing over her skin. "The next scene should be fairly easy. We'll go over it on location this afternoon. If you have any questions—"

"Just one," Parks interrupted. "Come here a minute." Without waiting for agreement, he drew her toward the dugout, stepped inside then just through the door that led to the locker rooms.

"What's the problem, Parks?" Brooke demanded. "I have to get into editing before the next shoot."

"Are we finished here for now?"

With an impatient sigh, Brooke gestured to the equipment being packed. "Obviously."

"Fine." Pressing her back against the doorway, Parks covered her mouth with his.

It was a proprietary kiss with whispers of violence. The frustrations of the past hours seeped into it as he finally let them free. There was the annoyance of wanting her—of being too far away to touch for days, then being close enough, but not being permitted to. There was the exasperation of her cool professional treatment of him while he had fought an insistent growing desire. And there was the banked fury at being put in the position of taking orders from a woman who dominated his thoughts and denied his body.

Yet it was more agitating than soothing to press his body against the softness of hers. She filled him—the exotic scent, the ripe woman-taste of her mouth, the silken skin over the sharp, strong bones of her face. Almost desperately, he pressed closer, plunged deeper. He would *not* be filled. He would find that corner, that secret place that would open her for him so that he could have her at last—body and mind. To do that he needed the edge of control, over himself, and over Brooke. Her strength made it a challenge—his desire made it a necessity.

"Hey, Brooke, want a ride to the . . . Whoops." E.J. poked his head into the dugout then retreated. As Parks's lips freed hers, she could hear the cameraman whistling gleefully as he strolled away. Furious that she had completely lost track of time and place, Brooke shoved against Parks's chest.

"Let go of me!"

"Why?"

Apparently her ice-pick stare more amused than wounded him. "Don't you *ever* pull something like that when I'm working," she hissed, shoving a second time as Parks blocked her exit.

"I asked if we were finished," Parks reminded her, then backed her into the wall again.

"When we're on the job," Brooke said evenly, "I'm the director, you're the product." He narrowed his eyes at her choice of words, but she continued, full steam. "You'll do *exactly* what I tell you."

"The camera's not rolling, Brooke."

"I won't have my crew speculating, circulating gossip that can undermine my authority or my credibility."

His own temper rose in direct balance with need. She only aroused him more when she challenged. "Aren't you more afraid that you enjoy being touched by me? Doesn't it infuriate you that when I kiss you, you don't really give a damn who's in charge?" He bent his head so that his lips were only a breath from hers. "I took your orders all morning, Ms. Gordon. Now it's my turn."

Her lancelike stare didn't falter as the quiet words fluttered over her lips. With the tip of his tongue he traced them, enjoying their taste and her own suppressed passion. Merging desire stung the air—they both felt it, they both tried to rise above it in the struggle for dominance. Yet they both became aware that it was the desire that would win over each of them.

His lips rubbed over hers, without pressure or force, taunting her to demand he stop, daring her to resist her own needs. Their eyes remained open and fixed on each other. Both pairs of irises darkened as passion tempted each of them to surrender.

"We have another shoot this afternoon," Brooke managed as she fought to keep her voice steady.

"When we're filming, I'll do what you tell me." He kissed her once, hard and quick. "Tonight," he added, dealing with his own heated blood, "we'll see."

CHAPTER 6

Brooke chose to shoot during the late-afternoon lull using day-for-night filters, rather than compete with the evening traffic. It was a quick scene, relatively simple and very glossy. The champagne-colored Rolls would drive up in front of the posh restaurant, Parks would alight, in the same outfit, but wearing a jacket—already sponged and pressed from the morning—then offer his hand to the sleekly dressed brunette. She would step from the car, showing considerable leg, then flash Parks a look before linking her arm through his. The scene would then fade out, with Parks's voice-over dubbed in, stating the motto for the campaign.

"De Marco. For the man who's going places."

The visual would be another twelve seconds, so that combined with the stadium segment, the intro and the tag at the end, the commercial would round out at thirty seconds.

"I want a long shot of the Rolls, E.J., then come in on Parks as he steps out. We don't want to lose the impact that he's wearing the same outfit he played ball in. Don't get hung up on the lady," she added dryly as she sent him a knowing look.

"Who me?" Pulling a Kings fielder's cap out of his back

pocket, he offered it to Brooke. "Want to wear it? Team spirit?"

Placing one hand on her hip, Brooke stared at him without any change of expression. With a quick chuckle, E.J. fit the cap over his own modified Afro.

"Okay, boss, I'm ready when you are."

As was her habit, Brooke rechecked the camera angle and the lighting before she signaled the first take. The Rolls cruised sedately to the curb. Brooke played the background music over in her head, trying to judge how it would fit. On cue, Parks climbed out, turning to offer his hand to the brunette still inside. Frowning, Brooke let the scene play out. It wasn't right. She saw why immediately but took the few minutes until the cut to work out how to approach Parks.

With a gesture, Brooke indicated that she would speak to Parks while the driver backed up the Rolls for the next take. Putting a hand on his arm, she led him away from the technicians. "Parks, you have to relax." Because handling fidgety actors was second nature to her, Brooke's voice and manner were markedly different from the morning session. Parks noted it and bristled anyway.

"I don't know what you mean."

She steered him well away from where a few interested pedestrians were loitering by a barricade. "Number one," she began, "you're plugging a good product. Try to believe in it."

"If I didn't think it was a good product, I wouldn't be doing this," he retorted, frowning over her shoulder at the huddle of lights.

"But you're not comfortable." When Brooke gave his shoulder a reassuring pat, Parks scowled at her. "If you insist on feeling like an idiot, it's going to show. Wait," she ordered as he started to speak. "This morning, you felt more at ease—the stadium, a bat in your hand. After the first couple of minutes, you started to play the game. That's all I want you to do now."

"Look, Brooke, I'm not an actor—"

"Who's asking you to act?" she countered. "God spare me from that." She knew she'd insulted him, so she tempered the comment with a smile. "Listen, you're a winner, out on the town in a chauffeured Rolls with a gorgeous woman. All I want you to do is have a good time and look rather pleased with yourself. You can pull it off, Parks. Loosen up."

"I wonder how you'd feel if someone asked you to field a line drive with twenty thousand people watching."

Brooke smiled again and tried not to think about the minutes ticking away. "You do that routinely," she pointed out, "because you concentrate on your job and forget those thousands of people."

"This is different," he muttered.

"Only if you let it be. Just let me see that same self-satisfied look on your face that you had when you hit that homer this morning. Pretend, Parks." Brooke straightened the collar of his shirt. "It's good for you."

"Did you know that Nina has the IQ of a soft-boiled egg?"

"Nina?"

"My date."

Brooke gave in to a sigh. "Stop being so temperamental; nobody's asking you to marry her."

Parks opened his mouth, then shut it again. No one had ever accused him of being temperamental. He'd never *been* temperamental. If his manager told him to take a three-and-one pitch, he took it. If the third base coach told him to steal home, he ran. Not because he was malleable, but because if he was signed with a team, he followed the rules. It didn't mean he always had to like them. With a quiet oath, he ran a hand through his hair and admitted that it wasn't so much what the orders were in this case, but who was laying them out. But then, the lights and cameras would eventually shut down.

"Fine, let's do it again." He gave Brooke the slow smile she'd learned not to trust before he walked toward the Rolls. Suspicious of his easy capitulation, Brooke turned back to stand beside E.J.

Parks gave her no more cause to complain, though they were more than two hours shooting the segment. Brooke found that she had more trouble with the professional actress—and a couple of fans who recognized Parks—than she had with him. It took three takes before she convinced Nina that she wasn't looking for glowing and adoring, but for sleek and aloof. Brooke wanted the contrast and ran everyone through the twelve seconds until she was certain she had it.

Then there was the matter of two fans who sneaked through the barricade to get Parks's autograph while the camera was still rolling. Parks obliged them, and though Brooke simmered at the interruption, she noted that he dispatched the fans with the charm of a seasoned diplomat. Grudgingly, she had to admit she couldn't have done better herself.

"That's a wrap," Brooke announced, arching her back. She'd been on her feet for over eight hours, bolting down a half a sandwich between segments. She felt pleased with the day's work, satisfied with Parks's progress and ravenous. "You can break down," she told the crew. "Good job. E.J., I've scheduled the editing and dubbing for tomorrow. If you want to see what we're going to do to your film, you can come in."

"It's Saturday."

"Yeah." She pulled the bill of the fielder's cap over his face. "We'll start working at ten. Nina . . ." Brooke took the actress's slim, smooth hand. "You were lovely, thank you.

Fred, make sure the Rolls gets back in one piece, or you'll have to face Claire. Bigelow, what's the new kid's name?" Brooke jerked her head at a young technician who was busily packing up lights.

"Silbey?"

With a nod, Brooke made a mental note of it. "He's good," she said briefly, then turned to Parks. "Well, you made it through the first one. We'll dub in the voice-over tomorrow. Any scars?"

"None that show."

"Maybe I shouldn't tell you that this one is the easiest on the schedule."

He met the humor in her eyes blandly. "Maybe you shouldn't."

"Where's your car?"

"Out at the stadium."

With a frown, Brooke checked her watch. "I'll give you a lift back there." She toyed with the idea of going by Thorton's first to take a quick look at the film, then discarded the idea. It would be better to look at it fresh in the morning. "I have to call Claire. . . . Well." Brooke shrugged. "That can wait. Any problems?" she asked to the crew in general.

"Tomorrow's Saturday," an aggrieved E.J. stated again as he packed up his equipment. "Woman, you just don't give a man a break."

"You don't have to come in," she reminded him, knowing he would. "Good night." With Parks beside her, Brooke started down the street.

"Do you make a habit of working weekends?" he asked, noting that after a long, hectic day she still moved as though she had urgent appointments to keep.

"When it's necessary. We're rushing this through to get it aired during the play-offs or, barring that, the series." She

shot him a look. "You'd better be in it." Still walking, she began to dig in the purse slung over her shoulder.

"I'll try to accommodate you. Want me to drive?"

With the keys in one hand, Brooke looked up in surprise.
"Have you been talking to E.J.?"

His brows drew together. "No. Why?"

"Nothing." Dismissing the thought, Brooke paused beside
her car. "Why do you want to drive?"

"It occurs to me that I may have had to stand in front of that
stupid camera off and on all day, but you haven't stopped for
over eight hours. It's a tough job."

"I'm a tough lady," she responded with a trace of defen-
siveness in her voice.

"Yeah." He grazed his knuckles over her cheek. "Iron."

"Just get in the car," Brooke muttered. After rounding the
hood, she climbed in, slamming the door only slightly. "It'll
take a little while to get across town in this traffic."

"I'm not in a hurry." Parks settled comfortably beside her.
"Can you cook?"

In the act of starting the car, Brooke frowned at him. "Can
I what?"

"Cook. You know." Parks pantomimed the act of stirring
a pan.

She laughed, shooting out of traffic with an exuberance
that made Parks wince. "Of course I can cook."

"How about your place?"

Brooke zipped through a yellow light. "What about my
place?" she asked cautiously.

"For dinner." Parks watched her shift into third as she
scooted around a Porsche. "It seems to me I'm entitled after
feeding you a couple times myself."

"You want me to cook for you?"

This time he laughed. She was going to fight him right

down to the wire. "Yeah. And then I'm going to make love to you."

Brooke hit the brakes, stopping the car inches away from another bumper. "Oh, really?"

"Oh, really," he repeated, meeting her dagger-eyed stare equally. "We both just punched out on the time clock. New game." He fingered the end of her braid. "New rules."

"And if I have some objection?"

"Why don't we talk about it someplace quiet?" With his thumb, he traced her lips. "Not afraid, are you?"

The taunt was enough. When the light changed, Brooke hit the accelerator, weaving through Los Angeles traffic with grim determination.

"Did you know that you drive like a maniac?" Parks observed.

"Yes."

"Just a passing comment," he murmured, then settled back against the seat.

Despite the infuriated woman beside him, Parks had the same sensation of tranquility when Brooke zoomed up in her driveway, braking with a teeth-jarring jolt, that he had had the first time he had seen her house. There was a tang of fall in the air—that spicy, woodsy fragrance you never smelled in Los Angeles. Some of the leaves had turned so that splashes of red and amber and orange competed with the customary California green. The shadows of trees reflected in the glass of the windows as the sun dipped lower in the sky. Along the base of the house the flowers had been allowed to grow bushy and wild. Whether it had been by intent or lack of time, her unkempt garden was eye-catching and perfectly suited to the lonely mountain spot.

Without a word, Brooke slammed out of her side of the
car. At a more leisurely pace, Parks followed suit. She was
furious, Parks noted with a pleased grin. All the better. He
didn't want an easy capitulation. From the first moment he
had come into contact with her, he had looked forward to
the struggle almost as much as he had looked forward to
the outcome. He'd never had any doubt what that would
be. When there was this much friction, and this much
spark between a man and a woman, they became enemies
or lovers. He had no intention of being Brooke's enemy.

Still keeping her stony silence, Brooke slipped the key into
the lock and turned it. Walking inside, she left him to follow
as he chose.

The fireplace caught his eye first. It was crafted from
large stone, dominating one wall. The fire set was shiny
brass, though dented and obviously old. Another wall was
all glass, rising from either side of the door to the peak of
the roof. Gazing at it, he felt not a loss of privacy but a basic
sense of security. Rocking gently on his heels, he studied the
rest of the main room.

A long armless sofa ranged in front of the fireplace,
crowded with dozens of pillows. In lieu of a table a large,
round hassock sat in front of it. Around this focal point a
few chairs were scattered. All the colors were muted—
ecrus, buffs, biscuits—set off by the surprising touches of
huge, brilliant peacock feathers in a brass urn, a scarlet af-
ghan tossed over the back of a chair, the vivid shades in the
hooked rug on the planked floor.

A shelf had been built into the east wall. Ignoring Brooke's
glare, Parks wandered to it. There was a small crystal but-
terfly that shivered in a rainbow of colors as the light struck
it. There was a chipped demitasse set that had come from one
of Brooke's yard sale jaunts along with a fat, grinning bear.
Parks noted a piece of Wedgwood next to a pink monkey

holding cymbals. It clapped them together gleefully when he flipped a switch. With a quick laugh, he flipped it off again. There were other treasures scattered haphazardly through the room, some priceless, some no more than department store whimsy.

Above his head, the second-floor balcony ran the length of the house. No closed-in spaces, he noted. He began to think the house itself would tell him more about Brooke than she would volunteer. The need for freedom of movement, the eclectic tastes, the combination of drab colors with the garish. It occurred to him that everything she owned would have been collected during the last ten years. But how much of the past had she brought with her?

Uncomfortable with Parks's silent, thorough survey, Brooke marched to a tiny corner cabinet to pull out a bottle. "You're free to take a tour," she said abruptly. "I'm going to have a drink."

"Whatever you're having's fine," Parks said with infuriating amiability. "You can show me around later." He proceeded to make himself at home on the low, spreading sofa. Leaning back, he glanced at the fireplace, observing by the ash that Brooke made good use of it. "Fire'd be nice," he said casually. "Got any wood?"

"Out back." Ungraciously, she stuck a glass under his nose.

"Thanks." After accepting it, Parks took her hand. "Sit down," he invited with a pleasantness that put Brooke's teeth on edge. "You've been on your feet all day."

"I'm fine," she began, then let out a gasp of surprise as Parks yanked her down beside him. Realizing she should have been prepared for the move despite his outward mellowness only fanned her already strained temper. "Who do you think you are," she began, "barging in here, expecting me to whip up dinner then fall into bed with you? If you—"

"Hungry?" Parks interrupted.

She sent him a searing look. "No."

With a shrug, he draped his arm behind her, propping his feet on the hassock. "You're usually ill-tempered when you are," he commented.

"I am *not* ill-tempered," Brooke raged. "And I am *not* hungry."

"Want some music?"

Brooke drew in a deep breath. How dare he sit there acting as though she were *his* guest? "No."

"You should relax." With firm fingers, he began to knead the base of her neck.

"I'm perfectly relaxed." She pushed his hand aside, disturbed by the sensation of warmth creeping down her spine.

"Brooke." Parks set his glass on the floor, then turned to her. "When you called me a few days ago, you accepted what you knew was going to happen between us."

"I said I would see you," she corrected and started to rise. Parks hand came back to her neck and held her still.

"Knowing what *seeing* me meant," he murmured. His eyes met the fury in her gaze for a moment, then drifted down to focus on her mouth. "You might have refused to let me come here tonight . . . but you didn't." Slowly, he brought his eyes back to hers in a long, intense look that had her stomach muscles quivering. "Are you going to tell me that you don't want me?"

She couldn't remember the last time she had felt the need to break eye contact. It took all her strength of will to keep from faltering. "I . . . I don't have to tell you anything. You might remember that this is my time, my house. And—"

"What are you afraid of?"

As he watched, the confusion in her eyes turned back to fury. "I'm not afraid of anything."

"Of making love to me," he continued quietly. "Or to anyone?"

Angry color flooded her cheeks as she bolted up from the sofa. She felt a combination of rage and hurt and fear that she hadn't experienced in more than a decade. He had no right to bring the insecurity tumbling back over her, no right to make her doubt herself as a woman. Tossing her head, Brooke glared at him. "You want to make love?" she snapped. "Fine." She turned on her heel and marched to the stairs leading to the second floor. Halfway up, she threw an angry look over her shoulder. "Coming?" she demanded, then continued on without waiting for his reply.

The fury carried her across the balcony and into her bedroom, where she stood in the center of the room, seething. Her gaze landed on the bed, but she averted it quickly as she heard the sound of Parks's footsteps approaching. It was all very simple, she told herself. They would go to bed and work this attraction or animosity or whatever it was out of their systems. It would clear the air. She sent Parks another killing look as he walked into the room. Fear prodded at her again. In defense, Brooke hastily began to undress.

It was on the tip of his tongue to tell her to stop, then Parks calmly followed her example. She was trembling and didn't even know it, he observed. For the moment, they would play it her way. As with the first night he had taken her out, Parks knew what Brooke expected. Though the angry fear urged him to comfort, he was aware that it would be refused. He didn't even glance over when she dropped her T-shirt into a heap on the floor. But he noticed that she had kept a small clutch of his hibiscus on her dresser.

Naked, Brooke stomped over to the bed and pulled off the quilt. Head high, brows arched, she turned to him. "Well?"

He looked at her. The surge of sharp desire caused him to go rigid to control it. She was long and softly rounded with fragile, china-doll skin. The proud almost challenging stance was only accented by the overall frailty—until one looked at her eyes. Stormy, they dared him to make the next move.

Parks wondered if she knew just how vulnerable she was and vowed, even as he planned to conquer, to protect. Taking his time, he walked to her until they stood face-to-face. Though her eyes never faltered, he saw the quick nervous swallow before she turned toward the bed. Parks caught her braid in his hand, forcing her to turn back. The fury in her eyes might have cooled the desire of most men. Parks smiled, comfortable with it.

"This time," he murmured as he began to unbind the braid, "I'll direct."

Brooke stood stiffly as he slowly freed her hair. Her skin tingled, as if waiting for his touch—but he never touched her. Deliberately, Parks drew out the process, working his way leisurely up the confined hair until Brooke thought she would burst. When he had finished, he spread it over her shoulders as if it were the only task he would ever perform.

"It's fabulous," Parks murmured, absorbed in its texture, at the way the slanting sunlight brought out the hidden gold within the red. Lifting a strand from her shoulder, he buried his nose in it, wanting to absorb the fragrance. Brooke felt her knees weaken, her muscles go lax. Would he ever touch her?

She kept her eyes on his face, trying to avoid a dangerous fascination with the tawny skin of his chest, the mat of dark gold hair and cords of muscles she had glimpsed in his bare shoulders. If she allowed herself to look, would she be able to prevent herself from touching? But when she noticed the thin gold chain around his neck, curiosity drove her to follow it down to the small gold circle that dangled from it. Because of this, she didn't see him shift ever so slightly to press his lips against the curve of her shoulder. The touch was a jolt, a branding shock that had her jerking back even as his hands spanned her waist.

"Relax." Fingers kneaded gently into flesh; warm lips nibbled it over his words. "I won't take you anywhere you don't want to go." Slowly, he ran the whisper-soft kisses over her shoulder, loitering at her throat. His fingertips ran down to her hips then back up in a rhythmic caress that could never soothe, but only arouse. He knew what he did to her—she knew her response was no secret. In a last attempt to hold her own, Brooke pressed her hands against his chest, arching back.

Parks still held her waist, but made no attempt to draw her back. Over the desire in his eyes, Brooke caught the light of humor. "Want me to stop?" he asked quietly. There was a trace of challenge in the question. She realized abruptly that whatever response she gave, she would still lose.

"Would you?" she countered, fighting the urge to run her suddenly sensitive fingertips over his naked chest.

It was his slow, dangerous smile. "Why don't you ask me and see?" Even as she opened her mouth to form an answer, his fastened on it. The kiss was soft and deep, the sort she knew a woman could drown in. Brooke had only the vague realization that her hands had crept up his chest to link around his neck, only the faintest knowledge that her body was melting into his. Then she was falling—or perhaps she was drowning—until the cool sheets were under her back and his weight was on her.

She didn't question how her body seemed to have become liquid, only reveled in the unaccustomed freedom of motion and space. His hands were so sure, so unhurried, as if he wished and waited for her total fluidity. With a deft caress, a strategic brush of lips, he was unlocking every restriction she had placed on herself. This pleasure was thick, fluent.

Brooke luxuriated in it, no longer caring what she gave up in order to receive. Weightless, helpless, she could only sigh as he took his mouth on a lazy journey down her body.

The flick of his tongue over her nipple brought a quick tug—not quite an ache—in her stomach. This pleasure was sharp, stunning. Then it was gone, leaving her dazed as he continued to range a moist trail over her.

His hands were never still, but moved so gently, almost magically, over her, that she could never pinpoint where the source of delight came from. It seemed to radiate through the whole of her, soothing, promising, luring. He caught the point of her breast between his teeth, causing a flash of heat to spring from her center out to her fingertips. But even as she gasped from it, arching, he moved on. He brushed his fingers over her inner thigh, almost absently, so that her skin was left heated then chilled. As fire and ice coursed through her, the sound of her own moan echoed in her head.

The quivering started—a drug wearing off. And the ache—unbearable, wonderful. She was no longer soothed, but throbbing and pleasure became exquisite torment. Suddenly her fingers were in his hair as she tried to press him closer. "Make love to me," she demanded as her breath started to tremble.

He continued with the same mind-destroying caresses. "Oh, I am," he murmured.

"Now." Brooke reached for him only to have him grip her wrists. His head lifted so that their eyes met. Even through a haze of passion she could see his intense concentration— that fierce warrior look.

"It's not so simple." He could feel her pulse hammering under his fingers, but he would give her no quick moment of pleasure. When he took her, she would never forget. Parks pressed his mouth to hers, not so gently. "I've only begun."

Still holding her wrists, he began a new journey over her,

with his mouth only. As he captured her breast again, taking it into the heated moistness of his mouth, she could only writhe beneath him in a frenzy that had nothing to do with a desire to escape. The breezy patience had left him to be replaced by a demand that would accept only one answer. It seemed he would feed on her skin, nipping, suckling, licking until she was half-mad from need so long suppressed. It seemed he would taste, and taste only, for hours, assuaging a steady greed she was powerless to refuse.

The heat suffused her, enervated her. Her skin trembled and grew moist from it. Down the hollow between her breasts, over the lean line of ribs to the subtle curve of hip he traced kisses until he felt her hands go limp and her pulse rage.

When his tongue plunged into the warm core of her, she shuddered convulsively, crying out with the first delirious peak. But he was relentless. Even as she struggled for breath, his hands began a new journey of possession.

With hers free, Brooke gripped his shoulders, hardly aware of the tensing of his muscles. There was no part of her body he hadn't explored, exploited, in his quest to have all of her. Now her surrender became agility and drive. Neither of them knew that her true capitulation came when she began her own demands.

Her hands sped over him, touching all she could reach while she twisted, wanting to taste—his mouth, his shoulder, the strong line of his jaw. Parks thought her scent intensified until it dominated all his senses—weakening and strengthening him at once. Her skin was moist and heated wherever his mouth nestled, bringing him another tantalizing image of white silk and forbidden passion. Husky murmurs and quick breathing broke the early-evening hush.

He was no longer thinking, nor was she. They had entered a place where thoughts were only sensations; sharp, aching, sweet and dark. Even as she fastened her mouth on his, Brooke trembled.

Then he was deep inside her, so swiftly that she dug her nails into his flesh in shock and pleasure. They merged, body to body, heart to heart, while all the sensations concentrated into one.

CHAPTER 7

Brooke luxuriated in the soft, warm security. As she hung between sleep and wakefulness she thought it was winter, and that she slept beneath a thick downy quilt. There was no need to get up, no need to face the cold. She could lie there for a whole lazy day and do nothing. She felt utterly peaceful, completely unburdened and pleasantly languid. Wanting to enjoy the sensations more, she struggled to shrug off sleep.

It wasn't winter, but early fall. There was no quilt, only a tangle of sheets that half covered her naked body as she curled into Parks. With sleep cleared from her mind, Brooke remembered everything—the first revelation of lovemaking, the surprise of having the secret door open without resistance, the hours of passion that had followed. There had been little talk, as the urgency to give and take had grown beyond the control of either of them. Time after time, fulfillment had led to rekindled desire, and desire to demand, until they had fallen asleep, wrapped tightly together.

Now, Brooke could remember her own insatiable thirst, the boundless energy and strength that had filled her. She remembered, too, Parks's ability to arouse her to desperation with patience . . . and that she had driven him beyond patience with a skill she had been unaware of possessing. But beyond the passion and pleasure, Brooke remembered one vital thing. She had needed him. This was something she had refused herself for years. To need meant dependence, dependence meant vulnerability. A woman who was vulnerable would always be hurt.

The night was behind her and dawn was breaking. In the misty gray light, Parks's face was relaxed, inches from hers, so that the warmth of his breath fluttered over her cheek. His arm was around her, his fingers curled into her hair, as if even in sleep he had to touch it. Her arm reached around to lock him close. They had slept, if only for a few hours, in a classic pose of possessing and possessed. But which one, Brooke thought hazily, was which?

With a sigh, Brooke closed her eyes. Not knowing was dangerous. The hours she had spent not caring put the independence she had taken for granted in jeopardy.

It was time to think again before it was too late, before emotions dominated her—those perilous emotions that urged her to burrow closer to Parks's warmth. If she were ever to stop the need for him from growing beyond her control, she had to do it now.

Brooke shifted in an attempt to separate her body from his. Parks tightened his hold and only brought her closer. "No," he murmured without opening his eyes. With sleepy slowness he ran his hand down the length of her naked back. "Too early to get up."

Brooke felt her breasts yield against his chest, felt the warmth in her stomach begin to smolder to heat. His lips were close—too close. The need to stay in the security of his arms was so strong it frightened her. Again Brooke tried to shift, and again Parks brought her back.

"Parks," she said, then was silenced by his lips.

Brooke told herself to struggle against the deep, musky morning kiss, but she didn't. She told herself to resist the gentle play of fingertips on her spine, but she couldn't. The gray dawn suddenly took on a rosy hue. The air seemed to grow thick. Even as he touched her, her skin quivered to be touched again. Don't! her brain shouted. Don't let this happen. But she was already sinking, and sinking quickly. She made a sound of protest that became a groan of pleasure.

Parks shifted so that his body lay across hers. Burying his face in her hair, he took his hand down the length of her; the slight swell of the side of her breast, the firm line of ribs and narrow waist, a flare of hip and long smooth thigh. He could feel the struggle going on inside her, sense her desire to separate herself from what had begun to happen between them since that first meeting of eyes. His quick flash of anger was tinged with unexpected hurt.

"Regrets already?" Lifting his head, he looked at her. Her eyes were dark, heavy with kindling passion. Her breathing was unsteady. But he knew she fought herself just as fiercely as she fought him. Her hands were on his shoulders, poised to push him away.

"This isn't smart," Brooke managed.

"No?" Controlling anger, ignoring the hurt, Parks brushed the hair from her cheek. "Why?"

Brooke met his eyes, because to look away would have admitted defeat. "It's not what I want."

"Let's be accurate." His voice was calm, his eyes steady. "It's not what you want to want."

"All right." Brooke shivered as his finger traced her ear. "It's not what I want to want. I have to be practical. We're going to be working together for quite a while. More technically, you'll be working for me. A solid professional relationship won't be possible if we're lovers."

"We are lovers," Parks pointed out, casually shifting so that the friction of his body on hers sent a shudder coursing through her.

"It won't be possible," Brooke continued, concentrating on keeping her voice steady, "if we go on being lovers."

Tilting his head, Parks smiled at her. "Why?"

"Because . . ." Brooke knew why. She knew dozens of logical reasons why, but no firm thought would form in her brain when he touched a light friendly kiss to her lips.

"Let me be practical a minute," Parks said after another quick kiss. "How often do you let yourself have fun?"

Brooke drew her brows together in annoyed confusion. "What do you mean?"

"You can work eight, twelve hours a day," Parks continued. "You can enjoy your job, be terrific at what you do, but you still need to throw a Frisbee now and again."

"Frisbee?" This brought on a baffled laugh that pleased him. The hands on his shoulders relaxed. "What are you talking about?"

"Fun, Brooke. A sense of the ridiculous, laziness, riding Ferris wheels. All those things that make working worthwhile."

She had the uncomfortable feeling she was being expertly led away from the subject at hand. "What does riding a Ferris wheel have to do with you and me making love?"

"Have you ever had a lover before?" Parks felt her stiffen but continued. "I don't mean someone you slept with, but someone you shared time with. I'm not asking you for any more than that." Even as he said it, Parks knew it wouldn't be true for long. He would ask for more, and she would fight him every step of the way. But then he had lived his life playing to win. "Throw a few Frisbees with me, Brooke. Ride a few waves. Let's see where it takes us."

Looking at him, she could feel her resistance melting. Before she could prevent it, her hand had lifted from his shoulder to brush at the hair that fell over his forehead. "You make it sound so simple," she murmured.

"Not simple." He took her other hand and pressed his lips to the palm. "Even fun isn't always simple. I want you . . . here." And his eyes came back to hers. "Naked, warm, daring me to arouse you. I want to drive with you with the top down and the wind in your hair. I want to see you caught in the rain, laughing." He ran whispering kisses over her face, then paused at her lips to drink long and deep. "I want to be with you, but I don't think it's going to be simple."

Rolling over, Parks cradled her head on his chest, allowing her to rest and think while he brushed his hands through her hair. His words had touched her in tiny vulnerable places she couldn't defend. Was she strong enough, she wondered, to try things his way without losing control? Fun, she thought. Yes, they could give each other that. He challenged her. Brooke had to admit that she had come to enjoy even the friction. What had he said once? That they could be friends before they were lovers. Odd, she mused, that both had happened almost before she realized it. Only the niggling fear that she was already afraid of losing him kept her from relaxing completely.

"I can't afford to fall in love with you," she murmured.

An odd way to put it, Parks reflected as he continued to stroke her hair. "Rule one," he drawled. "Party A will not fall in love with party B."

Making a fist, Brooke punched his shoulder. "Stop making me sound ridiculous."

"I'll try," he agreed amiably.

"Fun," she murmured, half to herself.

"A three-letter word meaning amusement, sport or recreation," Parks recited in a blandly didactic tone.

With a chuckle, Brooke lifted her head. "All right. I'll buy the Frisbee," she said before she pressed her mouth to his.

Parks cupped the back of her neck in his hand. "It's still too early to get up," he murmured.

Brooke's low laugh was muffled against his lips. "I'm not sleepy."

With a reluctant sigh, he closed his eyes. "Acting," he said thickly, "takes a lot out of you."

"Aw." Sympathetically, Brooke stroked his cheek. "I guess you'd better conserve your strength." She pressed a kiss to his jaw, then his collarbone, before continuing down his chest. Her fingers tangled with the gold chain he wore. "What's this for?"

Parks opened one eye to stare at the five-dollar gold piece that dangled from the chain Brooke held up. "Luck." He shut his eyes again. "My aunt gave it to me when I headed for the Florida training camp. She told my father he was a—" Parks reached back in his memory for the exact phrasing "—a stiff-necked old fool who thought in graphs and formulas, then gave me the gold piece and told me to go for it."

Brooke turned the shiny circle over in her palm. So he carried a little piece of the past with him, too, she mused. "Superstition?" she asked as she dropped the chain and pressed her lips to his chest.

"Luck," Parks corrected, enjoying the feel of her mouth on his skin, "has nothing to do with superstition."

"I see." She scraped her nails lightly down his side and heard his quick inhalation of breath. "Do you always wear it?"

"Mmm." She flicked her tongue over his nipple, bringing a low, involuntary groan from him. A sense of power whipped through her—light, freeing, tempting. His hands were buried in her hair again, seeking the flesh beneath. Brooke slid her body down, bringing them both a rippling slice of pleasure.

His scent was different, she discovered as she ran her lips over his skin. Different, she realized, because hers had mingled with it during the night. That was intimacy, as tangible as the act of love itself.

As the power stayed with her, she experimented. His body was strong and muscled beneath hers, tasting of man. He was taut and lean, his skin golden in the early-morning light. The palms that moved over her back were hard, calloused from his profession. Like the man, the body was disciplined, a product of that odd combination of pampering and outrageous demands any athlete subjects it to. She brushed her lips over the hard, flat stomach and felt the firm muscles quiver. Beneath her own smooth palms she could feel the sinewy strength of his thighs.

The knowledge of the pure physical strength he possessed excited her. With light touches and caresses, she could make this man breathe as though he had run to the point of collapse. With feathering kisses she could make this hardened athlete shudder with an inner weakness she alone was aware of. Though she didn't fully understand it, Brooke knew that she had given him something more than her body the night before, something more complex than surrender or passion. Without even knowing what the gift was, she wanted Parks to offer it in return.

Slowly, enjoying every movement of his body beneath hers, savoring each subtly different taste, she roamed up until her lips fastened greedily on his. How soft his mouth was. How nectarous, with a dark, secret cachet. Brooke savored it on her tongue, feeling it intensify until the draining, liquefying pleasure crept into her. Knowing she would lose that slim edge of control, she tore her mouth from his to bury it at his throat.

She felt the vibration of his groan against her lips, but she couldn't hear it. Her heartbeat raged in her head until all of her senses were confused. If it was morning, how could she feel this sultry night pleasure? If she was seducing him, how was she so thoroughly seduced? Her body pressed against his, matching itself to the slow, tortuous rhythm he set even as she raced tormenting kisses along his flesh. The heat seeping into her only seemed to add to the delirium of power, yet it wasn't enough. She was still searching for something so nebulous she wasn't certain she would recognize it when it was found. And desire, sharp bolts of desire, were causing everything but the quest for fulfillment to fade.

Parks gripped her hair in one hand to pull her head up. She had only a brief glimpse of his face—the eyes half-shut but darker and more intense than she had ever seen them—before he brought her mouth down to his and devoured. All will, all sense was seeping out of her.

"Brooke . . ." His hands were on her hips, urging her. "Now." The demand was wrenched from him, hoarse and urgent. She resisted, struggling to breathe, fighting to hold some part of herself separate. "I need you," he murmured before their lips met again. "I need you."

Then it was clear—for one breathless instant. She needed, and knew now she was needed in return. It was enough . . . perhaps everything. With a shuddering sound of relief and joy, she gave.

At nine fifty-five, Claire swept into the editing room. Neither the editors nor E.J. were surprised to see the head of Thorton Productions on the job on a Saturday morning. Anyone who had worked at Thorton more than a week knew that Claire wasn't a figurehead but an entity to be reckoned with. She wore one of her trim little suits, the color of crushed raspberries, and a trace of Parisian scent.

"Dave, Lila, E.J." Claire gave all three a quick nod before

heading toward the coffeepot. A newer member of the staff might have scurried to serve the boss, but those lounging near the control board knew better.

"Made it myself, Ms. Thorton," E.J. told her as she poured. "It won't taste like the battery acid these two cook up."

"I appreciate that, E.J.," she said dryly. Just the scent of it revived her. Claire inhaled it, telling herself only an old fool thought she could dance until three and still function the next day. Ah, but how nice it was to feel like a fool again, she thought with a slow smile. "I'm told that the shoot went well, with no major problems."

"Smooth as silk," E.J. stated. "Wait till you get a load of Parks knocking that sucker over the fence." He grinned reminiscently. "I won ten bucks off Brooke with that hit." His selective memory allowed him to forget that it had been his ten dollars in the first place.

Claire settled into a chair with a quiet sigh. "Is Brooke in yet?"

"Haven't seen her." E.J. began to whistle as he recalled Brooke leaving the location with Parks. Accustomed to his habits, Claire only lifted a brow.

"Are you set up, Dave?"

"Ready to run through it, Ms. Thorton. Want to see it from the top?"

"In a moment." Even as Claire checked her watch, she heard Brooke's voice in the corridor.

"As long as you understand you have absolutely no say in what gets cut and what stays in."

"I might have an intelligent comment to make."

"Parks, I'm serious."

His low chuckle rolled into the editing room just ahead of Brooke. "Morning," she said to the group at large. "Coffee hot?"

"E.J.'s special," Claire told her, watching Brooke over the

rim of her mug as she sipped. She looked different, Claire thought, then slid her eyes to Parks. And there was the reason, she concluded with a small smile. "Good morning, Parks."

Her face remained bland and friendly, but he recognized her thoughts. With a slight nod, he acknowledged them. "Hello, Claire," he said, abandoning formality as smoothly as he reached for a cup for himself. "I hope you don't mind me sitting in on this." Taking the pot, he poured Brooke's coffee, then his own. "Brooke has a few reservations."

"Amateurs," Brooke said precisely as she reached for the powdered cream, "have a tendency to be pains in the—"

"Yes, well I'm sure we're delighted to have Parks join us," Claire interrupted over E.J.'s chuckle. "Run it through, Dave. Let's see what we've got."

At her order, he flicked a series of buttons on the large control panel in front of him. Parks watched himself appear simultaneously on three monitors. He could hear Brooke's voice off camera, then the little man with the clapboard scooted in front of him announcing the scene and take.

"It's the third take that worked," Brooke announced as she settled on the arm of Claire's chair. "Casey at the bat didn't like the first pitch."

Her remark earned her a grin from Parks and a mild exclamation from Claire. "The lighting's very good." Claire studied the second take through narrowed eyes.

"The new boy, Silbey. He's got a nice touch. The clothes sell it." Brooke sipped while gesturing with her free hand. "Watch when he sets for the swing. . . . Yes." She gave a nod of approval. "Nice moves, no apparent restriction. He looks comfortable, efficient, sexy." Intent on the screen, Brooke didn't notice the look Parks tossed at her. "This is the one I want to use." She waited, silently, watching the replay of Parks's home run. The test swings, the concentration, the connection and follow-through, the satisfied grin and the shrug.

"I want to keep in the last bit," Brooke went on. "That gee-whiz shrug. It sells the whole business. That natural cockiness is its own appeal." Parks choked over his coffee, but Brooke ignored him. "As I see it, this segment is pretty clear-cut. The next I'm not so sure about. It's going to be effective. . . ."

Cupping his mug in both hands, Parks sat down. For the next two hours he watched himself on the screens of the monitors, listened to himself being weighed, dissected, judged. Though the latter disconcerted him initially, he found that watching himself didn't bring on the feeling of idiocy he'd been certain it would. He began to think he might find some enjoyment out of his two-year stint after all.

Though he'd heard himself picked apart and put back together countless times over the years—coaches, sports critics, other players—Parks couldn't find the same level of tolerance at hearing Brooke speak so matter-of-factly about his face and body, his gestures and expressions. All in all, he thought, it was as though he were the salable product, not the clothes he wore.

They ran the film back and forth, while Claire listened to input and made occasional comments. Yes, they would have to work in close-ups in the next shoot, his face was very good. It would be smart to fill another thirty-second spot with action to exploit the way he moved, showing the durability of the clothes as well as the versatility. They might try tennis shorts if his legs were any good.

At this Parks shot Brooke a deadly glance, half expecting her to offer her personal opinion. She caught it, then smothered a chuckle with a fit of coughing. Over Claire's head she gave him an innocent smile and an unexpectedly lewd wink. The quick response of his own body caused him to scowl at her. She was dressed like a waif, in baggy chinos and a sweater, her hair braided back and secured with a rubber band. From across the room he could smell the elusive, promising scent of her perfume.

"We taped his voice-over this morning," she told Claire. "I think you'll find his voice is good, though how he'll handle real dialogue remains to be seen. Do we have the graphics for the tag-on, Lila?"

"Right here." She flipped a series of switches. On the monitor now was the de Marco logo of a black-maned lion against a cool blue background. The signature line cartwheeled slowly onto the screen until it stopped below the cat. It held long enough for impact, then faded.

"Very classy," Brooke approved. "Then it's agreed? The third take from the first segment, the fifth from the second."

"We saved you guys from a lot of splicing," E.J. commented as he toyed with an unlit cigarette. "You should be able to put this together with your eyes closed."

"I'd appreciate it if you'd keep them open," Claire said as she rose. "Let me know when it's cut and dubbed. E.J., a splendid job, as always."

"Thanks, Ms. Thorton."

She handed him her empty mug. "On the camera work, too," she added. The editors snickered as she turned toward the door. "Parks, I hope you didn't find all this too boring."

"On the contrary . . ." He thought of the objective discussions on his anatomy. "It's been an education."

She gave him a mild smile of perfect understanding. "Brooke, my office, ten minutes." As an afterthought she glanced at her watch. "Oh, dear. Perhaps you'd like to join us for lunch, Parks."

"I appreciate it, but I have a few things I have to do."

"Well then." Patting his arm, she smiled again. "Best of

luck in the play-offs." She slipped away, leaving Brooke frowning after her.

"I probably won't get any lunch now," she muttered. "If you'd said yes, she'd have made reservations at Ma Maison."

"Sorry." Parks drew her out in the corridor. "Did that wink mean you approve of my legs?"

"Wink?" Brooke stared at him blankly. "I don't know what you're talking about. Winking during an editing session is very unprofessional."

He glanced at the door she had closed behind her. "The way you all talked in here, I felt that I was the product."

With a half laugh, Brooke shook her head. "Parks, you *are* the product."

His eyes came back to hers, surprising Brooke with the flare of anger. "No. I wear the product."

She opened her mouth, then closed it again on a cautious sigh. "It's really a matter of viewpoint," she said carefully. "From yours, from de Marco's, even from the consumers', the clothes are the product. From the viewpoints of your producer, your director, your cinematographer and so forth, you're as much the product as the clothes you wear because we have to see that both of you are salable. If I can't make you look good, what you're wearing might as well be flea market special."

He saw the logic but didn't care for it. "I won't be a commodity."

"Parks, you're a commodity every time you walk out on the diamond. This really isn't any different." Exasperated, she lifted her hands palms up. "You sell tickets to Kings games, baseball cards and fielder's caps. Don't be so damned sanctimonious about this."

"First it's temperamental, now it's sanctimonious," he muttered disgustedly. "I suppose what it comes down to is we look at this little . . . venture from two different perspectives."

Brooke felt a light flutter of fear inside her breast. "I told you," she said quietly, "that it would be difficult."

His eyes came back to her, recognizing the shield she was already prepared to bring down. Parks ran a finger down her cheek. "And I told you it would be fun." Leaning closer, he brushed his lips over hers. "We're both right. I have some things to do. Can I meet you back here later?"

Relaxing, Brooke told herself she had imagined the fear. "If you like. I'll probably be tied up until around five."

"Fine. You can cook me that dinner you promised me last night."

Brooke lifted her chin. "I never promised to cook you dinner," she corrected. "But perhaps I will."

"I'll buy the wine." Parks sent her a grin before he turned away.

"Wait." After a moment, Brooke went after him. "You don't have your car."

Parks shrugged. "I'll take a cab." He saw her hesitate then struggle with a decision.

"No," she said abruptly, digging in her bag. "You can use mine."

Parks took the keys, and her hand. He knew enough about her to realize offering the use of her car, or anything else important to her, wasn't a casual gesture. "Thank you."

Her color rose—the first truly self-conscious thing he had noticed about her. "You're welcome." Quickly, she drew her hand from his and turned away. "See you at five," she called over her shoulder without stopping.

Brooke felt a bit foolish as she rode the elevator to Claire's office. How could she have blushed over a simple thank-you for the loan of a car? She glanced up at the numbers flashing over the elevator door. Oh, he knew her too well, she realized, knew her too well when she'd hardly told him anything.

He didn't know she still had the copy of *Little Women* her second foster mother had given her. He didn't know that she had adored those temporary parents and had been devastated when a broken marriage had caused her to be placed in another foster home. He didn't know about the horrid little girl she had shared a room with during what she still considered the worst year of her life. Or the Richardsons, who had treated her more like a hired hand than a foster child. Or Clark.

With a sigh, Brooke rubbed her fingers over her forehead. She didn't like to remember—didn't like knowing that her growing feelings for Parks seemed to force her to face the past again. Oh, the hell with it, Brooke thought with a shake of her head. It *was* the past. And she was going to have enough trouble dealing with the present to dwell on it.

Steadier, she stepped out into the wide, carpeted corridor of Claire's floor. The receptionist, a pretty girl with lots of large healthy teeth, straightened in her chair at Brooke's approach. She'd worked on the top floor for over two years and was still more in awe of Brooke than of Claire.

"Good afternoon, Ms. Gordon."

"Hello, Sheila. Ms. Thorton's expecting me."

"Yes, ma'am." Sheila wouldn't have contradicted her if her life had depended on it.

Unaware of the impression she made, Brooke strode easily down the corridor and through a set of wide glass doors. Here, two secretaries, known as the twins only because of identical desks, labored away on word processors. The outer office was huge, scrupulously modern and cathedral quiet.

"Ms. Gordon." The first twin beamed a smile while a second one reached for the button on her intercom.

"She's expecting me," Brooke said simply and breezed by them into Claire's office. The door opened silently. Brooke was halfway across the pewter-colored carpet before she realized Claire was sound asleep at her desk. Totally stunned, Brooke stopped dead in her tracks and stared.

The chair Claire sat in was high-backed pale gray leather. Her desk was ebony, gleaming beneath stacks of neat papers. The glasses Claire wore for reading were held loosely in her hand. A Chinese "literary painting" in color wash and ink hung on the wall to her right, while behind her L.A. sunshine poured through a plate-glass window. Unsure what to do, Brooke considered leaving as quietly as she had come, then decided it was best to stay. Walking to the squashy leather chair facing the desk, she sat, then gently cleared her throat. Claire's eyes snapped open.

"Morning," Brooke said brightly and grinned at Claire's uncharacteristic confusion. "You'd do better on the sofa if you want a nap."

"Just resting my eyes."

"Mmm-hmm."

Ignoring the comment, Claire reached for the papers she had been reading before fatigue had won. "I wanted you to have a look at the script for the next de Marco spot."

"Okay." Brooke accepted the script automatically. "Claire, are you all right?"

"Don't I look all right?"

Deciding to take her literally, Brooke studied her. Except for the heavy eyes, she decided, Claire looked better than ever. Almost, Brooke mused, glowing. "You look marvelous."

"Well then." Claire smoothed her hair before she folded her hands.

"Didn't you sleep well last night?" Brooke persisted.

"As it happens, I was out late. Now the script."

"With Lee Dutton?" The thought went through her mind

and out her lips before she could stop it. Claire gave her a tolerant smile.

"As a matter of fact, yes."

Brooke set the script back on the desk. "Claire," she began, only to be interrupted by a knock on the door.

"Your lunch, Ms. Thorton." A tray was wheeled in by twin number one.

The scent of hot roast beef had Brooke rising. "Claire, I misjudged you." Lifting the cover from a hot plate, she inhaled. "Forgive me."

"Did you think I'd let you go hungry?" With a chuckle, Claire stood to move to the sofa. "Brooke, dear, I've known you too long. Bring me my salad and coffee like a good girl."

Nibbling on a potato wedge, Brooke obeyed. "Claire, I really want to talk with you about Lee Dutton."

"Of course." Claire speared a radish slice. "Sit down and eat, Brooke, pacing's bad for my digestion."

Plate in hand, Brooke approached the couch. She set it on the low coffee table, picked up half a roast beef sandwich and began. "Claire, are you actually dating Lee Dutton?"

"Does dating seem inappropriate to you for someone of my age, Brooke? Pass me that salt."

"No!" Flustered, Brooke looked down at Claire's outstretched hand. She gave her the salt shaker then took a defiant bite of her sandwich. "Don't be ridiculous," she muttered over it. "I can see you dating all manner of fabulous men. I have trouble seeing you out on the town with Lee Dutton."

"Why?"

Brooke shifted her shoulders uncomfortably. This wasn't how she had intended it to go. "Well, he's nice enough, and certainly sharp, but he seems sort of . . . well." Brooke sighed and tried again. "Let's put it this way: I can see Lee Dutton in the neighborhood bowling alley. I can't picture you there."

"No . . ." Claire pursed her lips in thought. "We haven't tried that yet."

"Claire!" Exasperated, Brooke rose and began to pace again. "I'm not getting through to you. Look, I don't want to interfere with your life—"

"No?" The mild smile had Brooke flopping back down on the couch.

"You matter to me."

Claire reached over to squeeze her hand. "I appreciate that, Brooke, I've been taking care of myself for a long time. I've even handled a few men."

A bit reassured, Brooke began to eat again. "I suppose if I thought you were really getting involved . . ."

"What makes you think I'm not?" At Brooke's gaping stare, Claire laughed.

"Claire, are you—are you . . ." She gestured, not quite certain she should put her thoughts into words.

"Sleeping with him?" Claire finished in her calm, cultured voice. "Not yet."

"Not yet," Brooke echoed numbly.

"Well, he hasn't asked me to." Claire took another bite of salad and chewed thoughtfully. "I thought he would by now, but he's quite conservative. Very sweet and old-fashioned. That's part of his appeal for me. He makes me feel very feminine. You can lose that at times in this business."

"Yes, I know." Brooke picked up her iced tea and stared into it. "Do you—are you in love with him?"

"I think I am." Claire settled back against the gray-and-rose patterned sofa. "I was only in love once before, really in love. I was your age, perhaps a bit younger." Her smile was soft for a moment, a girl's smile. "In all the years in between, I've never met anyone I was attracted to enough, comfortable enough with, trusted enough, to think of marrying."

Brooke took a long swallow of tea. She thought she

understood Claire's phrasing all too well. "You're thinking of marriage?"

"I'm thinking I'm almost fifty years old. I've built this up—" she gestured to indicate Thorton "—I have a comfortable home, a nice circle of friends and acquaintances, enough new challenges to keep me from dying of boredom, and suddenly I've found a man who makes me want to curl up in front of a fire after a long day." She smiled slowly and rather beautifully—not the girl's smile this time. "It's a good feeling." She let her eyes slide to Brooke, who was watching her closely. "I'd hate to see you have to wait twenty more years for it. Parks is a great deal more than mildly attracted to you."

For the third time, Brooke rose to pace the room. "We haven't known each other long," she began.

"You're a woman who knows her own mind, Brooke."

"Am I?" With a mordant smile, she turned back. "Perhaps I do know how I think, how I feel. I don't really know Parks, though. What if I give too much? What's to stop him from getting bored and moving on?"

Claire met her eyes steadily. "Don't compare him, Brooke. Don't make him pass tests for all those old hurts."

"Oh, Claire." Passing a hand through her hair, Brooke walked to stare out of the window. "That's the last thing I want to do."

"What's the first thing?"

"It's always been to have my own. To have my own so that nobody can come along and say, 'Whoops, you really only borrowed this, time to give it back.' " She laughed a little. "Silly, I suppose I've never really shaken that."

"And why should you?" Claire demanded. "We all want our own. And to get it, you and I both know there are a few basic risks involved."

"I'm afraid I'm falling in love with him," Brooke said

quietly. "And the closer I get, the more afraid I am that it's all going to crumble under my feet. I have a feeling I need this defense . . . that if I fall in love with him, I need this edge of control, this little pocket of power, to keep myself from getting demolished. Is that crazy?"

"No. You're not the kind of woman who gives herself completely without asking for something back. You did that once, but you were a child. You're a woman who needs a strong man, Brooke. One strong enough to take, strong enough not to take all." She smiled as Brooke turned to face her. "Give yourself a little time," she advised. "Things have a way of falling into place."

"Do they?"

Claire's smile widened. "Sometimes it only takes twenty years."

With a laugh, Brooke walked back to the sofa. "Thanks a lot."

CHAPTER 8

Brooke sat cross-legged on the softly faded Oriental rug in Claire's den. Sometime during the fourth inning she'd given up trying to sit in a chair. To her right, Lee and Claire sat on a two-cushioned brocade sofa. Billings had outdone herself by preparing her specialty, beef Wellington, then had been mutely offended when Brooke had done little more than shift the food around on her plate. Though she chided herself for being nervous, Brooke had been able to do nothing but worry about the outcome of the play-offs since Parks had taken off for the Valiants' home stadium.

She'd been able to catch part of the first afternoon game on her car radio as she had driven to a location shoot. One of the production crew had thought ahead, bringing a portable radio with an earplug, and had kept up a running commentary between takes. Brooke had felt overwhelming relief when the Kings had taken the first game, then frustration and more nerves when they had lost the second. Now, she watched the third on the television set in Claire's small, elegant den.

"That man was out at second," Brooke fumed, wriggling impotently on the faded royal-blue rug. "Anyone with two working eyes could see that."

As she launched her personal attack, the Kings' manager, a squat man with the face of a dyspeptic elf, argued with the second base umpire. If she hadn't been quite so furious herself, Brooke might have admired the manager's theatrical gestures as he spun around, rolled his eyes to heaven and pointed an accusing finger in the umpire's face. The umpire remained unmoved and the call stood. With the Kings holding on to a thin one-run lead, a runner on second with one out boded ill.

When the next batter sent one sailing over the fence and the slim lead changed hands, Brooke groaned. "I can't stand it," she decided, pounding her fists on the rug. "I just can't stand it."

"Brooke's become involved in the game," Claire murmured to Lee.

"So I've noticed." He dropped a light kiss on her cheek. "You smell wonderful!"

The sensation of blood rising to her cheeks was pleasant. She had been romanced by suave masters of the game in the more than twenty-five years of her womanhood, but she couldn't remember one who had made her feel quite the way Lee Dutton could. If they had been alone, she would have snuggled closer, but remembering Brooke, she merely squeezed his hand. "Have some wine, dear," she said to Brooke as she reached for the iced bottle beside her. "Good for the nerves."

Because she was breathing a sigh of relief as the next batter struck out, Brooke didn't acknowledge the teasing tone. "That's three out," she said as she took the cool glass from Claire.

"Two," Lee corrected.

"Only if you believe a nearsighted umpire," she countered, sipping. When he chuckled, she sent a grin over her shoulder. "At least I didn't call him a bum."

"Give yourself a little time," Lee advised, winking at Claire as she handed him a glass.

"You know, some of the players—" Brooke began, then broke off with a gasp as a smoking line drive was hit toward third. Her stomach muscles knotted instantly. Parks dove sideways, stretching his arm out toward the speeding ball. He nabbed it in the tip of his glove just before the length of his body connected with the hard Astroturf. Brooke thought she could feel the bone-rattling jolt herself.

"He got it!" Lee broke out of his casual pose with a jerk that nearly upset Claire's wine. "Look at that, look at that! He got it!" he repeated, pointing at the television image of Parks holding up the glove to show the catch while he still lay prone. "That young sonofa—" He caught himself, barely, and cleared his throat. "Parks is the best with a glove in the league," he decided. "In *both* leagues!" He leaned forward to pound Brooke companionably on the back. "Parks robbed him, kid. Stole a base hit from him as sure as God made little green apples."

Because she watched Parks stand up and brush himself off, Brooke relaxed. "I want to see it on replay," she murmured. "Slow motion."

"You'll see that play a dozen times before the night's through," Lee predicted. "And again on the eleven-o'clock news. Hey, lookie here." Grinning, he gestured to the set. "That's what I call classy timing."

Brooke shifted her concentration to the de Marco commercial. Of course she'd seen it a dozen times in the editing room, and again on television, but each time she watched, she searched for flaws. She studied the graphics as Parks's cool clear voice spoke out to her. "It's perfect," she said with a smile. "Absolutely perfect."

"How's the next one coming?" Lee asked Claire.

"It's just waiting for Parks to be available. We hope to shoot next week."

He settled back again, one arm around Claire. "I'm going to enjoy seeing that one play during the series."

"They still have two games to win," Brooke reminded him. "They're a run behind in this one, and—"

"The opera's not over till the fat lady sings," Lee said mildly.

Brooke swiveled her head to look at him. Claire was snug beside him, a crystal glass in one hand. Lee's paunch strained against the buttons of his checked shirt. The ankle of one leg rested on the knee of the other while his foot bounced up and down to some personal tune. Abruptly, Brooke saw them as a perfect match. "I like you, Lee," she said with a wide smile. "I really like you."

He blinked twice, then his lips curved hesitantly. "Well, thanks, kid."

She's just given us her blessing, Claire thought with an inward chuckle as she took Lee's hand in hers.

Brooke made her way through the airport crowd with steady determination. In addition to the usual flow of traffic at LAX, there were fans, mobs of fans, waiting to greet the incoming Kings team. Some carried handmade signs, others banners. There were, she noted with some amusement, a good number of truants in the Los Angeles school system that morning, not to mention a deficit in the workforce. After the twelve-inning victory, Brooke thought the players deserved a bit of adulation. She also wondered if she'd ever be able to fight her way through so that Parks would see her. The impulse to surprise him, she realized, had not been practical. A truant father hoisted a truant second-grader onto his shoulders. Brooke grinned. Maybe not practical, but it was going to be fun.

Pushing her sunglasses atop her head, Brooke narrowed her eyes against the sun and waited for the plane to touch down. As it stopped being a dot in the sky and took on form, she began to experience the first flicker of nerves. She fidgeted nervously with her bag while she stood, crushed shoulder to shoulder, with excited fans.

He'll be tired, she thought as dozens of conversations buzzed around her. He's probably looking forward to going home and sleeping for twenty-four hours. Brooke ran a hand through her hair. I should have told him I was coming. She shifted her weight to the other foot, curled her fingers around the chain link in front of her and watched the plane glide to a stop.

The moment the door opened, the cheering started, building, rising as the first men began to deplane. They waved back, looking tired and somehow vulnerable without their uniforms. Men, she thought. Simply men suffering from jet lag and perhaps a few hangovers. Then she smiled, deciding that the gladiators might have looked precisely the same the day after a bout.

As soon as she saw him, she felt warm. Beside Brooke, a teenager grabbed her companion and squealed.

"Oh, there's Parks Jones! He's bee-utiful."

Brooke swallowed a laugh as she thought of how Parks would react to the adjective.

"Every time I watch him, my knees get weak." The teenager pressed her lithe young body against the fence. "Did you see him in the commercial? When he smiled, it was like he was looking right *at* me. I nearly died."

Though she didn't take her eyes off Parks, Brooke smiled inwardly. My plan exactly, she thought, pleased with herself.

Why do I feel like a woman watching her man come home from the wars?

Though her sharp director's eye had seen a group of tense and tired men, the fans saw heroes. They cheered them. Some of the players merely waved and moved on, but most came up to the fence to exchange words, jokes, a touch of hands. Brooke watched Parks walk toward the barrier with a man she recognized as Snyder, the first baseman. She wondered, by the intensity of their discussion, if they were outlining infield strategy.

"It would only take twenty-five or thirty cans of shaving cream to fill his locker," Snyder insisted.

"Takes too long and evaporates too fast," Parks commented. "You've got to be practical, George."

Snyder swore mildly and lifted his hand in acknowledgment to a shout in the crowd. "Got a better idea?"

"Carbon dioxide." Parks scanned the crowd as they neared it. "Quick and efficient."

"Hey, yeah!" Pleased, Snyder gave him a slap on the back. "Knew your brains were good for something, Einstein."

"And as long as I help you work out the mechanics," Parks added, "my locker doesn't get filled with the thinking man's shaving cream."

"There's that, too," Snyder agreed. "Would you look at these people?" His grin widened. "Fantastic."

Parks started to agree, then spotted a mass of red hair touched with gold in the sunlight. The fatigue drained as though someone had pulled a cork. "Fantastic," he murmured and walked straight toward Brooke.

The teenager beside her made a moaning, melting sound and took a death grip on her friend's arm. "He's coming over here," she managed in a choked whisper. "Right over here. I know I'm going to die."

Brooke tilted her chin up so that her eyes would stay

level with his as he stopped on the other side of the fence. "Hi." Parks's hand closed over hers on the metal wire. The simple contact was as intimate as anything she had ever known.

"Hi." Brooke smiled slowly, accepting the flare of desire and the sense of closeness without question.

"Can I get a lift?"

"Anytime."

He pressed his lips to the fingers still curled around the wire. "Meet me inside? I have to get my baggage."

Out of the corner of her eye, Brooke saw the two teenage girls gawking. "Great catch last night."

He grinned before he stepped away. "Thanks."

Snyder caught him by the arm as Brooke melted back into the crowd. "Hey, I like that catch better."

"Off-limits," Parks said simply, making his way down the line of fans and outstretched hands.

"Aw, come on, Parks, we're teammates. All for one and one for all."

"Forget it."

"The trouble with Parks," Snyder began to tell a grandfatherly type behind the fence, "is he's selfish. I make his throws look good. I bite the bullet when he lines a hospital pitch at me. And what thanks do I get?" He sent Parks a hopeful smile. "You could at least introduce me."

Parks grinned as he signed a snatch of paper a fan thrust through a hole in the fence. "Nope."

It took him nearly thirty minutes to get away from the crowd and through the terminal. Impatience was growing in him. The simple touch of fingers outside had whetted his appetite for a great deal more. He'd never been lonely on the road before. Even if there was a rainout or an off day away from home, you were surrounded by people you knew. You became as close as a family—close enough to spend endless evenings together or opt to spend one alone without bruising feelings. No, he'd never been lonely. Until this time.

Parks couldn't count the times he had thought of her over the last four days, but he knew that everything had suddenly slipped back into focus the moment he had seen her standing there. Now he saw her again.

Brooke leaned back against a pillar near the baggage belt, Parks's suitcase at her feet. She smiled but didn't straighten as she saw him. She'd hate to have him know just how crazily her pulse was racing. "You travel light," she commented.

He cupped her face in his hand and, oblivious to the people milling around them, brought her close for a long, hard kiss.

"I missed you," he murmured against her mouth, then kissed her again.

There were enough of his teammates still loitering around to start up a chorus of approval.

"Excuse me." Snyder tapped Parks on the shoulder and grinned engagingly at Brooke. "I believe you've made a mistake. *I'm* George Snyder. This is our aging batboy." He gave Parks an affectionate pat.

"How do you do." Brooke extended her hand and had it enveloped in a huge, hard palm. "Too bad about those two strikeouts last night."

There were several jeers as Snyder winced. "Actually, I'm luring the Valiants into complacency."

"Oh." Amused, Brooke gave him a big smile. "You did very well."

"Sorry, Snyder, time for your shot." Parks signaled to two teammates, who agreeably hooked their arms through Snyder's to haul him away.

"Aw, come on, Jones, give me a break!" Good-naturedly, Snyder let himself be dragged away. "I just want to discuss my strategy with her."

"Goodbye, George." Brooke waved as Parks bent to retrieve his bag.

"Let's get out of here."

With her fingers laced through his, Brooke had no choice but to follow. "Parks, you might have introduced me to your friends."

"Dangerous men," he stated. "All dangerous men."

With a chuckle, she matched her pace to his. "Yes, I could see that. Especially the one holding a toddler on each hip."

"There are a few exceptions."

"Are you one?"

Parks caught her around the waist and drew her close against him. "Uh-uh."

"Oh, good. Want to come home with me and tell me your strategy?"

"That's the best offer I've had today." After tossing his bag in the rear of her car, Parks sprawled in the passenger seat. Accustomed to her driving pattern now, he relaxed and began to unwind by rambling about the previous day's game. Brooke said little, pleased to listen, glad that she had arranged to take the day off so that they could have a few hours together, alone.

"The commercial aired during each play-off game, you know," she commented as they headed out of town.

"How'd it look?" Parks laid his head back against the seat. God, it was good to know he didn't have to go anywhere or do anything for twenty-four hours.

"Fantastic." As the road opened up, so did the Datsun's throttle. "And I have it from the source that it plays very well."

"Hmm?"

"A teenager girl in that mob today." With near perfect mimicry, Brooke related the girl's comments. She caught Parks's automatic grimace at the term *bee-utiful* but swallowed a chuckle as she continued.

"Nice to know I devastate sixteen-year-old girls," he said dryly.

"You'd be surprised at the buying power of sixteen-year-old girls." With experienced ease, Brooke negotiated the curves on the narrowing road. "Not so much directly, certainly, but indirectly through their parents. And since they'd like their teenage boyfriends to make their knees weaken, too, they'll push them toward de Marco jeans, shirts, belts, *ad infinitum*." Tossing her hair back, she slid her eyes to his. "And you do have a great smile."

"Yeah." He gave a modest sigh. "I do."

Brooke stopped in her driveway with a deliberate jerk that had him swearing. Wisely slipping from the car before he could retaliate, she headed up the path.

"Just for that," Parks began as he dragged his bag out of the back, "I'm not going to give you the present I bought you."

At the door, Brooke turned, her grin changing to a look of bewilderment. "You bought me a present?"

Because she looked like a child who expected to be handed a brightly wrapped empty box, Parks treated it lightly. "I did. But I'm seriously considering keeping it myself now."

"What is it?"

"Are you going to open the door?"

Brooke shrugged, trying to pretend indifference as she turned the key. "There's a fire laid," she said as she breezed inside. "Why don't you light it while I get us some coffee?"

"Okay." Setting his bag down, Parks stretched travel-cramped muscles. With a wince, he pressed his fingers to the ribs still sore from their contact with Astroturf.

She'd brought some of her garden inside, he noted, spotting the bowl of vibrant mums and zinnias on the side table across the room. The table, he observed, was Queen Anne; the bowl, dimestore special. Grinning, he went to the hearth. The combination suited her—the exquisite and the practical.

Parks struck a match and set it to the carefully rolled paper beneath the kindling. Dry wood caught with a crackle and a *whoosh*. He inhaled the smell that brought back flickering images of the past; evenings in the cozy parlor of his family home, camping trips with his uncle and cousins, weekends in England at the home of a college friend. He wanted to add to the pictures now with the memory of Brooke lying in his arms in front of the simmering fire while they made slow, endless love.

When he heard her returning, Parks stood, turning to face her as she entered with a tray holding a bottle and two glasses. "I thought you might want wine instead."

Smiling, Parks took the tray from her. "Yes." After setting the tray on the hassock, Parks lifted the bottle, examining the label with a lifted brow. "Is this a celebration?"

"A precelebration," Brooke countered. "I expect you to win tomorrow." She picked up both glasses, holding them out. "And if you don't, we'll have had the wine in any case."

"Seems fair." Parks poured pale gold liquid into the stemmed glasses. Taking one from her, he clinked the rims together. "To the game?" he asked with a slow smile.

Brooke felt the quick nervous flutter in her stomach and nodded. "To the game," she agreed and drank. Her eyes widened but remained steady when he reached out to take a handful of her hair.

"I saw this in the sunlight," he murmured. "Even in that mob of people at the airport, I'm not sure what I would have done if that fence hadn't been in the way." He let it sift through his fingers. "It was a long four days, Brooke."

She nodded, taking his hand to draw him onto the sofa beside her. The curves of her body seemed to fit naturally against the lines of his. "You're tense," she said quietly.

"Postseason games." He drew her closer, knowing the nerves would gradually drain before they built again the next day. "Maybe the lucky ones are the players raking leaves in their backyards in October."

"But you don't really think so."

Parks laughed. "No, I don't really think so. The play-offs pump you up until you're ready to explode, but the series . . ." He trailed off with a shake of his head. He didn't want to let his mind run that far ahead. The rules were three out of five—they weren't there yet. For now he didn't want to think of it, but of the woman beside him, the quiet afternoon and the long evening ahead. He thought that he'd remember her this way, a little pensive, with the smell of woodsmoke and fall flowers mixing with her own perfume. His mind drifted lazily, comfortably, as he sipped the iced wine and watched the flames dance.

"Have you been busy?"

Brooke tilted her head in absent agreement. She didn't want to think of work any more than Parks did. "The usual," she said vaguely. "E.J. talked me into seeing a perfectly dreadful movie where the cast pranced around in mytholog-ical costumes and shot lightning bolts."

"Olympian Revenge?"

"It had a talking three-head dragon."

"That's the one. I caught it in Philadelphia last month when we had a rainout."

"I saw the mike in the frame three times."

Parks chuckled at her professional disdain. "Nobody else did," he assured her. "They were all asleep."

"Gross ineptitude keeps me awake." She leaned her head against his shoulder. It occurred to her how empty her home had been for the last few days, and how cozy it felt again. Brooke had never felt the need to share it before. In fact, she had always had a strong proprietary feeling about what was hers. Now, sitting quietly on the sofa, she realized she had already begun to give up her privacy, willingly and with total unawareness. Turning her head, she studied Parks's profile. "I missed you," she said at length.

He turned his head as well so that their lips were close, not quite touching. "I'd hoped you would." Then he shifted so that his mouth grazed her cheek. She trembled. Not yet, he told himself as the heat flared inside him. Not quite yet. "Maybe I'll give you that present after all."

Brooke's lips curved against his throat. "I don't believe you bought me anything at all."

Recognizing the ploy but willing to play, Parks rose. "You'll have to apologize for that," he said soberly as he walked to his suitcase. He flipped open the case then rummaged inside. When he stood again, Parks had a white box in his hands. Brooke regarded it curiously but with some of the wariness he had noted outside.

"What is it?"

"Open it and find out," he suggested, dropping it into her lap.

Brooke turned it over, examining the plain white box, testing it for weight. She wasn't a woman accustomed to spontaneous gifts and in the short time he had known her, Parks had already given her two. "You didn't have to—"

"You *have* to give your sister a Christmas present," he said mildly, sitting beside her again. "You're not my sister and it isn't Christmas."

Brooke frowned. "I'm not sure I understand the logic in that," she murmured then opened the lid. Packed in wads of tissue paper was a fat pink ceramic hippo with heavily lashed eyes, a flirtatious grin and varicolored polka dots. With a laugh, Brooke drew it out. "She's gorgeous!"

"She reminded me of you," Parks commented, pleased with the laugh and the look of humor in her eyes when she turned them to him.

"Is that so?" She held the hippo up again. "Well, she does have rather fetching eyes." Touched, she stroked the wide ceramic flank. "She really is sweet, Parks. What made you think of it?"

"I thought she'd fit into your menagerie." Seeing the puzzled look on her face, he gestured toward the shelf that held her monkey and bear. "Then there's that pig on the front door, the little carving of a jackrabbit in your bedroom, the china owl on the windowsill in the kitchen."

Comprehension came slowly. There were animals of varying types and materials scattered all through the house. She'd been collecting them for years without having the slightest idea what she was doing. But Parks had seen. Without an instant of warning to either of them, Brooke burst into tears.

Stunned, then alarmed, Parks reached for her, not having a clue what he would offer comfort for. Still, he'd seen enough tears from his sisters to know that logic often had nothing to do with tears. Ashamed, and unable to stem the flow, Brooke evaded his arms and rose. "No, no, please. Give me a minute. I *hate* to do this."

Even as he told himself to respect her wishes, Parks was going to her. Despite her resistance, he pulled her against him. "I can't stand to *see* you do it," he muttered; then, with a hint of exasperation, "Why are you doing it?"

"You'll think I'm stupid. I hate being stupid."

"Brooke." Firmly, he cupped a hand under her chin and lifted it. Tears rolled freely down her cheeks. Knowing no other remedy, he kissed her—the soft lips, the wet cheeks, the damp eyelids. What began as a blind effort to comfort grew to smoldering passion.

He could feel it build in him as his mouth sought hers again. His hands moved through her hair like those of a man making his tentative way through bolts of silk. She trembled against him—sobs or desire Parks was no longer sure as the kiss went deeper and deeper. She opened for him, more giving than he could remember. Her defenses were down, he reminded himself, fighting the impatience to fill his own needs quickly. His murmurs were quiet-pitched to soothe, his hands gently stroking to arouse.

Even recognizing her own vulnerability, Brooke didn't resist. She wanted to drift into that smoky, weightless world where every movement seemed to be in slow motion. She wanted to feel that fire and flash that left you breathless. She wanted the down-soft contentment that would lull you to sleep and linger in the morning.

As he lowered her to the floor, the scent of woodsmoke grew stronger. Brooke could hear the pop and hiss of the logs as flames ate at them. His long, patient kisses held her suspended—half in the reality of the wool rug beneath her back, the red flickers of firelight and sun on her closed lids, half in the world of dreams only lovers understand. While her mind floated, flirting with each separate sensation, he undressed her.

Parks took infinite care with the tiny round buttons of her blouse, as if he could wait until the seasons changed outside the tall windows. There was no time here, no winter, no spring, only one everlasting moment. Brooke slipped her hands under his shirt, fingertips gliding over the warmth and the strength. As patient as he, she drew the material up, over his shoulders, then discarded it.

Flesh against flesh, they lay before the fire while the sun streamed through the massive windows and pooled over them. Kisses grew longer, interrupted only for sighs, for murmurs.

She tasted the mellow warmth of wine on his tongue and was intoxicated.

Slowly, his mouth never leaving hers, Parks began to explore her body. Tiny, needlelike chills ran over her flesh, chasing the path of his hands. Feeling the light graze of his knuckles against the side of her breast, Brooke moaned, a liquid sound of pleasure. He took his tongue deeper into her mouth, gently exploiting this small weakness until the drug took full effect. She was limp, languid, utterly his. Then and only then did he give his lips the freedom to taste her skin again. It was as pungent as her scent, and somehow more erotic.

With moist, openmouthed kisses he savored her, entranced her. Then the quick pressure of his teeth on some sensitive spot would bring her sharply aware, gasping with the change. His lips would soothe again, lulling her back into pliancy. Again and again he yanked her toward the flame, then guided her back to the clouds, until Brooke was no longer certain which she most desired.

She felt him draw her slacks down over her hips while he pressed those soul-wrenching kisses along her stomach. A mindless excitement filled her, rendering her helpless to do any more than move as he requested. His breath was warm on her intimate flesh so that the long muscles in her thighs trembled then went lax.

Still his mouth moved slowly. The hands that had already discovered every secret point of pleasure continued to caress and linger, keeping her trapped beneath a thin sheet of silken passion. The power she had experienced before moved through her, but her mind was too dazed to recognize it. She felt herself balanced on a slender edge—desire's tightrope—and wanted to continue to walk it as much as she longed to fall headlong into the wild, churning sea below. Then he was above her again, his eyes looking down into hers for a long, long moment before his lips descended. He was waiting, and she understood. Their mouths still clinging, Brooke guided him inside her.

Her moan melted into his mouth, hot and passionate. Though she was clinging to him now with a sudden, fierce strength, Parks moved slowly. Brooke felt herself fill, fill to the desperate point of explosion. Then the shudders, racking, convulsive, until she seemed to slide back down some smooth cool path to the torrent again. Like a swimmer trapped in rushing white water, she was swept from peak to peak while he moved with tortuous slowness. She could feel the tight, tense control in him, hear it in the quick labored breaths that merged with hers as he prolonged the pleasure, and the agony. Then he murmured something—a prayer, a plea, an oath—and took them both tumbling off the tightrope.

He must have slept. Parks thought he had closed his eyes for only an instant, but when he opened them again, the slant of the sun was different. Brooke was beside him, her hair wrapping them to each other. Her eyes were wide and aware as she stared into his. She'd been watching him for nearly an hour. Parks smiled and pressed his mouth to her shoulder.

"Sorry. Did I fall asleep?"

"For a little while." She hid her face against his neck a moment. It was as though he had stripped off her flesh, exposing all her thoughts. She wasn't quite certain what she should do about it. "You must have been exhausted."

"Not anymore," he said truthfully. He felt alert, pumped with energy and . . . clean. The last made him give a quick shake of his head. He stroked a hand down her arm. "There was something I wanted to ask you before I got . . . distracted." Propping himself on his elbow, Parks looked down at her. "Why were you crying?"

Brooke moved her shoulders in a shrug and started to shift away. With a firm hand, Parks stopped her. He could feel the effort she was making to draw back from him, but he realized he could no longer permit it. Whether she knew it or not, she had given herself to him completely. He was going to hold her to it.

"Brooke, don't try to block me out," he said quietly. "It won't work anymore."

She started to protest, but the quiet, steady look in his eyes told her he spoke nothing less than the truth. That alone should have been a warning of where her heart was taking her. "It was a sweet thing to do," she said at length. "I'm not used to sweetness."

Parks lifted a brow. "That's part of it, perhaps. What's the rest?"

With a sigh, Brooke sat up. This time he let her. "I hadn't realized I'd been collecting." With both hands, she pushed her hair back, then wrapped her arms around her knees. "I overreacted when you pointed it out. I always wanted a dog, a cat, a bird, anything when I was growing up. It wasn't feasible the way I shifted around." She moved her shoulders again, causing her tumbled hair to shiver over her naked back. "It was kind of shattering to realize I was still compensating."

Parks felt a chord of sympathy and suppressed it. There was no quicker way to alienate her. "You've got your own home, your own life now. You could have anything you wanted." Reaching around her, he poured more wine for both of them. "You don't have to compensate." He sipped, studying her profile.

"No," she agreed in a murmur. "No, I don't."

"What kind of dog do you want?"

Brooke twirled the glass in her hand, then suddenly laughed. "Something homely," she said, turning to grin at him. "Something down-to-the-ground homely." She reached out, laying a hand on his cheek. "I didn't even thank you."

Parks considered, nodding solemnly as he took the glass from her hand. "No, you didn't." In a quick move, he had her rolling on top of him. "Why don't you thank me now?"

CHAPTER 9

Claire came down to give the set her final approval. At the far end of the studio, serenely indifferent to the piles of equipment, lights and shades, was a cozy living room scene. A deep, cushy sofa in shades of masculine brown was spotlighted as technicians made adjustments. On a table beside it was a Tiffany lamp which would appear to give the soft, sexy lighting the crew was working to achieve. Claire worked her way around cable and cases to a new angle.

Tasteful, she decided. And effective. De Marco was pleased with the first spot. So pleased, Claire thought with a mild grimace, that he had insisted his current inamorata appear in this one. Well, that was show business, she decided as she checked her watch. Brooke had moaned and groaned at the casting, then had given in with the mutter that at least he hadn't insisted they write her any dialogue.

The studio segment was being filmed first, though it would appear at the end of the ad when aired. Judging Parks's temperament, Brooke had decided to go with what would probably be the most difficult portion for him first, then ease him into the rest. And, Claire mused as she checked her watch, their luck was holding. The Kings would compete in the

World Series the following week, giving the commercials just that much more impact.

Outside the studio, a long buffet had been set up in the hall. E.J., the production coordinator and the assistant cameraman were already making the most of it. Brooke was in the studio, nibbling on a hunk of cheese as she supervised the finer details.

"Damn it, Bigelow, that light's flickering again. Change the bulb or get a new fixture in here. Silbey, let me see what kind of effect we get with that new gel."

Obediently, he hit a switch so that the light filtered through the colored sheet and came out warm and sultry. "Okay, not bad. Sound?"

The sound technician walked under the boom mike. With her face innocently bland, she began to recite a nursery rhyme with a few interesting variations. At the polite volley of applause, she curtsied.

"Any problems?" Claire asked as she moved to stand beside Brooke.

"We've smoothed them out. Your end?"

"Everyone's accounted for. The talent's changing." Absently, she straightened the hem of her sleeve. "I got a glimpse of de Marco's lady. She's gorgeous."

"Thank God," Brooke said with feeling. "Are we expecting him?"

"No." Claire smiled at the resigned tone of Brooke's voice. She heartily disliked relatives, friends or lovers hanging around a shoot. "He tells me Gina claims he would make her nervous, but he left no doubt she's to be given the royal, kid-glove treatment."

"I won't bite her," Brooke promised. "I ran through Parks's lines with him. He has it cold . . . if he doesn't fumble it on camera."

"He doesn't appear to be a fumbler."

Brooke smiled. "No. And I think he's starting to enjoy this whole business despite himself."

"Good. I have a script I want him to read." Above their heads on a ladder, someone cursed pungently. Claire's smooth features never registered she had even heard. "There's a part, a small one, I think he's perfect for."

Brooke turned to give Claire her full attention. "A feature?"

She nodded. "For cable. We won't be casting for another month or two, so he's got plenty of time to think about it. I'd like you to read it, too," she added casually.

"Sure." Mulling over the idea of Parks as an actor, Brooke turned to call out another instruction.

"You might like to direct it."

The order froze in her throat. "What?"

"I know you're happy directing commercials," Claire went on as if Brooke weren't gaping at her. "You've always said you enjoy creating the quick and intense, but this script might change your mind."

"Claire—" Brooke might have laughed if she hadn't been stunned "—I've never directed anything more complex than a sixty-second spot."

"Like the promo for the new fall shows you filmed last summer? Three major network stars told me you were one of the best they'd ever worked with." It was said dryly, hardly like a compliment. "I've wanted to ease you into something like this for a long time, but I didn't want to push." Claire patted her hand. "I'm still not pushing, just read the script."

After a moment, Brooke nodded. "All right, I'll read it."

"Good girl. Ah, there's Parks now." Her eyes ran over him with professional discrimination. "My, my," she murmured, "he does wear clothes well."

He looked as though he had chosen the pale blue cashmere sweater and slate-gray jeans at random, shrugging into them without a thought. That they fit with tailored precision wasn't nearly as important as the sense of rightness—that careless style that comes not from money but from basic class.

That he had, Brooke thought. Beneath the attractive face and athletic body was a sense of class that one was born with or one was not. It could never be taught. He held a glass of ginger ale in his hand, looking over the rim as he studied the room.

He found it crowded and cluttered and apparently disorganized but for the small island of order that was a sofa, table and lamp. He wondered fleetingly how anyone could work sanely around the coiled snakes of cable, huge black cases and poles of light. Then he saw Brooke. She could, he thought with a smile. She would simply steamroll over the chaos until she got exactly what she wanted. She might have wept like a child in his arms only a few nights before, but when she was on the job she was as tough as they came.

Perhaps, he mused, that was why he'd fallen in love with her—and perhaps that was why he was going to keep that little bit of information to himself for a while. If he'd nearly panicked when he'd realized it, Brooke would undoubtedly do so. She wasn't quite ready to sit trustingly in the palm of his hand.

Brooke moved toward him, eyes narrowed. Parks thought uncomfortably that she could always make him feel like a department store dummy when she looked at him that way. It was her director's look, appraising, searching for flaws, mulling over the angles.

"Well?" he said at length.

"You look marvelous." If she had noticed the faint irritation in his voice, she ignored it. Reaching up, she disheveled his hair a bit, then studied the effect. "Yes, very good. Nervous?"

"No."

Her face softened with a smile. "Don't frown, Parks, it won't help you get into the mood. Now . . ." Linking her arm in his, she began to lead him toward the set. "You know your lines, but we'll have cue cards in case you draw a blank, so there's nothing to worry about. The main thing we want is that sort of laid-back, understated machismo. Remember this is the end of the segment; the first scene you're on the field in uniform, then there's the business in the locker room while you're changing, then this. Soft lights, a little brandy, a beautiful woman."

"And I owe it all to de Marco," he said dryly.

"The woman in any case," she returned equably. "It's simply a statement that clothes suit a man's image. Hopefully, men will be convinced that de Marco's right for theirs. You'll sit here." Brooke gestured toward the end of the couch. "Give me that relaxed slouch of yours when you're unwinding. It's casual but not sloppy."

He frowned again, helplessly annoyed that she could dissect his every gesture and put a label on it. "Now?"

"Yes, please." Brooke stood back while Parks settled himself on the couch. "Yes, good. . . . Bring your elbow back just a bit on the arm. Okay." She smiled again. "That's what I want. You're getting very good at this, Parks."

"Thanks."

"You'll talk right into the camera this time," she told him, gesturing behind her to where the machine sat on a dolly. "Easy, relaxed. The girl will come up behind you, leaning over as she hands you the brandy snifter. Don't look at her, just touch her hand and keep talking. And smile," she added, looking at her watch. "Where is the girl?"

On cue, Gina entered, tall and voluptuous, followed by a stern-looking blonde and two men in business suits. Better than the photo de Marco sent over, Brooke noted, and that had been impressive. The woman was young, but not too young, a ripe twenty-five, Brooke estimated, with large sloe eyes and raven hair. Her body was curvy, shown to advantage in a clingy low-cut gown that stopped just short of censorship. She wouldn't get aloof from this one, Brooke mused, watching Gina make her way across the studio. Heat vibrated in every movement. This time she would go for pure sex—for the five and a half seconds Gina was on screen. For a thirty-second television ad, it would be more than enough.

Ignoring the appreciative mutters and elbowing of her crew, Brooke walked to meet de Marco's lady. "Hello." She extended her hand with a smile. "I'm Brooke Gordon, I'll be directing you."

"Gina Minianti," she purred in a voice that instantly made Brooke regret she'd have no lines.

"We're very pleased to have you, Ms. Minianti. Do you have any questions before we begin?"

Gina gave her a slight smile. *"Come?"*

"If there's anything you don't understand," Brooke began, only to have the blonde interrupt her.

"Signorina Minianti doesn't speak English, Ms. Gordon," she said briskly. "Weren't you informed?"

"Doesn't—" Breaking off, Brooke rolled her eyes to the ceiling. "Lovely."

"I'm Mr. de Marco's personal secretary. I'll be glad to translate."

Brooke gave the blonde a long hard look, then turned around. "Places," she called. "It's going to be a long day."

"A little stumbling block?" Parks murmured as she passed him.

"Shut up and sit down, Parks."

Controlling a grin, he stepped forward to take Gina's hand. "Signorina," he began, then caught Brooke's full attention when he continued in fluid Italian. Beaming, Gina answered in a rapid spate, gesturing freely with her other hand.

"She's excited," Parks commented, knowing Brooke had stopped in her tracks behind him.

"So I gathered."

"She's always wanted to do an American movie." He spoke to Gina again, something that made her throw back her magnificent head and laugh throatily. Turning, she dismissed the blonde with a flick of the wrist and tucked her arm through Parks's. When they faced her, the tawny Californian, the raven Italian, Brooke was struck with the perfection of the contrast. That five and a half seconds of film, she thought, was going to crackle like a forest fire—and sell one hell of a lot of de Marco merchandise.

"You seem to speak Italian well enough to suit her," Brooke commented.

"Apparently." He grinned again, noting that Brooke wasn't the least jealous but appraising, as if he and Gina were already in a view screen. "She'd like me to interpret for her."

"All right, tell her we'll run through it once to show her what she needs to do. Let's have the lights!" Striding to the set, Brooke waited impatiently while Gina and Parks strolled behind her, heads close as he relayed Brooke's instructions. "Sit down, Parks, and tell her to watch closely. I'll run through it with you." Parks settled on the couch as she had instructed him. "Take it from the top, just as if the camera were rolling."

He began, talking easily, as if to a few friends on a visit. Perfect, Brooke thought as she picked up the prop brandy snifter and walked into camera range behind the couch. She leaned over, letting her cheek come close to his as she offered it. Without glancing from the camera, Parks accepted it, raising the fingers of his other hand to run down the back of Brooke's as it rested on his shoulder. She straightened slowly, moving out of camera range as he finished the dialogue.

"Now ask her if she understands what she's to do," Brooke ordered.

Gina lifted an elegant hand at Parks's question, silently communicating "of course."

"Let's try one." Brooke backed behind E.J. and the assistants who would dolly the camera platform forward for the close-ups. "Quiet on the set," she called, effectively cutting off a few discreet murmurs. "Roll film. . . ." The clapper struck—Parks Jones for de Marco, scene three, take one. She narrowed her eyes at Parks. "Action."

He ran through it well enough for a first take, but Brooke decided he hadn't warmed to it yet. Gina followed instructions, bringing the snifter, leaning over him suggestively. Then she glanced up, startled, as the camera rolled in.

"Cut. Parks, explain to Gina not to look at the camera, please." She smiled at the woman, hoping she communicated patience and understanding. She needed a great deal of both by the fifth take. Instead of becoming more used to the camera, Gina seemed to be growing more unnerved. "Five minutes," Brooke announced. The hot lights switched off, and the crew began a pilgrimage toward the buffet. With another smile, Brooke gestured for Gina to join her and Parks on the sofa. "Parks, will you tell her she need only be natural. She's gorgeous, the few seconds she's going to be on film will make a tremendous impact."

Gina listened with brows knit, then tossed Brooke a smile. "*Grázie.*" Taking Parks's hand, she launched into a long, emotional torrent that turned out to be an apology for her clumsiness and a request for something cold to calm her nerves.

"Bring Signorina Minianti some orange juice," Brooke demanded. "Tell her she's not clumsy at all," Brooke continued diplomatically. "Ah, tell her to try to imagine you're lovers, and when the camera turns off—"

"I get the idea," Parks said with a grin. When he spoke to Gina again, she gave her throaty laugh then shook her head before she answered. "She says she'll try to imagine it," Parks relayed to Brooke, "but if she imagines it too well, Carlo will step on my face . . . or words to that effect."

"We have to sacrifice for our art," Brooke told him dryly. "Parks, it would help if you could put a little more steam into it."

"Steam?" he repeated, lifting a brow.

"A man who doesn't steam a bit with a woman like that hanging over his shoulder needs a transfusion." Rising, Brooke patted his shoulder. "See what you can do?"

"Anything for art," he returned, sending her a wolfish grin.

As E.J. sat behind his camera again, Brooke walked to stand at his shoulder. "Let's see if we can make one this time," she muttered.

"Boss, I can do this all day long." He focused his lens on Gina and sighed. "I think I've died and gone to heaven."

"De Marco might arrange it if you don't watch your step. Places!"

Better, she mused. Yes, definitely better as they completed the sixth take. But not perfect. She told Parks to ask Gina to give the camera a languid look before she slid Parks an under-the-lashes smile. The direction lost something in the interpretation. "Cut. Here, tell her to stand next to the camera and watch again." Brooke took Gina's place, moving behind him as he spoke, cupping the snifter of lukewarm tea. This time when Parks took it from her, he brought her other hand to his lips, pressing a soft kiss against it without breaking the rhythm of the dialogue. Brooke felt a jolt shoot up her arm and forgot to move away.

"Just seemed natural," Parks told her, linking his fingers through hers.

Brooke cleared her throat, aware that her crew was watching with avid interest. "Give it a try that way, then," she said matter-of-factly. She walked back to E.J., but when she turned, Parks's eyes were still on her. Brooke gave a quick, frustrated shake of her head. She knew that look. Slowly, the meaning crystal clear, Parks smiled.

"Places!" Brooke called in her own defense.

It took three more takes before she got just what she wanted. A hot but self-satisfied Gina gave Parks two exuberant kisses, one on each cheek, then came over and chattered something at Brooke. Glancing up at Parks, Brooke saw that amused and all too innocent look on his face.

"Just say thank you," he advised.

"Thank you," Brooke said obediently as Gina took her hand and squeezed it. She swept off with her entourage. "What was I thanking her for?" Brooke used the sleeve of her shirt to dry the sweat on her forehead.

"She was complimenting your taste."

"Oh?"

"She said your lover was magnificent."

Dropping her arm, Brooke stared at him. "Really?" she said coolly.

Parks grinned, gave a deprecatory shrug then strolled off to see if anything was left at the buffet.

Hands on her hips, Brooke stared after him. She wouldn't give him the satisfaction of letting her own smile escape. "Location, one hour," she called out.

Brooke had been right in thinking that the third brief scene of the commercial would be the most difficult to film. She shot the second scene next, crowding lights, equipment and crew into the Kings locker room. Claire had arranged, with a little negotiating, to have a few of the better-known of Parks's teammates available for background or cameos. Once Brooke got them settled down so that they stopped waving at the camera or making fictitious announcements into the mike, it began to work. And work well.

Because of the relative ease with which the segment was progressing, Brooke found the headache growing at the base of her skull unexplainable. True, the locker room was noisy between takes, and after the first hour of many bodies under hot lights, it *smelled* like a locker room, but this headache was pure tension.

At first she simply ignored it; then, when that became impossible, she grew annoyed with herself. There was nothing to be tense about. Parks did what he was told, pulling the cashmere sweater over his naked chest for each take. Arid every time he smiled at her, Brooke felt the headache pulse.

By the time the crew was setting up for the scene on the diamond, Brooke had convinced herself she had it under control. It was just a nagging ache, something she would take care of with a couple of aspirin when she got home. As she watched the sound technician work on a mike, she felt a beefy arm slip over her shoulders.

"Hi." Snyder grinned down at her, drawing an automatic smile of response from Brooke. He was, she thought, about as dangerous as a cocker spaniel.

"Ready for the next scene, George? You did very well before. Of course, you won't be on camera this time."

"Yeah, I wanted to mention that you're making a big mistake using Parks. Too skinny." He flexed a well-muscled arm.

Brooke gave his biceps a nod of approval. "I'm afraid I don't have anything to do with the casting."

"Too bad. Hey, now that I'm a star, are you going to pick me up at the airport?"

"Forget it, Snyder." Before Brooke could answer, Kinjinsky strolled over, a bat in one hand, a ball in the other. "She's out of your league." He grinned at Brooke, jerking his head at his teammate. "He specializes in belly dancers."

"Lies." Snyder looked amazingly like an overgrown choirboy. "All lies."

"When my daughter grows up," Kinjinsky said mildly, "I'm going to warn her about men like him." Walking to the plate, he tossed the ball up in the air then drilled it out to center field.

"Kinjinsky's the best fungo hitter on the team," Snyder told Brooke. "Too bad he has such trouble with a pitched ball."

"At least I can make it from first to second in under two and a half minutes," Kinjinsky tossed back.

Snyder, well used to ribbing about his base running, feigned an offended look. "I have this genetic anatomical problem," he explained to Brooke.

"Oh." Playing along, she looked sympathetic. "That's too bad."

"It's called a lead foot," Parks commented as he came up behind them.

Hearing his voice had the headache she'd nearly forgotten drumming again. She turned to find him watching her and his teammates with a lazily amused smile. Parks wore full uniform, the blazing white that brought out the gold of his skin. The navy cap shaded his eyes, giving him a cocky, assured look. Quietly possessive, his eyes skimmed over her. This time Brooke felt a flutter in her stomach in addition to the throb at the base of her neck.

"Just keeping your woman entertained," Snyder said genially.

"Brooke's her own woman." But there was something un-mistakably proprietary in the disclaimer.

Hearing it, Snyder realized there was something deeper here than he had imagined. So the lightning's finally hit the Iceman, he thought. Snyder had the wit to rib unmercifully and the nature of a man who mends the broken wings of small birds. "When she sees how good I come across on camera, you're going to be out of a job."

"De Marco doesn't have a line for sumo wrestlers," Parks countered.

"Gentlemen," Brooke spoke, cutting them off. "The crew's ready. George, if you'd take your place at first to give Parks his target."

"Ouch." He winced. "Try not to take that literally, Jones. I don't want to be on the disabled list next week."

"Mike." Brooke stepped over to Kinjinsky. "If you'll just hit them to Parks—don't make it too easy for him, I want to see a little effort."

With a grin, Kinjinsky tossed up another ball. "I'll see what I can do."

Nodding, Brooke walked toward the crew. "Places. Parks, any questions?"

"I think I can handle this one." He stepped up to third, au-tomatically kicking up a bit of dust with his spikes.

She looked through the lens, feeling another flutter in her stomach as she focused on Parks. Shifting his weight to one hip, he grinned at her. Brooke stepped back, gesturing to E.J.

"Hey, boss, you okay?"

"Yes, I'm fine. Roll film."

It went perfectly. Brooke knew she could have used the first take without a hitch, but opted for two more. They were equally smooth. Kinjinsky blasted the ball at Parks, enough to make him dive or leap before Parks in turn fired the ball at Snyder on first.

"Third take's the winner," E.J. announced when Brooke called the session a wrap.

"Yes." Unconsciously, she rubbed the back of her neck.

"He shouldn't have even caught it," E.J. went on, watching Brooke as he began to load his equipment.

"He seems to excel at doing the impossible," she murmured.

"Headache?"

"What?" Glancing down, she found E.J. watching her steadily. "It's nothing." Annoyed, she dropped her hand. Parks was already in a conference on the mound with his two teammates. He had his glove hand on his hip, grinning at Snyder's newest concept for a practical joke. "It's nothing," Brooke repeated in a mutter, reaching for one of the sodas in the ice chest.

It had to be nothing, she told herself as she tipped the bottle and drank deeply. Whatever was rolling around inside her was just a product of fatigue after a long day's work. She needed aspirin, a decent meal and eight hours' sleep. She needed to stay away from Parks.

The minute the thought entered her head, Brooke was infuriated. He has nothing to do with it, she told herself fiercely. I'm tired, I've been working too hard, I've— She caught E.J.'s speculative stare and bristled.

"Would you get out of here?"

His face cleared with a wide grin. "On my way. I'll drop off the film at editing."

With a curt nod, Brooke strode out to the mound to thank Snyder and Kinjinsky. She heard the tail of Snyder's brainstorm, something about frogs in the bullpen, before Parks turned to her.

"How'd it go?"

"Very well." Heat was running along her skin now, too physical, too tangible. She gave her attention to his teammates.

"I want to thank both of you. Without your help, it never would have gone so smoothly."

Snyder leaned his elbow on Kinjinsky's shoulder. "Just keep me in mind when you want something more than a pretty face in one of these commercials."

"I'll do that, George."

Parks waited through the rest of the small talk, adding comments easily though his concentration was all for Brooke. He waited until the ballplayers had wandered off toward the locker room before he took Brooke's chin in his hand. Closely, patiently, he examined her. "What's wrong?"

Brooke stepped away so that they were no longer touching. "Why should anything be wrong?" she countered. Her nerves had gone off like bells in her head at his touch. "It went very well. I think you'll be pleased with it when it's edited. With the two spots running throughout the series, we won't shoot another until November." Turning, she noted that most of the crew had gone. She found she wanted to be away before she and Parks were completely alone. "I have a few things to clear up back at the office, so—"

"Brooke." Parks cut her off cleanly. "Why are you upset?"

"I'm *not* upset!" Biting back fury, she whirled back to him. "It's been a long day, I'm tired. That's all."

Slowly, Parks shook his head. "Try again."

"Leave me alone," she said in a trembling undertone that told her, and him, just how close she was to the edge. "Just leave me alone."

Dropping his mitt to the ground, he took both her arms. "Not a chance. We can talk here, or we can go back to your place and hash it out. Your choice."

She shoved away from him. "There's nothing to hash out."

"Fine. Then let's go have dinner and see a movie."

"I told you I had work to do."

"Yeah." He nodded slowly. "You lied."

Sharp, bubbling anger filled her eyes. "I don't have to lie, all I have to do is tell you no."

"True enough," he agreed, holding on to his own temper. "Why are you angry with me?" His voice was calm, patient. His eyes weren't. The sun fell against his face, accenting that fierce sexuality.

"I'm not angry with you!" she nearly shouted.

"People usually shout when they're angry."

"I'm *not* shouting," she claimed as her voice rose.

Curiously, he tilted his head. "No? Then what are you doing?"

"I'm afraid I'm falling in love with you." Her expression became almost comically surprised after the words had tumbled out. She stared in simple disbelief, then covered her mouth with her hand as if to shove the words back inside.

"Oh, yeah?" He didn't smile as he took another step toward her. Something was scrambling inside his stomach like a squirrel in a cage. "Is that so?"

"No, I . . ." In defense, she looked around, only to find that she was alone with him now. Alone in his territory. The stands rose up like walls to trap them inside the field of grass and dirt. Brooke backed off the mound. "I don't want to stay here."

Parks merely matched his steps to hers. "Why afraid, Brooke?" He lifted his hand to her cheek, causing her to stop her retreat. "Why should a woman like you be afraid of being in love?"

"I know what happens!" she said suddenly with eyes that were dark and stormy in contrast to the trembling tone.

"Okay, why don't you tell me?"

"I'll stop thinking. I'll stop being careful." She ran an

agitated hand through her hair. "I'll give until I lose the edge, then when it's over I won't have anything left. Every time," she whispered, thinking of all the transient parents, thinking of Clark. "I won't let it happen to me again. I can't be involved with you for the fun of it, Parks. It just isn't working." Without being aware of the direction, Brooke had turned to pace to the third base bag. Parks felt the warmth of the gold piece against his chest and decided it was fate. Taking his time, he followed her. His percentage of errors at the corner was very small.

"You are involved with me, whether you're having fun at it or not."

She sent him a sharp glance. This wasn't the easygoing man but the warrior. Brooke straightened her shoulders. "That can be remedied."

"Try it," he challenged, calmly gripping her shirt in his hand and pulling her toward him.

Brooke threw her head back, infuriated, and perhaps more frightened than she had ever been in her life. "I won't see you again. If you can't work with me, take it up with Claire."

"Oh, I can work with you," he said softly. "I can even manage to take your orders without too much of a problem because you're damn good at what you do. I told you once before I'd follow your rules while the camera was on." He glanced around, silently relaying that there was no camera this time. "It's tough to beat a man on his own ground, Brooke, especially a man who's used to winning."

"I'm not a pennant, Parks," she said with amazing steadiness.

"No." With one hand still gripping her shirt, he traced the other gently down her cheek. "Pennants are won through teamwork. A woman's a one-on-one proposition. Seventh-inning stretch, Brooke. Time to take a quick breath before the game starts again." The hand on her cheek moved up to cup her neck. She wondered that he couldn't feel the sledge-hammers pounding there. Then he smiled, that slow danger-ous smile that always drew her. "I'm in love with you."

He said it so calmly, so simply, that it took her a moment to understand. Every muscle in her body went rigid. "Don't."

He lifted a brow. "Don't love you or don't tell you?"

"Stop." She put both hands on his chest in an attempt to push him away. "It's not a joke."

"No, it's not. What are you more afraid of?" he asked, studying her pale face. "Loving or being loved?"

Brooke shook her head. She'd been so careful to keep from crossing that thin line—been just as careful to keep others from crossing from the other side. Claire had done it, and E.J., she realized. There was love there. But *in* love . . . How could a tiny, two-letter word petrify her?

"You could ask me when," Parks murmured, kneading the tense muscles in her neck, "and I couldn't tell you. There wasn't a bolt of lightning, no bells, no violins. I can't even say it snuck up on me because I saw it coming. I didn't try to step out of the way." He shook his head before he lowered his mouth to hers. "You can't wish it away, Brooke."

The kiss rocked her back on her heels. It was hard and strong and demanding without the slightest hint of urgency. It was as if he knew she could go nowhere. She could fight him, Brooke thought. She could still fight him. But the tension was seeping out of her, filling her with a sense of free-dom she had thought she would never fully achieve. She was loved.

Feeling the change in her, Parks pulled back. He wouldn't win her with passion. His needs ran too deep to settle for that. Then her arms were around him, her cheek pressed against his chest in a gesture not of desire, but of trust. Perhaps the beginning of trust.

"Tell me again," she murmured. "Just tell me once more."

He held her close, stroking her hair while the breeze whispered through the empty stadium. "I love you."

With a sigh, Brooke stepped over the line. Lifting her head, she took his face in her hands. "I love you, Parks," she murmured before she urged his lips to take hers.

CHAPTER 10

Clubhouses have their own smell. Sweat, foot powder, the tang of liniments, the faint chemical aroma of whirlpools and the overlying fragrance of coffee. The mixture of odors was so much a part of his life, Parks never noticed it as he pulled on his sweatshirt. What he did notice was tension. That was inescapable. Even Snyder's determined foray of practical jokes couldn't break the curtain of nerves in the locker room that afternoon. When a team had spent months together—working, sweating, winning and losing—aiming toward one common goal, nothing could ease the nerves of facing the seventh game of the World Series.

If the momentum had been with them, the atmosphere would have been different. All the minor aches that plague the end of a season would barely have been noticed—the tired legs, the minor pulls. But the Kings had dropped the last two games to the Herons. A professional athlete knows that skill is not the only determining factor in winning. Momentum, luck, timing are all added for balance.

Even if the Kings could have claimed they'd fallen into a slump there might have been a little more cheer in the clubhouse. The simple fact was that they'd been outplayed. The number of hits between the opponents was almost even—but the Herons had made theirs count while the Kings had left their much needed runs stranded on base. Now it came down to the last chance for both teams. Then when it was over, they'd pick up their off-season lives.

Parks glanced at Snyder, who'd be on his charter boat in Florida the following week. Catching fish and swapping lies, he called it, Parks mused. Kinjinsky, getting heat applied to his ribs, would be playing winter ball in Puerto Rico. Maizor, the starting pitcher, would be getting ready to play daddy for the first time when his wife delivered in November. Some would go on the banquet circuit and the talk show circuit—depending on the outcome of today's game. Others would go back to quiet jobs until February and spring training.

And Parks Jones makes commercials, he reflected with a small grimace. But the idea didn't bring on the sense of foolishness it had only a few months before. It gave him a certain pleasure to act—though Brooke wouldn't call it that—in front of the camera. But he wasn't too thrilled with the poster deal Lee had cooked up.

He smiled a little as he drew on his spikes. Hype, Brooke had called it, saying simply it was part of the game. She was right, of course; she usually was about that aspect of things. But Parks didn't think he'd ever be completely comfortable with the way she could look him over with those calm eyes and sum him up with a few choice words. Wouldn't it disconcert any man to have fallen in love with a woman who could so accurately interpret his every expression, body move or careless word? Face it, Jones, he told himself, you could have picked an easier woman. Could have, he reflected, but didn't. And since Brooke Gordon was who and what he wanted, she was worth the effort it took to have her, and to keep her. He wasn't so complacent that he believed he had truly done either yet.

Yes, she loved him, but her trust was a very tenuous thing. He sensed that she waited for him to make a move so that she could make a countermove. And so the match continued. Fair enough, he decided; they were both programmed to compete. He didn't want to control her . . . did he? With a frown, Parks pulled a bat out of his locker and examined it carefully. If he had to answer the question honestly, he'd say he wasn't sure. She still challenged him—as she had from the very first moment. Now, mixed with the challenge were so many emotions it was difficult to separate them.

He'd been angry when Brooke wouldn't change her schedule and fly East during the games at the Herons' home stadium. And when he'd become angry, she'd become very cool. Her work, she had told him, couldn't be set aside to suit him or even herself . . . any more than his could. Even though he'd understood, Parks had been angry. He had simply wanted her there, wanted to know she was in the stands so that he could look up and see her. He had wanted to know she was there when the long game was over. Pure selfishness, he admitted. They both had an ample share of that.

With a grim smile Parks ran a hand down the smooth barrel of the bat. She'd told him it wouldn't be easy. Brooke had been her own person long before he had pushed his way into her life. Circumstances had made her the person she was— though they were circumstances she had still not made completely clear to him. Still it was that person—the strong, the vulnerable, the practical and the private, whom he had fallen for. Yet he couldn't quite get over the urge he had at times to shake her and tell her they were going to do it his way.

He supposed what epitomized their situation at this point was their living arrangement. He had all but moved in with her, though neither one of them had discussed it. But he knew Brooke considered the house hers. Therefore, Parks was living with her, but they weren't living together. He wasn't certain his patience would last long enough to break through that final thin wall—without leaving the entrance hole a bit jagged.

With a quiet oath he reached into the locker and grabbed a batting glove, sticking it in his back pocket. If he had to use a bit of dynamite, he decided, he would.

"Hey, Jones, infield practice."

"Yeah." He grabbed his mitt, sliding his hand into its familiar smoothness. He was going to handle Brooke, he told himself. But first there was a pennant to win.

Alternately cursing and drumming her fingers against the steering wheel, Brooke cruised the parking lot in search of a space. "I knew we should've left earlier," she muttered. "We'll be lucky to get anything within a mile of the stadium."

Leaning back against the seat, E.J. interrupted his humming long enough to comment. "Still fifteen minutes before game time."

"When somebody gets you a free ticket," Brooke said precisely, "the least you can do is be ready when they pick you up. There's one!" Brooke gunned the motor and slipped between two parked cars with inches to spare. Hitting the brake, she glanced at her companion. "You can open your eyes now, E.J.," she said dryly.

Cautiously, one at a time, he did so. "Okay. . . ." He looked at the car beside him. "Now how do we get out?"

"Open the door and inhale," she advised, wiggling out her side. "And hurry up, will you? I don't want to miss them taking the field."

"I've noticed your interest in baseball's increased over the summer, boss." Thankful for his thin frame, E.J. squeezed out of the Datsun.

"It's an interesting game."

"Yeah?" Joining her, he grinned.

"Careful, E.J., I still have your ticket. I could scalp it twenty times before we reach the door."

"Aw, come on, Brooke, you can tell your friend what's already in the papers."

She scowled at that, stuffing her hands in her pockets. There'd been pictures of her and Parks, tantalizing little articles and hints in every paper she'd looked at for more than a week. In L.A., gossip carried quickly—a hot ballplayer and his attractive director were definitely food for gossip.

"I even caught a bit in one of the trades," E.J. went on, blithely ignoring the storm clouds in Brooke's eyes. "Speculation is that Parks might take up, ah . . . show business," he said, giving her another grin, "seriously."

"Claire has a part for him if he wants it," Brooke returned, evading his obvious meaning. "It's small but meaty. I didn't want to go into it in depth with Parks until after the series. He has enough on his mind."

"Yeah, I'd say the man's had a few things on his mind for some time now."

"E.J.," Brooke began warningly as she passed over her tickets.

"You know," he continued when they fought their way through the inside crowd, "I've always wondered when somebody'd come along who'd shake that cool of yours a little."

"Is that so?" She didn't want to be amused, so she slipped her sunglasses down to conceal the humor in her eyes. "And you apparently think someone has?"

"Honey, you can't get within ten feet of the two of you and not feel the steam. I've been thinking . . ." He fussed with the front of his T-shirt as if straightening a tie. "As your close friend and associate, maybe I should ask Mr. Jones his intentions."

"Just try it, E.J., and I'll break all of your lenses." Caught between amusement and irritation, Brooke plopped down in her seat. "Sit down and buy me a hot dog."

He signaled. "What do you want on it?"

"All I can get."

"Come on, Brooke." He fished in his pocket for a couple of bills, exchanging them for hot dogs and cold drinks. "Buddy to buddy, how serious is it?"

"Not going to let up, are you?"

"I care."

Brooke glanced over at him. He was smiling, not the wise-cracking grin she so often saw on his face, but a simple smile of friendship. It was, perhaps, the only weapon she had no defense against. "I'm in love with him," she said quietly. "I guess that's pretty damn serious."

"Grade-A serious," he agreed. "Congratulations."

"Am I supposed to feel like I'm walking on a cliff?" she demanded, only half joking.

"Don't know." E.J. took a considering bite of his hot dog. "Never had the experience."

"Never been in love, E.J.?" Leaning back in her seat, Brooke grinned. "You?"

"Nope. That's why I spend so much time looking." He gave a heavy sigh. "It's a tough business, Brooke."

"Yeah." She took off his fielder's cap and swatted him with it. "I bet it is. Now shut up, they're going to announce the starting lineup."

A tough business, she thought again. Well, he wasn't far wrong, even if he had been joking. Looking for love was a lonely occupation, one she'd given up—or thought she'd given up—years before. Finding it—or having it tickle you from behind—was even tougher. Once it found you it clung, no matter how much you tried to shake it off. But she wasn't trying to shake it off, Brooke mused. She was just trying to understand how it fit and make a few adjustments. The fabric kept changing.

"Playing third and batting fourth, number twenty-nine, Parks Jones."

The already boisterous crowd went frantic as Parks jogged out on the field to take his place in the lineup. When he stood beside Snyder, he let his eyes drift over. They locked on Brooke's. With a smile, he gave the customary tip of his cap. It was a gesture for the crowd, but she knew it had been aimed at her personally. It was all the acknowledgment he would give her until it was over. It was all she expected.

"I'm going to outhit you today, Iceman," Snyder warned, grinning at the crowd. "Then Brooke's going to realize her mistake."

Parks never took his eyes off her. "She's going to marry me."

Snyder's jaw dropped. "No kidding! Well, hey . . ."

"She just doesn't know it yet," Parks added in a murmur. He slapped hands with the right fielder, batting fifth. "But she will."

Brooke detected a change in Parks's smile, something subtle, but to her unmistakable. Narrowing her eyes, she tried to decipher it. "He's up to something," she muttered.

E.J. perfected a shot with a small still camera. "What?"

"Nothing." She swirled her drink so that ice chunks banged together. "Nothing."

A well-known blues singer stepped up to the mike to sing the national anthem. Two lines of athletes removed their caps. The crowd rose, silent for what would be the last time in more than two hours. The excitement was so tangible Brooke thought she could reach out into the warm October air and grab a handful of nerves. It built and built until it exploded with cheers and shouts and whistles as the last note of the song trembled. The Kings took the field.

Sportscasters are fond of saying that the seventh game of the World Series is the ultimate in sports events—the pinnacle test of teamwork and individual effort. This was no exception. In the first inning, Brooke saw the Kings' center fielder charge a ball, stretching forward to catch it on the run then holding on to it as the momentum carried him into a forward roll. She saw the Herons shortstop seem to throw heart and body after a ball to prevent it from going through the hole for a base hit. At the end of the fourth, the teams had one run apiece, each on solo home runs.

Brooke had seen Parks guard his position at third, stealing, as Lee would have put it, two certain base hits and starting the execution of a clutch double play. Watching him, Brooke realized he played this game just as he played every other—with total concentration, with steady determination. If he had nerves, if somewhere in his mind was the thought that this was *the* game, it didn't show. As he stepped up to bat, she leaned out on the rail.

Before he stepped into the box, Parks ran a hand up and down his bat as though checking for splinters. He was waiting for calm, not the calm of the shouting fans but inner calm. In his mind's eye he could see Brooke leaning on the rail, her hair tumbling over her shoulders, her eyes cool and direct. The knot of tension in his stomach eased.

When he stepped up to the plate, his predominant thought was to advance the runner. With Snyder on first, he'd have to put it well out of the infield. And they'd be pitching him carefully. Both times he had come to bat, Parks had clipped a single through the hole between third and short.

Parks took his stance and looked directly into the pitcher's eyes. He watched the windup, saw the ball hurtling toward him, shifted his weight, then checked his swing. The slider missed the corner. Ball one.

Stepping out of the box, Parks knocked the bat against his

spikes to clear them of dirt. Yeah, they were going to be careful what they gave him. But he could get Snyder to second just as easily on a walk as on a hit. The trouble was, second wasn't a sure scoring position for Snyder.

The second pitch missed, low and outside. Parks checked the signal from the third base coach. He didn't allow his eyes to drift over to where Brooke sat. Parks knew even that brief contact would destroy his concentration.

The next pitch came in on him, nearly catching him on the knuckles then bouncing foul. The crowd demanded a hit. Parks checked Snyder, who was keeping very cozy with the bag, before he stepped into the box again.

Hoping to even the count, the pitcher tried another fast curve. In that fraction of a second, Parks shifted his weight. Wrists square and unbroken, he connected, letting his hips bring the bat around. He had the satisfaction of hearing the ball crack off the bat before the crowd was on its feet, screaming.

The ball sailed over center field, and though three men gave chase, no one reached it before it smashed into the dirt of the warning track and bounced high over the wall. With the fans roaring on all sides, Parks settled for the ground-rule double. There was sweat trickling down his back, but he barely felt it. He thought once that if he'd pulled the ball a bit to the right, it would have gone over clean, scoring two. Then he forgot it.

With Snyder on third, he couldn't take a sizable lead, so he contented himself with putting only a couple of feet between himself and the bag. The odds that Farlo would sacrifice to score Snyder were slim. The outfielder could spray a ball to all fields, but he wasn't a power hitter. Parks crouched, shaking his arms to keep the muscles loose.

Farlo fell behind quickly, fouling off two pitches and frustrating the crowd. Parks simply refused to think of the possibility of being stranded on base again. The infield was playing them tight, looking for that ground ball that could be turned into a double play.

Parks saw the pitch, judged it to be a low curve and tensed. Farlo showed his teeth and smacked it to right field. Parks was running on instinct before he consciously told his feet to move. The third base coach was waving him on. Years of training had Parks rounding third at top speed and heading home without hesitation or question. He saw the catcher crouched, ready to receive the ball, shielding the plate like a human wall. It flashed through Parks's mind that the Herons' right fielder was known for his arm and his precision before he threw himself at the plate in a feet-first slide that had dirt billowing in the clouds. He felt the red flash of pain as his body connected with the catcher, heard his opponent's *whoosh* of air at the hit and saw the small white ball swallowed by the mitt.

They were a tangle of bodies and mutual pain as the umpire spread his arms. "Safe!"

The crowd went wild, stranger pounded on stranger, beer sloshed over cups. Brooke found that E.J. had grabbed her for a quick dance. His camera cut into her chest but it was several moments before she felt it.

"My man!" E.J. shouted, whirling her into the man on her right, who tossed his box of popcorn into the air.

No, she thought breathlessly. *My* man.

At the plate, Parks didn't concentrate on the adulation of the crowd, but on drawing enough breath into his lungs so he could stand again. The catcher's knee had slammed solidly into his ribs. Rising, he gave his uniform a perfunctory brush then headed to the dugout, where his teammates waited for him. This time, he allowed his eyes to find her. She was standing, her arms still around E.J. But her face softened with a smile that was only for him.

Touching his cap, he disappeared into the dugout. The trainer had the cold spray ready for his ribs.

Parks had forgotten his aches long before he had taken his defensive position in the top of the ninth. The Herons had whittled their lead down to one run with some blood and guts baserunning in the seventh. Since then, both teams had held like rocks. But now, Maizor was in trouble.

With only one out, he had a runner on second and a power hitter coming to the plate. We could walk him and put him on, Parks considered as the catcher tipped back his mask on his way to the mound for a conference. But the Herons had more big bats in the lineup and a few pinch hitters who couldn't be underestimated. Parks sauntered over to the mound, noting as he did that Maizor was strung tight.

"Gonna go for him?" Parks asked as the catcher chewed on a wad of gum the size of a golf ball.

"Yeah, Maizor's gonna take care of him, aren't you, Slick?"

"Sure." He turned the ball over and over in his hand. "We all want a ride in Jones's new sports car."

Parks took the mention of the Most Valuable Player Award with a shrug. They were still two outs away, and all three men knew it. "One thing." He adjusted his cap. "Don't let him hit it toward me."

Maizor swore and grinned and visibly relaxed. "Let's play ball."

Over his shoulder, Maizor checked the runner on second. Satisfied that his lead wasn't too greedy, he fired the ball at the plate. Parks could almost hear the rush of the wind as the bat cut, just over the ball. Kinjinsky called out, telling him to bear down and do it again. He did, but this time the batter got a solid piece of it.

As if a button had been pushed, Parks went for it, lunging from his side as Kinjinsky dashed to cover him. He had only seconds to judge the speed and the height. Even as he let his body fall in the direction of the ball, he felt the runner pass him on his way to third. Landing on his knees, Parks caught in on the short bounce. Without taking the time to rise, he fired the ball toward third. Kinjinsky nabbed it and held his ground as the runner slid into him.

"Still trying to make the easy plays look hard," the short-stop commented as they passed each other. They were both coated with dirt and sweat. "One more, baby, just one more."

Parks let the long, mixed roar of the crowd wash over him as he crouched at third. His face was utterly impassive. The tying run was on first. By the time the count reached three and two, being on the diamond was like being in the eye of a hurricane. Noise and turbulence whirled around them from the stands. On the field, the tension was dead silent.

Maizor went inside, handcuffing the batter. The ball was hit, drifting foul. Parks gave chase as it drifted toward the seats, running at full speed as though the wall weren't looming up in front of him. He could get it, he knew he could get it—if an excited fan didn't reach over and make a grab.

With his free hand, he caught the rail and lifted his glove. He felt the impact of the ball as he closed his leather over it. While the crowd started to scream, he found he was looking directly into Brooke's eyes. The foul had all but fallen into her lap.

"Nice catch." Leaning over, she kissed him full on the mouth.

Then one of his teammates had him around the waist, and the rest was madness.

Parks had more champagne dumped on him than he could possibly have drunk. It mixed with sweat and washed some of the grime away. Snyder had positioned himself on top of a locker and from there emptied two bottles on anyone in sight—reporters and league brass included. Accused of showboating, Parks was tossed, fully dressed, into the whirlpool. Grateful, he stripped and remained where he was with half a bottle of champagne. From there he gave interviews while the water beat the aches from his body and bedlam raged around him.

The pitch on his double had been an outside fast ball. Yeah, his slide into home had been risky, considering the arm of the right fielder, but he'd had a good lead. He continued to answer questions as Snyder, in a champagne-drenched uniform, was not so gently assisted into the whirlpool with him. Parks slid down farther in the soothing water and drained the cold wine straight from the bottle. Yes, the redhead in the stands was Brooke Gordon, his director on the de Marco commercials. Parks smiled as Snyder wisecracked the reporters' attention to himself. Teammates might poke and prod into each other's business, but they protected their own.

Parks closed his eyes a moment, just a moment. He wanted to recapture that instant when she had leaned over and touched her lips to his. Everything had been heightened in that split second of victory. He had thought he could hear each individual shout from the crowd. He'd seen the sunlight glint on the chipped paint of the railing, felt the baking heat as his hand had wrapped around it. Then he'd seen her eyes, close, soft, beautiful. Her voice had been quiet, conveying excitement, humor and love all in two words. When they had touched his, her lips had been warm and smooth, and for an instant that had been all he had felt. Just the silky texture of her lips. He hadn't even heard the last out called. When he'd been dragged back on the field by his teammates, she had simply lowered her chin to the rail and smiled at him. *Later.* He had heard her thought as clearly as if she had spoken it.

It took two hours to urge the last reporter out of the clubhouse. The players were quieting. The first rush of victory was over, replaced by a mellowness that would very quickly become nostalgia. The year was over. There'd be no more infield practice, batting practice, night rides on planes with card games and snoring. They were in a business where today was over quickly and tomorrow took all their efforts. Now there wasn't a tomorrow, but next year.

Some were sitting, talking quietly on the benches in the midst of the locker room litter, as Parks dressed. He glanced at the second-string catcher, a boy of barely nineteen, completing his first year in the majors. He held his shin guards in his hands as if he couldn't bear to part with them. Parks put his mitt into his duffel bag and felt suddenly old.

"How're the ribs?" Kinjinsky asked as he slung his own bag over his shoulder.

"Fine." Parks gestured to the boy on the bench. "The kid's barely old enough to vote."

"Yeah." Kinjinsky, a ripe thirty-two, grinned. "It's hell, isn't it?" They both laughed as Parks closed his locker for the last time that year. "See you in the spring, Jones. My woman's waiting for me."

Parks zipped up his bag while the thought warmed in him. He, too, had a woman, and it would take him thirty minutes to drive to the mountains.

"Hey, Parks." Snyder caught him before he'd reached the door. "You really going to marry her?"

"As soon as I can talk her into it."

Snyder nodded, not questioning the phrasing of the answer. "Give me a call when you set it up. I'm the best man."

With a smile, Parks held out a hand and shook the beefy one. "Damned if you're not, George." He walked into the corridor, closing the door on the clubhouse and the season.

When he emerged outside, it was dusk. Only a few fans lingered, but he signed autographs for them and gave them the time they wanted. Parks thought idly about picking up another bottle of champagne for himself and Brooke as he signed his name to the bill of a twelve-year-old's battered hat. Champagne, a fire burning low, candles. It seemed like a good setting to propose marriage. It was going to be tonight, because tonight he didn't think he could lose.

The parking lot was all but deserted. The overhead lights were just flickering on as twilight deepened. Then he saw her. Brooke was sitting on the hood of his car, spotlighted in the flood of a security light, her hair like tongues of flame around her strong-boned, delicate-skinned face. Love welled up in him, a fierce possessive love that took his breath away. Except for the lips that curved, she didn't move. He realized then she had been watching him for some time. He struggled to regain some control over his muscles before he continued toward her.

"If I'd known you were waiting here, I'd have come out sooner." He felt the ache in his ribs again, but not from the bruise this time. This was from a need he was still not quite used to.

"I told E.J. to take my car. I didn't mind waiting." Reaching up, she put both hands on his shoulders. "Congratulations."

Very deliberately, Parks set his bag down on the asphalt then dove his hands into her hair. Their eyes held briefly, endlessly, before he lowered his mouth and took what he needed.

His emotions were more finely tuned than he had realized. All the pleasure of victory, the weariness that came from winning it, the dregs of excitement and tension surfaced, to be doubled then swept away by one all-encompassing need. Brooke. How was he to have known that she would grow to be everything—and all things? A bit unnerved by the intensity, Parks drew away. A man couldn't win when his knees were buckling. He ran his knuckles down her cheek, wanting to see that very faint, very arousing clouding of her eyes.

"I love you."

At his words, Brooke rested her head against his chest and breathed deeply. She could smell his shower on him, some subtle soap fragrance that spoke of gymnasiums and locker rooms that were inhabited only by men. For some reason, it made her feel acutely a woman. The light grew dimmer as they remained, held close and silent.

"Too tired to celebrate?" she murmured.

"Uh-uh." He kissed her hair.

"Good." Drawing away, she slid from the hood. "I'll buy you dinner to start it off." Brooke opened the passenger door and smiled. "Hungry?"

Until that moment, Parks hadn't realized that he was starving. What little he'd eaten before the game had been devoured by nerves. "Yeah. Do I get to pick the place?"

"Sky's the limit."

Fifteen minutes later, Brooke gazed around the garishly colored Hamburger Heaven. "You know," she mused, studying the overhead lights that were shaped like sesame seed rolls. "I'd forgotten your penchant for junk food."

"A hundred percent pure beef," Parks claimed, picking up an enormous double-decker sandwich.

"If you believe that, you believe anything."

Grinning, he offered her a French fry. "Cynic."

"If you call me names, I won't read you the sports page." She put her hand over the folded paper she'd just bought. "Then you won't hear the accolades the press have heaped on you." When he shrugged, unconcerned, she opened the paper. "Well, I want to hear them." With one hand on her milk shake, Brooke began to thumb her way through. "Here . . . Oh." She stopped dead and scowled.

"What is it?" Parks leaned over. On the front page were two pictures, side by side. The first was of his over-the-seats catch of the final out. The second was of Brooke's impulsive kiss. The caption read:

JONES SCORES . . . TWICE

"Cute," he decided, "considering I didn't score but snagged a pop fly." He twisted his head, skimming down the article which ran through the highlights of the game—critiques and praise. "Hmm. . . . 'And Jones ended it with a race to the rail, snagging Hennesey's long foul out of the seats in one of the finest plays of the afternoon. As usual, the MVP makes the impossible look routine. He got his reward from the luscious redhead—' " here he shot Brooke a brief glance " '—Brooke Gordon, a successful commercial director who's been seen with the third baseman on and off the set.' "

"I really hate that," Brooke said with such vehemence that Parks looked up in surprise.

"Hate what?"

"Having my picture splashed around that way. And this—this half-baked speculation. This, and that silly business in the *Times* a couple days ago."

"The one that called you a willowy, titian-haired beauty with smoky eyes?"

"It's not funny, Parks." Brooke shoved the paper aside.

"It's not tragic, either," he pointed out.

"They should mind their own business."

Leaning back, Parks nibbled on a fry. "You'd probably be the first to tell me that being in the public eye makes you public property."

Brooke scowled at that, knowing they were precisely her words when they'd discussed the poster deal. "*You're* in the public eye," she countered. "It's the way you make your living. *I* don't. I work behind the camera, and I have a right to my privacy."

"Ever heard of guilty by association?" He smiled before she could retort. Instead of a curt remark, she let out a long sigh. "At least they're accurate," he added. "I've often thought of you as a beauty myself."

Brooke picked up her cheeseburger, frowned, then bit into it. "I still don't like it," she muttered. "I think . . ." She shrugged, not certain how foolish she was going to sound. "I've always been a little overly sensitive about my privacy, and now . . . what's happening between us is too important for me to want to share with anyone who has fifty cents for a paper."

Parks leaned forward again and took her hand. "That's nice," he said softly. "That's very nice."

The tone of his voice had fresh emotion rising in her. "I don't want to hole up like a couple of hermits, Parks, but I don't want every move we make to be on the evening news, either."

With a bit more nonchalance than he was feeling at the moment, he shrugged and began to eat again. "Romance is news. . . . So's divorce, when it involves public people."

"It's not going to ease up with the de Marco campaign, either, or if you decide to take that part in the film." She took another French fry out of its paper scoop and glared at it. "The hotter you are, the more the press will buzz around. It's maddening."

"I could break my contract," he suggested.

"Don't be ridiculous."

"There's another solution," he considered, watching Brooke swallow the French fry and reach for another.

"What?"

"We could get married. Want some salt for those?"

Brooke stared at him, then found she had to search for her voice. "What did you say?"

"I asked if you wanted some salt." Parks offered her a tiny paper packet. "No?" he said when she neither answered nor moved. "I also said we could get married."

"Married?" Brooke echoed stupidly. "You and me?"

"The press would ease off after a while. Quietly married couples don't make the news the same way lovers do. Human nature." He pushed his sandwich aside and leaned toward her.

"What do you think?"

"I think you're crazy," Brooke managed in a whisper. "And I don't think this is funny."

Parks gripped her arm when she started to scoot out of the booth. "I'm not joking."

"You—you want to get married so we won't get our picture in the paper?"

"I don't give a damn if we get our picture in the paper or not, you do."

"So you want to get married to—to placate me." She stopped struggling against his hold on her arm, but her eyes filled with fury.

"I've never had any intention of placating you," he countered. "I couldn't placate you if I dedicated my life to it. I want to get married because I'm in love with you. I'm *going* to marry you," he corrected, suddenly angry, "if I have to drag you, kicking and screaming."

"Is that so?"

"Yes, that's exactly so. You might as well get used to it."

"Maybe I don't want to get married." Brooke shoved the food in front of them aside. "What about that?"

"Too bad." He leaned back, eyeing her with the same

simmering temper with which she eyed him. "*I* want to get married."

"And that's supposed to be enough, huh?"

"It's enough for me."

Brooke crossed her arms over her chest and glared at him. "Kicking and screaming?"

"If that's the way you want it."

"I can bite, too."

"So can I."

Her heart was thudding against her ribs, but Brooke realized it wasn't from anger. No, it had nothing to do with anger. He was sitting there, across a laminated table littered with food from a twelve-year-old's fantasy, telling her he was going to marry her whether she liked it or not. Brooke discovered, somewhat to her own amazement, that she liked it just fine. But she wasn't going to make it easy for him.

"Maybe winning the series went to your head, Parks. It's going to take more than a temper tantrum to get me to marry you."

"What do you want?" he demanded. "Candlelight and soft music?" Annoyed that he had scuttled his own plans, he leaned over again and grabbed her hands. "You're not the kind of woman who needs scenery, Brooke. You know just how easy it is to come by and how little it means. What the hell do you want?"

"Take two," she said very calmly. "You know your motivation," she began in her cool director's voice, "but this time tone down the force and try for a little finesse. Ask," she suggested, looking into his eyes, "don't tell."

He felt the anger, or perhaps it had been fear, slide out of him. The hands that held hers gentled. "Brooke—" he lifted a hand and pressed her fingers to his lips "—will you marry me?" Parks smiled over their joined hands. "How was that?"

Brooke laced the fingers with hers. "Perfect."

CHAPTER 11

What was she doing? In a sudden panic, Brooke stared at herself in the free standing long-length mirror. How could things be happening so fast and be so much out of her control? A year ago—no, even six months ago—she hadn't known Parks Jones existed. In something under an hour, she would be married to him. Committed. For life. Forever.

From somewhere deep inside her brain came a panicked call to run and run fast. Brooke hadn't realized she'd made a move until she was summarily jerked back into place.

"Be still, Ms. Gordon," Billings ordered firmly. "There are two dozen of these little buttons if there's one." She used a complaining tone, though privately she thought Brooke's choice of an ivory satin gown with its snug bodice and flowing skirt was inspired. A good, traditional wedding dress, she decided, not one of those flighty trouser suits or miniskirted affairs in scarlet or fuchsia. Billings continued to fasten the range of tiny pearl buttons in back.

"Stand still now," she ordered again as Brooke fidgeted.

"Billings," Brooke said weakly, "I really think I'm going to be sick."

The housekeeper looked up at Brooke's reflection. Her face was pale, her eyes huge, made darker by the merest touch of slate-gray shadow. In Billings's staunch opinion, a bride was supposed to look ready to faint. "Nonsense," she said briskly. "Just a case of the flutters."

"Flutters," Brooke repeated, creasing her brow. "I never flutter. That's ridiculous."

The Englishwoman smiled fleetingly as Brooke straightened her shoulders. "Flutters, jitters, nerves—every woman born has them on her wedding day."

"Well, I don't," she claimed as her stomach muscles quivered.

Billings only sniffed as she finished her fastening. "There now, that's the last one."

"Thank God," Brooke muttered, heading for a chair before Billings caught her.

"No, you don't. You're not putting creases in that skirt."

"Billings, for heaven's sake—"

"A woman has to suffer now and again."

Brooke's opinion was a short four-letter word. Lifting a brow, Billings picked up a hairbrush from the vanity. "A fine way for a blushing bride to talk."

"I'm not a blushing bride." Brooke swept away before Billings could apply the brush. "I'm twenty-eight years old," she continued, pacing. "I must be crazy, I must be absolutely crazy. No sane woman agrees to marry a man in a fast-food restaurant."

"You're getting married in Ms. Thorton's garden," Billings corrected. "And it's quite a lovely day for it."

The practical tone caused Brooke to scowl. "And I should never have let her talk me into that, either."

"Hah!" The exclamation had Brooke's brows lifting. Billings gestured threateningly with the hairbrush. "Hah!" she said again, effectively closing Brooke's mouth. "No one talks you into anything. You're a hardheaded, stubborn, single-minded young woman, and you're shaking in your shoes because there's a hardheaded, stubborn, single-minded young man downstairs who's going to give you a run for your money."

"I certainly am not shaking in my shoes," Brooke corrected, insulted. Billings saw the faint pink flush rise to the pale cheeks.

"Scared to death."

Brooke stuck both fists on her hips. "I am most certainly not afraid of Parks Jones."

"Hah!" Billings repeated as she pulled over a footstool. Climbing on it, she began to draw the brush through Brooke's hair. "You'll probably stammer and quake when you take your vows, just like some silly girl who doesn't know her own mind."

"I've never stammered in my life." Enunciating each word precisely, Brooke glared at their twin reflections in the mirror. "And nothing makes me quake."

"We'll just see about that, won't we?" Rather pleased with herself, Billings arranged Brooke's mane of hair into a cunningly tumbled mass. In this, she secured a delicate clip of pale pink-and-white hibiscus. She had fussed that lily of the valley or rosebuds would have been more suitable, but secretly thought these flowers were stunning.

"Now, where are those lovely pearl drops Ms. Thorton gave you?"

"Over there." Still fuming, Brooke pointed to the tiny jeweler's box that held Claire's gift.

They should have eloped as Parks had suggested, Brooke thought. What had made her think she wanted all this fuss and bother? What had made her think she wanted to get married in the first place? As her nerves started jumping again, she caught Billings's ironic stare. Brooke lifted her chin.

"Well, put them on," the housekeeper ordered, holding the pink-blushed pearls in her palm. "It was very clever of Mr. Jones to send you flowers to match them."

"If you like him so much, why don't you marry him?" Brooke muttered, fastening the earrings with fingers that refused to stop trembling.

"I suppose you'll do," Billings said briskly, swallowing a lump in her throat. "Even without a proper veil and train." She wanted badly to press a kiss to Brooke's cheek, but knew it would weaken both of them. "Come along, then," she said instead. "It's time."

I could still call it off, Brooke thought as she let Billings draw her down the hall. There's still time. No one can make me go through with this. The little skips of nerves in her stomach had increased to thumps. There's absolutely nothing that can make me walk out into that garden. What was the phrase? she wondered. Marry in haste, repent at leisure? This was certainly haste.

It had only been four days since Parks had asked her. Four days. Maybe the big mistake had been in telling Claire. Good God, she'd never seen anyone move so fast once they'd gotten the bit between their teeth. Brooke decided she must have been in a state of shock to have let Claire sweep her along with plans and arrangements. An intimate ceremony in her terraced garden, a champagne reception. *Elope?* Claire had brushed that aside with a wave of her hand. Elopements were for silly teenagers. And wouldn't a three-piece ensemble be lovely? Brooke had found herself caught up. And now she was just caught.

But no, Brooke corrected as she and Billings reached the foot of the stairs. All she had to do was turn around and head for the door. She could get into her car and just drive away. That was the coward's way. Straightening her shoulders,

Brooke rejected it. She wouldn't run, she would simply walk outside and explain very calmly she had changed her mind. Yes, that's all it would take. I'm very sorry, she practiced mentally, but I've decided not to get married after all. She'd be very calm and very firm.

"Oh, Brooke, you look lovely." And there was Claire, dressed in powder-blue silk with the sheen of tears in her eyes.

"Claire, I—"

"Absolutely lovely. I wish you'd let me have them play the wedding march."

"No, I—"

"It doesn't matter, as long as you're happy." Claire pressed her cheek to Brooke's. "Isn't it silly, I feel just like a mother. Imagine having your first pangs of motherhood at my age."

"Oh, Claire."

"No, no, I'm not going to get sloppy and sentimental and ruin my face." Sniffling, she drew away. "It's not every day I'm maid of honor."

"Claire, I want to—"

"They're waiting, Ms. Thorton."

"Yes, yes, of course." Giving Brooke's hand a quick squeeze, she went out on the terrace.

"Now you, Ms. Gordon." Brooke stood where she was, wondering if the coward's way wasn't basically sound. Billings put a firm hand on her back and pushed. Brooke found herself out on the terrace facing Parks.

He took her hand. He was firm as he brought hers to his lips. She noticed his eyes, smiling, sure. He was in a pearl-gray suit, more formal than anything she had seen him wear. But his eyes held that complete intensity she knew they had when he waited for a pitch. She found herself walking with him to the center of the terrace that was surrounded by flowers and the ornamental trees Claire loved.

Still time, Brooke thought as the minister began to speak in a calm, clear voice. But she couldn't open her mouth to stop what was already happening.

She'd remember the scent always. Jasmine and vanilla, and the sweet drift of baby roses. But she didn't see the flowers because her eyes were locked on Parks's. He was repeating the words the minister spoke, the traditional words spoken countless times by countless couples. But she heard them as if they were uttered for the first time.

Love, honor, cherish.

She felt the ring slip onto her finger. Felt, but again didn't see because she couldn't take her eyes from his. From the branches of a weeping cherry, a bird began to trill.

She heard her own voice, strong and assured, repeat the same promises. And her hand, with no trembling, placed the symbol of the promise on Parks's finger.

A pledge, a promise, a gift. Then their lips moved together, sealing it.

I was going to run, she remembered.

"I'd have caught you," Parks murmured against her mouth.

Astonished and annoyed, Brooke drew back. He was grinning at her, his hands still caught in her hair. To the confusion of the others in the quiet, fragrant garden, Brooke cursed then threw her arms around his neck and laughed.

"Hey." Snyder gave Parks a firm shove. "Give somebody else a chance."

Claire's idea of a small gathering was the epitome of a producer's understatement. Though Brooke didn't bother to count heads, she knew there were well over a hundred "absolutely essential guests." She found she didn't mind—the glitter was her gift to Claire. There was a bubbly fountain of champagne, a five-tiered pink-and-white cake and silver platters of food that for once Brooke had no interest in. Which turned out for the best, as she was swept from one person's arms to another, kissed, hugged and congratulated until it all became a blur of color and sound.

She met Parks's mother, a tiny, exquisite woman who kissed her cheek then burst into tears. His father crushed Brooke in a hug and murmured that now that Parks was married, he would stop the nonsense and come into the company. She found herself inheriting a family in a lump—a large, confusing family that didn't quite fit any of the imaginings of her youth. And through it all, she had barely more than glimpses of Parks as she was passed from cousin to cousin to be weighed, measured and discussed like a fascinating new acquisition.

"Leave the girl be a minute." A sturdy, pewter-haired woman swept the others aside with an imperious wave of her hand. "These Joneses are a silly bunch." She sighed, then summed Brooke up with one long look. "I'm your aunt Lorraine," she said and extended her hand.

Brooke accepted the handshake, knowing instinctively the gesture was somehow more sincere and more intimate than all the kisses she had received. Then with a flash of insight, she knew. "The gold piece."

Lorraine smiled, pleased. "Told you about that, did he? Well, he's a good boy . . . more or less." A straight, no-nonsense brow lifted. "And he won't bully you, will he?"

With a grin, Brooke shook her head. "No, ma'am, he won't."

Lorraine nodded, giving Brooke's hand a quick pat. "Good. I'll expect a visit in six months. It takes a couple that long to work out the first kinks. Now, if I were you, I'd get my husband and sneak out of this rabble." With this advice, she strode away. Brooke had her first twinge of genuine kinship.

Even so, it seemed like hours before they could slip away.

Brooke had intended to steal back upstairs and change, but Parks had seen his opportunity and had pulled her outside, bundled her into his car and driven off. Now he stopped the car in the driveway of the A-frame and sighed.

"We made it."

"It was rude," Brooke mused.

"Yeah."

"And very smart." Leaning over, she kissed him. "Especially since you managed to cop a bottle of champagne on the way."

"Quick hands," he explained as he stepped from the car.

Brooke chuckled, but felt a fresh ripple of unease as they walked up the path. Parks's hand was closed over hers. She could feel the slight, unfamiliar pressure of her wedding ring against her skin. "One problem," she began, pushing the feeling aside. "You dragged me out of there without my purse." She glanced at the door, then back at Parks. "No keys."

Parks reached in his pocket and drew out his own. A faint frown creased her brow as she remembered he had a key to the door now. A key to her life. Though he noticed her reaction, Parks said nothing, only slipping the key into the lock. It opened silently. He swept her up into his arms, and with her laughter, the subtle disharmony was forgotten.

"I hadn't realized you were such a traditionalist," Brooke murmured, nuzzling at his neck, "but . . ." She trailed off at the sound of high, sharp yapping. Astonished, she looked down to see a small brown dog with a black muzzle racing around Parks's feet, making occasional dives for his ankles. "What's that?" she managed.

"Your wedding present." With his toe, he nudged the puppy, sending him rolling over on his back. "Homely enough?"

Brooke stared down at the pushed-in mongrel face. "Oh, Parks," she whispered, close to tears. "You fool."

"E.J. should've dropped him off about an hour ago, if he was on schedule. Guy at the pound thought I was crazy when I told him I wanted something down-to-the-ground homely."

"Oh, I love you!" Brooke squeezed his neck fiercely then wriggled out of his arms. In her satin wedding dress, she knelt on the floor to play with the puppy.

She looked young, Parks thought, too young, as she buried her face in the little dog's fur. Why would he constantly expose her vulnerabilities then be uncertain how to handle them? There was so much sweetness in her, and yet, was he somehow more comfortable with the vinegar she could serve him? It was the mix, Parks thought as he knelt to join her, the fascinating mix he couldn't resist.

"Our first child." Brooke chuckled when the puppy lay in exhausted slumber on the rug.

"He has your nose."

"And your feet," she retorted. "He's going to be enormous from the size of them."

"Maybe you can cast him in a few dog food commercials," he commented as he drew Brooke to her feet. Gently he kissed her cheek, then trailed his lips over her chin to the other one. He felt the sudden tremble of her breath on his skin. "Champagne's getting warm," he murmured.

"I'm not thirsty."

He was leading her slowly toward the stairs, still planting those soft, whispering kisses over her face on the journey, leaving her lips—her heating, seeking lips—subtly tormented. And they started to climb the stairs, without rush or hurry, while Parks began unfastening that long range of tiny buttons.

"How many are there?" he murmured against her mouth.

"Dozens," Brooke answered, loosening his tie as they reached the halfway point.

His fingers were nimble. Before they reached the door of the bedroom, he had the gown loosened to her waist. Brooke pushed the jacket from his shoulder, and with her teeth nipping at his neck, tugged his shirt from the waistband of his pants.

"Are you ever going to kiss me?" she demanded breathlessly.

"Mmm-hmm." But he only drove her mad by running his lips over her shoulder as he nudged the satin aside. Then he drew it from her, running his hands slowly down her body until the material was only a pool of white at her feet. He toyed with the bits of lace she wore, tiny, filmy wisps designed to torment men. And even as they tormented him, Parks fought for control. There was always that last struggle for control before he found he was lost in her.

Her fingers slid down his naked ribs to brush over his stomach before she found the hook to his trousers. She heard his quick, indrawn breath before his hands became more demanding. Needing, wanting, she pulled him with her onto the bed.

Why should there be such desperation when they were now so securely bound to each other? Though neither of them understood it, they both felt it. The urgency to touch, taste. To possess. Gentleness was abandoned while hungry, primitive passion took its place. The teasing kisses stopped with a hard, burning pressure of mouth on mouth. Her hands sought, as skillfully as his, to find weaknesses. Every moan brought a fresh thrill of arousal, each sigh an increase of tortuous desire until neither knew if the sounds were from pleasure or desperation. And both refused to succumb to the fire.

He found her breast taut and firm. Greedily, his mouth sought it, sending a tearing thread of delight into the core of her. Even as she moaned in surrender, her hands pressed him closer, her body moving sinuously under his until he was lost in the taste of her.

Flesh heated against flesh. The pace quickened. Faster, faster until they were breathless and clinging but still not ready to yield. She ran her hands over his damp back, over the roping of muscles that accented his superior strength. But physical strength meant nothing in the inescapable quicksand of passion. They were both trapped in it, both equally incapable of freeing themselves.

With sudden strength, she shifted, so that they were tangled together, side by side. Her mouth fastened on his, devouring as eagerly as she was devoured, taking as mindlessly as she was taken. Her hair fell over them, curtaining their faces so that Parks couldn't breathe without breathing her. If he had been capable of thought, he might have imagined himself absorbed by her. But there was no thought for either of them, and the need had grown too great to be resisted.

She went willingly when he shifted her, drawing his mouth down to hers even as he entered her with something close to violence. Then there was only speed and heat, driving them beyond everything but each other.

S hould I need you more each time?" Brooke wondered aloud.

"Mmm." Parks didn't want to move from the warm comfort of her body. It yielded under his, pressed deep into the mattress. "Just don't stop."

It was dusk. The light filtering through the windows was soft—and soon it would be night. Her wedding night. Yet she still felt only like a lover. How would it be to feel like a wife? Lifting her hand, she stared at the band on her finger. It was encrusted with diamonds and sapphires that glowed softly in the room's twilight. "I don't want it to be different tomorrow," she thought aloud. "I don't want it to change."

Parks raised his head. "Everything changes. You'll get mad if I use all the hot water for my shower. I'll get mad if you've drunk the last of the coffee."

Brooke laughed. "You have a way of simplifying things."

"Those are the nuts and bolts of a relationship, Mrs. Jones," he claimed and kissed her.

The eyes that had begun to close for the kiss opened wide. "Jones," she repeated. "I'd forgotten about that part of it." She considered for a minute. "It makes me think of your mother . . . though of course she was very nice."

Parks gave a muffled chuckle. "Don't worry. Just remember she lives three hundred miles away."

Brooke rolled over until she lay on top of him. "You have a very nice family."

"Yeah, and we don't want to get tangled up with them any more than we have to."

"Well . . ." Brooke laid her head on his chest. "No. At least not too soon," she added, thinking of his aunt. She relaxed again as he began to lazily stroke her hair. "Parks?"

"Hmm?"

"I'm glad we decided to come here instead of flying off somewhere."

"We'll go to Maui for a couple of weeks around Christmas. I want you to see my place there."

Brooke thought of her schedule if she decided to take Claire up on the feature for cable. Somehow or other, she'd managed to get the two weeks. "I love you."

His hand stopped a moment, then pressed her closer. They

were three words she didn't say often. "Did I tell you how beautiful you looked when Billings shoved you out on the terrace?"

Brooke's head shot up. "You saw that?"

Grinning he traced her ear with his fingertip. "Funny, I didn't expect you to be as terrified as I was."

Brooke regarded him a moment, then a smile curved on her lips. "Were you really?"

"A half hour before the wedding, I'd run up a list of all the reasons why we should call it off."

She lifted a brow. "Were there many?"

"I lost count," he told her, ignoring the narrowing of her eyes. "I could only think of one good reason to go through with it."

"Oh, really?" Her chin came up as she tossed her head. "And what was that?"

"I love you."

Brooke dropped her forehead onto his. "That's it, huh?"

"The only one I could think of." He slid a hand down to her hip. "Though one or two others are beginning to occur to me."

"Mmm. Like it being good for the campaign." She began to nuzzle, just behind his ear.

"Oh, sure. That's top on my list." He groaned when the first shudder rippled through him. "Right next to having somebody to sort my socks."

"You can forget that one," Brooke murmured, moving down to his shoulder. "But there's always having an in with the director when you do that part for cable."

"Haven't decided to do it." His legs tangled with hers as they altered positions. "Have you?"

"Not yet." Her thoughts began to drift as he cupped her breast. "But you should."

"Why?"

Lazily, her eyes opened to look into his. "I shouldn't tell you."

Intrigued, he propped himself on his elbow and toyed with her hair. "Why not?"

She sighed a little, while managing to convey a shrug. "The last thing you need is someone feeding your ego."

"Go ahead." He kissed her nose. "I can take it."

"Damn it, Parks, you're good."

He stopped in the action of twining her hair around his finger and stared at her. "What did you say?"

Brooke shifted again. "Well, I don't mean you can *act*," she began. "Don't start getting delusions."

He grinned, enjoying her ironic lift of brow. "That's more like it."

"You have good camera presence," she went on. "Do you have any idea how many big stars stay big simply by playing themselves?" Parks grunted, more interested in the curve of her shoulder. "You know how to play yourself, Parks," Brooke persisted, drawing him back for a moment. "And if you were to stick to parts, at least for a while, that suited you . . . well, when you really are ready to retire from base-ball you could walk right into a movie career."

He started to laugh, then stopped when he saw the look in her eyes. "You're not joking."

Brooke stared at him, then let out a long breath. "I'm really going to hate myself when I've got to deal with you as a director in a couple of weeks, but you're very, very good, and you should think about it. And if you get a star complex when I tell you to run through some business on camera a half a dozen times, I'll . . ."

"What?" he challenged.

"Something," Brooke said ominously. "Something despi-cable."

He gave her a wicked grin. "Promise?"

Since she couldn't stop the laugh, she rolled him over forcibly so that she was lying across him again. "Yeah. And now I'm going to make love to you until your bones dissolve."

"Is this in my contract?" he demanded.

"You better believe it."

CHAPTER 12

Though it was November, Los Angeles was suffering from a heat wave that fried tempers and melted patience. Brooke's was no exception. She and Parks had had ten long, isolated days before she had begun work again—but they hadn't been trouble-free. Nothing's trouble-free, Brooke reminded herself as she knotted her blouse beneath her breasts. What fool thought a honeymoon would be? She had, she admitted ruefully as the camera crane was unloaded. But then how much thought had she really given to adjustments, to changes and, as Parks had termed it, the nuts-and-bolts business that made up a marriage?

She had accepted his name, and though she would keep her own professionally, it was Brooke Jones that she would sign to all legal documents. He had given up his apartment and moved into her house. She had his name, he had her key. Why did she feel she was tallying a balance sheet? Frustrated, Brooke wiped her forearm over her brow.

Was that what marriage was, she wondered, a series of checks and balances? With her marriage barely three weeks old, she should be blissfully happy, glowing. Instead, Brooke felt frustrated, annoyed and unsettled—perhaps more unsettled because she knew Parks was no more blissfully happy than she.

With a shake of her head, she told herself to put it aside. Bringing her personal problems to work wouldn't solve them—and more than likely it would make them worse, since she was directing Parks.

"Let's go up, E.J., I want to see the angle." Sitting in the basket beside him, she gave the crane operator a nod to take them up.

Below them, the beach spread gold. The surf kicked up, white and frothy, catching the glint of the sun and rainbowing through the lens. She thought she could feel the heat steam from the metal casing of the camera. "All right, I'll want a wide shot when he starts, then zoom in, but not too tight. At this angle, we'll get a good profile of the horse. The palomino's a nice contrast with the jeans. Set the speed. I want it slow enough so they see every muscle ripple."

"On Parks or the horse?" E.J. asked with a grin.

"On both," Brooke answered curtly, nodding to be brought down. Wiping her palms on the seat of her pants, she strode over to where Parks waited. He wore nothing but snug, low-slung de Marco jeans. "We're ready for you."

"All right." Parks gave her a long, steady look as he hooked his thumbs in his front pockets. He wasn't sure why he was dissatisfied, or why he felt the need to annoy her. The friction had been growing between them for the past few days, building and shifting like some electric storm. But there'd been no boom of thunder, no slash of lightning to release the pressure. "What do you want?"

"You've seen the script," she reminded him.

"Aren't you going to give me my motivation?"

"Don't be a smart aleck, Parks," she snapped. "It's too damn hot."

"Just want to make sure I've got the right mood so you won't make me do it a half dozen times."

Temper flared in her eyes and was forcefully suppressed. She wouldn't let him taunt her into a public sniping. "You'll do it two dozen times if I feel it's necessary," she said as calmly as possible. "Now get on the horse, gallop straight down the beach in the shallows. And enjoy it."

"Is that an order?" he murmured, deceptively mild.

"It's a direction," she returned evenly. "I'm the director, you're the talent. Got it?"

"Yeah, I got it." Catching her close, he crushed her mouth with his. He felt the dampness of her blouse under his palm, the angry rigidity of her body and the yielding softness of her breasts. Why was he angry? he wondered even as his temper inched higher. Why did he feel he was dragging her close and shoving her away at the same time? "Got that?" he demanded as he turned and swung onto the horse.

She glared at him, a half-naked man astride a golden horse, as he smiled down at her with the cocky assurance she both loved and detested. Making him pay for that small victory would be a pleasure. Turning on her heel, Brooke strode back to her crew. "Take one," she ordered, then waited, turning ideas for vengeance over in her mind. She took the bullhorn her assistant handed her. "Places!" Parks led the palomino into the surf. Brooke stared at him, forcing herself to put her personal feelings on hold while she thought and felt and saw only as a director. "Roll film, and . . . action!"

He's magnificent, Brooke thought with a twin surge of pride and irritation. He took the horse into an easy, rolling gallop, kicking up the surf so that the streams of water rose high. Beads glistened on his skin, darkly tanned so that he and the palomino merged into one golden form. Parks's hair and the horse's mane lifted in the wind the motion caused. Strength, an elegance of movement and the simplicity of two beautiful animals. Brooke didn't need special effects to show her how it would look in slow motion.

"Cut. E.J.?"

"Fantastic," he called down. "Sales of de Marco jeans just went up ten percent."

"Let's make sure." Pulling her damp shirt away from her back, Brooke walked to where Parks waited, astride the horse. It had been fantastic, she mused, but not perfect. Spotting her, Parks broke off his conversation with the palomino's trainer.

"Well?"

"It looked pretty good. Let's do it again."

"Why?"

Ignoring the question, she absently patted the gelding's smooth throat. "I want you to look down the beach as you ride . . . all the way down." She didn't want that comfortable, freewheeling sexuality this time, but a dash of aloofness, the solitary-man appeal flavored with the sensuality any female over twelve would recognize.

He shifted in the saddle, his eyes never leaving hers. "Why?"

"Ride the horse, Parks," she countered. "Let me sell the jeans."

Very slowly, he dismounted. The trainer quickly remembered something he had to do somewhere else. Behind them, the crew became very busy. Parks held the reins in one hand while he and Brooke measured each other. "Ever considered asking?" he said quietly.

"Ever considered following directions?" she tossed back.

He felt the salt spray drying on his skin. "Too bad you've never been a team player, Brooke."

"This isn't a ball game," she retorted, firing up. "We all have our jobs to do. Yours is whatever I tell you it is."

The flash of anger in his eyes suited her mood. She wanted

a fight, a rip-roaring screamer that would tear through the tension of their last few days together. Planting her feet, Brooke prepared to attack and defend.

"No," he said with a sudden deadly calm that put her at a disadvantage, "it's not. My job is to endorse de Marco."

"And that's what I'm telling you to do." She forced herself to match his tone, though she badly wanted to shout. "If you want to be a prima donna, wait until after we wrap. Take your complaints and talk to your agent."

His hand snaked out to grab her arm before she could stalk away. "I'm talking to my wife."

Heart hammering in her throat, she looked down at the hand that held her. "Your director," Brooke icily corrected, meeting his eyes. "My crew's hot, Parks. I'd like to finish this before someone faints from heat exhaustion."

His grip tightened. But he saw that her face was flushed from the heat and damp with sweat. "We're not finished with this," he told her as he released her arm. "This time, you're going to take a good hard look at the rules." Swinging onto the horse, Parks rode away before she could think of an appropriate comment.

Brooke frowned after him as she stalked back to the crane. "Take two."

He could have given no logical, succinct explanation for his anger. Parks only knew he was furious. He had only one motivation as he stalked down the corridors to Brooke's office—to have it out with her. He wasn't certain what *it* was, but he would have had it out with her on location if she hadn't been gone before he'd realized it. Though he wasn't thrilled about coming to terms with her in her office, he'd had plenty of experience in meeting a challenge on the opposition's home field. All it meant was that he would take the offensive first.

Brushing by her secretary without a word, Parks pushed open the door to Brooke's office. Empty.

"I'm sorry, Mr. Jones." The secretary hurried up to him, warned by the dangerous light in his eye. "Ms. Gordon . . . Mrs. Jones isn't in."

"Where?" Parks demanded curtly.

"I—Perhaps Ms. Thorton's office. If you'll wait, I'll check for you. . . ." But he was already heading out with a long, determined stride that had her chewing on the nail of her forefinger. It looked like Brooke was in trouble. And some people have all the luck, the secretary mused before she went back to her desk.

In less than five minutes, Parks walked by the twins in Claire's outer office and opened her door without knocking. "Where's Brooke?" he demanded, not bothering to greet Claire or his agent.

"Good afternoon, Parks," Claire said easily. "Tea?" She continued to pour Lee's cup as if a furious man weren't at that moment glaring at her.

Parks gave the classic little tea service a brief glance. "I'm looking for Brooke."

"You've missed her, I'm afraid." Claire sipped her tea, then offered Lee a plate of macaroons. "She was in and out a half an hour ago. Would you like a cookie, Parks?"

"No. . . ." He managed to get a tenuous hold on his manners. "Thanks. Where did she go?"

Claire nibbled on a macaroon, then dusted her fingers on a pink linen napkin. "Didn't she say she was going home, Lee?"

"Yep. And she wasn't in any better mood than Parks is." He sent his client a bland smile before he wolfed down a cookie.

"No, she wasn't, was she?" Claire folded her hands on her lap. "Tell me, dear, are you two having a tiff?"

"No, we're not having a tiff," Parks muttered, not certain

what they were having. It occurred to him suddenly how cozy his agent and his producer were on the small two-cushioned sofa. "What are you two having?" he countered.

"Tea." Claire smiled her dry smile.

"Why don't you have a seat and cool off," Lee invited. "You look like you've just played nine full innings."

"We were shooting on the beach," Parks murmured. Did Lee Dutton have his arm around Claire Thorton, or was he seeing things?

"It went well?" Claire asked, noting his expression, amused by the reason for it.

"Apparently Brooke was satisfied."

"Apparently," Claire murmured, then shot him a level stare. "When are you and Brooke going to relax and enjoy yourselves?"

Parks's speculative look changed to a frown. "What do you mean?"

"I mean I've never in my life seen two people spend so much time poking at each other."

"Is that what you call it?" Parks muttered, stuffing his hands in his pockets.

"For want of a better term." Claire set her teacup carefully in its saucer. "I realize, of course, that the power game is a founding part of your relationship, and provides its own stimulation, but don't you think it's time you became a family as well as opponents?" Keeping her eyes level, Claire settled into the crook of Lee's arm.

Parks stared at her for nearly a full minute. Power game, he repeated silently. Well yes, it was an intricate part of what they were to each other. They had both looked for strength, challenge, and would have walked the other way if they hadn't found the combination. But as for the rest—a family . . . Was that what was niggling at the back of his mind?

Wasn't it true that he couldn't resolve himself to the

fact that they were living in *her* house, surrounded by *her* things? He still felt uncomfortably like a guest. Even as fresh annoyance grew, he remembered their discussing a trip to Maui. He had told Brooke he wanted her to see *his* place. But . . . Even as he searched for an excuse, he knew he wouldn't find one.

Turning, Parks paced to the window and scowled out. "I don't think Brooke's ready for a family relationship." The brief, undignified answer Claire gave him had Parks turning back, half-amused. Lee merely reached forward and snatched another cookie.

"She's looked for one all of her life. If you know anything about her, you know that." Suddenly angry, Claire rose. "Is it possible for two people to live together and not understand the other's needs, the other's hurts? How much has she told you about how she grew up?"

"Barely anything," Parks began. "She—"

"How much did you ask?" Claire demanded. "Don't tell me you didn't want to pry," she said quickly, cutting him off. "You're her husband, it's your business to pry. You can be civilized enough to respect her privacy and never touch on what she really needs from you."

"I know that she needs to know she can make her own place," he tossed back. "I know that it doesn't matter if it's a chipped cup or a Hepplewhite table, as long as it's hers."

"Things!" Claire raged. "Yes, she needs things. God knows she never had them as a child, and the child in her still hurts because of it. But they're only a symbol of what she really wants. Brooke walked in here, an eighteen-year-old adult with nothing more than a few dollars in her pocket and a lot of guts. Someone she thought she loved had taken everything from her, and she wasn't ever going to let that happen again." Her mouth tightened, her eyes frosting over at the memory. "It's your job to show her that it won't."

"I don't want to *take* anything from her," Parks retorted heatedly.

"But you want her to give," Claire shot back.

"Of course I do, damn it. I love her."

"Then listen to me. Brooke's struggled all her life to have something of her own, to have some*one* of her own. She has the things. She's earned them. If you want to share them with her, share her life, you'd better have something pretty special to offer in return. Love isn't enough."

"What is?" Parks tossed back, furious at being lectured by someone half his size.

"You'd better figure it out."

Parks measured her another moment. "All right," he said coolly and left without another word.

Lee rose from the sofa to stand beside Claire. Her pampered skin was flushed with temper, her faded blue eyes icy. "You know," he mused as he studied her, "I've never seen you in full gear before."

"I don't often lose my temper." Claire fluffed at her hair. "Young people," she stated, as if the two words explained everything.

"Yeah." Taking her shoulders, he turned her to face him. "They don't know a good thing when they've got it." His puckish round face creased with a grin. "How'd you like to spend the rest of your life with an overweight theatrical agent?"

The ice melted from Claire's eyes, but the flush remained. "Lee, I thought you'd never ask."

Parks was fighting his way through L.A. traffic when he heard the first report of the fire. His anger at Claire, his frustration that she had spoken no more than the truth, was switched off instantly as he caught the tail end of a news broadcast reporting brush fires in Liberty Canyon—less than an hour away from Brooke's isolated A-frame. No, there wasn't anger now, but a sick sense of fear that had his palms slipping damply on the wheel.

Had she gone home? he wondered frantically as he sped around a cruising Ferrari. Would she have the television set on, the radio, or would she be in one of her solitary moods? After a hot, enervating day on location, she would often simply shower and sleep for an hour. Recharging, he had called it jokingly. Now the idea terrified him.

As he drove higher, he began to scent the fragrance of dry leaves burning. A faint haze of smoke rose into the sky to the east. Thirty minutes, Parks estimated as he pressed his foot on the accelerator. Forty, if they were lucky. It would take him nearly half that to get there.

There was no wind to hurry the fire along, he reminded himself, fighting to keep calm. They weren't calling it a firestorm . . . not yet. Brooke was probably already packing up her most important things—he might even meet her on the road on her way down. Any minute she could come zipping around one of the curves in the road leading back down the mountain. They'd get a hotel, talk this business out. Claire was right, he hadn't dug deep enough. Once he had promised himself he would learn the whole woman. It was long past time to make good on the promise.

Parks could almost taste the smoke now, the thick black smoke that led the way for the fire. He saw a pack of small animals—rabbits, raccoons, a fox—race down the road on the other side in their migration to lower elevation. It was close, then, he thought, too close. Why in God's name wasn't she speeding down the road toward safety? He drove the last fifteen miles in a blur of speed and fear.

Parks only took the time to register that Brooke's car was in the driveway before he was out of his own and racing toward the house. She had to be asleep, he decided, not to know the fire was closing in. Even without the radio on, the haze of smoke and smell of burning brought the news. He burst through the front door, calling her name.

The house was silent. There was no sound of hurried movement, of drawers slamming, nothing to indicate frantic packing. Parks was racing up the stairs two at a time when he heard the dog barking. He swore, but kept going. He'd forgotten the dog completely in his fear for Brooke. And the fear grew again when he saw the bed was empty. He was racing through the second floor, still calling, when a movement outside the window caught his eye.

Rain? he thought, pausing long enough to stare. No, water—but not rain. Going to the window, he saw her. Relief was immediately overlapped by irritation, and irritation by fury. What the hell was she doing standing in the backyard watering the lawn when the smoke was thick enough to block out the trees to the east?

With a quick jerk, he pulled up the window and shouted through the screen. "Brooke, what the hell are you doing?"

She jolted, then looked up. "Oh, Parks, thank God! Come down and help, there isn't much time. Close the window!" she shouted. "The sparks could get inside. *Hurry!*"

He moved, and moved quickly, intending on shaking her until she rattled then dragging her to the car. Halfway down the stairs, he leaped over the banister and headed to the back door. "What the hell are you doing?" he demanded again. Then, instead of shaking her, he found he was holding her tight enough to make her bones crack. If he hadn't heard the radio, if she'd been sleeping . . . *If.* A thousand ifs ran through his mind as his mouth came down frantically on hers.

It was the sudden howl of wind that brought him back. A sudden ripple of terror ran down his spine. The wind would speed the fire and feed the flames. Brush fire became firestorm. "We've got to get out of here."

He had dragged her nearly two feet before he realized she was fighting him. "No!" With a show of pure strength, Brooke broke away from him then picked up the hose she had dropped.

"Damn it, Brooke, we can't have more than fifteen minutes."

He took her arm again and again she broke away. "I know how much time there is." She aimed the spray of water toward the house again, soaking the wood. The sound drummed in the air over the growing fierceness of the wind.

For the first time, Parks noticed that she was wet and filthy and wearing only a bathrobe. She'd just been stepping from the shower when the special report on the radio had warned her of the approaching fire. He looked at the dirt and grass stains on the silk of her robe and realized what she'd been doing. The land around the house had been cleared. She'd done it with her hands. He saw the scratches and dried blood on them and on her legs and ankles. Now, with the puppy barking frantically around her, she was wetting down the house.

"Are you crazy!" he demanded as the first flash of admiration was drowned in fresh fury. Parks grabbed her arm again, ripping the shoulder seam of her robe. "Do you know what a firestorm is?"

"I know what it is." Her elbow connected with his ribs as she struggled away. "If you won't help, stay out of my way; half the house hasn't been wetted down yet."

"You're getting out of here." Parks pulled the hose out of her hand and started dragging her. "If I have to knock you unconscious."

Brooke shocked them both by planting her fist solidly on his jaw. The blow was enough to free her so that she stumbled back, losing her balance and landing on all fours.

"I said stay out of my way," she hissed, then choked as the smoke clogged her lungs.

Parks dragged her to her feet. His eyes were as wild with fear and fury as hers. "You idiot, are you going to fight a firestorm with a garden hose? It's wood and glass!" he shouted as he shook her. "Wood and glass," he repeated, coughing as he threw a hand toward the house. "Is it worth dying for?"

"It's worth fighting for!" she shouted back against smoke and wind as the tears started to flow. "I won't give in to the fire, I *won't!*" She began fighting him again, more desperately than before.

"Damn it, Brooke, stop!" He took her shoulders until his fingers bit into her flesh. "There isn't time."

"The fire won't have it. Not our home, don't you understand?" Her voice rose, not in hysteria but in fierce determination. "Not *our* home."

Parks stopped shaking her, again finding that his arms had wrapped around to hold her close. Understanding flooded through him, and in its wake came every emotion he'd ever experienced. Is that what Claire had meant, he wondered, when she'd said love wasn't enough? Love was enough for beginning, but sustaining took every feeling a human being was capable of. *Our home*, she had said. And with the two words Brooke had cemented everything.

He drew her away. The tears were streaming, her breath was labored. Her eyes were rimmed with red but steady. He knew he had never felt more for another, and never would. And suddenly he knew that questions and answers weren't necessary for him to know the whole woman. Without speaking, he let her go and picked up the hose himself. Brooke stayed where she was while he turned the water onto the house. With the back of her wrist, she wiped the stinging tears from her face.

"Parks . . ."

He turned, smiling the grim gladiator smile. "It's worth fighting for." Brooke let out a shuddering sigh as she closed her hand over his. "We'll need towels to breathe through, a couple of blankets. Get them while I hose down the rest of the house."

It seemed like hours passed while they worked together, soaking the wood and each other, the dog, again and again while the smoke grew thicker. The wind screamed, threatening to rip the blanket Parks had tossed over her out of her hands. The heat, Brooke thought. She wouldn't be able to bear the heat. But the flames still held off. There were moments she almost believed the fire would veer away, then she would be choking on the smoke and taking her turn with the hose until she couldn't think at all. There was only one goal—to save the house she'd shared with Parks—the symbol of everything she had ever needed. Home, family, love.

With the towels pressed to their faces, they worked their way around and around the house, soaking the roof, the sides, all the surfaces the heat seemed to dry again so quickly. They no longer spoke, but worked systematically. Two pairs of arms, two sets of legs, working with one mind—to protect what was theirs.

Parks saw the flames first, and was almost too awed to move. It wasn't a furnace, he thought, or an oven. It was hell. And it was racing toward them. Great, greedy towers of fire belched out of the main body like spears. And in the midst of unbearable heat, he felt the icy sweat of human fear.

"No more." In a quick move, he grabbed Brooke's arm and scooped up the puppy.

"What are you doing? We can't leave now." Stumbling and choking, Brooke fought to free herself.

"If we don't leave now, we could be dead." He pushed Brooke into his car and shoved the puppy into her arms. "Damn it, Brooke, we've done all we can." His hands were slick with sweat as he turned the key. "Nothing you can buy is worth dying for."

"You don't understand!" With the back of her hand she smeared grime and tears together on her face. "Everything—everything I have is back there. I can't let the fire take it all—everything that means anything to me."

"Everything," he repeated in a murmur. Parks stopped the car to stare at her with red-rimmed, stinging eyes. "All right, if that's how you feel, I'll go back and do what I can." His voice was curiously flat and emotionless. "But, by God, you stay here. I won't risk you."

Before she could take in what he'd said or what he was doing, he was gone. For a moment, the hysteria had complete control. She trembled with it, unable to move or think. The fire was going to take her home, all her possessions. She'd be left with nothing, just as she had been so many times before. How could she face it again after all the years of struggling, of work, of wanting?

The puppy squirmed in her arms and whimpered. Blankly, Brooke stared down at him. What was she doing sitting there when her house was in danger? She had to go back, go back and save . . . Parks.

Fear froze her, then had her springing from the car and racing through the smoke. She'd sent him back—he'd gone back for her. For what? she thought desperately. What was she trying to save? Wood and glass—that's what he'd called it. It was nothing more. He was her home, the real home she'd searched for all her life. She shouted for him, sobbing as the smoke blocked everything from view.

She could hear the fire—or the wind. Brooke was no longer certain one was separate from the other. All that was clear now was that if she lost him now, she truly lost everything. So she shouted his name again and again, fighting her way through the smoke to get to him.

For an instant she could no longer breathe, no longer be certain where she was or where to run. An image flashed through her mind, one of herself as a young girl approaching a small two-story house where she would spend a year of her life. She couldn't remember the names of the people who would be her parents for those twelve months, only that sense of disorientation and loneliness. She'd always felt as lonely going in as she had coming out. She'd always been separate, always an outsider, until she'd met Parks.

She saw him racing back to her, misted through the curtain of smoke. Before she could separate one image from another, she was in his arms.

"What happened?" he demanded. "I heard you shouting, I thought—" He buried his face against her neck a moment as the fear ebbed. "Damn it, Brooke, I told you to stay in the car."

"Not without you. Please, let's go." She was dragging on his arm, pulling him back down the road toward the car.

"The house—"

"Means nothing," she said fiercely. "Nothing does without you." Before he could react, Brooke was climbing into the driver's seat herself. The moment Parks was beside her, she started down the twisting road.

After nearly a mile, the smoke thinned. It was then Brooke felt the reaction set in with shudders and fresh tears. Pulling off the road, she laid her head on the steering wheel and wept.

"Brooke." Gently, he brushed a hand over her wet, tangled hair. "I'm sorry. I know the house was important to you. We don't know yet that it's gone or beyond repair. We can—"

"Damn the house!" Lifting her head, she looked at him

with eyes that were both angry and desolate. "I must've been crazy to act that way. To send you back there when . . ." Trailing off, she swore and slammed out of the car. Slowly, Parks got out and followed her.

"Brooke."

"You're the most important thing in my life." She turned to him then, taking deep breaths to keep the tears back. "I don't expect you to believe that after the way I behaved, but it's true. I couldn't let go of the house, the things, because I'd waited so long to have them. I needed the identity they gave me." Because the words were painful, she swallowed. "For so long everything I had was only mine on loan. All I could think of was that if I didn't keep that house, those things, I'd be lost again. I don't expect you to understand—"

"I will understand." He took her face in his hands. "If you'll let me."

She let out a long, shuddering breath. "I never belonged anywhere, to anyone. Ever. It makes you afraid to trust. I always told myself that there'd be a day when I'd have my own things, my own place—I wouldn't have to share them, I wouldn't have to ask. It was something I promised myself because I couldn't have survived without that one hope. I forgot to let go of that when I didn't need it anymore."

"Maybe." He stroked a thumb over her cheek. "Or maybe you had without realizing it. Back there, you called it *our* home."

"Parks." She reached up to place her hands on him. "I don't care if the house is gone, if everything in it's gone. I have everything I need, everything I love, right here in my hands."

They were wet, filthy, exhausted. Alive. Parks looked at her blackened face and matted hair, the red-rimmed eyes. She'd never looked more beautiful to him. Throats raw from smoke, eyes stinging, he reached for her. Together, they fell to the grass.

Brooke was laughing and weeping as he kissed her. Her face was streaked with soot and tears, but his lips raced wildly over it. Passion met passion. Bruises were unfelt as they touched each other while a need, as volatile as the fire they had challenged, raged through them. When the tatters of her robe were gone, his sodden clothes joined it, they lay tangled, naked on the grass. Again and again, their mouths clung, drawing the strength and victory of the moment from each other, climbing beyond the smoke and stench of the fire left behind to a clean, bright world.

She knew she had never been so aware, so stunningly alive. Her body seemed to hum from a thousand pulses that grew more erratic as he touched her. With her arms tight around him, his body pressed against hers, she felt the sensation of absolute trust. He would protect, she would defend, against any outside forces that threatened. During the fire, they had ceased to be a man and a woman. They had become a unit. Somewhere beneath the swirling passion, Brooke felt peace. She had found her own.

They made love while the smoke broke into mists above their heads. And when they were spent, they clung still, unwilling to break the unity so newly discovered.

"You've hurt yourself," Parks murmured, touching a bruise on her shoulder.

"I don't feel hurt." She buried her lips at his throat and knew she would never forget the smell of smoke and ash and loving. "I hit you."

"Yeah, I noticed."

Hearing the grin in his voice, she closed her eyes. "You were only thinking of me. I'm sorry."

"Now you're thinking of us." He pressed his lips to her temple. "I'm glad."

"We won," she whispered.

Parks lifted his head to look down at her. Taking his

thumb, he rubbed a streak of soot from her skin. It was the color of her eyes, he thought, seeing it on his own flesh. "We won, Brooke."

"Everything."

His lips curved before he brought them down to hers. "Everything."

She cradled his head on her shoulder, gently stroking his hair. Tiny pieces of ash continued to float above her like memories. "I said once I didn't want anything to change. . . . I was afraid to let it change. I was wrong." Closing her eyes, she let herself absorb his closeness. "It's not quite the same now."

"Better," he murmured. "It makes a difference. It'll always make a difference."

She sighed, knowing the contentment she had always searched for was irrevocably bound up in one man, one love. "But we'll still play the game, won't we?"

This time when he lifted his head, he grinned. Brooke's lips curved in response. "By our own rules."